Blood Trials

Iris Kain

Acknowledgments:
Shakespeare, William. *Macbeth*. 5.1.31.
Shakespeare, William. *A Midsummer Night's Dream*. 3.2.1375.

ISBN: 978-1-957244-10-5

Also by Iris Kain

Blood Tribe: Book #1 of the Blood Tribe Trilogy

Blood Treason: Book #3 of the Blood Tribe Trilogy

Shadow Hunter

Eternal Spring

Offshoot

The Murphy Blackwell Chronicles:

Sour

Sweet

Salty

For my dear friend Kim.
Beta friend extraordinaire
Cats and rainbows, too.

Blood Trials

Sana's 2nd Edition Name Change

Usually, when a character shows up in a book for the first time, there isn't much backstory about how their name came about. Not so with Sana—perhaps the most important woman in *Blood Trials*. Her name has had a few hiccups along the way, which is why she has a new one in the second edition of this book.

I wrote *Blood Trials'* predecessor, *Blood Tribe*, many moons ago—most of it in 2003, before my son was born. When I started *Trials*, Maysun Khatri needed an American daughter. A friend of mine in Germany had the name Karin. I liked the unique spelling, so I gave it to Maysun's daughter.

Well, then the 2020s rolled around, and the name *Karen* took on a whole new meaning—a self-important woman of white privilege. Ugh. And while there are thousands of incredible women named Karen out there, because of the new (and frankly silly) cultural interpretation of the name, Karin got a name change before the first edition of *Blood Trials* was published.

I consulted the almighty oracle, Google, for ideas. What did I know about Maysun's daughter? Well, Maysun's character is Indian. Her daughter had… well, special traits. (*Spoilers!*) When I added those details to my search, I came across a beautiful name that fit: Amara.

Quick backstory here: when I wrote the *Blood Tribe* series, I avoided all things vampire. No movies, no books, no TV shows—nothing. I didn't want anyone else's mythos to leak into my story by accident. Yes, Michael and David are named in honor of characters from my favorite horror movie, *The Lost Boys*, and the Renfields are called that because of R. M. Renfield from Bram Stoker's *Dracula*. But that's the extent of my intentional hat-tipping. Michael and David's characters are nothing like the ones from the 1987 movie. I was determined to be as unique as possible, even while writing about one of the most popular myths in history: vampires.

Consequently, I missed out on lots of movies and shows—including a little series you may have heard of: *The Vampire Diaries*. When I finally got around to watching it (in 2023—talk about late to the party), I hit season five and my heart sank. They also used the name Amara for a character, probably for the same reasons I did. By then, I'd already released the first edition of *Blood Trials*, complete with Amara as Maysun's daughter.

Well, crap. It was time for another name change.

Could I have left it the same? Sure. But it felt weird, given the popularity of *The Vampire Diaries*. And dammit, I'd tried so hard to be unique.

So, I went back to the Googlebox and asked it for an Indian name that would suit Maysun's gifted daughter. That's when I found *Sana*, which means "brilliance" or "exceptional talent." I'm pretty sure that by the end of this book, readers will agree it suits her.

If the name Sana has already been used somewhere else to name a vampire, I don't even want to hear about it. It probably has. As Ecclesiastes says, "There is nothing new under the sun." All I ask is that if it has, please forgive me and move on. I think two name changes is plenty.

—Iris Kain

Character List

Sana Huett = Child of Maysun Khatri and Eoghan O'Rourke (see below). Attacked by vampires at a young age, Sana hasn't changed into a vampire, despite swapping blood with vampires.

Angelo Vargas = Vampire lieutenant to David Sheen, direct descendant of Joseph Cartaphilus. One of the vampires trying to turn Sana Huett into a vampire.

Bellina = Head of the Southeastern United States region of the *Shévet ha Dam (*former confederate states and all of Texas).

Blu = Birth name Babu Latif Ubora. Five-hundred(ish) year-old vampire and friend to Michael Graves and Vivian Black. Known for his blue-tipped hair. Met Vivian centuries before, during her time as a princess.

Brantley = Table underling who assists in capturing young Savannah vampires.

Bully Bosworth = Witch and friend to Michael Graves and Vivian Black.

Charles Dunning = Former lieutenant to Joseph Cartaphilus (also identified as Jude Shepherd), now host to the Maleficence. Once known as Oisian Drummann, a Scottish serial killer, Charles was a founding member of the *Shévet ha Dam.*

Crystal Novak = Adopted sister to Harmony Novak. Capable of aerocleaving (joining two locations through a tear in the fabric of space).

David Sheen = Leader of a small group of dark vampires, including Angelo Vargas and Perry Taylor. A direct descendant of Joseph Cartaphilus, David and Angelo have been friends since the 1960s, and Perry joined them in the 1980s.

Detective Kenneth Jewell = The detective investigating Sana's case.

Domevlo Ghedi = African *Shévet ha Dam* representative and one of the earliest members of the Table.

Dominick = Minion to the Table who assists in capturing young Savannah vampires.

Dorian Bradley = Also called DB or "Dragon Boy" by his friends Crystal, Harmony, and Tristan, Dorian can create fire with his breath (torch tongue).

Doyle Christy = Helped Michael and Vivian while they were in Germany. Provided false documents and entertainment. Also, a liaison for the Blood Tribe.

Ealdred D'Eath = Australian replacement Table member for Peter Ford, who died in the battle between Vivian and Jude.

Eoghan O'Rourke = Lover to Maysun Khatri (see below), Eoghan inherits the Balance. His alternate personality is Kip MacConin.

Errando Medina = South American delegate of the *Shévet ha Dam*

Gina = One of the original members of Michael's and Lukas' family Gina fell victim to Joseph Cartaphilus and sired Lukas.

Hatshepsut Keket = African (Togolese) *Shévet ha Dam* representative.

Harmony Novak = Another, younger vessel of the Balance (she calls it the Harmony). Adopted sister to Crystal Novak. Harmony has held her power for around 2 years.

Joseph Cartaphilus = Former gatekeeper to Pontius Pilate, father of the vampire race, cursed to contain the Maleficence that must remain on the earth until Armageddon. He took Vivian hostage during the time of Jesus of Nazareth. Identified in the current era as Jude Shepherd.

Kip MacConin = see Eoghan O'Rourke

Krieg = Spawn of a vampire and a giant, Krieg is a transporter hired by the *Shévet ha Dam* to move humans and vampires below the radar—literally and figuratively.

Linda Goodson = Friend to Michael Graves' vampire family, who held a memorial for her. Died at the hand of a drunk patron of the dance club where she worked as a dancer.

Lightning = Superhuman capable of creating electrical charges with his hands.

Lukas Graves = Michael's son and the family member who took Vivian in upon arrival at Michael's safe house. Pseudonym: Scott Moriarty.

Luzon Quiboloy = Minion to the Table who assists in capturing young Savannah vampires.

Mateo Gutierrez = Police officer in the Piper, South Carolina police force when Sana is brought in for questioning in her husband's death.

Maysun Khatri = Vessel of the Balance that holds the earth in equilibrium. Has many forms, but is often seen as a vampire Maysun.

Megan Jameson = Vampire girlfriend to Lukas Graves, also his blood progeny. Pseudonym: Ilsa Wolfe.

Michael Graves = Vivian's lover. Patriarch of the family that took Vivian in when she escaped from Cartaphilus. Pseudonym: Dillon Moriarty.

Perry Eoin Taylor = David's vampire progeny and the youngest vampire in his group who attempted to turn Sana when she was young.

Shévet ha Dam = Blood Tribe (not a character), the global network of vampires rooted in the Maleficence that allows humans to die for food.

Shui Cheng = Young self-appointed Asian representative of the Table.

Susan Batista = A member of the *Shévet ha Dam* employed by Charles Dunning for information that needs tracking down by technological means.

Talya Ananenko = Young Russian vampire who attempts to become part of the *Shévet ha Dam*.

Thom Huett = Sana's husband. Killed by David Sheen and Angelo Vargas.

Tristan Williams = Friend to Crystal, Harmony Novak, and Dorian Bradley (Dragon Boy [DB]). Tristan has magical abilities, including creating an invisibility veil and throwing fire from his hands.

Vivian Black = Born Jerusha, also called Bettina, Princess Katerina, among other names. Two-thousand-year-old vampire, former captive of Joseph Cartaphilus, and the primary host of the Source

Wynda Moireach = United Kingdom (Scottish) *Shévet ha Dam* representative.

The Story So Far

Book one, *Blood Tribe,* opens in 1943. Vivian Black learns that her best friend, Ruth, has died a horrific death, having been drained of blood, and Vivian's mother, Rose, seems to have a mysterious connection to a man named Cartaphilus. The man Vivian met the night Ruth died, Jude, swiftly seduces her, and she finds herself unable to turn away, despite her reservations about his secrecy.

Then Vivian awakens in a crypt, terrified and without a memory. She discovers several decades have passed since she met Jude, who she now understands is an evil man. She escapes to Savannah, Georgia, where she stays in a safe house with Lukas, a human; Michael, Lukas' father; and their friend, Gina. Lukas explains to Vivian that the *Shévet ha Dam,* or Blood Tribe, is a murderous group of vampires with Jude—who was born Joseph Cartaphilus—as its leader. Vivian learns then that she is also a vampire.

Jude tells the leaders of the Shévet ha Dam that Vivian is not just any escaped plaything—she is Jerusha, his only full-blooded child, whose strength surpasses theirs.

A "Renfield"—a zombie-like follower of the Blood Tribe addicted to vampire blood—tracks down Vivian and attacks her. Realizing it is only a matter of time until the Tribe finds her, Vivian and Michael flee to Germany.

Jude tracks Vivian to Savannah, where he finds and enslaves Gina to gather information about Vivian. He orders Gina to turn Lukas into a vampire.

Charles Dunning, Jude's lieutenant, summons favored Table members to a meeting, where he claims Vivian may be the key to overthrowing Jude. Although Jude has been cursed to walk the earth until Armageddon, Charles feels he sees how to kill Jude without triggering it.

Vivian discovers that her mother, Rose, is still alive. Vivian convinces Michael to head back to the States, both to help her reconnect with Rose and to discover why he can't reach Lukas.

Meanwhile, Lukas and Gina meet with Jude. Jude attacks Gina and toys with Lukas. Lukas escapes, but barely. Injured, Lukas collapses on the steps of a River Street candy shop. He meets Megan, who takes him inside the shop to bandage his knee. Lukas gives in to his hunger, drinks her blood, and then panics when he sees she is dying. Desperate to save her life, Lukas gives her his blood and changes her into a vampire.

Vivian, Michael, and Blu—Michael's friend—meet with Vivian's mother, Rose, only to discover she isn't really Rose's daughter. Her entire past was a mind trick Jude invented to keep her sated until he came for her again. *Shévet ha Dam* members attack Vivian, and her suppressed memories return. She is Jerusha, a Hebrew woman seduced by Joseph Cartaphilus after Yeshua had cursed him to walk the earth until Armageddon. Joseph was the first vampire, and she was the second.

Vivian, Michael, and Blu head to Savannah to confront Jude, unaware that Maysun and Charles have lured hundreds of vampires there for a battle centuries in the making.

Now in touch with the Source—a power for good—Vivian fears for Blu and Michael's lives and heads to Savannah alone. Blu and Michael meet Krieg, a vampire transporter whose job is to ensure they make it to Savannah in time for battle.

With Gina under his influence, Jude believes Lukas is one domino away—and with Lukas would come Michael, and then Vivian.

During the battle, Jude finally realizes his feelings for Vivian are more than lust and a thirst for power. That recognition changes his essence, severing his connection to the Maleficence. The power he wielded for two thousand years is expelled, and Joseph Cartaphilus dies.

Epilogue:

Charles lands at Savannah's airport, seething with disappointment over missing the battle. Furious and filled with hate, he becomes the new embodiment of the Maleficence.

Chapter One

October, 2006

Through a fog of bloodlust and ecstasy, Sana Huett heard two voices on the floor above engaged in an angry debate. It distracted her from the handsome young man between her thighs on the bed. Her lover's pale, cool body sent pleasure from her core to her slim fingertips as she writhed over him, but Sana was too unfocused to fully enjoy the experience.

She shook her head and tried to clear her mind, but her thoughts moved like water striders on the surface of a still pond. One minute, she was intent on her lover, awash in desire, enjoying his strength and boundless vigor; the next moment, the conversation above interrupted her with annoying, insistent words.

It wasn't until her lover placed his hands on either side of her rib cage that Sana noticed she was struggling to keep her balance. His hands held her steady as her shoulders and head swayed. She felt pleasantly drunk, but had a hard time concerning herself about it.

I didn't have any alcohol, did I? Her mind reeled with the unsteady, disjointed pace of the inebriated. She struggled to remember, but her thoughts bobbed and tumbled in a sea of confusion. She couldn't recall her lover's name. Or where she'd met him. Or how they'd wound up naked in the finished basement room of… *It is my house, isn't it?* She giggled.

Her head lolled, and the young man sat up and caught it tenderly in his hand. Sana grinned, and he returned it with interest. His elongated eyeteeth sent excited chills from her neck to her toes, and the sight of his tongue against them only heightened the thrill.

Vampire! But god, he's so beautiful. So, so beautiful. Hair as dark as raven's wings, eyes like bright turquoise, his light skin contrasted against her toffee-color. *But what is his damn name? Why can't I…?*

This has to be a dream. Vampires aren't real. And I'd never sleep with a stranger.

The sharp-toothed man below her drove his pelvis into her with earnest, sending waves of delight from her core through her body and making it impossible not to cry out. He gave her a smile that managed to be both shy and self-satisfied with her reaction.

The voice from the floor above spoke, interrupting her enjoyment. Though the accent was English, the tone casual, it set Sana's heart racing, this time in fear.

That voice. I know that voice!

Sana jerked upright, but her lover grasped her with gentle hands and brought her focus back to him. He met her eyes in his wide blue ones, and she lost the impression that she'd been on the verge of an important realization. She couldn't resist her lover's pull.

And why would I want to? It's a dream. I might as well enjoy it. She relaxed, her body a puddle of bliss and desire as she stretched into a reclining pose. The man below her enfolded her in his muscular arms and entered her again.

Cedar-paneled walls surrounded her in the windowless room. Colors appeared ostentatious in the amber light of the bedside lamp: the off-ivory vase of the nightstand, the hazel swirls in the painting to her left, the yellow of the lamp, all of it blinding and frustratingly distracting.

The brilliance was fleeting. Soon, the colors dimmed, along with the throbbing of blood pumping in her veins, the smell of pine cleaner and laundry soap, and the musky odor of sex. She blinked until the colors became less murky and wished her thoughts would do the same.

A voice growled, clearly frustrated. She'd recognize Thom's irritated tone anywhere.

Damn that conversation. I wish they'd stop talking.

The voices drew her with a slow but powerful force, like a tide to the moon. The deepest voice unsettled her, making her heart flutter in a way that was both familiar and terrifying.

That voice. It sounds like the one that's always running inside my head, but it's talking to Thomas!

Thomas. Her husband. *My husband? Then why am I—?* Her breath caught in her throat, and her stomach clenched in guilt as her eyes dropped to the breathtaking young man she lay with. How had she forgotten she was married?

A sharp scratch on her breast set off another overwhelming wave of euphoria, but she fought the emotion. She tried to picture Thom, but all that came to mind was a muscular arm in a button-down shirt encircling her waist, a condescending voice, and a space where she assumed love belonged. No details. No face. No smile.

A familiar metallic odor hit her nostrils and, with it, a rapture that stunned her. Her mouth opened, and she felt an odd pulling at the gums above her eyeteeth. *What is that smell?*

She willed herself to block out all the hectic stimuli and shake the confusion, but it was as if she was under the influence of a hypnotic drug. Her vision blurred, and her muscles froze as she struggled to regain her senses.

Shutting her mind to the overpowering lust and desire wasn't easy. It was simpler to lie still and enjoy the carnal waves running through her body with her lover's every touch. The clearer her mind grew, the more panicked she became. She needed answers, but with solutions came a life-altering truth. She sensed more than she saw it, like touching a scalding doorknob and knowing a house fire lay behind the door.

I have to see. I have to! This can't be right. Was I drugged? Is this even real, or is it a dream? I have to fight it! Wake up, dammit!

The flesh below her was too genuine not to be real. When her eyes met her lover's concerned ones, she realized he didn't like the level of clear-headedness he saw there.

He sat up, pulled back the collar of her button-down shirt, and sank his sharp eyeteeth into her neck. Sana cried out in a mix of suffering and enjoyment, and the grip she'd had on reality slipped away.

David Sheen stood in the Huett foyer with Sana's husband, Thom, tied to a heavy wooden kitchen chair two feet away. A third man, Angelo Vargas, lazed on the couch, picking at his nails and letting the shredded cuticle bits flutter to the rug. The man tied to a chair in the next room was not worthy of his attention.

"Sorry about the restraints," David said, allowing himself to come frustratingly close to kicking distance so he could feel Thom's ill humor. "Couldn't be helped, you know."

"So you say."

Dark-haired and dark-eyed, the three could have been mistaken for brothers: angular faces, all on the taller side of average, muscular,

straight teeth. Handsome, David supposed. Their hair was a little different. Angelo had shoulder-length straight hair lighter than the others and
dark green eyes. Both Thom and David had shorter, wavy hair, but David's was a tad longer than Thom's professional style. It was the way
they carried themselves that made each of them distinct. Angelo's attitude was one of indifference to the point of soullessness. David had a
feral quality that straitlaced Thom could never pull off. David often
wondered if it was their similarity in appearance which initially drew
Sana to Thom. He suspected the woman remembered more about her
fugues than she let on.

"Well, I couldn't have you running about the house mucking things
up," David continued.

"Mucking things up? My wife's downstairs fucking a kid—"

"He looks young, but he's not. Physically, he's kind of stuck, but
he's not truly seventeen."

"Seventeen? Aw, jeez. Statutory rape. Great. Fucking great. He's a
damned kid, and you miscreants—"

"Gentlemen."

"Bullshit. None of you are fucking gentlemen. Gentlemen don't let
women fuck children in basements. You and your friend are up here
having coffee—"

"Tea."

Thom scowled, tired of his captor's persistent correction of trivial
details during Thomas' remonstration.

"Shut the hell up," he snapped.

"Listen, Thomas. You're not in a position to quarrel now, are you?
Tied up and all? I understand that you're cross, but if you'd let me explain—"

"There's nothing you can say that would explain this. Nothing."

David dragged a second chair away from the dining room table and
sat on it backward, chest to the backrest, elbows slung over the top. He
raised his brows cockily and heaved an exaggerated sigh. Thom's head
sank to his chest, and his nostrils flared like an angry bull.

"I told you, Thomas, He's not underage. But you've been a right arse
since we arrived, and you won't listen. Are you ready to hear about how
your wife met us?" he asked, "Or are you still too cross to hear? You
might find the tale interesting."

Thom turned his chin to the wall. Although he tried to appear disin-
terested, his eyes gave away his curiosity, incapable as they were of not

flicking back and forth from the other man's face to the wall and back. David smiled. This was the point in the script he'd been waiting for.

"Well then, allow me to fill you in on a few details about your wife she's never told you. What she couldn't tell you, because when she's with you, she can't remember."

Chapter Two

It had been three weeks since Charles Dunning had sucked the life out of a human, and his normally ageless complexion showed it. His drawn skin looked as furrowed as a well-used map of the Grand Canyon, and every noise or question directed his way by the Renfields—his vamp-addicted minions—scuttling about his home unpacking his belongings made him irritable.

This was no way to begin ruling the undead. The *Shévet ha Dam*, or Blood Tribe, the global vampire organization that kept vampires and other dark souls hidden from humankind, had been rudderless for far too long. Since Maysun Khatri hadn't stepped up, it was long past time he took the helm. After all, the Maleficence, the dark force that had empowered his predecessor, had chosen Charles as its host. If Maysun *did* turn up and claim her position as the leader of the *Shévet ha Dam*, he'd kill her.

Maysun was the oldest living vampire in the Tribe after the previous leader of the Tribe, Joseph Cartaphilus, died. Logic and protocol dictated that it was her duty to take over the *Shévet ha Dam* once Jerusha had killed her sire. Or was Jerusha still calling herself Vivian Black? Did it matter? A flower that went by either name reeked of the Source and had killed Cartaphilus.

Although Charles, not Jerusha, was the one who'd driven the wedge within the ranks of the *Shévet ha Dam*, he saw no reason to blame himself for its collapse. If Cartaphilus—then known as Jude Shepherd—hadn't kept Jerusha as his slave for centuries, the Tribe's division and Jude's death wouldn't have been necessary. Jude had made the mistake of feeding Jerusha on his blood and had made her incredibly powerful, mistakenly believing he could control a creature who was his spiritual opposite.

At two thousand years old, Vivian was now the oldest vampire on earth with a power that Michael and his family could only marvel. Only Cartaphilus had been older and more potent. When the former doorkeeper to a man called Pontius Pilate was cursed by a young teacher named Jesus to walk the earth until Armageddon, Cartaphilus had become the first of the earth's walking dead—and the father of the vampire race. Sensing the good in Jerusha—the young Hebrew woman Vivian had once been—Joseph had taken her captive, planning to abuse her at his leisure for centuries.

But fate worked in mysterious ways. The Maleficence that powered Joseph—who, years later, called himself Jude Shepherd—had an opponent, one that had found a home in pure-hearted Jerusha. The Source, which loves all beings, found a way into Joseph's heart through Vivian. Two thousand years after he captured her, she used the Source to help Joseph recognize his suppressed adoration for her. With his acceptance of this love, Jude Shepherd rejected the Maleficence and became a mortal far overdue for death.

Cartaphilus was a love-struck fucking fool. And Maysun is a damn fool as well if she doesn't want to take her place in the Tribe. It shows her weakness. She may as well lie down and let us tear her to pieces. It would be quicker.

Despite Charles' exploitation of all the resources the Tribe offered, he hadn't found Maysun. She had vanished, untraceable despite his global psychic reach. Rumors abounded that she'd died in the war, but she'd survived long enough to call him after the Blood War had turned to dust in the Savannah sun. She'd made a passing comment about a holiday, and Charles had agreed she needed to take time off. Days later, he'd learned his plan to track Maysun down and kill her while she was on vacation had become impossible. She had vanished. Perhaps she knew death waited for her. Charles held the deepest and darkest power on earth. And he who held the Maleficence ruled the Tribe, regardless of age.

That was nearly ten years ago. If she'd taken a summer holiday, it had long since expired. While ten years wasn't much when compared with eternity, it was far too long to let the Tribe continue without a figurehead. He suspected Maysun was dead, but if she was dead, he resented not having the chance to be the one to thrust the proverbial—or literal—stake into her heart. Still, Charles needed to be confident that Maysun had no designs on leading the Tribe herself before stepping into the role of leader. It was a role he very much looked forward to taking on.

For centuries, Charles had watched as vampires hid from humans in the shadows and the dark of night. Despite their power, they hid like cockroaches in the dark and scuttled away from humans, never revealing their presence. Jude had never embraced the potential glorious authority of the Tribe. Charles would not make that mistake. It was time for vampires to take their proper role on the earth.

The flurry of Renfields bustling around his new Sedona home made his typical quiet hobbies impossible. Their nervous haste as they fluttered, unpacking box after box in room after room, was the type of frantic motion that made him edgy. That he was famished only exacerbated his irritability.

He could have eaten sooner, but the move from Houston had made hunting difficult, more an interruption than a need. He was fifteen hundred years old and descended directly from Joseph Cartaphilus, the two-thousand-year-old father of vampires. A trek into the daylight would not kill him, especially if he used photoprotection—a special sunblock designed by Blood Tribe scientists to extend the time a bloodsucker could endure sunlight. If his skin endured a day in the Arizona sun, it might grow a little pink, no more.

A vampire with his age and blood lineage had the strength to go weeks without food, but his stamina and power to resist sunlight waned as the stolen blood aged in his veins. Now, the combination of the emptiness in his stomach and the unforgiving desert sun gave him a headache.

Many of his younger kin thought him crazy, relocating to a town where the sun was a near-constant presence. He didn't care. He'd considered many factors when deciding where to purchase his new home. Once he assumed the head of the Tribe, it would house their headquarters as well. If aspiring members of the Table were powerful enough to be part of his company, he expected them to have no hesitation about negotiating miles of the desert instead of their previous meeting place in Atlanta.

"Mr. Dunning?"

Charles turned and faced a tiny Renfield, a meek, slim female who, had she been fully human, seemed the type to be more comfortable in a library than moving and unpacking boxes.

"Yes?"

"Your—your…" she held up a tall, mirrored glass case. Charles eyed his reflection in the back: slicked-back, dark-brown hair, an oval face that, years ago, had often been mistaken for the actor Tyrone Power. His eyes twitched from his wan reflection to the inquisitive Renfield impatiently.

"The great room, please," he said with a fluid wave of his hand. "Near the mantel. And be careful with the crystal that goes inside once you find it."

She nodded and waddled off with the heavy case in her arms, the top teetering over her head, causing her to lean back as she crossed the room. Charles winced, expecting her to drop it at any moment as she swerved to avoid boxes in her path. Renfields were stronger than humans thanks to the vampire blood they drank, but a Renfield her size still had her limits.

He wished his servants had set up the wet bar, but the dusted surfaces remained empty, still waiting for his collection of bottles, shakers, strainers, and jiggers. He longed for a highball. The taste of liquor was bland to his undead palate, and getting drunk nearly impossible, but indulging in a single-malt Scotch or a good Kentucky bourbon was a pleasant habit that left a comforting warmth in his stomach that helped him forget his need to hunt for a while.

After crossing an expanse of adobe-colored tile, he opened the glass door to the patio and stepped outside. The tile floor was several degrees warmer than the air; the heat was palpable through his suede slippers. Though the sunset was long past, the bricks retained the Arizona heat, and the radiating warmth caressed his exposed ankles.

Leaning forward, he put his elbows on the concrete balustrade and took in the lush view, one of the many features that had sold him on his home. From any window or door, one might see mountains, red rocks, city, desert, or forest, depending on the elevation of the window and the direction one faced. This patio held his favorite panorama. In the distance, piles of red rock, dyed purple with night, held up the heavens like mismatched columns. Mere yards from the iron railing he leaned on, the Coconino National Forest began. The fragrance of ponderosa pines filtered through the night air. In the center, a single, lifeless tree broke through the foliage and reached for the sky like a blackened hand.

He was lucky to find a home in the area that he found attractive. Most Sedona architecture was mission-style, which he'd never much liked. This mansion—purchased for a mere three and a quarter million—was

French, with a red brick walk and plenty of lush landscaping, which he didn't doubt would cost him a fortune to maintain and put him at odds with the local water authorities.

His home was nearly 8,000 square feet of rambling brick and tile and was far enough from town for privacy. He'd have his pick of humans in Sedona proper when he was ready to hunt. Flagstaff lay a quick flight to the north, Phoenix was an easy night's journey, and Los Angeles—his favorite hunting ground of late—was reasonably nearby.

Tonight, hunting had to wait. Her opportunity had passed. He'd been more than generous. It was time to reunite those who'd survived the battle that killed Cartaphilus and assume his responsibility as leader. Years of rumors and internal power struggles had left the Blood Tribe's Table disjointed. Charles had already chosen who he intended to head the groups—hadn't the Maleficence chosen him as its host?—but he had waited politely, if impatiently. He knew how to play the game. He'd made most of the rules.

It was time to gather them together again. He had sent his charges across his American territory to round up vampires unaffiliated with the Tribe—usually ones too cowardly or soft-hearted to kill. They were to provide them with a choice: join the Tribe and become killers, or die. Tonight, that would become an international initiative once the Table learned Charles held the Maleficence.

Charles considered using telepathy, but dismissed it. Telepathy was a trick Jude had used often, and while effective, thoughts were fleeting, emotions too easily buried. No, he needed to see the looks on their faces when he told them he was taking over as the leader of the Blood Tribe. The most fleeting expression revealed a plethora of moods.

One by one, he called. He heard new voices in place of the familiar ones as he paced and extended invitation after invitation to his new home. He'd arranged for a party for the Table the following evening, and would they kindly come? A few sounded surprised to hear from him, especially by telephone. Others expressed pleasure, or sounded a little too eager to reconnect with other Table members. He mentally cat-alogued each response, every hesitancy, every vocal nuance for later consideration.

His last call complete, he wandered into his den and sank into a plush leather armchair in front of the wide stone fireplace. If he was going to head his cherished Blood Tribe, he needed to appoint someone in his previous position as head of the U.S. division. He'd saved that role for one particular man—one Charles had firmly in hand. A vampire of dubious scruples who had high esteem and a higher level of fear of Charles.

He dialed Doyle Christy's number.

Chapter Three

Dawn rose in a brisk, late Scottish October. Maysun Khatri propped herself up on her elbows and used the few moments before her lover awoke to appreciate his handsome sleeping features bathed in the early sunlight.

Eoghan always looked most peaceful in the few minutes before waking up. Pale skin smattered with freckles made him look boyish, though he was nearing fifty. Once a fiery orange, his hair was now salted with white. Heavy lids covered eyes so blue they made the clearest winter sky dull in comparison. Crow's feet, softened as he slept, showed at the corners. Not long ago, those corners had been young and smooth. She remembered those days, and many in between, fondly.

Softly, she ran her fingers through his hair. Her own hair, the color of polished onyx, lay in a puddle on the mattress next to his. She considered his long, strong limbs and thought about allowing herself to be wrapped in them one last time, but decided against it; she didn't want to lose her nerve. She swung her legs over the side of the bed and dug her toes into her fuzzy pink slippers.

They had spent much of the past thirty-six years together, during which he'd never married, never proposed. If it was because he waited for her to say she was ready, she had never tried to find out. Those years were a drop in an overflowing bucket. On the upcoming December twenty-third, Maysun would reach sixteen hundred and seventy-four years old.

Eoghan sighed and murmured in his sleep. Maysun's lips curled into a smile as she headed through the antique-filled flat to put on the tea. Her nervous stomach churned at the thought of food or drink, but it was routine for the two of them to start with a cup as they discussed what they might do with the day.

What we might do with the day, she thought as she took the kettle from its base next to the stove, nearly dropping it on the way to the sink. She added the water, placed the electric kettle back into its base, and pushed the button at the bottom of the handle to start it. She retrieved two cheery yellow mugs from the cabinet and added bags of breakfast tea. *Am I getting nervous? Are my emotions returning already?*

Robotically, she collected the newspaper from the stoop, brushing her dark hair back over her shoulder as she stood. A breeze stirred the hem of her robe, and a look to her left told her it was going to be another rainy day. She paused for a moment, taking in the cool morning air and the view of the Firth of Clyde. A gray sky met gray water, and she couldn't see the Isle of Arran across the Clyde. Closer to home, the road shone black with moisture, and collected condensation dripped from her neighbor's gabled roofs.

Instead of putting the newspaper at Eoghan's place at the table, she threw it into the recycling bin. *We won't need it today.*

She desperately wished her stomach would stop dancing as she paced the kitchen, her eyes constantly surveying the neighbor's lawn through the window instead of paying mind to her task. As she added toasted crumpets thick with butter and fresh strawberries to a large plate for breakfast, she noted puddles growing in what was once their tiny garden. Beads of water clung to clotheslines made useless by the weather. A striped cat, agitated by the drizzle, shook his tiger-like head.

Why am I nervous? I shouldn't be worried. Or is it because… because the change is coming?

She let out a curt laugh. The change was coming. The flow of emotions suppressed for so long was only one of a thousand signs.

The kettle clicked, and the light turned off, so she tipped the boiling water into their mugs. Eoghan's voice disrupted her reverie.

"Morning, Luv."

She jerked and nearly burned herself with boiling water. She paused a moment to let her heart return to its normal pace before setting the teapot on its base.

"Good morning, Darling."

Eoghan stood in the doorframe, scratched at the red hair on his chest, and smiled. Maysun smiled back, a nervous and false twist of the lips. She took a moment to read his thoughts to see what he was thinking—if he'd picked up on her nerves. He was taking in her appearance, her black eyes, her arched brows. Thinking about kissing her full lips, how he loved her face, and how he enjoyed caressing the slight cleft in her chin with his thumb. She backed out of his mind and left him to his thoughts.

"Tea on?" he asked, more out of habit than inattentiveness.

"It is, but it'll be a moment," she said, taking a seat at the table. "It's steeping."

Eoghan sat in the chair closest to her, noted the absence of the newspaper, and went to rise and fetch it.

"Sit, please," she said, placing her hand atop his arm. "I need to talk to you."

Her voice sounded more desperate than she wanted, probably more desperate than he'd ever heard from her before. He sat, a concerned wrinkle forming in the center of his brow.

"What is it, May?" he asked.

Maysun rose and tended the tea, adding lemon to both cups and honey to Eoghan's. It was easier to approach the subject with her back to him, not to see his face as she spoke.

"Eoghan, how long have we known each other?"

"All of my life, May. Why?"

Gripping the mugs and her courage, she pivoted carefully and sat at the breakfast table, placing the mugs on cloth placemats.

"You were a young man when we met, Eoghan," she said. "In your early twenties, I think."

He disagreed with a shake of his head. "I wasn't alive before I met you, May."

Maysun's nutmeg skin hid the blush that touched her cheeks. No doubt about it, her emotions were returning.

"Eoghan, have you ever wondered why I never married you?"

His blue eyes clouded but never wavered. "I never asked."

"Yes, but why?"

It was his turn to look embarrassed. "You were hardly ever around to ask. Your work had you off all the time, and I… figured I'd wait until you were done gallivanting about. Maybe then you'd be ready. Or maybe you couldn't bring yourself to marry a daft git who spells 'Owen' with half the alphabet and not a single bloody double-u."

Maysun took a sip of hot tea and replaced the cup onto the mat with delicate hands. His joke was an old one, but it still made her heart light to hear the way his brogue rolled the last word.

"My travels are done now, Eoghan," she said. "But for you, they're only beginning."

Eoghan, who was about to lift his cup, paused. "I don't understand."

"Allow me to explain," she said, "but please keep an open mind." She sat upright and made sure his eyes met hers before she spoke. "I am the Balance."

"The… Balance? Is this something to do with your job?"

Maysun tipped her head in a nod. "This is going to sound incredible. Unbelievable. All I ask is that you let me finish."

Eoghan, puzzled, agreed.

"On the earth, there is a constant struggle," Maysun said. "A battle between what is moral and good and what is evil and dark. For a very long time, it has been my job to make sure the scales of the world don't tip too heavily in either direction. I've traveled the world over to influence world leaders and ordinary people to make decisions that affect the entire planet. I, and others like me, keep the earth in Balance."

He blinked. "I'm not sure I understand. That is, I understand, but…?" He stopped, his confusion and misgiving clear in his handsome face.

"That is where I go when I am not with you. I travel to wherever I am needed."

Lifting his hand to his mouth, Eoghan touched his lips and then returned his hand to the table. Crossed his arms. Tipped his chair back, then let it fall heavily. Turned to face her, his arm slung across the back of his chair.

"But there are over—what—six? Seven billion people on the planet? How can you keep them all from doing what they shouldn't and still have time to have a normal life?"

"Six billion, nine hundred eighty-eight thousand and…" her eyes tipped to the right, "one hundred. As of now. And I'm not involved with every single person. Only those whose impact on the world cannot be ignored."

"Like Hitler?" Eoghan asked. "Stalin? Saddam Hussein?"

She nodded. "And Einstein, Thomas Edison, and Ada Lovelace. And others as well. Sometimes, a single, small action performed by a seemingly inconsequential person has the most extraordinary consequences.

"There are other sources of power. One is called the Source or the Light—that is the power for good. The other, which is evil, is called the Maleficence, or the Darkness. They have both had many other names. These energies are available to anyone who asks—in varying amounts.

My job, the Balance, is an embodiment. I live to ensure that those who hold the greatest command don't gain too much power."

Conversation lapsed, and Eoghan's expression pained her. He appeared mystified at her words, and troubled, too. Maysun knew he was weighing them, trying to decide if he believed her or not. Although the power she wielded had told her he was open to the story because he trusted her, she still found her heart beating faster than normal. How long would it take to convince him?

"What do you do as the Balance?" he asked. "How did you change the—the—" his hands waved in uncharacteristic uncertainty as he searched for the words and failed.

"It varied," she said. "Sometimes, I was no more than a servant who said the right word at the right time, planted an idea in the head of a great—or terrible—man or woman. I've been the scriptwriter of dreams. Other times, I played the part of a confidant, a friend."

"A lover?"

She shrugged. "If the job called for it."

He let out a long sigh. "How long have you been doing this?"

"Sixteen hundred and four years."

"I—I'm not sure I—" he stopped, peered into her eyes, and shut his mouth. "May, what's all this for now? In over thirty years, you've never so much as fibbed to me, so it must be true. But why are you telling me now?"

This is the hard part. Oh, let me have the strength.

"Because it's time for you to take my place."

Eoghan froze. "What? Take your place? How on earth—?"

"You'll know. With the power comes the understanding of how to do what must be done."

"You can do that? Hand over your power?"

She made a small dip with her head. Eoghan blinked.

"Why me, May?"

"In all my time, I have never met a man like you, Eoghan. You have a staunch character, with a definite concept of right and wrong. You never waver when it comes time to make a hard call, no matter how difficult.

"As to why today and not five years from now or ten years ago, let me share a brief story. A man filled with the Maleficence was cursed to remain on earth until Armageddon. His name was Joseph Cartaphilus. He was a vampire, and a leader of the *Shévet ha Dam*, a global network of vampires called the Blood Tribe."

"A vampire? Are vampires real? Blood-sucking vampires?"

"Yes. I am not the only extraordinary type of being that has evaded detection by humanity. When dealing with Joseph Cartaphilus, I took on the appearance and powers of a vampire. The power of the Balance allows me to become any of these creatures and assume their abilities.

"Earlier this year, Cartaphilus died, but not before he rejected the Maleficence within him. That power found a new home in another vampire, his lieutenant, Charles Dunning. For years, Charles has waited for me to take control of the *Shévet ha Dam* because I am older than he, but I have held the Earth in balance by not stepping forward. Charles has decided to move forward. He will do his best to unite the Blood Tribe under him, and to overrun the world with the undead. He can identify me, and may come looking for me once he's recognized the part I played in the Blood War. And that's alright. My time as the Balance is over.

"Eoghan, the earth is filled with creatures most of humankind has only read about in books or seen in movies: vampires, werewolves, ghosts, and so many other creatures they've never realized. It will be up to you to make sure that these things don't get out of hand."

"That the world stays balanced."

Maysun tipped her head. That he didn't express disbelief at her claim that the paranormal existed was promising. She watched as the Adam's apple in Eoghan's throat bobbed. The poor man looked more frightened than she'd ever seen him. It was difficult for her not to console him.

"Not much point in saying no, is there?" he joked.

She let out a small laugh. "I already knew you'd say yes." His blue eyes reflected how touched he was that she understood she could trust him with this—literally the balance of the entire world.

Chapter Four

It was a strange memorial service. Michael Graves and his partner, Vivian Black, didn't hold it in a church. Too many newly turned vampires in Savannah clung to the mistaken belief that the sight of a cross threatened their health. Some avoided cemeteries for the same reason—they had faith in the myth that once a vampire stepped foot in a cemetery, they may never step out. It wasn't true, but the old vampire's tale lingered.

Instead, they held it at their empty townhome on Jones Street. They'd cleared the living area of furniture except for a handful of chairs covered in red velvet and a couple of large ficus plants in brass pots in the rear corners. White candles glowed atop a glossy black table covered in white roses and baby's breath. A smiling black-and-white photograph of their friend Linda Goodson, taken last spring at the Sidewalk Arts Festival, had been enlarged into an eight-by-ten portrait that rested in the center of the decorations.

Vivian guessed that about two hundred mourners had gathered in the home and courtyard to remember Linda, a handful of vampires, many unsuspecting humans, and a handful of humans who knew and accepted them. The number didn't surprise her. Linda had been a well-liked vampire in Savannah's club scene. She balanced her life as a vampire well with her job as a dancer at the Pink Peacock, a local strip club.

A sigh escaped Michael's lips, a sound he rarely uttered but had been making a lot in the two days since their friend's passing. He flicked the last of a cigarette at a glass ashtray, and several gray snowflakes fluttered onto the sleeve of his long, black button-down and black slacks. He squashed the butt and brushed at them with pale hands until his clothes were tidy. He rarely smoked anymore, but the stress of the past few days had worn him down and driven him back into his bad habit.

"Think they're ready?" he asked, surveying the crowd.

Vivian shrugged her narrow shoulders, surprised at his indecisiveness. "As ready as they can be. Have you decided what you're going to say?"

He fidgeted a little—another uncommon behavior—and ran his tongue over eyeteeth he was still too young to retract. The hand that held hers was atypically warm with nervousness. He'd hunted that night to keep his appearance as human as possible, and the fresh blood elevated his temperature for a while and added to his color. Michael had been pale when he died, and being undead didn't help. Vivian had been a young Hebrew woman during the time of Christ, and although she'd been blond and blue-eyed when Michael met her, she'd returned to her natural appearance rather than maintain the façade.

"I'm pretty sure. Short and to the point," he said. "I…" His hands turned palms up, then dropped to his sides. "What can I say? It's Linda, and she's gone. She'd hate the idea of us holding a funeral for her. It's not our way. But so many of her friends seemed to need closure…"

Vivian nodded and embraced him briefly, letting go before he lost control of the emotions he'd reigned in for the service.

He let a determined breath out through his nose and said, "Okay. It's time."

Michael meandered his way through the crowd. Conversations died to a murmur as he assumed a place beside Linda's photograph at the head of the room. He needed no microphone; a hush settled when they saw he was about to speak. Everyone in that room knew Michael Graves, only to them he was Dillon Moriarty, a man renowned among Savannah's party set.

Michael glanced to where Vivian stood at the back of the room and gave her a meager smile.

"I'd say good evening, but we we're all here for the same sad reason," he said somberly. "Uh, I know many of you by name, and for those of you I haven't met yet, welcome.

"We're family here. If not by the familial bond that links a few of us, then by our love for Linda." He paused as his voice cracked, broke eye contact with the room, composed himself, and stood straight. "It's hard to believe she's gone. I was as shocked as you. She was always so vibrant. It's hard to wrap my mind around the fact that anyone so full of life could be gone."

He paused and shuffled a little. "Um, I won't take much of your time.

If I knew Linda, she'd be appalled at the thought of us crying over her and taking turns saying eulogies and sharing stories one by one while the rest of the room stayed quiet. She was a tough woman, and not too prone to sentimentality. So, with that in mind, there's a big open bar in the kitchen and plenty of beer in the fridge. Help yourselves, and let's spend the rest of the night—or, as much as you're inclined to spend here—sharing memories about Linda in a way she'd be proud to see us sharing them. Drunk."

A wave of polite laughter passed over the group, and a few applauded. Michael motioned with his head, then with his hand, showing that he was serious. He finally resorted to making shooing motions to urge the crowd to the back of the house, where folding tables of high-proof alcohol and two refrigerators—one in the kitchen, another in the garden—full of beer and white wine awaited. There were enough kegs to stock a bar—or at least enough to get around two hundred young people drunk and a handful of vampires mildly intoxicated. Slowly, the group made its way back, already chatting among themselves with relief that they hadn't been required to sit through a drawn-out service.

Michael stepped down and took his place next to a smiling Vivian. He wound his hand through the arm of her sweater and interlaced his fingers with hers.

"She wouldn't have wanted it any other way," Vivian said. She wrapped her arms around him and rested her head on his shoulder for a moment. When his energy regained its evenness and he seemed comforted, they joined the last of the mourner-partiers at the tail end of the procession. She noticed a nearly empty bottle of Wild Turkey was already making its way through the pack as if crowd-surfing.

That was Linda's favorite whiskey.

"Vivian?"

Tears burned her eyes. "Sorry. Just remembering."

Thick, dark fingers snatched the bottle of Turkey before it reached them. The enormous hand belonged to Bully Bosworth, the bouncer at the Pink Peacock, and Linda's biggest fane save her boyfriend, Rob. Bully's bulk, scarcely hidden tonight under a striped polo shirt, would easily give competition to the average NFL center.

Bully tipped the bottle vertically and pulled a few long gulps that Vivian suspected burned his human throat.

"It's gonna take more than that to do you in, Bull," Michael said with an affectionate pat on his arm.

Bully's round face showed none of his usual joviality.

"Ain't nothing I coulda done for her," he said, voice thick with grief. His eyes stayed low. "She was here one second, gone the next... Poof." Large tears broke free and dripped down his face, almost iridescent against his dark skin. "I can't believe I lost her. I didn't have time—"

"There wasn't anything you could do," Michael said. "In some ways, we're more vulnerable than humans. Linda was a young one. She didn't stand a chance."

Bully shrugged his massive shoulders as another tear made its way to his chin. He wiped it away with the back of a hand.

"Worst part is that sorry-ass mofo really think he got away with murder." To which Michael could offer no consolation.

Two nights ago, Linda had proven that death awaited immortals as easily as it did humans. One of her regular customers, an irritable redneck fueled by kamikazes and libido, had become furious when the stripper with the sexy librarian stage persona had refused to offer him more than a lap dance for his hundred-dollar tip. Murderously outraged, he'd driven a number two pencil straight into her heart before Bully could intervene.

He'd had no way to tell he'd be getting away with the murder he was about to commit. As soon as the tip hit home in the young vampire's heart, Linda ashed. No trace of her body, save what little clothes she'd been wearing, attested to her former existence.

Bully, Linda's friend and a bouncer, had positioned himself in the private room when the incident had happened. He was aware of Linda's vampirism, so the way she died hadn't shocked him—only that he'd failed to prevent her death from happening.

"You can't blame yourself for that," Vivian said, gently touching Bully's forearm. "Linda wouldn't want you to, and neither do we."

The sincere tone of her words lessened the tension in his face, and he patted her hand with his. "Appreciate you, Viv."

"Nothing to thank me for. It's true."

The sound of a shouting male voice drew their attention to the kitchen door. Michael's son, Lukas Graves—six-foot, ten inches tall, blond, and thick as a grizzly—wended his way through the crowd to the front of the house, one arm suspended horizontally, the other clutching a bottle of Jack Daniels aloft. The spectacle made Vivian smile. She did not doubt that Megan Jameson was draped under his lower arm, hidden by the crowd. Less than a year ago, Lukas had sired her in a desperate effort to save her life after nearly draining her in his tremendous hunger for blood as a freshly-turned vampire. His hunger and inexperience had nearly killed her. Instead, he now had a best friend, girlfriend, and progeny.

"Make way! Make way!" Lukas shouted. The crowd parted before him like rush hour traffic slowly making room for an ambulance. Still, it took him much less time to cross the room than it would have most people. Whether it was his height, his volume, or because he was the son of Michael Graves, Vivian wasn't sure. Probably all three.

Seeing them side-by-side, no one would guess Lukas and Michael were father and son. While they appeared roughly the same age, the physical similarity was limited to their confident posture. Michael was of average height and fit build, with deep brown eyes and dark brown hair contrasting with his pale complexion. His square jaw and cleft chin were exceptionally masculine, unlike his son's rounder, more youthful face. Lukas was tall, built like a Norse god, and had a face framed by curly, dirty-blond hair that accented his other childlike attributes: a smattering of sandy freckles and a mischievous grin.

A little over thirty years ago, a member of the *Shévet ha Dam* had sired Michael and left him alone with his dead wife and toddler. Michael had struggled to survive and had protected Lukas from others like him, vampires who relied on human blood for life. He'd made a family out of a devoted group of other undead stragglers like himself, vampires who refrained from killing the way the Blood Tribe did.

After Vivian escaped from Cartaphilus, Michael's small family nearly unraveled. Jude had turned their friend Gina into his slave, and sired Lukas. Gina had died in the Blood War; Vivian saved Lukas.

Once at his father's side, Lukas sighed and dropped the whiskey bottle as if it had suddenly gained ten pounds. His face reflected a maturity that losing friends gave a young man. He hadn't aged physically as a vampire, but his eyes matured in ways that physiology could not measure.

Megan, usually outspoken and quick-witted, was atypically silent tonight. Vivian wished she and Megan had gotten closer over the past few months, but she imagined it was hard to bond with a vampire two thousand years old.

"Bully," Lukas said in greeting to the man at Vivian's side. Bully nodded, but remained silent.

Lukas inhaled deeply, raised the bottle once, and crowed, "To

Linda!" Across the home, shouts of the toast echoed deafeningly, and bottles and disposable red and blue cups were tapped together and up-ended.

Once Lukas had drunk his fill, he handed Bully the bottle, already half empty. Bully, who had killed off the Wild Turkey, accepted the fresh bottle and tipped the bottom to the ceiling.

Megan swallowed and blinked, her eyes panning the crowd. "When do we leave?"

"As soon as the last of the revelers go home," Michael said. "All we'll have to do is hit up an ATM so I can replace the cash we've spent on this." His hand motioned to the crowd.

Megan cocked a skeptical eyebrow above a blue eye flecked with gold. "It'll be almost morning then," she noted. "Shouldn't we wait until tomorrow night?"

Michael shook his head. "The sooner, the better. The windows on the Jeep are tinted, and the three of us have had plenty to drink tonight. Thanks to Doyle, we have photoprotection. We'll be alright."

"Where you headed?" Bully asked.

Michael shrugged. "I thought we'd try Massachusetts," he said. "I hear it's nice this time of year. Very busy. Lots of crowds to get lost in."

Bully managed a smile that almost looked genuine. "Salem at Halloween? Man, that's straight up perfect. Y'all tell 'em Bully said Hey."

"Do you have friends or family there, Bully?" Vivian asked.

"Nah, not really. But anybody who love folks walking the line between this world and the next? That's fam to me." He pulled a wallet the size of a paperback book from a back pocket and withdrew a business card. In white lettering on a navy background, it read, "Deshawn J. Bulworth, Personal Bodyguard, Thaumaturgist Extraordinaire." His e-mail address, home, and cell phone numbers were listed in the corner with a post office box number. He extended his hand to Michael.

"Y'all need anything—don't matter what—you hit me up. You hear?" he asked.

"Thaumaturgist?" Michael said, grinning as he put the card into his wallet. "Good word. Didn't know you had a business card, much less a day job. I can't see you in a cape waving a wand around and performing sleight of hand."

Bully didn't hear. He lifted the bottle to his lips once more, his deep brown eyes bloodshot and sorrowful.

Chapter Five

"Name's David Sheen, by the way," David said .
Thom looked away and pretended not to listen, but his posture belied his act. David took a few steps, leaned against the wall, crossed one ankle over the other, and went on.

"She was fourteen when we found her. Of course, we didn't know she was fourteen. She easily looked eighteen, easy, and acted older than that. Carried herself older than that. Precocious little thing, your Sana. Took us a bit to clock her age. If we'd known, well… things might've gone a bit differently. We were sent to find her, not turn her. Not that we managed either properly."

"Turn her?" Thom asked.

David snorted but didn't answer. "Oh, keep up, would you? Our old buddy Ralph fell in love with her in less than a minute, I'd wager. Stupid git. Of course, he hid her from us. He knew what would happen if Angelo and I found out. We were freshly turned then. Perry—the one downstairs with your wife—he was barely shaving when I sired him. Angelo over there, he was twenty-six. I was nearly thirty.

"Anyway, Ralph wasn't a good liar, and I could sift through his thoughts easier than flour. After he'd ducked us a few nights and snuck off, I decided to take Angelo and Perry to see what Ralph was up to. That was when we first saw Sana.

"'Bet he's filling her head with fairy stories about living forever. I bet that's what she's after.' Angelo says. I can still picture him, squatting behind the fountain, never taking his jealous eyes off 'em.

"Fucked up as it sounded, we talked ourselves into believing Angelo was right. Ralph had become a traitor. And it made us mad. We were a family that had stood together when our sire left us alone to find a fourteen-year-old girl in this tiny South Carolina town. We had no idea Sana was the one we'd been looking for.

"Ralph walked her home. We trailed them. Watched her sneak into the basement window. Ralph made sure she got in without waking daddy dearest. As soon as he turned around—"

"Grabbed the bastard," Angelo growled, his eyes flashing.

David smirked. "By the hair. You should've seen Ralph's face. He knew the jig was up."

Thom's upper lip curled, but he said nothing—whether from shock or disdain was unclear.

"I stepped between him and the window, made sure he couldn't see her. He looked like an underfed, frightened animal. He didn't fight. He couldn't; he was too weak. It'd been a while since he'd fed. Ralph had been on his best behavior since he met Sana.

"'Thought you'd get yourself a little friend, Ralphie?' I asked. He didn't say anything. I smiled, and he looked more scared. I snapped my fingers and pointed to the window Sana had climbed through.

"In ten seconds, all four of us slipped into her window, silent as ghosts. Her back was turned. She was already half undressed for bed, in a long white t-shirt. Bare legs. She didn't see us in the mirror—that's a choice we can make once we're strong enough, which we were. She didn't see us, didn't hear us. Then she turned around. I can only assume what went through her mind when she saw the four of us standing there.

"Jude, my sire, taught me a few tricks in his time, and mind control was my favorite. Always has been. Hypnosis is subtle, and the way we can make mortals comply is beautiful.

"I approached her first. Perry and Angelo held Ralph back. Ralph had never been a fighter before, and I have to admit, he impressed me with what he managed, but he was too feeble from blood deprivation. Still, I wouldn't have thought he'd had that much spunk.

"I ran a finger under her chin and smiled. Something was weird when I went into her mind—an absence like a cold spirit—but I thought nothing of it. I motioned to the bed. She went, complacent as could be.

"'Hold on to the headboard,' I said. She did, and gripped it fiercely, like she knew what was coming. I ran my hands up her calves to her thighs. She trembled, and I loved that. It smells delicious, fear.

"Then I struck. I sank my teeth into Sana's femoral artery, and I drank, careful not to drink too much. I called Perry over when I was done.

'Not to the death,' I said. 'But close.' He obeyed. Always did. Sweet lad, Perry."

There was an almost fatherly pride in his tone.

"They always heeded me. Next to Jude, our sire, I'm the closest thing to a father they have.

"Angelo brought Ralph forward. The man was barely standing. I opened his neck with a nail and pressed it to her lips. Blood's easier to swallow when you don't have a choice. She drank. And that was that."

"Ralph kicked and fought, but it didn't work. Blood coated her lips and slipped down her throat. She swallowed, and it was done. We might have drained her, but Ralph was her sire.

"Wasn't going to let the others go hungry. Told them to have their fill—so long as they didn't drain her. They fed. She faded. I topped her back off with Ralph's blood. Over and over. Whenever she wore down, I forced more of Ralph's blood into her. Ralph tried to pull us off, but pushing him away was like swatting at a fly.

"By the end, she was trembling, pale as death. Ralph's cheeks were streaked with tears. Bloodied his own lip biting down to stay silent. He knew if her father walked in, we'd kill them both.

"When dawn had nearly arrived, I turned to Ralph with a sneer.

"'Do her,' I said. Ralph could only shake his head.

I scoffed. 'Don't kill her,' I said. 'I want you to break her in.'

"He shook his head again.

"'I'll do it,' Angelo offered. His hands were already going for his belt.

"I shook my head. 'Ralph will do it. He'll do it, or I'll do it for him. And if I have to do it, I'll kill her when I'm done.'

"Ralph dropped to his knees and sobbed. Damn him for a hero, he refused.

"'Then kill her,' I said, 'or I will. And you won't like the way I do. And then I'll kill you, too.'

I meant every word, and I can only imagine the sort of death he imagined I had in mind for her. Chances are that whatever he pictured, I'd planned worse. He crawled into her bed like the beaten dog he was and sank his teeth into her neck.

"'Wake,' I whispered. And she did. Her eyes grew enormous with panic.

"She screamed. God, how she screamed when she saw Ralph on top of her, and it got louder when she realized there were three more of us watching, and there was blood all over her. Her conscious mind didn't get what had happened, but the sight of Ralph with his teeth sunk into her neck gave her a fair idea. She hit him, and she cried.

"Ralph leaped off and put his hands in front of him, waved, begged for her forgiveness. Sana made sounds that weren't words, her sentences nothing but sadness and anger. Then she surprised us all.

"She lunged forward and bit him in the neck. She'd only had vampire blood in her veins a couple of hours, but her teeth had already popped. Sana learned fast, that little minx. Of course, she was probably starving, newly turned and all.

"Ralph cried out and fell. He was a hell of a sight there, dropped to his knees by a tiny female covered with bruises and bite marks. She drank like she was starving, and he didn't fight her off. I guess he thought he deserved it.

"Then we heard footsteps on the stairs.

"'Let's go,' I barked. And Sana stood and watched, panting, angry, with more blood spilling down onto that white t-shirt. She recognized the odds were not in her favor—three of us, one of her. Angelo pulled Ralph's body out the window, and it ashed as soon as the light of dawn hit it. She'd drained him dry.

"I waited, standing at the edge of her room, defying her to confront me.

"Our sire Jude—the first vampire—gave us all particular abilities. I learned to use mine quickly and well, one of which is the power to make myself invisible. I was there one minute, and then—poof—I wasn't.

"I think that's when Sana lost it.

"Then her dad came in. Chunky little sod wanted answers. Asked who'd done it. Didn't like seeing someone else's fingerprints on his prize.

"Her lip shook. Her eyes watered, and tears poured down her bruised cheeks as she hyperventilated.

"'Sana? Sana, who did this?'

"She drew in a shuddering breath.

"'N-n-n-nobody,' she said. 'There's nobody there.'"

Chapter Six

Centuries before in India, a Brahmin teacher had entrusted Maysun with the power of the Balance. Although she had little idea what had inspired him to pass that power onto her, when the moment passed, she understood how and why he'd done it. Likewise, Maysun needed no instructions to guide her in transferring her power to Eoghan. She placed her fingertips on Eoghan's temples and simply wished for it.

She felt like a shore, the tide slowly ebbing away, indifferent to the lives it touched. A part of her that had appreciated the power and responsibility ached to grasp at the riptides of strength draining from her and funneling into Eoghan, edging out and obscuring his most profound signs of age, making it difficult to gauge.

A physical change began in her, too. First, her toes and feet tingled. It took several moments to realize it was because she could feel the cold again. Then, her limbs grew heavy as the vitality she held made its way from the rest of her body and traveled down her arms and fingers into Eoghan's waiting vessel. Her neck fell forward as her shoulders weakened, and she fought her buckling legs.

When the change finished, Maysun's legs wobbled. She gripped the back of Eoghan's chair before the need to collapse won. The process might have taken five minutes, but to her body, it seemed like hours. When she opened her eyes, stars danced before them.

She backed to a chair, stumbling as she went, and fell into it as soon as her knees touched the edge of the seat. Her eyes blinked as the world grew fuzzy. The view didn't improve. Her eyes had aged, and her vision blurry.

Oh yes. This is what it's like to be tired and old. She had forgotten.

With the power of the Balance had come supernatural strength and endurance, the ability to work days at a time without sleep, the power to block out pain, and the inability to age. But memory had often been sacrificed in service of the greater good. She'd matured several years as her agelessness moved to Eoghan. Did she now look like the seventy-year-old woman who'd inherited the job from the Brahmin priest? Her hands and arms looked only slightly different. Fate had been kind; it did not repay her for her service with a dying body.

Eoghan opened his sky-blue eyes and gazed around the room. She knew what he was seeing: the entire universe in the space of one tiny kitchen. While his eyes took in the table, the tins of tea, and her, the knowledge of continents flowed through him as easily as oxygen to his lungs. Her rediscovered human thoughts struck her as remarkably mundane.

His gaze fell on hers. "Brilliant," he murmured. He continued to study her as if she were the source of his newfound insight. Then his brows furrowed. "Maysun…"

"It's alright," she said. "You'll get used to it in time."

"But why don't I feel… I mean, why can't I—?"

"You can't afford to have the emotions you did," she explained. "Life as the Balance means not letting your emotions disrupt the equilibrium that keeps the Earth stable. If you did, it would be hard not to let the earth become overrun with good and unable to understand what a gift it is."

Eoghan paused, visibly upset—or as upset as his newly dwindled emotions allowed. In time, his feelings would recede until they all but vanished. Now, the power flowing through him was growing, conquering the last vestiges of lingering humanity.

"Did you ever love me?" he asked.

Surprised by the question, Maysun had to consider her answer. Eoghan would sense a spurious reply. Not that she intended to lie, but she'd gotten into the habit of dancing around the truth.

"As much as I could," she finally replied.

He processed her answer with a blink of his heavy-lidded eyes.

"Can I die, then?"

She smiled, aware of the oddly exhausted muscles in her face. "You tell me."

Eoghan considered it like a young man pondering the solution to a riddle. She wondered if it felt the same to him as it had to her as he prodded the fabric of the Universe in search of answers.

"Aye, I can die," he finally said, "But I'll know how not to. Where to be, and where not to be, what to say, when to hold my tongue. It's all there. The ways to prolong life. It's there, too."

She tipped her head in a bow, affirming his answer.

"I have to go," he said, standing and weaving, a little punch-drunk with power that animated him with a pressing need to be where the Balance called.

"I understand," she said, wanting to stand as well, but unable.

Eoghan started to the door but stopped at the edge of the kitchen, his hand extended short of the knob.

"Do you ever get used to it?" he asked, a childlike expression on his ageless face. "All these thoughts… all this knowing. Feels like there's always something to be done, always somewhere else to be."

"You learn to choose your battles," she said. "Otherwise, you'd never rest. There are many places you'll need to be, and at times it will seem as though there's too much to do, that life asks too much of you. You'll learn to handle it."

He put his hand on the doorknob.

"Thank you for trusting me," he said.

She wanted to say so much. Now that her humanity had returned, so had her exhaustion, her age, and the emotional weight of everything she had done. More than that, years of pent-up emotions had come back; the weight of all the times she'd had to act in unethical ways, all those times she'd fought battles she wouldn't have otherwise supported, all the guilt for the immoral acts she'd committed in the name of balancing the good with the evil.

And, sitting there in the tiny kitchen in Scotland, Maysun stared into the eyes of the lover she'd held close for over three decades. Now that she had gotten in touch with her heart, she saw how good he had been for her. How much better he had been *to* her than any other man. For the first time, she felt the depth of her love for him, and it was awe-inspiring. The sensation was more potent than what she'd wielded as the Balance. Like all the emotions she'd suppressed for centuries had come back as this single emotion—her love for Eoghan. It was beautiful. Intoxicating. Heartbreaking.

Aware that tears flowed down her cheeks and burned her eyes, her throat constricted as she choked on emotion, she forced herself to speak one more time before her lover walked out of the door and, very likely, out of her life forever.

"I love you," she breathed.

He looked down, unable to say what wouldn't be true. If he returned the sentiment, he would be lying, and they would both know it. Eoghan had never lied to her, and he wouldn't start now.

"My heart's always been yours," he murmured. He closed the door behind him.

Chapter Seven

Thom's head had dropped to his chest. He closed his eyes and feigned sleep, but his gut roiled.

Anger. Frustration. Irritation. All directed at the cocky assholes who swaggered around his house telling ridiculous vampire stories.

Who were these men, and why did they have so much interest in Sana? For all he knew, she might have taken turns fucking each of them. The woman never talked! She locked herself up in her studio at all hours, attacking canvases as if they held the secret to life.

He'd tried to be patient with her. She never bitched about all of his overtime, all the travel, all the time apart. But it was hard not to ask her why she didn't give up and live like a regular housewife. What was wrong with romance novels and watching Lifetime movies? Why didn't she join a gym or a club or volunteer like his coworker's wives? It wasn't like her work was selling much. Unfortunately, she'd had enough success to keep her flinging paint.

If she weren't such a damn tiger in bed, he probably would've walked years ago. Or at least have had a decent affair instead of a handful of flings with younger women he saw around the office.

Once he realized that David's story had ended, he lifted his head and gave the man a bewildered look.

"You're telling me she's a *vampire*?" Thom asked.

"No," David said, his face reflecting an odd emotion that might have been disgust. "Well, not the way we are. See, that's what's thrown a real spanner in the works. Most days, she's nearly human. She holds a job, if you call her painting a job."

Thom scoffed. David regarded him with a smirk and went on. "She doesn't drink blood nearly enough to qualify. She's an addict, sure. And she's got a bit of our power."

"Power? Sana?" Thom sneered. "Oh, that's bullshit. Like what?"

David ignored him. "She lost her mind a little that night too, but she hides it well. She thinks she went crazy and did it herself. All those bruises, the bite marks—she thinks she's gone mental and she's hiding it. Like our presence. For years, she's sensed us; her vampire blood won't let her ignore that we're there, following her around. After a while, we became a bit bored, and we started teasing her a bit for fun. But she thinks it's because she's crazy, so she ignores us. Easy enough to do. I've taught my boys to be invisible or out of sight most of the time.

"We can read her thoughts, just as she reads ours when we let her. She thinks she's a functioning schizophrenic, the only person she knows who invented imaginary friends as a teenager."

"Not to mention that she married a man who looks like you, Dave." Angelo sat up a little and then shrank back down at a fierce look from his blood brother.

"Thanks, Ange." He studied Thomas, noting the likeness. "Yeah, there's that, too."

"What's any of this got to do with what's happening in the basement?" Thom snapped.

"Vampire blood is addicting to humans. Very addicting. Most of the time, she does fine without it, though. Better than most I've known—and I've seen more than a few Renfields. But there are days she remembers. Vividly. And when she remembers, she craves it. And when she craves it, she goes… well, a little barmy."

"What do you mean? Like fucking seventeen-year-olds in the basement crazy?"

"I told you—Perry's not really seventeen. It's when he was turned. Vamps don't age, remember? And Sana is part vampire. Ever notice how your wife doesn't seem to age like other people?"

Thomas hesitated, not wanting to concede any part of David's story. "We've only been together five years."

"Well, how old is she? Thirty-three, right? And she only looks as though she's in her early twenties? It's the vampire blood. She's not a perfect vampire, though, so I'm guessing she'll age, but much slower."

The basement door opened, and a young man—dark-haired like David, but paler, with vivid turquoise eyes—stepped out, a sated look on his face and a fresh, very human bite mark on his neck Thomas glared. *If she's a vampire, where are her fangs?*

"Cheers," the young man said to David.

"No problem, mate." David turned to Thomas. "He looks young, but Perry here is closer to her age than you are. Renfields—well, Sana's not a Renfield—"

"You keep saying that. What the fuck is a Renfield?"

"Vampire servant."

"Looks like she's serving you fine," Thom snarled. "I should've known there was a reason she didn't mind me working all those hours."

"No, Thomas, you're not *listening*. She's not herself right now. My mates and me, we call it when her fangs come out. Sana's not a philanderer by nature. Unlike you. When she gets like this, she's detached from reality. Her fangs have come out, and she needed to feed."

Thomas digested the story and tried to figure out what parts were truth, and what parts fiction. How had David known he cheated? How far back did all of this go? After a minute, he gave in and spoke.

"You're telling me all this bullshit, but she's never acted like this since we've been together."

"She has. You've never been around. We've always relocated you in time. Business trips. Family emergencies. Trysts with women from the club or the office. All planned."

The truth in David's words sank in, and the color left Thomas' cheeks. "You staged that accident with my cousin last year?"

"And your father's emergency surgery. Yes."

"And—"

"That little affair during the New Year holiday the year you and Sana moved in together. That was us as well. I won't tell her if you don't. Never have before." His smug expression and ribald attitude enraged Thomas. He let out a frustrated breath, yanked at his restraints until his legs and arms grew raw with rope burn, and finally gave up.

Breathing heavily, he lifted his head. "What are you trying to tell me?"

"It means that Sana will need blood. Vampire blood, so you can't help—not that I suspect you'd offer. We've tried, but the human stuff doesn't pack a punch no matter how much we give her. And it seems she doesn't just want the blood. She craves sex. To her, it's all one dependence. Perry here was the one to help her out this year. He often is. She seems to like him."

"Cor, Dave!" the young man said. "Why don't you hand him a pointy stick and toss him at my heart?"

Angelo sniggered. "What's the matter, Perrywinkle?" he chortled. "Afraid you'll get a splinter?"

"Not—not funny, Ange," Perry snapped defensively. Perry's hands balled at his sides, but he avoided eye contact with the older vampire.

David made a motion that ended the banter. "Perry," he said softly, "no stake would cash your chips in."

"Easy for you to say," Perry said in a huff. "You're first generation."

David put a paternal hand on Perry's forearm. "And you are my son," he said, "In all ways that matter. Do you think I'd let anything happen to you?"

Perry looked away, embarrassed.

Thom fidgeted in his chair and scowled, unmoved by the display of affection from these men who, up to this point, had shown nothing other than snide condescension. Ready to put the focus back on him and the problem with his wife, he leaned over to catch David's attention. "And what if I don't want to let her do this? Can't I give her the blood? The sex? What's wrong with me doing it for her?"

"Are you really this thick? You're *not a vampire*, Thomas," David said. "She wouldn't get what she needs from you. We could change that." He gave Thom an appreciative leer. "You're already good-looking and heartless. You'd fit right in. Hell, we could even share her."

And be a freak like you? No way. "I can't forbid this from happening? I can't not let her go?"

David shrugged, amused. If Thomas didn't know better, he'd have thought the man had read his thoughts.

Thomas shook his head. Share Sana? No. She might not be much, but she was beautiful, and she was *his*. "There's got to be another way…"

"It's a hell of a concept, I understand. But if it's any condolence, her experience with Perry was nothing more to her than a nice little dream. She won't believe it happened—she never does. Tomorrow, she'll push it all to the back of her mind like a pleasant fantasy. It's all part of her denial of what she is."

"And what's that?"

"A creature with a killer's instinct. Like me." His eyes caught the light with a devil's gleam. The pupils grew until the irises went from brown to black. "But, unlike Sana, I can get what I need from you."

Thom noticed his sagging jaw, and he snapped his mouth shut.

"It's your choice, Thomas," David said. "You can let us stick around, cooperate with us when it comes time to take Sana for a drink. I like you. Hell, as I said, you can become one of us. Or you can die."

Thomas waited long enough to make it appear that he'd considered the offer. "Untie me," he said.

David produced a pocketknife from his jeans and cut the ropes with quick flicks of his wrist. Thomas stood, his fists balled at his sides, ready to strike one of them, or all of them at once. From behind clenched teeth, he struggled to find his voice. When he did, the words emerged garbled with anger. "You can go to—"

One motion from David and the air around Thom thickened. He was no longer restrained, but it was as if the ropes bound him once more. David's eyes bore into his: large, inky black… hypnotic. Handsome. God, so handsome. Thom found his breath short, his heartbeat deafening.

"Perry?" David asked, never breaking his eye contact with Thom.

Perry held up a palm and waggled his head. "No. I'm good."

With barely a twitch of David's hand, Angelo crossed the space between couch and Thom's side without appearing in any of the intervening space.

As Angelo's teeth penetrated the skin at Thom's throat, David broke the stare. Thom had barely enough time to break from his trance to realize he was screaming.

Chapter Eight

Charles hated mysteries, and he resented Jude for leaving so many behind, all in need of unraveling. For instance, the mystery of why Maysun had ever been chosen for the Table, despite her habit of vanishing for long, untraceable stretches of time. Why had Jude allowed so many small bands of renegades to live outside of the Tribe? Why had he created Jerusha and kept her alive when he must have known she could be his undoing?

Now, Charles resented the interruption into his delightful mental broadcast. He'd been channeling the thoughts and activities of vampires he'd charged with rounding up the rebels. One had shoved a young vampire into the sunlight for the pleasure of watching it ash in the light. *That one has potential.* A smile turned his lips up at the corner when another mental transmission intruded: the vampires following Jude's strange little project had decided to feed on—and sleep with—the woman they'd been tracking. Tonight, they'd killed her husband. The impressions he received from them were of pheromones and blood, sex, lust, power, anger, fear. The impressions he understood; the assignment to follow the woman for decades, he did not.

Another damned mystery. Why had Jude left three impetuous vampires stranded in an upper-middle-class town in South Carolina for years to monitor one woman? Three rebellious, bloodthirsty vampires who had followed Jude's orders for a decade and a half without argument. Not so much as a complaint. *Why?* Was it because they were as addicted to this Sana woman as she was to them? Why? She wasn't a vampire.

Why was it that *he,* Charles, could always sense it—every time the young vampires sated the woman? He was often thousands of miles away. He shared no direct ties with her or them. There was no logical reason for it. If Charles bore a connection to every vampire Jude had fathered over the centuries, he'd feel like a switchboard that never stopped lighting up. No, it wasn't the lusty British boys he sensed, it was her. What was it about Sana that alerted him?

When Jude had told Charles about Sana, Charles worried she would grow into another Jerusha situation—a plaything that Jude fed with his ancient blood alone until she became dependent and blind to his abuse, but also incredibly powerful. Unlike Jerusha, Charles would have had the advantage of age over Sana—at least at first. If Jude fed her a steady diet of his blood alone, he suspected that her strength would, in time, outpace his.

It never came to that, though. The companions Jude had assigned this odd duty monitored her from afar, but they occasionally toyed with her and diluted Jude's blood with their own. They trailed her and taunted her and reported back diligently. Why had Jude bothered? Why did they, when there was a world of young women and men for them to enjoy?

Charles believed that what fascinated Jude was their inability to turn her. Perhaps he believed that her resistance was a sign that she held a secret in her physiology to healing vampirism. The idea had merit. Not that Jude would want to become human again, but the threat of taking immortality away from another vampire, forcing them to live deprived of their potential for eternity, could be a weapon in Jude's arsenal. The *Shévet ha Dam* lab that created photoprotection, the tool that kept younger vampires safe from the sun, studied other things. Perhaps it was time to pay closer attention to what the lab was brewing—and what part this woman might be playing in it.

As the last human revelers slept, a handful of vampires lingering at Linda's farewell nursed half-empty bottles of whiskey, wine, and beer. Exceptional metabolism gave them impressive healing, but made it a bitch to get properly drunk.

Michael finished the last of his Courvoisier and set the snifter down. An empty stretch of wooden table showed where over seventy liquor bottles once stood, wet half-moons from cold beer bottles the only evidence of what had been there. Vivian expected the kegs in the garden were similarly empty.

"So," Michael said and stopped.

"So," Vivian echoed. Lukas and Megan caught her eye from across the smoke-filled room full of sleeping bodies, and she smiled at them solemnly. They gave her sleepy acknowledgements of small waves involving the slight lifting of fingers.

"It's daylight. Everyone here is probably going to be crashing here for the rest of the morning, so we have time to talk," Michael observed, keeping his voice low, so the conversation stayed between them. "I think it's time that we come up with a plan. We've been talking about moving forward with different things, but it's like we're all not sure what to do. Megan's quit her job. Lukas has cut his hacking into the Tribe's websites down to a couple of times a week. And hell, I've been floating around in a haze, acting like I'm on autopilot." His hands floated up from his sides in a shrug and dropped. "We need something to do. We've been resting on our laurels since the war, waiting for the Blood Tribe to make a move rather than being proactive. Not that I want to be the one to start problems, but confrontation is inevitable, and we're acting like we're helpless."

Vivian considered his comments, her head tipping to the side. "It is a relief that they have waited this long, but given what Lukas has said he's found out about their lack of leadership, not entirely surprising. I could channel the Source. It will give us at least an idea of where to start."

Michael looked relieved at her suggestion, the tightness at the corners of his mouth and eyes easing. He scanned their surroundings. "Do you need a quieter room?"

"This will do," Vivian said, a smile playing at the corner of her mouth. She found one of the few chairs free from debris with a lone jacket draped across the back, and she took care not to disturb it as she sat on the edge of the cushion.

Megan, watching what was now a familiar sight, noted a couple of petite half-awake humans murmuring, their heads nearly touching. Curled into an oversized chair, they looked like a pair of Gemini twins representing polar opposite, yet connected, personalities. One of them had honey-colored hair and tawny skin, and the other's hair hung in tight, dark curls around a fair face.

The two young women, noting Vivian's somber expression, stopped speaking.

"Is she gonna—?" the dark-haired one said.

"Shh!" Megan hissed.

Abashed, they shushed.

Vivian drew herself up, sent her shoulders back, and closed her wide brown eyes, raising her face to the heavens. Only her toes touched the floor, and her arms draped loosely at her sides. Wavy brown hair tumbled down to the center of her back as she slowed her breathing. The atmosphere in the room grew charged, and energy filled the air, stirring it slightly, like the soft breeze of a slowly turning fan. Vivian exhaled and heard Megan's thoughts: *I think I saw her breath!*

She blocked out any other interruptions and reached for the Source.

A fount of energy filled her with love and knowledge so strong it lifted her from her chair until she hovered above the seat. An electric charge flickered under her skin, and tiny lightning bolts set her body afire from within until she glowed with a faint, ethereal light. An irrepressible smile covered her face. She hovered for a moment, then allowed herself to drift back to the chair as the answers she sought found their way to her. The smile faded, and the room grew dark again.

"Wow," breathed one of the women at Megan's side, so emphatically that her tight, curls shook. "That was cool."

"Amazingly cool," agreed her fairer-haired friend.

Vivian stretched like she'd woken from a long nap, arching her back as she reached her slender arms over her head. She regarded the two young women in the chair interestedly, but she communicated nothing to them other than sending them a faint smile of acknowledgment.

"You've gotten quite good at that," Michael said. "What did you see?"

"I think it is time to go into another room first," Vivian suggested. Michael followed her from room to room, seeking privacy but always finding slumbering people. Lukas and Megan trailed them as they searched. The four of them wound up squeezing into a bathroom. Vivian and Michael perched on the edge of the claw-footed bathtub, Megan sat on the lid of the commode, and Lukas leaned against the countertop. It was the first time that night Megan had been farther than two steps from Lukas.

The positive energy from the Source that had left Vivian with an expression of bliss became tinged with unease as she shared the flood of emotion and images she'd seen.

"It was the weirdest thing," she murmured. "This connection was one of the most powerful connections I can remember making, but I don't understand it. Doyle's in trouble—that I'm sure of. Charles has plans to draw him in; he may already have. And there's more. The Balance has shifted."

"You mean it's in favor of evil?" Megan asked, her voice rising in fear. Vivian shook her head.

"No, I mean the actual Balance—the—uh—the job. Maysun's gone. Well, not gone, but she left her post. Someone new took her place. I could feel her the way I do any other human. And I don't know who she gave it to. I guess I'm not supposed to."

The four of them regarded one another and considered the implications of Vivian's discovery.

Michael tilted his head in Lukas' direction. "Get on your computer. See what you can find out. If the Balance has shifted, that may mean there's some news you can uncover in the Tribe. In the meantime, we should probably pack and be ready to move out by tomorrow morning at the latest."

"Why leave?" Megan asked. "Don't we want to confront them?"

"Not until we learn Charles' weakness."

"If he has one," Lukas added.

Megan frowned. "What if he doesn't have one?"

"Then killing him might mean the beginning of Armageddon."

Chapter Nine

Sana stirred after eight, judging from the glowing blue-green numbers of the nightstand clock. She wasn't sure whether it was eight a.m. or eight at night. At times like this, she wished she'd been born with an internal clock and a normal circadian rhythm. Hers had stopped ticking twenty years ago.

What am I doing down here? I came down to start a load of laundry and... She ran a hand through her hair, trying to tousle it back into place, but her fingers snagged on an unusual number of tangles. She flinched and tugged the ends of her hair until she could finger-comb through it. *I must have gotten tired again and conked out in the guest room. Ugh! I'm always doing that. How long have I been asleep?*

She sat up and stretched, unable to fight back a grin. Normally, the first few minutes after waking were her least favorite of any day, full of taut muscles and brain fog. But not this time. Her nap had left her more alive than she'd felt in weeks—months. The only problem was that she couldn't recall choosing to take a nap, lying down, or doing other activities resulting in body parts being slightly sore in ways that typically involved her husband. Perhaps she'd had an erotic dream.

IT'S BECAUSE YOU'RE CRAZY, SANA. YOUR MIND DOESN'T WORK PROPERLY. YOU HAVE A SPLIT PERSONALITY. YOU'RE SCHITZO.

Shut up shut up shut up.

Had she spent the entire night in the basement? And why hadn't Thom woken her up? He'd have left for work about half an hour ago if it was morning. If it was late, he should've been home for well over an hour. Either way, she should've heard from him. Thom wasn't a doting husband, but he always told her when he arrived home. His silence was odd. Thom was typically a little overbearing, often more like a father than a husband. Not her adopted father, thank God. That guy had been positively creepy. More like the way a regular father behaved, she supposed. That was part of why she cared about Thom—at least he acted concerned, even if his interest was more out of a need to be aware of where she was at all times. As long as he knew where she was, she was free to do what she wanted, for the most part.

In too good a mood to ponder it, she rose and noted that once again, she'd splattered her shirt with paint. Rust-colored stains covered the top of her white peasant blouse. What was she working on again? Oh yes, the portrait. Her dream men on canvas—the one that looked like a cheesy romance book cover. Thom hated it.

Another shirt ruined. It's white—bleach might do the job. Maybe I can save it.

She headed for the laundry room alongside the basement guest room, started the water, added the detergent and bleach, stripped her shirt off, daubed it with stain remover, and noted with disappointment the paint had seeped through and stained her brassiere as well. Her fifty-dollar brassiere. Her *white* fifty-dollar brassiere. *Great. Now I have to add that to the wash, too. And I'm not walking around the house naked.*

Looking around for a top to wear, she noted one of Thom's sweaters drying on the wooden fold-out rack. She removed the bra, treated the stains, and tossed it in with the rest of the whites. Then she slipped Thom's green cable-knit sweater over her slim, brown shoulders and headed up the staircase.

The door creaked as she pushed it open, but apart from that, pale shadows and silence loomed—no sign of Thom. The kitchen was as dark as she'd left it. The television was silent. No footsteps, no greeting from Thom as she made her way into the living room.

She caught herself tiptoeing and stopped. Why was she sneaking around in her own home? Why did the air feel *wrong*—heavy, foul, contaminated? A metallic sensation tanged in the back of her dry throat, and her eyes scanned the rooms, but for whom, or what, she did not know. Her irrational fear made no sense. Logically, she grasped she was alone, but it didn't feel that way.

It never felt that way.

It must be daytime. The sun is up, and Thom's gone to work. If it was p.m. the sun would already be down.

ARE YOU SURE? WHAT MAKES YOU AN EXPERT ON WHAT TIME THE SUN RISES AND SETS IN SOUTH CAROLINA?

I'm sure, she thought, flushing as she argued with one of the never-silent voices that plagued her mind. *I woke up when Thom did before he went to work last week. The sun was up then.*

BUT THAT WAS LAST WEEK, another voice taunted. MAYBE IT SETS EARLIER NOW.

Which it would; the days were getting shorter this time of year, but that wasn't the point. The sun came through the windows in the mornings. She wanted to tell the voices to shut up—what did they care about such asinine details as sunrises and sunsets?—but she didn't. Arguing was too much like admitting she heard them. It seemed the voices took constant steps to whittle away her self-confidence, which made no sense. The voices were part of her—why would she sabotage her sanity?

Part of her supposed it had to do with her adopted father. The years of "accidentally" caressed breasts and blatant brushes against her bottom with his pelvis as he passed by her in their galley kitchen. How well she recognized that confidence made a woman attractive and desirable. Exactly what Sana strove to avoid. Male gazes made her queasy—except when she craved them.

That's me—the living, breathing contradiction.

She turned her head; no one was there. *Right. I'm alone.* So why didn't she believe it?

Thom usually spent his last few minutes before work in the recliner, one hand on the remote, the other on a folded newspaper, but the chair was empty. What was on the television at this time of day? His morning news shows, probably. Thom loved to start his day with a dose of daily news bulletins and ink-black coffee. The screen was black. The television was off, not muted. The open drapes let in the faint light of the breaking sun, enough for Sana to see that the living room was empty.

Why didn't she feel alone?

Thom might have called in sick. Right. Thom, workaholic extraordinaire, avoider of spouses, and nearly all social occasions, had called in sick. That was about as likely as… well, as likely as the voices in her head being real.

"Thom?"

The emptiness swallowed her voice. A lump of fear rose in her throat, and Sana tried to push it down, but she only succeeded in bringing up the taste of blood.

The drapes are open, and the sun isn't high. The neighbors will see inside as soon as you turn on the lights. Anyone who wants to see what you're doing will be able to see.

SHUT THE CURTAINS. SHUT THEM SHUT THEM SHUT THEM.

Not bothering to hit the light switch—if she did, the entire neighborhood could watch—Sana scampered into the living room, set on closing the drapes, protecting her privacy, and keeping those pesky, nosy folks from seeing what she was doing.

Her foot hit a slick patch on the hardwood past the recliner, and she fell hard onto her hip and elbow. Her mouth opened in pain, but no sound came out, just a sharp exhale of surprise and hurt. She pulled her elbow out of the sticky mess and noted woefully that a thick coat of red paint coated her slacks and Thom's sweater.

Not again. Wait... paint? I never paint in the living room.

She looked down into unseeing eyes of her husband, his body carelessly tossed into a heap, his throat brutally removed by an animal. It *had* to be an animal; no human could've torn it out so savagely.

DON'T BE STUPID, SANA. HOW COULD AN ANIMAL GET INTO THE HOUSE? DO YOU SEE ANY BROKEN WINDOWS OR ANIMAL TRACKS? HEAR ANY NOISE COMING THROUGH THE FRONT DOOR? YOU DID IT. YOU.

Sana let out panicked whimpers of disgust and fear, fumbling to her feet in the slippery, sticky, gory mess. The back of her throat burned as she choked back vomit. Not thinking of her safety, not wondering for a second if Thom's killer was still in the house, she raced to the phone and lifted it with a bloodstained hand, punching 9-1-1 with trembling fingers before she thought too long and screamed.

Chapter Ten

Maysun couldn't remember the last time she'd had a proper night's sleep. Over the past few centuries, she'd used time deep in meditation to catalog people's lives, deciding whose troubles she needed to put right or complicate. While her body rested, her mind surveyed thousands of potential issues, and she'd choose the most pressing ones. She'd sorted events and lifelines like a defragmenting computer, categorizing them by significance from "Most Likely to Intervene" to "Worth Monitoring."

Often, she'd forgo sleep, passing the hours with people who lived most of their lives in the dark. She wasn't a regular human in need of recovery.

Until now.

After Eoghan left that morning, she realized how human she was. Although Her body longed for rest, but her mind wouldn't shut off.

The pain of her love for Eoghan was multiplied by losing him the same day she realized how potent that love could have been. Watching him walk away, knowing what lay ahead, had been heart-wrenching. She passed the morning pacing and worrying, wondering if she should reach out to him to make sure he was alright, but knowing that doing so would be more for her benefit than his. The result was a combination of mental exhaustion and physical sleeplessness, an aching heart, and a restless mind. She managed a short nap and jerked awake with a start, her heart in her throat. She felt terribly odd, but the oddness came as a result of being human again.

As the sun reached its crest, she left her apartment and wandered down to the beach, watching the choppy waves as they lapped on the shore, occasionally glimpsing blue in the iron-gray sky. The chill in the air was unfamiliar, and she reveled in her sharpened senses. She reveled in thoughts unburdened by constant insights into people's lives, but part of her missed the hectic pace her mind used to keep.

You've prepared for a relaxing retirement, but you've spent most of your life in a frenzy. You can't change that in one morning.

She strolled down South Beach Esplanade, which paralleled a lonely stretch of shore, and studied the rocks and sea. The Isle of Arran loomed in the distance, a blue-gray mountain surrounded by mists.

A happy-looking middle-aged couple passed, heading the other direction. She was plump and dark-haired, with a touch of gray in her wavy locks; he was slightly older, also with gray hair but a face nearly unmarked by time. Maysun thought of Eoghan and his newly rejuvenated face. The couple passed her holding hands, smiling, and chatting in the brogue she'd grown to love. Maysun nodded in their direction and longed for the familiarity they shared.

At lunchtime, she discovered to her delight that she was genuinely hungry. She headed for a pub on the coast and ordered the daily special— a messy roast beef hoagie paired with chips—from a man with kind gray eyes and a friendly grin. As she took her paper-wrapped goods to one of a handful of empty metal tables nearby, a flash of percipience struck her. She froze, arms outstretched to catch her balance as she braced herself for the flood of information that typically came with the onslaught of a mental news bulletin.

Nothing came. It was gone as soon as it struck.

An echo? Perhaps I'm still adjusting. The thought nearly made her laugh. No doubt it'd take months to grow used to the banality of humanity again. After living life at the Balance's frenetic pace, the serenity of calm thoughts and breezy shorelines was almost like going deaf.

"Alright?" the man behind the counter asked. He sounded ready to rush to her aid if need be. Maysun hesitated, waited until her heartrate settled to answer, and gave him a humble grin.

"Yes," she said with practiced sincerity, "I'm fine. Got a bit pissed last night—still feeling it, I think."

The gray-eyed make gave a hearty chuckle and offered a few hangover cures he swore would solve her illness. Maysun thanked him, took a seat at the table, and fought the urge to laugh again as reality set in.

It was no echo of her former power coming to haunt her. Her flash of "intuition" was nothing more than the flash of a dream she'd had during her hasty nap, a strange sequence of events that unraveled in discombobulated bits and pieces. A man in a brown suit. A gray room. A table not unlike the one she sat at now. The feeling that she was being interrogated. A young man who made her confused and aroused at the same time.

She popped a chip in her mouth—salty, vinegary perfection—and grinned.

I guess getting worked up over a dream is a little strange, but it's probably to be expected that I'd have visions of accusations or imprisonment after the acts I've done to keep the earth in Balance.

Her armchair psychoanalysis done, she found herself pleased to have found the answer to her problem in a minute's worth of pop psychology. She tucked in and enjoyed her lunch as she watched people passing by without so much as a hint into their personal lives.

She spent the day shopping in Glasgow weaving among everyday people and reacquainting herself with life among humankind. After returning home, she treated herself with a cool glass of chardonnay before pulling the last of her satchels from the car and dumped them in the entry of her seaside flat. Exhausted, she eyed the bags for a moment and then shook her head.

Unpack tomorrow. Take the rest of the night off. Don't do a damn thing—except a bath. With more wine. And bubbles.

Turning her back on the bursting bags, she sat on the couch with a book she'd picked up on Sauchiehall Street, but it couldn't hold her attention. Frustrated, she set the book down, lifted the remote, and spent ten minutes randomly flipping from station to mind-numbing station, but none of it numbed her mind the way she'd hoped it would.

For, try as she might—and she'd spent the whole day trying— she couldn't shake the sense that her dream had been more than a dream. Something was wrong. And she didn't need the power of the Balance to tell her she was right.

"Mrs. Huett, you understand my problem," the detective said, flipping a corner of his notes in a fidgety little gesture—one Sana assumed was meant to make him seem vulnerable, the kind of guy in whom she'd want to confide her secrets. Under any other circumstances, she would have found Detective Jewell cuddly; the man looked like a basset hound in a cheap brown suit. Droopy, coffee-colored eyes. Sagging jowls. A mouth that looked like it wanted to smile but couldn't quite commit.

As it stood, several hours into an interrogation, he looked more like a bloodhound out to tree her.

He sat up and cocked his head—another dog-like gesture. "Your husband's murdered in your own home, and you can't explain where you were when it happened."

Sana squirmed in her seat, then made herself stop for fear the motion made her appear guilty. When the cops arrived, she'd readily answered their questions. The idea of calling a lawyer hadn't crossed her mind; her only concern was helping them catch whoever had killed Thom. The problem was, although she'd never budged from her story— her true story—it sounded too convenient to be factual. Now, as it neared evening, she was tired of defending herself against a man skilled in the art of twisting words into evidence, especially when there was no way to confirm an intruder that only she knew existed. She was not the most likely suspect—she was the *only* suspect. And that was part of her problem.

"I told you. I was asleep."

"While your home was broken into and your husband tied to a chair and killed." He leaned back in his chair, started to put his hands behind his head, stopped. A bewildered expression crossed his face. "Mrs. Huett, there was no sign of forced entry. All the doors were locked and dead bolted. You said it yourself."

Sana had no reply to that. The lack of break-in evidence mystified her as much as anyone else, as did every other facet of that strange, horrible morning, which had drawn out until the late afternoon. Dragged in for her "statement," with Thom's body, they soon inundated her with questions and ultimately herded her into an interrogation room. Left alone at first in the chilly, drab room, Sana had wondered what she'd done wrong, what she'd said, how she transformed from bereaved wife to murder suspect.

The questions had started simply enough. Did Thom have any enemies? Not that she knew. Had he changed anything recently—new habits, new friends? No. Hell, Thom never had friends, only a handful of work colleagues he golfed with a couple of Sundays a month. He had friends when they first married, but that stopped after a few of his contemporaries had eyed Sana too appreciatively for Thom's comfort. Would anyone at work have a reason to be angry with him? Thom had never discussed his job with her. He didn't mind spending his money on her, but he never let her hold the checkbook. She didn't care. Thom was all business, and she was all art, and they'd both preferred it that way.

She had a credit card with a generous spending limit, and he never questioned her when she used it. It had been a suitable arrangement.

"You're pretty well-off financially, am I correct?" Detective Jewell had asked.

"We do alright, I guess," she replied warily. "I don't handle the finances."

"Why not?"

"I'm an artist," she said with a dismissive wave, as if that answered the question.

"Do you bring in much money?" he asked, trying and failing to sound casual.

"My painting is mostly a hobby, but I've sold a couple of pieces."

"But you'd like to," Jewell had said, "Maybe open a studio one day?"

Seeing this as an opportunity to prove her willingness to contribute to the household, she'd jumped in readily. "Well, I think every artist has a dream of opening a studio one day."

"Does your husband have any life insurance?"

Understanding now where this was heading, Sana's face fell. *Better tell him and get it over with, she thought. Otherwise, he'll assume you're covering up when he finds out later. And he'll find out.*

"Yes, we both do."

"Can I ask how much?"

Her protective posture wilted under the detective's scrutiny. If she lied, he'd sense it. He was too good at his job for her to bluff. She might as well continue being honest.

"A million and a half dollars," she admitted.

Jewell was trying so hard to appear the good guy, Sana wanted to scream.

"You don't handle the finances, but you know how much life insurance your husband has?"

This guy's too good, Sana thought. *He's building a case where there shouldn't be one. And he's right; it is weird that I remember about Thom's insurance. How do I prove it wasn't me?*

"Thom said he wanted to make sure there was enough to pay off the house and all of our bills and enough to live off for a while until I got on my feet. And we recently had the amount changed. It used to be less, but Thom said he wanted to be sure I had enough to pay off the house in case…" She found herself not sure if she wanted to cry or scream, but either way, it was hard to push syllables around the tightness in her throat. "He had me sign some papers. That's when I saw the amount."

"Hmm," Jewell said, placing his hand on his chin. Sana, who'd never had a sincere homicidal urge, now wanted to strangle him. Not to death, just enough to vent her frustration.

At around five-thirty in the evening, the door popped open. A young Latino police officer stuck his head in the room with an apologetic expression.

"Detective Jewell?" he said. "Phone call."

Jewell pushed the chair back onto all four legs with a screech that jangled Sana's already frazzled nerves. Jewell muttered a hasty word in exit and left.

Alone, at last, Sana washed her face with dry hands. She covered her mouth and blinked back tears. Catching her reflection in a mirror she suspected hid more cops behind it, she saw a stressed-out woman whose day had gone from nightmare to something out of a Fuseli painting. Her long, dark hair was lank, and her face looked sunken.

What had happened? She had awoken feeling phenomenal. But during her rejuvenating slumber, someone had broken into her home and killed her husband without her awareness. Now she almost believed she was guilty. How had she remained oblivious?

Why didn't he scream? Or had he? She might not have loved Thom, but her heart broke with the thought that she'd allowed him to die without trying to stop it.

Pulling her stare from her disheveled reflection, she realized for the first time in hours, since the moment the police had asked her those first innocuous questions at the station house, she was finally alone.

She folded her arms on the cold table, laid her head down, and cried.

Chapter Eleven

"We shouldn't be here," Harmony Novak said. Her calm tone made it sound more like an observation (*NO Skating NO Skateboarding ENFORCED*) than a warning. It was dawn, and there was almost no one on the sidewalk that early on a clear Savannah Sunday morning. Her friend Tristan LeClair and her sister Crystal both knew if they were in danger, Tristan would likely foresee it, or Harmony would get a ping from *the* Harmony she held within her. Harmony's mouth twisted in frustration as they ignored her. Sometimes having supernatural powers was weird.

Tristan pivoted his Vans on the lip of his skateboard and balanced dexterously on the end. Crystal and Harmony watched from their seats on the concrete steps as he tried, again, to do a skateboard stunt on the lip of the bottom step of the Civic Center. What had he called it? A Nollie nose something. Harmony had never had a head for skate terms, no matter how often she hung with Tristan, which was often. She and Crystal had spent most of their growing-up years together with the same foster mother and called one another sisters. Clairvoyant Tristan had joined their duo in high school along with their fire-breathing friend Dorian Bradley—jokingly called Dragon Boy, or DB—who was sleeping off a night shift waiting tables back at their collective apartment. The four of them shared bills, groceries, teasing, time, and devotion with their makeshift superpowered family. They were inseparable.

As expected, Tristan wound up stopping the board instead of sliding and toppled to the pavement with a grunt. His long, dark bangs flopped into his light brown eyes, and he blew them away with a puff. He looked so much like a kid when he did that. Harmony found it hard to believe he was nearly thirty. So were she and Crystal, and Harmony felt so… *old*.

"We should go meet with Vivian and Michael and… well,

everyone," Harmony suggested. The memory of sitting with Crystal in the oversized chair watching Vivian connect with the Source lingered in her memory like a scene from a favorite movie. The way she floated, practically *glowed,* as she came in contact with the power that Harmony would never experience—it left an impression.

"We will," Crystal said, twisting a curly dark lock around her finger. "Tristan told us this day was coming, and you'd know if we were meant to be there right this second. I think you're being paranoid. Besides, sitting on the steps of the Civic Center isn't a crime," she added, noting Harmony's worried glance at the warning sign.

"Maybe not," Harmony said, "But it looks funny—us loitering. And there *are* rules against skateboarding."

Crystal watched with interest as Tristan grunted and failed to pop his board onto the rail again. His board clattered noisily, and he landed with a huff, skinning his elbows. "Just as well," she said. "Those knobby things on the end would kill you."

Tristan groaned and lifted his lean torso from the staircase with another huff at his long bangs. "What knobby things?"

Harmony shook her head. It was no wonder he and Dorian had been friends with her and Crystal for so long. The four of them had drawn to one another like filings to a magnet the first week of high school; supernatural humans who wanted to use their abilities to help people, but were still learning how.

Harmony's brain took a startling detour away from the fresh, green air surrounding her in the square. Colors, sounds, and scents spun through her mind like a carnival hit by a sudden tornado. She braced herself, the sensation of her hands on the concrete grounding her in reality. Her gut lurched, and she leaned forward, anticipating a bucketful of whatever it was she'd eaten last to make a reverse trip in return for the insight that pummeled her brain like a bass drum.

"What is it, Harmony?" Crystal asked. "Are you getting another one of your… thingies?"

Harmony nodded and pulled her straight golden hair back to be safe. Her stomach heaved, then churned again, but no visions appeared behind her eyes, no guidance, only a sense that a major player behind the Darkness was coming. Very major. The worst being she'd seen in her life. And he, like they, weren't a typical human.

When she was confident the spell had passed, she sat up and gently wrapped her arms around her stomach. At times it was inconvenient knowing things before anyone else. Having a clue when Tristan would get a new bruise was fine, but knowing that a being firmly rooted in the Darkness was heading their way was another matter.

When she found her voice, she said, "It was a weird one." She snuffled and wished for a tissue, opting instead to use her sleeve, since she had no choice. "Like… it doesn't involve me. Not exactly."

"Like that time back in March?" Crystal asked, her short frame leaning forward. Tristan's surprised face swiveled to meet hers and then went back to Harmony, who nodded.

"Yeah, like in March, when events moved so crazy between the Divine and Darkness, but we weren't supposed to get involved. Only this time…."

Tristan, giving up on becoming the next Tony Hawk for the moment, pulled himself forward and leaned his sinewy frame on his board. Freckled features peered from behind his hair. "This time what? Is my premonition coming true?"

Harmony shook her head, trying to clear the low buzzing that clung to her ears like static from a weak radio signal; voices came in broken, distorted. She wished it was more distinct, but the sound of the breeze through the live oak trees and the occasional car passing through the square muffled the sound. "Not yet. It's stronger this time. I can almost hear a transmission. But it's different."

"How?" Crystal asked.

Harmony's shoulders dropped. It wasn't easy explaining when she didn't experience emotions the way the others did. "Like it's special. Not from my usual direction. It has a distinct quality to it."

"But it's not the Darkness pulling you over to its side?"

"Not right now," Harmony said. Tristan wrinkled his nose. They all knew that her job required her to take on unpleasant tasks from time to time, but none of them liked it.

"Maybe you'll be leaving us soon," Crystal said worriedly, her brows lifted, her head falling to the side.

"Or this time," Tristan said eagerly, "we get involved."

"Just us?" Crystal scoffed. "Man, if it's as big as that shit in March, I hope we're not alone."

A short, heavyset woman rounded the sidewalk, her feet seeming to float over the asphalt despite her bulk, which propelled her like a juggernaut. Though Harmony had no fear, she didn't doubt this woman was sinister and that the lives of her family were in danger from seeing her.

"Tristan!" she hissed, her voice as loud a stage-whisper as she dared. She grabbed her sister and rushed to Tristan's side. There was nothing to hide behind, exposed as they were on the wide sidewalk, but that didn't matter. Crystal and Harmony grasped the edges of Tristan's shirt. Tristan waved his right hand in his fluid, delicate manner, and they vanished to the outside world.

Inside their protective bubble, Harmony viewed the woman through an iridescent sheen. The creature that glided over the asphalt had a thick head of brown hair that rivaled Crystal's, a dark dress, and dark designer sunglasses that hid her eyes. To a human, she might have been a businesswoman on her way to work.

"Vampire," Tristan breathed, his voice wavering as he held his protection charm over them. "She's got the Darkness in her."

"She's *bad*. Even I can feel it," Crystal said

Behind the woman, other vampires rounded the corner. A young man with smooth skin the color of fall oak leaves held two younger vampires captive before him. Lastly, a vampire in a light linen suit strode past, the jacket flapping around his thin legs as he walked. The linen-clad vampire had a middle-aged face, but every aspect of him—his carriage, his aura, the cunning in his stare—screamed ancient.

"That's Evan," Crystal said, pointing to one of the captive vamps. "And Tina. What are they doing with them?"

"They're so *old*," Harmony said in awe. She'd never seen vampires so ancient, aside from Vivian. She was familiar with a handful of unusual beings—she and her friends were good examples—but these were older and more malevolent than any of them. They wore their evil like a banner on their souls. Like the major player she'd seen in her vision.

Crystal held up her hand in a motion of silence as the older vampires argued.

"Who are you to question me?" the one in linen said, his voice surprisingly deep. "I report to Charles, not you. And I say we kill them now. We can't drag them through the streets like this. This is not the way of the *Shévet ha Dam*. We cannot risk exposure."

"And I say we bring them to Charles," the brown-skinned one snapped.

The woman scoffed in frustration. "Dominick, you can try to take them from us and run off to Charles if you want to. I'm not going to go against Charles. We were told to capture and question them. To give them a choice. Not to deliver them to Charles for him to deal with."

Dominick's jaw cocked angrily, and he stormed off. The woman and the suited man continued down the street until they were beyond the eye-shot of Tristan's bubble. He released his spell, and the world grew clear again.

"What was that about?" Crystal asked.

Harmony let out a slow breath. "Vampires are killing vampires," she said. "That's what it is about."

"But Evan and Tina—"

"They're planning to kill them if they make the wrong choice—whatever that means," Harmony said. "The question is where? And why?"

"Harmony, if you don't have a clue, there's no way *we're* going to," Tristan observed with a slight shrug. He spun his skateboard between his palm and the pavement. "I can't touch the Darkness, and my premonitions only work if I do that spell."

"I don't know why, either," Crystal said, "but as to where…" The sisters looked at one another. Crystal took a long time to examine Harmony's face, though what she expected to find there, Harmony couldn't speculate. "And you got no guidance on this, no…"

"No," Harmony said, her hands outstretched. "I'm telling you; I've gotten no guidance saying it's time for us to intervene."

Crystal frowned. "We can't stand here while Evan and Tina get killed!"

Tristan's contemplative face watched the sisters argue as he waited for Crystal to offer him direction. Harmony, as usual, waited for the word from Crystal.

"Though she be but little, she is fierce," thought Harmony—a Shakespeare line that always came to mind when she looked at her sister.

Crystal puffed up as she faced her Harmony, daring her to disagree. "I'm going to do it."

Chapter Twelve

Doyle pressed the *off* button on his phone and ran a hand over his bald head. He wished he'd taken the call in the living room instead of the kitchen—the stool he'd perched on didn't feel as sturdy as it had when he'd first sat on it, but his slender frame wasn't what threatened it. The tiny Hilton Head townhouse seemed much smaller, the white walls pressing in like the padded walls of a madhouse cell.

Pen in one hand, phone in the other, Doyle stared at the page of frantic scribbles in his handwriting as the letters became a jumbled muddle. Judging from the call, his wildest dream was about to come true, and it terrified him.

He'd only been awake about an hour, and it had already been a weird day. He hated that Charles operated during normal human hours. It was so… unvampiric.

Charles rarely called during Doyle's vacations, but this one had already been disrupted three times in forty-eight hours. Unusual, but not terribly out of the ordinary. The first call he'd ignored, hoping he could get away with pretending he hadn't noticed, since it was during the day, when he usually slept. The next had taken place in the evening shortly after he'd woken up, and when he heard what Charles had to say, he'd nearly asked if Dunning was kidding. This time, after three cups of strong Ethiopian coffee, Doyle comprehended that the man was sincere—his intentions for Doyle were genuine, thought-out, and planned. Despite that, it sounded hard to believe.

Head of the U.S. division? *But that makes no sense! I haven't lived in the States for the past twenty years!*

He recalled a conversation he'd had with Charles months earlier at Café Wiedmann, in downtown Kaiserslautern, Doyle's hometown in southwest Germany. Day days before Jude's death, he'd sat at one of the few outdoor iron tables available in the cold weather. Charles had asked Doyle about his thoughts on Vivian. Doyle remembered the exchange exactly.

"She... she made me feel bad about one or two things. She made me feel like I wasn't living up to my potential."

"And you are not."

Which was true, and he hadn't resented Jude's lieutenant for saying so. Doyle knew his honor was nonexistent, and Charles often implied that he'd been aware of Doyle's indiscretions when he'd helped friends outside the clan. But if Charles thought he was a traitor who wasn't living up to his potential, why was he putting Doyle on the Table instead of killing him? Was it an attempt to draw out untapped talents? What other motive could he have?

He knows I brought Michael and Vivian supplies while they were hiding from the Tribe in Germany, gave them fake IDs, brought them tickets when they needed to leave. I've supplied them with photoprotection for years. I've was the biggest traitor—next to Charles—that Jude had.

During the call, he'd tried to send out subtle psychic antennae to get an idea of Charles' emotions, what drove him to seek Doyle out for such a big job. All he got in return was a dead space where Charles' thoughts should have been. He hadn't expected much. Despite his age, Doyle's vampiric gifts were woefully underdeveloped.

Why didn't Maysun call me? Shouldn't she be heading the Tribe? Where in the hell has she been all this time?

As the facts tallied up in Doyle's mind, the phone dropped from his hand and thumped onto the tile floor. The sound of gently crashing waves from outside the French doors sounded like thunder preceding a hurricane. Doyle's head felt thick as setting concrete—how had he been so stupid? Dead air where Charles should have been. Charles appointing Doyle to his old position despite his lies. No word from Maysun.

Charles had become the Maleficence's new host, and he was taking over the Tribe! It explained everything. *Did he kill Maysun? God, I hope not. She was cool.*

The idea of Maysun's slain body lying at Charles' feet sent a tremor down his neck and set his fingers shaking. Maysun had over five hundred years on Charles. If Maysun was dead, the Maleficence must have added a substantial amount of strength, speed, and cleverness to the intimidating talents Charles already wielded. How indestructible was he now?

Charles had tolerated Doyle's rebellion when he was against Jude. What was his opinion about Doyle's independent streak now that he was in charge of the Tribe?

Was this offer bait to get him close enough to kill?

Doyle's teeth chattered, and he rubbed his arms as if they were cold, an inconvenience he hadn't suffered in decades. The clock across the room read 9:08 in the morning. He had almost no time to catch the private jet Charles had chartered to take him from the tiny Hilton Head airport to Sedona. To Charles' side. To the Blood Tribe. *Why did he have to do this during the daytime?* Doyle burned quickly despite his age, which hovered around the century mark, and use of photoprotection. Usually, a vampire of his era could stay out in the sun for at least a couple of hours without effect, but not Doyle. His photosensitivity was often a source of embarrassment. No matter how often he fed or slathered on the buffer, he still grew pink.

I could run. I know people who make IDs. I could catch a flight back to Germany and—and they'd have me tracked down and killed in a day—two, tops. They all know you, and they'd turn you in as soon as they learn Charles has plans for you.

There was no backing out without dying. He rubbed his arms again, but the notion that Freon flowed through his veins didn't subside.

Closing his eyes, Doyle saw a dozen scenarios where he tried to escape, but each resulted in him dead, usually with his neck in Charles' mouth. His survival instinct was on high alert, but he had nowhere to run. For once, he was grateful that his body was undead—if not, his heart wouldn't have stood a chance. Guaranteed heart attack—if his heart still worked.

He snorted. *Too many hospital dramas.* His eyes shifted from corner to corner of his luxury vacation home as if looking for an escape route. Beige walls with light blue accents. Impersonal paintings of seashells and ocean sunrises on the walls. He usually thought better that way, scanning his familiar surroundings, but not today. *No copping out, then. But what would staying in the Tribe mean?*

More bloodshed. More death. Being at Charles' right hand, as Charles had been with Jude, presented an ugly alternative. Live like Charles—commanding the U.S. part of the Blood Tribe, giving orders, killing humans—or die. Those were the choices.

Doyle closed his eyes, but the images lingered, pressed into his retina like phosphenes. His heart now seemed weighted with the imaginary concrete that had thickened his mind moments before.

Maybe it was better if he remained in the Tribe. Who'd warn Vivian what Charles was doing if he died or ran off?

Does she know Charles is leading the Shévet ha Dam? Don't be stupid. Of course she does! But she doesn't have a way to see what he's doing. I could be that person.

Eventually, it'd cost him his life, and there was no guarantee that Vivian would trust him once she learned he'd taken Charles' old position. His choices were minimal, though, and siding with the Tribe for a while ensured that he'd live longer than the alternative. Possibly long enough to come up with a solution.

Chapter Thirteen

"Mrs. Huett?" A voice called. Sana stirred, then jerked awake, disoriented at first by the unfamiliar room. She felt the same grogginess she used to get after a night of too much reveling—but this wasn't a hangover. Her mouth wasn't coated in stale alcohol residue, and she had the distinct impression that whatever had landed her here hadn't been fun.

Four gray walls settled into focus, too far apart for a cell, but not by much. The police station. *That's right. I came back in to answer more questions and... Oh god, Thom!*

The last two days had been a sleepless haze of phone calls and staring blankly at the hotel walls in disbelief. She hadn't returned to her home, opting instead to stay at a quiet place nearby while her home was turned over for clues and then cleaned. Despite not having answered their questions satisfactorily, she hadn't been detained.

The sleepless hours had caught up with her, and she'd drifted off in her chair. Her cheeks warmed, and she averted her eyes from his direct gaze. *What sort of monster sleeps at the police station after her husband is murdered?*

The young Hispanic man who'd pulled Detective Jewell away to the phone yesterday stood in the doorway behind her, his face apologetic. Sana wondered what he was sorry for—that he'd woken her up, or that she'd been through such a horrible past couple of days. She caught his name on the brassy plate of his uniform: Sergeant Gutierrez. He was handsome, if young. She suddenly wished she had makeup on—then instantly felt ridiculous. She might be single now, but only because she'd been made a widow.

She rubbed her eyes, tossed her hair into place as well as she could, then fought with a yawn and lost.

"Where do I go now?" she asked. "No, wait. I should call our lawyer before I say much else." *Our lawyer. Now he's my lawyer. And I should've called him way before this. God, I was so stupid! I said all that stuff and now they can use any of it to accuse me of whatever they want! They read me my Miranda rights, didn't they?* She tried to remember, but the past few hours had been such a blur, and the police were so unassuming at first that she wasn't sure if they'd read her her rights. She had thought nothing of their questions initially, and when she saw where their questioning was headed, it was too late.

Sergeant Gutierrez gave her a wary smile that caught her off guard. She liked him despite herself.

"That won't be necessary, ma'am," he said. "We've got a suspect. He, uh… turned himself in. Said he killed your husband. I suspect you'll be able to go home soon."

"He what? You what?" Sana's hand flew to her chest as the weight that had been there vanished, replaced by a mixed sensation of elation and a hard to define emotion bordering on disbelief. Her stomach churning like a combination of acid and butterflies. Part of her found it impossible to believe that anyone would take the blame for a crime when the police already had a suspect. It didn't seem right, but she wasn't in a position to argue.

YOU DON'T BELIEVE HIM BECAUSE YOU KILLED THOM, SANA. NO ONE ELSE CAN ADMIT TO A MURDER YOU COMMITTED.

Don't be stupid. I'd remember if I killed him.

YEAH, LIKE YOU REMEMBER LYING DOWN FOR A NAP.

So what if I don't remember? I was tired.

OR YOU BLOCKED OUT WHAT YOU DID. REMEMBER THE "PAINT" ON YOUR CLOTHES?

Sana shook her head, trying to knock loose the stubborn voices that buzzed like flies in her skull. She hated when her mind took off like this.

She avoided the sergeant's eyes, which were watching her for a reaction. The police may have detained a suspect, but that didn't mean she was off the hook. Maybe they thought she'd hired him to snuff Thom. Isn't that what all the potentially rich widows did in television cop shows? Hire a hitman for the dirty work?

Don't let him see what you're thinking! He'll lock you up and they'll have your sanity evaluated, and then everyone will know you hear voices! He'll see that you're crazy, and they'll never let you out of here. WHO DO YOU THINK YOU'RE FOOLING? HE ALREADY KNOWS.

She swallowed a huge lump of fear in her throat. "What time is it?" she asked, forcing her voice into something resembling calm. It sounded shaky and tense to her ears, but if Gutierrez noticed, he hid it well.

"It's a little after nine o'clock, ma'am," he said.

"Wow," she murmured. She wiped her face, scratched her head, let her hair fall back over her eyes. "I can't believe I fell asleep."

"Ma'am?"

She shook her head. "Nothing." Extremely self-conscious, she grasped her elbows and pulled them close together. "Um… is there any way I might have a cup of coffee?"

"There's orange juice or water," he said. "I'd steer clear of the coffee. It's not very good. Reminds me of burned chestnuts, or something… burnt."

Sana allowed herself a polite laugh and accepted his offer of juice, which he brought to her moments later in a coffee mug emblazoned with an Army unit symbol. He left her alone to finish the drink, which she sipped slowly. Her nervous, sleep-starved stomach threatened mutiny at every sour drop.

When she finished, she rinsed the cup out in the water fountain before seeking Gutierrez in the cluttered office maze. She found him in a drab-walled bullpen filled with gray metal desks and threadbare chairs. A large U.S. flag drooped in the corner. A Mr. Coffee machine and a few chipped mugs stood on a plastic tray atop a set of metal filing cabinets. It looked like a dismal place to spend one's time. About three officers, besides Gutierrez, were doing that. They buzzed around the coffeepot, exchanging hellos and smiling. A few noticed as she walked into the room, but none moved to stop her. One greasy-haired one did a thorough inspection, saw her wedding ring, and looked away with a nasty smirk.

Sana approached Sergeant Gutierrez and held out the mug.

"I—I didn't wash it. I just rinsed it out."

"That's fine," he said, accepting it.

She avoided his eyes, sure they would show that he still suspected her of wrongdoing. She noticed he wore a plain gold wedding band and hoped that none of the other cops thought she was there as a visitor. Of course, if they didn't suspect it was a casual visit, they would know why she was there, and that wasn't a pleasant idea, either.

DON'T BE STUPID. THIS ISN'T A HUGE NEW YORK CITY PRECINCT WHERE PEOPLE GET LOST IN THE SHUFFLE. OF COURSE THEY KNOW WHY YOU'RE HERE. AND THEY ALL THINK YOU DID IT.

"Am I free to go?" she asked. She wasn't prepared to believe they were ready to release her after the barrage of questions she'd endured.

"The clean-up team is probably done. I called the crime scene guys, and they said they cleared out some time ago. I can call and check, make sure it's clear." He paused, and his face grew apologetic again. "Do you need a ride home? Or would you rather go back to your hotel?"

Sana shrugged and kept her face pointing toward the flag, noting how the blue and red had faded and the white was a dingy gray. "I'll walk. It's not that far. Is it nice outside?"

He nodded. "October in South Carolina. It's beautiful. Let me make that call for you, huh? Make sure it's clear?"

Her eyes, desperate to avoid meeting the sergeant's, dodged from desk to desk as she nodded.

As she waited, an officer brought in a gorgeous fair-skinned young man, perhaps twenty at the oldest, with brilliant blue eyes and a head full of straight, messy, black hair. Cuffs shackled his wrists behind him as a burly officer led him to a desk on the far side of the room. The officer pulled out a chair, and the young man sat, spinning his chair a quarter turn as he did and coming eye to eye with her.

The handcuffed young man was, without question, the most beautiful creature she'd ever seen. Sana wanted to gawk, walk straight over, say hello, and to lose herself in his aquamarine eyes for the rest of her life. He looked like the man of her dreams.

MORE LIKE YOUR NIGHTMARES.

What has he done to be here?

"Who—who is that?" Sana asked, pointing out the young man as discreetly as possible. Gutierrez turned from his call to see where she was gesturing and turned back around quickly, a guilty expression on his handsome face. He put his palm over the mouthpiece so the person on the other end of the phone couldn't hear.

"I'm afraid I can't tell you," he replied quickly. Too quickly.

He's hiding something, she thought. *That man must have committed a crime, and I'm only a civilian, so he can't tell me.*

THERE ARE NO OTHER CRIMINALS HERE, SANA. WHO DO

YOU THINK HE IS?

Lightning struck. The blood drained from her face swiftly as she understood without a doubt who it was and what he had done.

"He's the man who killed Thom," she breathed. The sergeant's lack of verbal response and guilty expression were all the answers she needed.

"Do you recognize him, Miss Huett?" Gutierrez asked, hanging up.

"I… I don't think so," she stammered. And while she didn't, she did. *That doesn't make sense. How can he look so familiar if I've never seen him before?*

"Are you sure?" he pressed. Sana shook her head, her brows furrowed as she strained to recall where she might have seen the young man before. There was the slightest of vague, unnamable, frustrating impressions, like trying to recall a single word in a foreign language or a long-lost name of a childhood schoolmate among millions of memories tucked away.

A vision slammed into her: the shackled young man whispering in her ear, slick with sweat, his hips bucking beneath her. Her knees buckled. She tried to catch her hand on Gutierrez's arm, but her grip was weak, and she continued downward. The sergeant caught her as her longest tresses grazed the floor. He eased her into a chair and sent another officer to bring her a cup of water, reassuring her the whole time that she was going to be alright.

As he took the cup from another officer, he leaned forward, placing it cautiously into Sana's trembling hand. "Are you alright?"

Sana nodded. "It's the shock, I guess." She fanned herself. When had the room gotten so hot? She lifted the cool liquid to her lips. Cold water traced an icy path down her throat, setting off a full-body shiver.

His brow remained furrowed, but he took his place at his desk. While he was engaged at his computer, Sana studied the young man. She studied the pale hands that had spilled Thom's blood, the eyes that had watched her husband's last expression flicker and vanish, the ears that heard the last word he spoke, or perhaps his screams of terror. In her mind, she could almost trace the sharp line of his jaw, almost remember the press of those slender lips against hers.

How was it she knew the most intimate of details? The cross pattern of his chest hair, the faint lift of a mole on his cheek, the subtle rise beneath her touch.

He was too stunning to look like a murderer. Too young, too perfect.

Don't be an idiot. Plenty of killers are attractive. Hell, some have an advantage from it. Think about all those true crime shows you've watched.

He was too young to be one of Thom's coworkers. How had he chosen her husband as his target? What motivation did he have for killing a man who'd led such a bland existence? He couldn't have known Thom well—she'd remember if he'd ever set foot in their house. So, why?

Not that she'd known Thom well, either. They'd been married for over five years, but it had taken her less than one to recognize that she was a trophy wife, a beautiful showpiece to sit at his elbow at social functions and keep her undereducated mouth shut, lest she embarrass him. She'd suffered through it because Thom supported the artwork she loved, both financially and verbally, and because the outside world terrified her. He seemed proud to tell his associates that his wife was an artist. What Sana heard every time he repeated her career choice was, "I can afford to support my wife's hobby."

They'd never shared an emotional bond, though she wasn't sure their lack of connection wasn't her fault. Thom was a distant man, yes, but he tried to behave as though he cared. It was possible the reason they hadn't bonded was her fault. Still, a guilty little voice deep inside her whispered thanks that he was gone.

The young man turned and caught her staring. Sana told herself to look away. She didn't. A thrill at their connection set her heart galloping. A shudder made its way from her hair to her toes, and though part of her saw him as Thom's killer, another part of her wished they were alone in the room together, doing things she had no business envisioning them doing atop one of the cold metal desks. As they faced each other unblinkingly, she heard a voice echoing in her head.

I DIDN'T DO IT, SANA. I DIDN'T. PLEASE BELIEVE ME!

Her knees weakened again. That voice—it had to be hers. It sounded so much like one of her trick voices, those schizophrenic, audial hallucinations she had. But she wanted to believe it was him!

It was crazy. *She* was crazy. Sana would never lie with a killer. But her instincts didn't believe it. But she believed that she'd seen that young man before. She wished she remembered how and where.

And why.

In the shadows of the hall, she heard the faint rustling of two unseen bodies and the laughter of two voices she knew all too well echoing in her mind.

Chapter Fourteen

"For the record, I don't think this is a good idea," Harmony said, her eyes catching the light and making them shine like gold. "Crystal, your only skill is aerocleaving, which is great for helping us escape, but you have no clue how to fight. Tristan's magic will take out two. Three, if he's lucky and his aim is good. And I can't choose a side."

Crystal glared. "You're going to sit on the bench and let those vamps kill our friends? Thanks a lot. Tristan?"

Tristan nodded and rubbed his hands together, closing his eyes as he murmured the words that gave him confidence and conjured his power. He rocked from toe to heel, toe to heel, then stopped, wiggled his fingers at his side, his eyes closed, his face tipped to the heavens. He looked like an angelic sorcerer with his longish hair, smooth skin, and wide-spaced eyes.

"What about DB?" Harmony asked. "He might be helpful." Harmony couldn't influence Crystal's decision, but she wanted to give her sister the opportunity to consider bringing their dragon-like friend with them to help.

Crystal frowned. "By the time we find him and explain what's going on, it might be too late!" Crystal scanned the area for anyone watching before turning from Harmony, inhaling deeply, and bracing herself. Though the air was still, Harmony's hair stood as if lightning had struck nearby, and a wave of energy washed over her as Tristan tapped into the wellspring of his power.

Crystal caught Harmony smiling as the Divine animated the surrounding air. "I can't believe you're going to stand this one out."

Harmony rolled her eyes. Her mother had told her never to act without guidance, and the last transmission she'd picked up, although dramatic, didn't indicate it was time for her to intervene. *What* did *it mean? A dark force is coming—that makes no sense. It's already here!*

Crystal lifted her arm, stretched out her index finger, and a point of light appeared. As she lowered her arm, the glowing spot stretched and arched, forming a radiant finger-width line in the air. A sound like ripping parchment broke the morning stillness, and the landscape visible in the inch beyond peeked through the tear in the framework of space. Crystal stretched the taut, split fabric into an oddly shaped doorway. The odor of searing flesh and fiery blood reached Harmony, and she wrinkled her nose.

Against her better judgment, Harmony stepped toward the line of light and pulled at it, helping her sister extend the hole. Her hands burned at the frayed edge, so she shifted her grip to lessen the sting.

Beyond the tear lay a wide, dusty room in what looked like an abandoned warehouse that she'd never seen before. Tristan took a deep breath and stepped through, ducking almost in half to avoid touching the edges of the hole. Crystal followed, holding the aperture open with both hands as she moved.

Oh, what the hell, Harmony thought, and with a slight shake of her head, she dove in after. A gust of wind announced the closing hole as they released it.

Before her was a vista from hell. Every young vampire for miles around had been rounded up before being beaten and bloodied. Now, they awaited their judgement at the end of the wide, gray room. Harmony guessed there had to be at least fifty of them. At the rim of the circle of young vampires, four elder vampires circled like vultures, eyeing their prisoners smugly. Three of them Harmony recognized from the steps of the Civic Center. The fourth was unfamiliar, tall, blond, apathetic, his wavy hair held in place by a leather cowboy hat.

Only the boarded windows saved the younger vampires from the rays of the morning sun, which would soon kill them all.

"Why don't they fight back? They have them outnumbered." Crystal whispered, not wanting to draw attention to their presence.

"Because," a voice said, making the three of them jump. The brown-haired, dark-suited female who stood about fifty feet away turned in their direction with a dour expression. Without her sunglasses, her eyes were small with icy irises. "They have seen what happens if they try."

It was then that Harmony noticed the piles of ashes to her left inches shy of a wide beam of sun shining through a wide crack in the boards. The gray flakes rose and twisted in the air like dust motes. How many had they killed already? One? Ten? Twenty?

She has no plan, and they are wildly outclassed. What was she think-ing?

Crystal groaned, and her hands became slack at her side. He body stood like a marionette awaiting the tugging of strings. The black-clad woman stared at her, unblinking, and Harmony knew the fight between the two of them had turned inward and had become a battle of minds. The ancient vampire was infiltrating Crystal's thoughts—and from the look of it, she was winning.

The sound of crunching stones on the concrete floor drew Harmony's eyes to her sister's feet. Incredibly, they stepped forward as Crystal fought the urge, leaned back, her hands pressed to her temples. Her eyes pressed tightly closed as her head shook against an unseen enemy invading her in a way she could not defend against. Her arms extended before her to block an assault without a physical form.

"No. No! NO!"

Tristan's breath came in brief spurts, and he flailed his hands at the vampire who had seized his friend with mental tentacles, but panic was not conducive to channeling. Like a crazed mime, he thrashed, clapped, and poked air at the woman strolling toward Crystal, his hands trembling as he struggled. The other senior vampires watched with amusement, their attention divided between guarding their detainees and the diversion provided by the newcomers.

Harmony shot Tristan a look, and he read volumes in her eyes.

"I'm *trying*, I'm *trying*!" he said, his voice high in panic. Drops of sweat burst onto his forehead as the one eye visible from behind his bangs darted from his hands to Crystal to the oncoming vampire.

When not more than twenty feet separated Crystal from the oncoming vampire, Harmony frowned. That raised-hackle sensation of charged energy grew again.

"Aha!" Tristan exclaimed, bolder now as he stepped forward and threw what looked like a blue bolt of lightning at his opponent. The vampire staggered and regained her footing, but the effect was not a total loss. Her hypnotic hold on Crystal broke, allowing the young woman to run back to her friends.

"We can't take them," Harmony said, the words in a rush. "Not all three of them. They're too damned old. You are seriously outmatched." Twenty feet, she calculated, between the vampire stalking toward them and counting down. *I should have talked Crystal out of this infernal plan. This was such an idiotic idea!*

"Can we break their hold on the others?" Tristan asked.

"How?" Harmony asked, her eyes glued to the woman. *Why doesn't she jump?* Harmony wondered. *Is she getting off on our fear?*

"We gotta jet," Crystal said, extending her finger again.

No kidding. This whole idea was terrible.

Ten feet.

Tristan, his confidence restored by his last blow, now stretched his hands out flat. His mouth bent into a sort of cocky half-grin. Tristan's connection to his power was so strong she felt light enough to float. The memory of Vivian hovering in her seat at her Jones Street townhome flashed back to her.

Her ears rang with a familiar sensation from Tristan's practice sessions, the same one she sensed when Tristan hurled glowing yellow balls at various targets balanced on a sawhorse in the alley behind their apartment.

Fire. Good idea, Tristan!

Crystal slashed at the air behind them with a herky-jerky rip. The hole that emerged was a much smaller one this time; in her alarm, she'd not lengthened the line. She and Harmony grabbed opposite sides of the ragged light and yanked frantically to stretch the hole bigger.

Poof. Red-orange balls of fire shot from Tristan's glowing palms and hit their attacker mid-center; she cried in pain, and the eerie, half-human sound made Harmony cringe.

You should've gone for the head, Tris!

Harmony's skin sizzled as she yanked the doorway open, the air thick with the stench of burning flesh. Agony lanced through the fresh welts on her palms. Next to her, Crystal worked at expanding the bottom of the door. Her face grimaced with pain and fear.

A scream erupted from behind them, and though Harmony didn't sense panic or fear like a normal human, chills triggered by her sympathetic nervous system raced down her spine, and her heart pounded hard in her ears. Her body didn't need to fear to want to live.

The fiery bloodsucker had reached Tristan and now clutched him in a bloodsucking embrace. How could she not feel and yet desire for Tristan not to die? Was this guidance or a residual emotion from their desperate, poorly thought-out scheme?

No. It was time for her to step in. Why now, when the damage was done and no one was saved?

"Hold the door," Harmony said. "I'll help him." Crystal nodded, her eyes wide in surprise, and Harmony let go.

Harmony raced across the dusty floor to cover the distance, but she was too late. Knowing his death was imminent, Tristan gripped the vampire in an embrace. He ignited his hands at her back, her hair, every spot in reach, bathing her in a fire that consumed him, too. Smoke from charred hair and clothing made Harmony squint as she fought to separate her friend from the now ashing vampire.

Crystal's voice cried out from behind her, the sound thick with emotion. *"Tristan! No!"*

The demon howled and yanked her body loose. She retreated a few steps, giving Harmony a chance to grab her friend and pull him toward their escape route. For the first time in this ill-conceived adventure, she drew on her power to give her strength so she could drag Tristan's burnt body with them back through the hole. As she retreated, her hands blistered again and the stench and smoke rising from Tristan's body sent her sinuses pounding and made her gag for the second time that morning. The pain of her thrice-burned hands now radiated up her wrists and into her forearms.

She backed over the threshold, not caring where Crystal had brought them—anywhere was fine. A Turkish prison would have been better than that abandoned room in Savannah, Georgia.

Crystal stepped through and dropped her hold on the line.

Whoosh.

The smell of burning flesh and charred clothing rode on the gust of air filling their small apartment. Crystal had brought them home. The sounds of gasping sobs came from near Harmony's elbow. Her sister knelt beside Tristan, her charred hands gently patting the embers still glowing on his blackened body. His red, raw skin looked sickeningly like charred hamburger.

Their friend DB leaped from the comic-strewn futon to their side, spilling the graphic novels in a paper waterfall as he cleared the distance in two bounds of his long legs. His golden eyes clouded in his bronze face as they swept from the closed gap to Tristan, Crystal, Harmony, and back to Tristan. He held his tanned arms out toward Tristan's scorched torso and then drew them back as if burned as well.

"Holy mother of God," he breathed. "How did this happen?"

No one answered. There would be time for an explanation later. Now, Tristan's eyes stared blankly at a point only he saw, his jaw slack in an oval face so pale each freckle stood out like a star on a clear night.

DB yanked a phone from his pocket and dialed 9-1-1, but his face held little hope that help would come through in time.

"I'm sorry," Crystal said, clinging to Tristan's limp form and rocking him back and forth like a mother with an injured child. If his damaged body was too hot to hold, she didn't show it. "I'm sorry. I'm so, so sorry."

Tristan lay in her lap, his eyes darting but not seeing, his mouth moving but not uttering audible words. She swayed back and forth and repeated the apology like a mantra as fat tears dropped from her chin. One landed on a smoldering pocket of Tristan's t-shirt and sizzled. Harmony watched helplessly as the drama unfolded.

DB began giving his information as rapidly to the emergency operator as she allowed.

Crystal turned to her sister. "Can't you help?" she asked, her voice thick. "Can't you use your power to—?"

Harmony shook her head, sure to be more stubborn than typical. "I can't, Crystal."

"DB?"

Tears scored his face as well, falling freely onto the tops of his Vans. He covered the mouthpiece of the phone long enough to say, "I can't mend his burns, Crissy. My ability to heal from my own burns is self-generated. I can't—I can't project it. Fuck!" The operator came back on the line, and DB answered her questions in rapid-fire responses, his face drooping in grief as he watched his friend fading while they stood by, helpless.

Crystal's tears, a rare sight, flowed freely. Tristan was failing.

A tide of knowledge overcame Harmony. It was time for her to step forward, to become *the* Harmony. As if seeing herself through another's eyes, she crept forward and sat down at Tristan's head. Placing her hands at his feverish temples, she used both her power and his to allow him to utter his final premonition.

"A battle is coming." The words emerged from her throat, but it was Tristan's voice, his tempo from her lips, weak and thin. "Fight against the Darkness. The Divine blessed you with your strengths and gave you the urge to stand against the Darkness. Don't let what happened to me keep you from fighting. Please."

His face slackened, and his body went still. Harmony perceived his essence drifting upward, spiraling free of his body, dispersing into a cloud of something too vast to define or follow. Then he was gone.

"I think he died," DB informed the operator in hushed tones, sobs shaking his shoulders as the sound of response sirens arose.

"No!" Crystal sobbed. "No! No! NO!" She gently slid Tristan's form from her lap to the floor and started to position his head for CPR.

DB set the phone face down on the floor, crouched at Crystal's side and lifted her carefully from under Tristan's limp body. Crystal beat at his chest, each impact making a loud *thump* until her tired shoulders slumped in hopelessness. DB pulled her closer, stroked her wild, dark curls, and made soothing shushing noised until she collapsed in his arms. Harmony picked up the phone and answered the dispatcher's questions as she watched impassively, her soul, if not her heart, grieving Tristan's absence.

Chapter Fifteen

iper, South Carolina, was not Mateo Gutierrez's idea of a dream assignment. As a native of San Diego, he found it too sleepy—and far too inland—to make him happy. Without the surf to ride, his arms and legs lost much of their former strength, and his balance was off—in every sense of the word. Fortunately, he had Carlotta.

His wife of eight years, he and Carlotta had married in her hometown of Piper surrounded by her friends, family, and the few of his siblings who could afford the trip. Immediately after the vows, her father offered Carlotta a job at his law firm—an offer too good to refuse, especially days after passing the bar.

"You understand, don't you?" she said, her melodious voice pleading, her hazel eyes golden in the setting Carolina sun. "It's only until I build a reputation. Then we can go back to San Diego, and I'll hang up my shingle."

As usual, Mateo gave in. He never could resist when her eyes sparkled like that—and that radiant smile, crooked tooth and all, always did him in. He had to admit it was a dream gig for a new lawyer. And he could do police work anywhere with an opening. There had been a spot on the force in Piper, and he took the three-week course to become state certified as an officer. He'd been there ever since.

He picked up the keys to the tiny cell block and strode to the rear of the precinct. "And, meanwhile, I'm stuck in this boring backwater town," he mumbled.

Gutierrez was in charge of headcount. Today, there were a whopping two heads to tally, which was two more than usual. One was a drunk who Smitty had hauled out of his car and brought in so the drunk could sleep it off away from the streets. The other, the young Englishman, was unusual. More than unusual. Murder. In Piper! And, of course, he turned himself in. Mateo found it hard not to laugh despite the morbid circumstances. Not even the murders here needed much work.

He'd known—well, he'd suspected—from the moment the police had escorted Sana into the precinct that she hadn't committed the crime. No cop liked to admit that they jumped to conclusions, but in her case, he'd guessed right. Her eyes were vacant, but not the empty stare of a psychopath—more like a haunted, scared woman. Like she'd experienced fear every day of her life and still held on to her childhood innocence.

Not so innocent that she hadn't turned his head. Not at first. At first, she'd seemed disheveled, her thoughts as scrambled as her hair. But once she'd composed herself—there was a quality about the way she carried herself that he'd found incredibly attractive. He feared for a moment that she might come on to him.

Which was a crazy thought. She lost her husband this morning, and here I am wondering how I'm going to turn her down—no, if I'd be able to turn her down. How messed up is that?

He bit his lip and set his mind on Carlotta. It helped, but the ghost of Sana still lingered, rivaling for his wife's spot in his thoughts that day. Well, it'd take a while to forget a woman that striking. And she was striking. He was devoted, but he wasn't blind.

He lifted the clipboard from the nail outside the cell block and unlocked the outer door. Four individual cells lay beyond. Well-lit and clean, they reminded him of the lodges at that childhood campground his parents once dragged him to. Andrew Sinclair laid on a cot on the immediate left, his drunken snores resonating on the concrete walls. On the right—

Mateo hesitated. Typically, they placed those waiting for release or transfer in the cells closest to the door. It saved having to take five steps to the next cell. But the self-admitted murderer—Perry Eoin Taylor—wasn't in the cell to the right.

That's weird, Mateo thought. *Nobody here ever breaks routine. Huh. Maybe the toilet's busted.*

He took the five steps and peered into the next cell. Flat cot, untouched institutional bedding. No one hiding underneath.

Mateo turned. The left cell was every bit as empty.

He took the five steps back to Sinclair's cell. The man was alone.

He hustled between all four cells, careful not to touch anything in case they needed prints. There was no sign of force on any of the locks. No inexplicable gaps in the concrete wall. And yet—

Taylor's gone!

"Whassa matter, sarge?" Sinclair mumbled, sitting up groggily. Gutierrez nearly answered before remembering himself. Instead, he dashed out of the cellblock, locking it firmly behind him before alerting anyone of the jailbreak.

Standing on the shores of the Firth of Clyde near Maysun's flat had always been a spiritual experience for Eoghan, but never more than now. In place of the sweeping breezes, crashing waves, and the view of the Isle that once stirred him as a human, it was now insight flooding his mind, his body, his cells, his very spirit. His recently acquired talent exhilarated him. With a flick of his eyes toward the few pedestrians crossing his path at this late hour, he absorbed their lives from birth to now, their secrets, their fears.

What to try now? Well, what can I do? As soon as the question formed, an answer came. *Brilliant.*

He eyed the Isle of Arran, a looming, purple shadow in the distance, and in a heartbeat, he stood on its shores. Yesterday, he would've lost his balance and fallen into the water. Instead, he stepped gracefully onto the beach. Maintaining his equilibrium came as natural as breathing. *Amazing.*

In the distance, lights twinkled in a few homes on the shores of the sleepy town of Troon. Maysun was awake, hovering in the twilight before sleep. The awareness didn't trouble him. A small part of his mind still raged at life's unfairness, longing to lie in her bronze arms once more. Though he sensed that small, furious presence in the back of his mind shaking its tiny fist, the emotions never reached the places that once triggered his human responses. Anger, distress, sadness. Emotions were a luxury—one he couldn't afford.

He didn't need emotions to recognize the Isle's beauty: azure waters, soaring mountains, the vast expanse of green grass under the cloudy sky. He noticed it, but the sight no longer made his heart soar; instead, there was a one-ness with the surrounding land, an understanding of each particle of the universe and his place within it. And while part of him registered the hollow space where emotion used to live, the time for sentiment had passed. For now. Maysun had done this for centuries.

He sighed. *At least something still works. Apparently, I still need oxygen.*

A vision surfaced: a young woman, Stateside. Dark-skinned like Maysun—perhaps slightly lighter. Recently widowed. Something important was coming, and she was at the heart of it. A woman named Sana.

He knew exactly where he had to go.

Chapter Sixteen

Sana's energy drained as she pulled her overnight bag from the Camry's trunk. The warmth of the unseasonably hot day faded as the sun dipped behind the neighborhood trees. It would be night soon. The night was when she grew most alive, the most connected with the world around her. When the sun took its nightly dip beyond the horizon, as the temperature dropped and darkness covered the world, her body came alive.

She loved the solitude of night, though she never felt alone. The voices were always there. Her voices. Sometimes, they comforted her—not with words, but simply by being there, a constant presence saving her from the emptiness of her loveless marriage.

She never understood why so few people saw beauty in the darkest hours. Who hadn't taken a stroll down a starlit road, danced in the moonlight with their love, or wished on a star to do so? The night was a beautiful time to be alive, to dream while awake.

Her visual and mental acuity, dexterity, and stamina sharpened the darker her environment. Her whole body improved.

SANA.

The awareness of the voices in her head.

SANA!

She turned subtly, afraid that someone might catch her looking, but, as usual, there was no one nearby to hear. About a block away, she saw a red-haired man, but the voice was too close to be coming from him.

Leave me alone!

YOU DID IT, SANA. YOU KILLED THOM.

No, I didn't!

AWW, YOU NEVER LISTEN TO US.

That's because you lie all the time! Why do you do this to me?

A surge of anger shot through her, and Sana cut the conversation off.

What was the point in arguing with herself? In the distance, she heard the faint sound of heckles, but the voices no longer dominated her thoughts. That was good.

Her house loomed nearby, a large, two-story red brick foursquare in a row of brick foursquares. She picked up her pace, anxious to be home. If she lost control and yelled at the voices—which she rarely did, but at times anger got the better of her—at least there'd be no one to see. Not that there were many people on Piper's lonely streets. A couple of people who preferred to power walk to their jobs at the big hotels on the river, and the occasional jogger.

Just a few more steps. Hey, wasn't that red-haired guy farther back?
NO, CRAZY WOMAN.

The wavering reply sent a chill through her. For once, the voice didn't sound confident. Her voices were always cocky. Hearing doubt in one of them was unsettling, even if it was only a subconscious part of her. If her voices came unglued, might it not be an omen of what was to come? A complete loss of sanity, perhaps?

The door to her neighbor's porch swung open, and Melanie Winslow, her chubby, gray-haired neighbor, emerged with her tiny Yorkie, Trotter, in tow. Melanie had bundled to the neck in an emerald cashmere cape and scarf despite the relatively mild autumn weather. Her wardrobe made Sana aware of her short sleeves and bare arms. Why wasn't she colder?

"Sana!" Melanie cried, her round face lighting up. Gray bangs blew into her eyes, and she swatted them away with her leash hand, giving Trotter an unpleasant jerk off his feet. "What a pleasant surprise. I haven't seen you out lately. Are you alright? I saw the police cars outside, and I've been worried about you and Thom."

"I'm—I'm not," Sana said, slowing down reluctantly. "I mean… I'm coming home now. It's been a terrible past few hours."

Melanie's brows rose, and Sana could tell if she didn't disentangle herself from Melanie's conversational clutches, she'd be stuck explaining every minute of her morning despite Trotter's incessant tugs at his mistress's hand.

The setting sun emerged from beyond the trees, and a few golden setting rays struck Sana in the face. She winced and moved forward, edging toward her door.

"I—can we talk later?"

Assured those explanations were forthcoming, Melanie's face

brightened. "Sure! Sure. Trotter, heel!" Melanie gave her leash a commanding tug, but Trotter, as usual, paid no mind, yanking and fighting toward his favorite telephone pole. "Why don't we do coffee later? Or tea? I bought this wonderful Chai from the corner coffee shop—you know—that Indian place?"

"Sure, Melanie," Sana said. "But I've got to go, now. I'm exhausted."

"Poor thing," Melanie cooed. "You *look* exhausted. Does this have to do with the police—?"

"I am… exhausted. We'll talk later."

She strode to her door and wondered for a moment where her keys were. It took a full minute of searching—minutes she would have sworn weighed on her like sandbags—before she found them in a side pocket of her purse.

She shut the door behind her and leaned on it heavily. Home… but not really. Though it was hers, it had always felt more like Thom's, and with Thom gone, the home had lost its soul. Hadn't Thom picked the neighborhood? Chosen the building? Urged Sana into agreeing that it was perfect for them, despite her preference for a smaller place downtown? Still, once the life insurance came through, it'd be hers without mortgage payments. He'd made sure that if he died, she'd be taken care of—she'd told Detective Jewell the truth about that. About everything.

NO, YOU DIDN'T.

The draft that followed her from outdoors passed, and the smell of astringent cleaner hit her nostrils. It only took a second of wondering what she was smelling before a graphic picture of what it was and why she smelled it triggered the urge to vomit. She raced across the living room and through the kitchen to their guest bath. Acidic orange juice scorched her throat as it made a return trip up her esophagus. As she vomited, tears fell into the porcelain bowl. She mourned the loss of her husband. She mourned Thom with sobs that wracked her body. Strangely, the sense that someone nearby watched—and even sympathized—brought her comfort. Maybe they cared.

Don't be stupid. Hallucinations don't have compassion.

She pulled the lid to the commode down and, after wiping her mouth with toilet paper, she laid her arms and head atop it. It took several minutes for her body to relax, minutes when her newly emptied stomach cried out to be filled.

What can I eat that will stay down? Comfort food. The only nourishment that had a chance of keeping down.

She rose on shaky legs, and half walked, half staggered to the refrigerator.

Comfort food.

She looked past the pasta salad and the vegetables. Milk, creamer, applesauce. No, no, no. Hot dogs. Close.

Two thawed porterhouse steaks lay on the bottom shelf, the dinner she'd planned for her and Thom that night. She withdrew the plate, grateful that she hadn't marinated them yet.

Comfort food.

She crossed the kitchen, laid them on the granite countertop, and pulled back the plastic wrap.

THAT'S IT, SANA. YOU KNOW YOU WANT IT.

She would have sworn hands caressed her triceps as she wrenched a chunk of raw meat from the rest of the steak. Popping it into her mouth, she groaned in delight as the blood from the uncooked meat trickled down her throat.

"Oh… that's good," she said aloud. She tore off another chunk. And another.

When nearly all the steak was gone, her fatigue vanished, replaced by something primal—vitality, and an unnerving flicker of arousal.

How sick are you? That is so fucking wrong! Your husband died last night, and here you are getting off on the taste of raw meat! She wiped her hands on her pants, leaving cold, wet spots on her slacks. *Think about trees, good books, the way the wind smells in the fall…*

And she tried. But the trees became phallic symbols, the books turned into lusty romances, and the wind became the sensation of her sweater brushing against her breasts.

My sweater? But—

Her bra was unhooked, though she didn't remember doing it.

Oh, God, not again.

She tore open the cabinet, grabbed the Ambien, shook one into her hand. Then another. She swallowed them dry, dashed to the cabinet, chased it with a glass of water, and marched purposefully to her room.

She gathered her blankets and swore to sleep. She wouldn't touch herself—not when her husband had been dead less than two days.

She wouldn't masturbate, but she had no doubt she would dream. The fantasy men would come again tonight, those blurry creatures that hovered between twilight and solidity, and they would touch her…

As the drug claimed her exhausted body, Sana saw the shadowy bodies emerge from the corners of her room. A muscular, tanned male with dark, wavy hair turned to his companion, another male of similar description, but more leonine, with straight hair.

"I thought you were going to go give her a hug, Angelo," the short-haired one said. David, Sana thought, glad to be asleep at last.

"Cut me some slack, will you?" the second replied. "She ran for her pills again. Same as always. Out cold now."

David shook his head. "That raw meat got her going. Probably had our little Perry on the brain."

Angelo shook his head, and from behind them, Sana saw one more form emerge before the drug pulled her into its spell of sweet oblivion. Average height, only a little taller than her, with a pale face and bright blue eyes. Perry. The breathtaking young man from the police station.

Angelo smirked. "Yes, and now we get to have a drink."

Chapter Seventeen

Eoghan watched as the trio of vampires trailed Sana, taunting her telepathically while staying out of sight. Her face struggled to remain neutral, but her mouth dipped at the corners, and her eyes darted, instinctively scanning for the source of the chatter. They were only twenty feet behind her, but Eoghan saw how Sana kept glancing over her shoulder, searching for what she sensed was real on a primal level, yet couldn't prove.

He saw them, but to her, they existed only in her mind. As long as they stayed hidden, she would believe they were only voices. When they chose to emerge from the mists, they convinced her they were dreams, hallucinations, or a twisted fantasy. They'd been at it for years—twenty years come October.

The poor girl. It's a miracle she's not cracked. How has she stayed sane?

The question was not rhetorical, so the Universe provided an answer. His stream of consciousness became a cascade of unraveling pictures. He had to close his eyes against the deluge of information or risk falling. Maysun. Birth. Daughter. Maysun's daughter.

Our daughter. That's how she's kept from losing her sanity. She's more than human, born of the Balance. She's—

Eoghan saw her birth and Maysun's sacrifice as she handed the child over to humans she trusted. The adopted family's death, and the foster home that stepped in. A new mother who worked too much and a father who saw a nearly ripe fruit in Sana. The night of what should have been her introduction to an undead life. She was emotionally scarred and mentally fragile, but she'd inherited a power her foster father—and most men—both feared and desired. And not just men. The vampires who tracked her from the station house to her home sensed it, too.

The vampires who hounded her were responsible for Thom's death, but convincing her she'd had a hand in it was their new goal.

Twenty years of blood and voices. And now I'm here to change everything.

He glanced across the street from Sana's home and used his power to relocate, watching as she spoke with her neighbor, and watched her talk to her neighbor while the troop of young vampires snickered and watched. Judging from the posture of the tallest and oldest one, his thumbs slung into the belt loops of his Levi's, he was the leader. David.

David was the man to meet.

Night. The stars above were enormous—so bright and numerous, Charles fancied he could read by their light. It was the kind of night that made him ache to take flight, to vanish into the wind and hunt beneath the stars. A night to kill. To soar in the dark heavens with moonlight on his skin as cool air roared in his ears. It was a night to revel in the darkness.

Instead, business called.

Charles resisted the compulsion to glare at half of the young undead that had sauntered into his home. One of them, a blond female from Russia who'd introduced herself as Talya—no last name offered, but he read telepathically that it was Ananenko—was a child of only three hundred. Two others were only decades older than she. These were the self-proclaimed leaders of continents! And why? Because they were the descendants of those who'd died in battle, blood children or grandchildren who'd brazenly assumed the position their sire had occupied by heir apparent rights. *Petty fools.*

They'd strode into his home cloaked in a false sense of security—one Charles could smell more clearly than the blood on their breath and the thick coats of photoprotection on their skin. They took seats around the long, mahogany table he'd had delivered from Jude's underground vault in Atlanta.

No one spoke. Impertinent youth mingled with the old, their arrogance poorly masked beneath a thin veil of obsequiousness. Shui Cheng, who'd replaced one of Charles's old allies in Asia, flaunted a smugness so repugnant Charles longed to kill him for the simple joy of setting an example. He refrained. For now.

A few faces were familiar. Errando Medina—the chubby Central

American leader with his fake wire-rimmed glasses, and Wynda Moireach, the stunning, glamorous blond from the United Kingdom, had both sided with him during his mutiny from Jude. Domevlo Ghedi and Hatshepsut Keket, both of Africa, had not. The mistrust on Domevlo's face was a mere glimpse of what churned behind those dark, unblinking eyes. Hatshepsut seemed willing to hear what Charles had to say. She sat gracefully in a chair, swooping her skirts around dainty bronze ankles like low wings.

Mistrust. Rage. Suspicion. As if Cartaphilus had never left.

Charles stepped forward.

"I see you have all found my new home without a problem," he said. "Welcome. This meeting is critical to the future of the *Shévet ha Dam*. Your roles in it—whatever they may become—are important. Though likely not as important as some of you seem to think—" he allowed his gaze to travel to Cheng, "but important, nevertheless. Maysun Khatri is the oldest of the Tribe, but has forgone her right to assemble the Table. As Jude's lieutenant, I feel it is time for me to assume the title of the Tribe's leader."

"Charles, my apologies for my brazenness," Domevlo said, "but you, who were so maligned with the *Shévet ha Dam*, seem a strange choice as ruler, no matter what your position was during Jude's reign."

"I understand your concern," Charles said, taking a seat at the head of the table. "I was partially to blame for Jude losing his life, and I assisted Jerusha to that end. As it turned out, she did not need my support." He fought to keep the anger from his voice. "I had a few friends who helped her avoid Jude until she was ready to destroy him—"

"But the world didn't end," Wynda said with an appreciative pat on the table as emphasis. "Your theory was right."

"It was," Charles said. "It was not Jude, but the power within him that, if destroyed, would have shattered the world as we know it. The power which now finds its home in me."

Any doubt on the faces of those around him vanished. As the principal body of the Maleficence, Charles had cemented his title, and resisting him was pointless. Charles was the oldest one present, and the strongest. Combined with the Maleficence, his power was easily double that of anyone in the room—and killing him meant the end of the world. Charles felt no love, and there was no weakness to exorcise.

Cheng scoffed. "Prove it."

The smile crossing Charles' face drove away the arrogance painted on Cheng's features.

"Gladly," Charles said. The sound of gasps from across the room stretched his smile further. Eduardo muttered a word in Spanish that Charles understood to mean "fool."

Charles stood, opening the mental floodgate that allowed the black river of the Maleficence to flow through him. In an instant, he ascended to the crux of the second-story ceiling above. Looking down, he envisaged the world as he wished it.

The lights weakened, then died. As they did, Charles sent the depth of his vision into the mind of everyone present. Vampires emerging from the shadows and night to take their rightful places at the pinnacle of the evolutionary chain. Using the vast resources the *Shévet ha Dam* had accrued over a multitude of centuries to overturn governments. Using their vast strength, speed, and cunning to defeat even the keenest military—either by defeat or by creating a global army of the undead. Butchering humans like livestock whenever the need arose, and enjoying the Death Rush at any time, any place they desired.

Death. The only life. Charles' black heart soared.

Cheng raised a hand. "Stop. Please. Stop."

Charles landed on the parquet floor with a gentle thump. Around them, lights flickered back to their former brilliance.

"Some of you belong at this Table," Charles said, giving Domevlo and Hatshepsut a small bow of recognition and eyeing other familiar faces. Turning to the new, he said, "And others do not."

"I don't—" Ananenko said, sitting up in her chair like an affronted student.

"You will keep your fool mouth shut ," Charles snapped, "or I'll end you where you sit.

Ananenko saw he was sincere and stopped.

"I cannot believe the gall! You young fools believed though you are under five hundred years old, you might have the privilege of sitting at my Table."

"But there was—" Ananenko said, but stopped when, like lightning, Charles shoved the mahogany barrier soaring over their heads and across the room like particleboard. He flew to her side in an instant, wrenched her head back, exposed her neck, and drained her body of life.

Finished, he wrenched her head from her shoulders with his hands and let the body tumble to the floor, casting her head after it like a macabre trophy. Charles ensured that the two red puncture marks stared up at Cheng like angry crimson eyes when the body fell. The gray eyes in her head stared blankly at the feet of those around her. No blood flowed from her corpse.

"I will not be interrupted," Charles stated, his voice deadly calm. He resumed his position at the head of the Table, though the table itself now laid leaning against the far wall. Studying only at those whose faces were familiar, he said, "Has anyone seen or heard from Maysun Khatri?"

Heads turned to one another, searching for answers, but no recognition registered on any of them.

"In that case, for now, I will leave you with two missions," Charles said. "One is for my old and trusted acquaintances. You will help me search for any vampires not in the Blood Tribe. Dismantle every insurgent faction. All vampires must join us or die. How, I'll leave for to you to decide. I have already begun this using the troops I have in the United States, and you will do likewise in your territories.

"As for you," he turned to face Cheng and the other youths, one a young female from the Philippines, the other a male from Australia. "I don't care how closely descended you are to Cartaphilus. You have no business in my home. The only reason I do not kill you this instant is so you can follow my instructions. This is not a time for mutiny. Not if the *Shévet ha Dam* is going to survive."

He motioned to a darkened hall behind him. Four vampires emerged—three old, undead souls who stood next to the youths, and one younger, bald, and thin. With a nod from Charles, the elders wrenched the three younger ones from their places and assumed the chairs. The young one standing at Charles' elbow waited near the chair Charles used to occupy.

Turning to the uprooted youths, Charles said, "Get the table. Put it back where it was."

They scuttled to do as they were told, silent save for the scraping of chairs and table legs, until the proper heads of state were where they belonged. The young ones stood at their sides like properly heeled dogs.

"Ladies and gentleman," Charles said, standing so he could show as he went, "allow me to introduce—or, rather, reintroduce—Ealdred D'Eath of Australia," he patted a tall, Nordic-looking man on the shoulder, "Luzon Quiboloy of the Philippines," he gave a short, stout, fierce-looking woman a half-hearted half embrace, "Lan Chiu of China," he nodded to a stern-looking Asian with an exceptionally wide nose, "and

Doyle Christy of the United States." Christy stepped forward with apparent reluctance. Lean, with hollow cheeks, narrow blue eyes, and a straight smile, he tipped his shaved head as if expecting to be thrown into a feeding frenzy.

Charles turned to Cheng, defying him to ask what Christy was doing there, a being barely over a century old that hadn't lived Stateside for over two decades. Cheng's blood reeked of Jude; on the outside, he might be three generations separated, but Charles wagered it was less. If any of the youths had power, it'd be him. Cheng, however, demonstrated a newfound civility Charles hadn't expected. He barely moved.

"You have met the Table," Charles barked. "Scour your territories. Report your progress daily. Track every enemy you eliminate. You have your missions and are dismissed."

Everybody but Christy lifted smoothly from their places and headed, as one, to the exit. Charles walked them to the door and watched as they took flight from his walkway. Cheng made a display of the ease with which his wings emerged from his lean back and gave Christy a contemptuous scowl before launching himself at the starry sky.

Then they were gone, and for the first time in the week since he'd moved in, the house was silent.

Charles closed the door and sighed. Doyle sat in his chair, a dazed expression on his face.

No sign of Maysun. By rights, the Table should be hers. Where is she? Perhaps he should seek a replacement for the Middle Eastern sector of the Tribe.

No. Not yet. She may turn up. And I can't allow the only vampire older than myself to roam unchecked.

It had been a long night, and it was only the beginning. He had given the Tribe a mission, one he planned on following as well. His plan had always been to usurp Joseph. Now, Jerusha and her little clan of rebels had proven that allowing vampires to roam freely was not in the best interests of the *Shévet ha Dam*. Charles had looked after the Blood Tribe for a thousand years. That it took only one female—granted, one who was the second strongest of their kind—to nearly undo what he'd spent centuries putting together maddened him.

Vivian infuriated him. *Vivian. Jerusha. Katerina. Whoever she may be this go-around. It doesn't matter. She needs to die.*

She'd rejected his help, but more importantly, she'd come close to unraveling his life's work. He'd see her destroyed, preferably at his hand. Soon. He only needed to track her down. Although he had the Table working for him, they didn't have the Maleficence, his experience, or his wisdom. Shielded by the Source she was beyond his reach, at least telepathically. But he might be able to follow clues others would miss. This wasn't a task he was willing to risk to incompetence.

Killing Vivian would be a fantastic was to start his reign.

Facing her with less than his full reservoir of energy would be foolhardy, though. He called his pilot and told him to ready the plane for Savannah, the last place Vivian had called home.

Chapter Eighteen

"We can't sit back anymore!" Crystal cried, pacing the floor of their cramped apartment. From the kitchen counter to the living room couch, and back again. She hadn't stopped since she hopped out of bed that morning.

Harmony wrestled with the moment. These were her friends—but duty came first.

"You heard Tristan!" Crystal snapped, grabbing Harmony's shoulders and shaking her. "He said we have to fight!"

"He channels the Divine," Harmony said coolly. "I don't have that luxury. I have to—"

"Listen to the fucking Universe. Like I haven't heard that before," Crystal snapped. Harmony's rigidity only fueled Crystal's passion. She raced to a closet, threw back the door, grabbed a backpack, marched to her bedroom, and started shoving fistfuls of clothing inside without regard for organization or style.

Harmony stood in the bedroom doorway. Crystal's frustration rolled off her in waves so strong, Harmony saw them shimmer in the air like heat rising off asphalt.

"What are you doing?" Harmony asked.

"I'm going to Michael and Vivian," Crystal growled. "They'll go fix whatever's happening, and I'm going with them. We saw young vamps herded like cattle. You saw those ashes. They've already killed some—and the rest are next. Tristan's already dead. Stay here if you want. I won't sit by and—"

"Okay. We'll go."

Crystal froze, one hand buried in the backpack, the other clenched around a nylon strap. She blinked, confused, disbelieving. She raised her head from her half-packed bag.

"Seriously?"

Harmony nodded. "I needed to find out for sure. Now I know."

Crystal's jaw jutted out. "You didn't know a second ago?"

Harmony sighed, and Crystal sensed the impatience in it. "I did. You weren't listening."

Crystal was unsure whether to punch her or sigh with relief. Harmony would never—could never—let emotion interfere with duty. Even so, her sister's stolid presence at her side reassured her. So much in her life was tumultuous; Harmony's presence had somehow managed to be the one thing that remained somewhat constant.

"Well, shit," Crystal muttered, squaring her shoulders and tossing her dark curls back. "Let's fucking go."

"So, we agree?" Michael asked from his seat while Vivian perched on the chair's arm beside him. "Find Doyle and get him away from Charles? That will be our first step?"

"He risked his life for you and Viv," Lukas said. "I'd say it's time to return the favor. He might have been a bit shady, but he came through when it counted and picked the right side."

Megan nodded from the crook of Lukas' arm. She looked downright tiny beside him despite being five-foot-five. "How are we going to find him?" she asked.

Vivian frowned. "He's buried too deep in the Maleficence. I can't touch him psychically. Lukas?"

Lukas' head swiveled her way.

"Can you hack into the Tribe database again? See what they've got on him?"

Lukas nodded, slid his arm out from behind Megan, and stood. As he did, the sound of ripping material caught their ears. He contorted himself into a twist to see if his pants had torn, his expression baffled. Megan smirked, but it didn't quite reach her eyes.

The sound of frantic whispering drew their attention to the kitchen, where a golden, otherworldly light had appeared. Brows furrowed, Michael, Vivian, Lukas, and Megan hastened to inspect it as three people— two tiny and female, one a tall, bronze-skinned male, tumbled through a supernatural doorway lined with jagged, white-hot light. Once they released the light, the portal sealed behind them as if it'd never been.

It was the two women from earlier who'd seen Vivian connect with the Source. They stood with their companion, their cheeks red with embarrassment. Dainty, neither of them over five feet tall, they stood dwarfed by Lukas, who cast a broad shadow on them from the light coming from the living room. Their male friend stood closer, protectively.

"Can we help you with something?" Lukas asked, narrowing his eyes.

The three of them shared an awkward glance that spoke volumes. The dark-haired one took charge by unspoken agreement.

"Uh… actually, we were gonna ask you the same thing."

"I'm sorry?" Michael said.

"We want to help you," the dark-haired one continued. "Me—uh, I'm Crystal Novak, and this is my sister, Harmony. Adopted sister. We're both adopted." Her hands flew in dizzying motions as she spoke. "This is our friend DB—Dorian Bradley. We call him Dragon Boy," Crystal said.

"Does he morph into a lizard?" asked Lukas.

"No, but he can breathe fire."

DB puffed a smoke ring that rose lazily in the air and viewed Vivian and her family with subtle humor, a twinkle in his golden eyes, and a lopsided grin.

"Fire-breathing friends," Megan said, her eyebrows raised, giving the newcomers a skeptical once-over.

"Good to have at a barbecue," Lukas quipped.

"Or when you need to flambé a vampire," said Michael. "It's one of the few reputed methods that'll kill 'em."

"Charmed," Harmony injected with an awkward half-smile.

"We're human," Crystal said. "DB and I are… superpowered. Although Harmony can live an awfully long time, I've been told, but she'll be human again, eventually. I'm, uh… I'm an aerocleaver."

"A what?" Michael asked.

"We made the word up because we don't think there is a word for what I do," Crystal said, her discomfiture growing stronger the more she babbled on. "I… uh…" her hands moved toward where the bright light had been.

"She's a spatio-temporal connector," Harmony offered smoothly. Her explanation was met with blank stares from the four vampires.

Harmony cocked her head and added without blinking, "She can cut holes into the fabric of space and connect any two points on the earth."

"Handy," Lukas said, impressed.

"Sort of," Crystal said, put at ease by her sister's handy contribution to the conversation. "Makes vacations a breeze," Crystal said with a shrug.

Vivian had to grin. "And what is your skill, Harmony?"

Harmony licked her lips with a mouth that neither smiled nor frowned. "I can't say. Not yet." She pushed up the sleeves of her blouse before crossing her arms in front of her chest and gave them a half-shrug. "But I will when I need to. If I need to."

Megan's expression grew cloudy. "How can we be sure you're not working with the Blood Tribe?"

"She's not," Vivian said, fascinated. "I can't feel her at all!"

"What do you mean?" Michael asked. His muscles tensed, prepared to pounce on the newcomers.

"It's not like Charles or any of the others. I'm aware of Charles' existence. The thought of him makes me uneasy. She's absent. Like a void."

"Bad?" Megan asked.

"No… not negative… but intriguing," Vivian's lips turned up in curiosity. She might get no answers from Harmony about where her abilities lay, but the Source told her that accepting the newcomers worked in the Universe's favor, so she rested in that knowledge.

"We had another friend, Tristan," Crystal said. "Tristan was a human with special powers, too."

"What kind?" Michael asked.

"Prophecy. And he could turn energy into a ball and use it as a weapon."

"You said 'had a friend' and 'could,'" Michael observed. "Where is he?"

"He died a few hours ago," Harmony replied. The candor in her voice was odd, almost robotic. "Killed by vampires. They were rounding younger vampires up and killing them."

Conversation lapsed, and heads turned from Harmony, whose expression refused to emote, to Vivian. There were a thousand questions, but which to ask first? As Vivian's family gave them their full consideration, Harmony drew herself to her full, if slight, height.

Crystal waved her hands at them beseechingly, her eyes tearful as her sister assumed a posture similar to the one Vivian had recently used. Head back, eyes closed, she inhaled deeply and then swooned. The tanned, golden-eyed boy placed a hand on either side of her, prepared to catch her. Harmony drew a sharp breath, one Michael heard duplicated by Vivian.

"Balance," Vivian said. "She's in the Balance."

"Oh, great, *now* we can trust her," Megan scowled, but Lukas shushed her and put a gentle hand on top of hers. Megan glowered, but remained silent.

Harmony's eyes flew open, but her placid features revealed little. Vivian's body became unsteady. Michael took her elbow with a distracted arm.

"Who's Charles?" Harmony said, her voice in a rush.

"Charles Dunning, head of the Blood Tribe, the primary host of the Maleficence," Vivian said. Michael questioned Vivian's trust—especially in someone she couldn't read—but held his tongue.

"You mean the Darkness?" Crystal asked. Vivian blinked and nodded in confirmation. Maleficence, Darkness, it was all the same.

"He's coming," Harmony said.

"How long do we have?" Michael asked, but Harmony's head was already shaking, her eyes wide with panic.

"Now," Harmony said gravely. "We need to leave now."

"Time for me to show you what I can do," Crystal said. She drew up her hand outside the bathroom and pulled it down. A ray of light shot across the kitchen, setting the room aglow.

"Grab the bags," Michael told Lukas. "Megan, you and Vivian get everyone out of here."

Lukas grinned. "Back into the fray. Finally."

Chapter Nineteen

Doyle felt anything but honored after his first meeting with Charles. Less than a year ago, he'd have amputated a limb if it meant he could attend a meeting with the prestigious group. Now that he'd endured the scornful stares of the vampire elite, the idea of Charles appointing him head of the U.S. division was even more unfathomable. He sat in Charles' vast living area staring at the empty table in the adjoining room, his mind awhirl.

Him. Of all people, Charles had chosen *him* to lead the U.S. division. Why? He was remarkably young by Table standards. Sure, the war had thinned the herd—but not so badly Charles was out of options. There were still at least fifty older members of the Tribe who lived in the States more competent than he.

It wasn't a matter of his devotion. Doyle's dedication to the Tribe was suspect; he'd proven that by helping Vivian and Michael many times. Never mind that helping them had ultimately worked in Charles' favor when he plotted to kill Jude, anyway.

So why? What quality did Doyle have better than any of the ancient ones?

You're his lapdog. Always have been. Always said yes. You'll be a figurehead—a little stoolie who will go running to the Big Man when anyone misbehaves.

A tall glass of *Das Schwarze*—a thick, oil-black German beer Charles had imported for him—rested on the table by his knee. He took a long sip, but the beer, as dark as it was, still lacked flavor.

Anything but blood lacked taste. He closed his eyes and envisioned sinking his teeth into the jugular of a squirming human, but his eyeteeth failed to elongate the way they used to. The struggle, the Death Rush—lately, it lacked the punch for him. The satisfaction wasn't there. Instead, it left him feeling…

Guilty.

The word landed like a sack of wet concrete. Guilt? Doyle Christy? The two ideas had always been so contrary before. His lack of remorse had drawn him to Charles' attention. Death, cheating, scheming, it was all part of the sport. Now the first, at least, seemed to have lost its ability to give him pleasure. The Death Rush was still a rush, but the guilt it left behind churned in his gut for hours, sometimes days, dulling the short-lived thrill.

Is the Maleficence's hold on me weakening? And if it is, where does that leave me? Not part of the Table. Not head of the U.S., for sure. Probably not alive.

Did Charles sense the cracks forming? Was that why he wanted to keep him so close? Did he hope that giving him a job with authority might bring him back into the fold? Or did Charles care that much for him—for anyone?

Probably not. I'm as disposable as anyone else in the Tribe. He cringed, remembering Ananenko's blank stare after Charles drained her.

He needed to get a hold of Vivian, to warn her about Charles' flight to Savannah and his plan for the renegades. Her family, Blu, all of their friends and acquaintances, were in peril. His fingers twitched at the phone on his hip, but he didn't detach it from its clip. No doubt the phone Charles had issued him was tapped, linked to the Tribe network. Telepathy was straight out—Charles was only in the next room. Not that Doyle was too good at it, anyway.

A thought occurred to him. *What if Charles is counting on me to lead him to Vivian? Of course! Keep your friends close, and your enemies closer, that whole thing. He knows I care. He's waiting for me to screw up and lead him straight to her.*

His long fingernails, tight within his fists, pressed into his palms. How long did he have to warn her? A few hours? Charles undoubtedly had the best private jet on the market. It wouldn't take long for them to reach Savannah.

I have to warn Vivian. But how?

"Doyle?"

He looked up. Charles stood with one eyebrow cocked, body angled toward the door. Had he been reading his thoughts? He hadn't sensed Charles in his head but… *God, I'm so stupid.*

But if Charles had heard his musings, he showed no displeasure. He must not have bothered. And why would he? What was he to Charles but a puppet?

"Time to go," Charles said, his expression taciturn, as always.

Doyle stood, suppressing a sigh of relief.

Maysun lurched upright, hands outstretched to shove away an unseen assailant she was certain hovered in the gloom. A psychic link to her attacker revealed his intent as clearly as if she were watching a film. He wasn't there to kill her. What the man wanted was worse than death. He wanted to rule over her, to control her body and spirit. He wanted to drive her out of her mind with fear.

Her hands flailed at empty air while her heart pounded in her ears. A scream died in her throat as her eyes adjusted to the scant light.

There were no attackers. She was alone, an empty spot where Eoghan used to lie in the bed next to her. Her eyes took a moment to focus.

Royal blue bedspread. Blue jacquard curtains hanging over a tall window, blocking out nearly all the daylight. Plush, white carpet. A matching antique bed and dresser. Strange. She hadn't expected to be back in her flat, but where else would she be now that her life as the Balance was over?

The dream she'd had was so vivid, her heart still thundered, her teeth clenched in an unspoken scream. In her dream, she wasn't in any of the homes she'd lived in across the globe. She wasn't anywhere she remembered seeing before.

I'd forgotten what nightmares were like. She released a long breath and her tension left with it. *That was so real.* She'd opened the door to many others' dreams and nightmares over the centuries, but always from the safely insulated position of the Balance. She experienced the dreams with the dreamers, but the sensation left once her eyes opened. With her nightmare, it took several minutes before her sympathetic nervous system finally recognized her panic was a false alarm. Her heart rate slowed, and her breathing grew deeper. The first prolonged sleep she'd had in centuries, and she was rewarded with a nightmare so vile it was enough to put her off sleep for a long while.

It was harder rising from bed than usual—perhaps because it was the first time she'd awoken since she'd regained her mortality. She'd slept hours longer than she'd expected to; the bedside clock read a quarter past eight. Her head felt fuzzy, her muscles sore; her blistered feet ached from yesterday's shopping trip. She swallowed and winced. A sharp tang of copper hit her tongue. Her face screwed up in recognition.

Blood? But how…?

Maysun shuffled to the bathroom and pulled back her upper and lower lips to study her teeth and gums, but she saw no trace of blood. She was sure she'd tasted it.

She released her lip and leaned in to study her reflection. *I probably irritated my gums clenching my teeth in my sleep. I'll have to be sure to take better care of them now that I'm human again.*

A nagging thought lingered. Perhaps it was merely the dream. Maybe the scent and taste of blood in her mouth had triggered a memory from her time as a vampire. Now that she was alert, the dream had faded, save for the lingering unease.

It's been so long since my dreams were merely an overactive imagination. I can't recall normal ones. Could it have been more than a nightmare?

She squeezed toothpaste onto her brush and scrubbed her teeth until baking soda and mint replaced the aftertaste of blood and sour morning breath.

The problem was that the dream had seemed *too* real. Though it'd been centuries since she'd had dreams, she'd caused many in the minds of others. Few dreams had that level of clarity, and those belonged to precognitives.

If she were clairvoyant, why didn't she remember? And if it wasn't hers… whose life had she seen?

Chapter Twenty

Sana woke from a fitful morning sleep, crusted tears on her cheeks and a familiar foul taste in her mouth. Her clock confirmed that she'd slept a good portion of the day away—not an uncommon occurrence after nights when the painting muse struck. Her body ached like she'd been beaten unconscious instead of simply falling asleep. She cringed and peeled her tongue from the roof of her mouth.

Slowly, she sat up, slightly dizzy and bleary-eyed from the residual effect of the Ambien. The clock on her night table told her it was a little after noon. Irregular hours were nothing new, but the weight pressing on her chest told her this wasn't post-painting exhaustion. Her world took several seconds before coming back into focus and when it did, Sana wished to return to her odd dreams of blood and hunger.

Thom. Murdered in their home while she slept, unaware, only yards away. She'd have to arrange for his burial today. *What do I even do? I've never handled death before. I'm not sure where to start. Oh! The lawyer. I've got to call Darrin. Oh God, is he going to be mad I didn't call sooner? The funeral home. Damn, I should have done that yesterday. And the insurance people. Or will that only make me look suspicious again? Oh, hell!*

She swung her legs over the side of her bed and searched for her slippers. They weren't where she remembered them, but many days, nothing was.

At least this time I have an excuse. Stress screws with memory.

She heard a chuckle and turned, but, as usual, no one was there. Only the window, blinds drawn against the sun, stood where the voice had come from.

NO, YOUR POOR SHORT-TERM MEMORY ABOUT THOM'S DEATH IS BECAUSE YOU DON'T WANT TO REMEMBER, a familiar voice said. Not hers. Not the one tied to vocal cords. This was one of the masculine ones that haunted her. She closed her eyes and braced herself, preparing her mind to defend itself from an onslaught of vicious put-downs and attacks on her self-esteem. None came.

She walked around the foot of their bed—her bed—to the master bath. It struck her as strange, her habit of rising from her side. Thom's half was closer to the bathroom; it would've made sense to roll to that side. Instead, she'd made the roundabout trip. *Habit*, she supposed. *How long until I get used to having that huge bed all to myself?*

DON'T WORRY, SANA, a voice said WE'LL ALWAYS BE THERE TO SHARE YOUR BED WITH YOU. WE'LL NEVER LEAVE.

Is that supposed to surprise me? she shot back mentally, venom thick in the thought. *I'm so used to you poking around in my head that if you left, I wouldn't know what to do!*

Without flipping the light switch, she covered the steps to the sink by the light of the streetlamp light filtering through the beveled window. She turned the brass knob, held her hands under the gooseneck faucet, and splashed her face, determined to ignore whatever comeback surfaced. Nothing came. A smirk played at her lips, and she snorted. *That's telling me.*

She heard the soft click of the bedroom door. Or imagined it. Usually, faint door sounds were an indication that she was about to enjoy a length of time without her intrusive monologue. *Good.* Today she could get work done. Maybe longer than today. Sometimes the voices stayed away for weeks at a time. Then, when she dared to hope her sanity had returned, they'd come back.

She brushed her teeth, wincing at the overpowering mint toothpaste. It was one of those mornings when no matter what she used to clean out her mouth—multipurpose toothpaste, expensive rinses, flavored floss— the taste of copper persisted.

She took a long, hot shower and nearly drained the container of lavender-scented soap while trying to remove the dried sweat that lingered on her skin. Her hands moved mechanically over her skin.

As her hands traced the curve of her neck, she found two sets of closely spaced new scabs. Her mouth turned down. Once again, she'd clawed herself in her sleep. Before her arousal? After? During?

Turning her hands over, she studied under her fingernails, where the telltale half-circle of blood lingered at the deepest part of three fingernails, before the pink. She grabbed her fingernail brush and scrubbed until the blood was gone and her fingertips turned pink. *Out, damn spot!*

She toweled off, headed back to her walk-in closet, and dressed in faded, paint-smeared jeans and a white t-shirt, which she covered with a worn, red flannel rolled to the elbows.

A million things to do, but before she tackled them, she needed a few moments of sanity. Only one place on earth gave her that sort of calm, the mental and spiritual serenity she craved.

She scaled the stairs to her studio—four broad, high walls so white and pristine they could have been glossy enamel. The far wall held a clean, stainless-steel sink set deeply into a small, white counter. Two enormous floor-to-ceiling windows with rectangular mullions gave her a view of the tops of the neighbor's homes and the pasture and green hills beyond. White tile floors, gauzy curtains, and tin ceiling tiles completed the sterile, almost surgical feel. The only color was in the center of the room: the vibrant hues of Sana's paintings, palettes, drop cloths, and easels and a worktable smeared with paint on the legs from many paintbrushes dropped in anger, frustration, or clumsiness.

It'd been three days since she'd last entered, and the air smelled musty and stagnant. Sana crossed to the windows and cranked them wide, letting in the crisp fall air. The oak trees in the distance glowed orange against the gray autumn sky, brightening with the rising sun. She inhaled deeply as a wind gust blew under the pane, breathing in with it the moisture and traffic and the distant fragrance of fallen leaves.

Voices rose from below the window, a nearly one-sided dialog of men deciding where to go. She followed the conversation, her eyes trying to bore through the walls, searching for the dominant speaker as if he was in the room. And why not? She recognized that voice.

Now you're becoming paranoid. That's probably not your imagination, somebody that sounds a lot like one of the fantasy voices you've created. It's probably the voice you based one of your imaginary friends on. Except that it couldn't be. The voices in her head had been the same years before she'd met Thom and moved into her house.

Donning a paint-smeared apron pulled from a hook on the back of the closet door, she marched to the center of the room, picked up her easel, and studied her latest work. In the pencil outline, three young, shirtless men in tattered jeans tore through the black corners of her canvas amid a smoky swirl that might have been moonlight. Each face revealed a passion that might have been fury. Or hunger.

Chapter Twenty-one

Eoghan trailed the young men at a distance, watching their stride, their pride, their enthusiasm. He had to draw close to them, learn about them, and earn their zeal. He had to become one of them.

More facts, drawn from David's mind, clued Eoghan in on the perfect costume. Lineage, age, respectable names, the right people. As a cascade of images burst through his mind, his body reacted, attuning itself and making the changes.

His body, already muscular, regained its springy gait and leaner proportions of youth. His hair resumed its youthful hue with each step until it shone in the sunlight like fire. The crow's feet faded, leaving him no older than his late twenties. Last came his eyeteeth—elongating into a subtle, demonic overbite.

His change into a vampire was more than superficial. The Balancing act now required that he take on a vampire's chemistry to blend properly. His blood churned with immortal power, and his skin prickled under the sun's touch. Not too much. He had to appear old enough to impress them and descended from the proper "family." Eoghan made himself appear as a vampire of around a century, but one with Table lineage—which he identified now, thanks to David. Power, but not antiquity. Just what these young ones understood.

He rifled through their minds like annotated files, key thoughts already highlighted. David Sheen, the eldest, was the most complex, intelligent, cunning, and wicked. That he was leader made sense; his drive was more significant, and the other two relied on his guidance. Angelo Vargas, the lieutenant, held his position through more than ass-kissing. He had an inordinate amount of resentment and hate, even for a vampire. His savagery had earned respect, not only from David; it was the standard to which Perry Taylor—the youngest one—was expected to reach. A mere babe to those in his family who'd been nearly ten years older when they'd been turned, Perry masked his softer heart under a thick façade of toughness and reticence. His victims' deaths were a means to survive, not a pleasure. Like Sana, his bond with David's clan was forced, but fear of death and concern for Sana's safety cemented Perry's tie. No one escaped David's hand—not if they valued their survival—but Perry wouldn't dream of leaving while Sana's fate was uncertain.

The research took seconds. The necessary conversation downloaded into his mind like a script. He gleaned how to penetrate David's clan long enough to be one of this tightly-knit group. Of course, it helped that he British and looked, walked, and smelled like a vampire. He stepped up his pace. The pieces of this game were nearly in place.

David and his clique sat on the inside steps of a fountain, a dried, half-circle of yellow brick in the center of the park shielded by trees to the left and a large brick building to the front. A sidewalk, about five paces wide, paralleled the street to the right of the fountain, continuing its course around the entire park.

A human rapidly approached them on the sidewalk, a worn canvas bag under his armpit. The man was single. His only connection to this earth was a mother with dementia, who didn't recall who he was more often than not. No children. Minimal universal impact.

The timing was crucial to avoid police intervention. Several pedestrians milled about the park at this hour. Joggers peppered the sidewalk at uneven intervals, dog-walkers, a woman on her way to back to work after a lunch break, taking a shortcut through the thick, green grass. Eoghan placed them like dots on a map, timed his strike, and slipped behind a broad oak tree trunk.

He heard the patter of the human's feet as he hustled down the sidewalk. When Eoghan saw the first glimpse of flesh and dark clothing around the tree, he struck, pulling him from his feet and covering his mouth simultaneously. Only a quick, muffled huff of air escaped his victim's lips. With a speed and ease he'd never experienced in a human body, Eoghan dashed with his prey behind the brick building, swift enough that no human eyes saw, but ensuring that David and his mates detected him. He ducked behind a six-foot-tall half-circle of holly bushes and struck, sinking his teeth into the pale flesh exposed above the collar.

Blood flowed through his veins stronger than any whiskey high. His knees weakened. After a few long draughts, he forced himself to toss the body to the ground. His first impulse was to gather the half-dead body into his arms again and sink his teeth in once more, to suck the man dry until his cheeks were florid and his veins sang with warmth and life.

So I can feel, even as the Balance, when I'm a vampire. He willed his heart to slow, the adrenaline to ease, and to his surprise, his body heeded his thoughts. *I'll have to be careful. This might become addicting. God, to feel!* His body, having parted with emotions for a day, reveled in his restored senses. How much worse would it be if he'd been without them for a month? A year? Good God, a decade?

As he stood panting over the mugger's body with blood trickling from his chin, David rounded the corner of the brick structure that had blocked his view, followed by Angelo and Perry.

David's head was slightly down, eyeing Eoghan's quarry. He only raised it slightly to ask, "Alright?"

Eoghan gave a quick nod as the boys circled the body, and his breathing returned to normal.

Angelo shook his head. "Well, now you're snookered," Angelo sneered. "You've got a body dead out here in public. I mean, it's hidden, sure, but someone will find it. You know how the Tribe feels about that, mate."

"No worries," Eoghan replied. Using his wide, sharp index fingernail, he created a deep gash in his front arm and dripped the blood into the gaping mouth of the dying man who was too weak to turn his head. When a small amount had collected in the back of his throat, the dying man swallowed reflexively. The blood hit his stomach, and the newborn vampire's body smoldered in the bright mid-day sun.

"Now that's brilliant," Perry said with a laugh. "Why'n't we ever do that?"

"'Cause it *smells*, you twit," Angelo replied, waving his hand in front of his face with exaggerated sweeps. Although the words sounded harsh, his expression revealed an appreciation for Eoghan's brazen, casual act of siring solely for disposal convenience.

Within five very long, silent minutes, the body had ashed. David nudged the corpse with the white toe of his Converse. The first breeze in several minutes caught the ashes and sent them spiraling in the wind. David watched as they fluttered away and then returned his gaze to Eoghan.

"Snag him, half kill him, give him a sip, and Bob's your uncle," David said. "Problem solved. Brilliant. I've never done that."

"Bit risky," Eoghan admitted. "What if they live?"

David nudged another piece of the ashy corpse and watched the bits fly. "Still."

He and Eoghan eyed each other squarely. Eoghan didn't blink. Neither did David.

"David Sheen," the other man said, extending his arm. Eoghan took it and gave it a strong shake. "Angelo Vargas, Perry Taylor," David added with a nod to each.

"Kip MacConin," Eoghan said, shaking firmly. "Pleasure." The name seemed to come from thin air, but it stuck as soon as he uttered it. His vampire name—at least for now.

"So, Kip," David said, "What brings you to our little corner of the world?"

"You, actually," Eoghan replied.

David nodded. "Alright."

Eoghan and his new acquaintances emerged from behind the tall holly bushes, and as the young vampires dangled their legs into the dry fountain, David turned to Eoghan.

"How many years do you have?" David asked.

"One hundred six. You?"

"Just over forty."

Eoghan feigned surprise, his eyes glancing at the sun high overhead. "You're not well-fed," Eoghan said. "I smell no recent blood or photo-protection on you. How do you survive the daylight?"

"Sired by the Old Man himself," David said. "Angelo, too. Perry's mine." Eoghan gave an understanding bob of his head.

"Children of Cartaphilus. That explains why I've been asked to come."

Only the slightest tugging of a smile pulled at the right corner of his lip revealed David's pride and eagerness.

"I'm a mate of Charles Dunning," Eoghan began.

"The Yank head of the *Shévet ha Dam*."

"Mmm. And it's supreme head, now."

David's thick eyebrows raised; shock covered his handsome face. Angelo and Perry's heads swiveled at the news, but they remained mute, letting David handle business.

"And Jude?"

"Dead. Killed by his eldest child, Jerusha."

"Explains a few things. How'd it go down?"

"That's not the story I'm here to tell you," Eoghan said.

David shifted his position with a forceful kick of his foot, and he placed a tanned hand on the hip of his Levi's as he glared at the sunlight breaking through the trees. His sire had died, and he plainly longed to hear the details of what had happened, who had carried it out. But he refused to ask.

"Go on."

"This is about Sana."

His curiosity about Jude's death momentarily forgotten, David shot Eoghan a baffled look. "Sana?"

"About what she is. How she's resisted both vampirism and insanity despite your ploys."

David nodded, subtly urging Eoghan to continue.

"Sana is the daughter of a human man and the Balance," Eoghan went on. "She was raised by humans and has never learned her roots. She never met her mother—"

David chuckled. "Wait. Are you telling me we tried to turn the daughter of the Balance? All this time, we've been fucking around with the daughter of the Balance?"

Eoghan met his eyes, but said nothing, his placid expression both frustrating David and earning his respect.

David chuckled again, but cut it short. "Well, that's a bloody enormous cock-up? Can't turn a woman without buggering it up." He eyed his fingernails for a moment and then replaced the hand on his hip. "So that's why she hasn't become a complete nutter." He chuckled and stared at the bricks near his feet. For a vampire who'd a moment ago discovered he'd probably been on the wrong side of a globally influential force, he took it well.

David finally looked up. "Tell me about Charles Dunning."

Chapter Twenty-two

Maysun drifted through the late morning in a half-fugue, likely the result of her first true sleep in centuries. After a cup of strong coffee, she decided to clear her foggy mind with a lukewarm bubble bath, another stomach-eroding cup of joe, and a good book. *A motivational non-fiction book should do the trick.*

She shed her nightdress and brushed through long ebony hair as the tub filled with lilac-scented bubbles. She tied her hair into a knot at the crown, set it in place with a pair of antique ivory chopsticks, eyed her reflection with mild admiration, and then turned her attention to the steaming tub. She checked the temperature and adjusted the knob, so the incoming flow wasn't as hot. From the closet, she retrieved a large, purple, fluffy towel, which she set on the edge of the bathtub for when she was finished.

Humming to herself, she angled her toes to the water. A memory hit like a boxer's punch, dragging her under like a white-water current. Her father. The image of him, short-statured, with large, heavy-lidded eyes, came as clearly as the image she'd seen in the mirror moments ago. When she was six, her father had drowned in a tidal wave while she visited relatives farther inland with her mother. They'd returned home weeks later only to find their small village destroyed, their home swept away. Her father had been accounted for among the dead villagers and buried in a mass grave.

His voice was so friendly. So kind. Maysun remembered the way his hands looked—his fingers were thin and short, his palms callused.

The pressure of tears became a trail down to her chin as they broke free, only to be replaced by more. It'd been nearly two thousand years, but the memory wrenched her heart as it had when she was that little girl called Ishani, seeing her ravaged, waterlogged home for the first time and hearing from a villager that she'd never see her father again.

She braced herself on the cool tile; her fingers squeaked and slipped against the condensation. Her balance wavered as the images of her youth took the place of the ivory walls around her. The stench of sewage, rotting wood, death, and mildew replaced the soapy bathroom. The sound of her mother's grieving wail overcame the sound of the water pouring from the spout.

Maysun brought herself back to the present by force of will and detected pressure in her temples and clenched jaw. Why now? She'd been human for a full twenty-four hours. Why hadn't these memories arrived sooner? Was her body still recovering, pulling all the thoughts she'd suppressed as the Balance to the forefront and putting them into their rightful, more human places? That had to be it.

I'd better be cautious. If every returning memory hits me like that one, I'm in for a rocky time. Days of flashbacks—perhaps weeks.

Once composed, she eased herself cautiously into the water. She maintained three points of contact in case another memory swept in and threatened her balance. The fragrance of lilac was cloying, sickeningly sweet after the stench from her memory. Like gorging on rich food after days of fasting—too sweet to savor. She wrinkled her nose as she eased herself back and wished she'd chosen another fragrance. It was too late to change it now.

She grabbed a sponge and soap and lathered distractedly. How many memories might hit her with that level of emotion? Might she be sideswiped by incidences she'd suppressed during her time as the Balance? Cautiously closeting specific experiences was part of life as the Balance. The Universe worked hard to maintain its equilibrium, and some memories were best left locked away.

She made an effort to remember more about her childhood in India, pulling up memories from centuries ago. Her mother had lived only ten years more than her father, grieving his loss every day, then had died of what they then considered old age. These were relatively easy memories to deal with, the natural order of life.

Family.

A flash hit her like cerebral lightning, stealing her breath. *My daughter! Sana!*

Her hand flew to her forehead, sprinkling her face with bubbles and hot water. Lilac foam touched her open lips, and a bitter taste of soap filled her mouth as tears sprung to her eyes. She had closeted the memory of her daughter.

My child? What did I...? Why...?

Sana. Her daughter. Guided by the Balance, she had allowed Eoghan to impregnate her. As a mother, her ability to perform her job as the Balance would be affected, so she'd maintained a disconnected standpoint from her offspring. She'd carried the child to term, and after delivery, she'd handed the child to a couple who hadn't the ability to create their own before locking the memory of her daughter away.

I treated her like a doll—another pawn in the Balance's grand game. But why? What does my child have to do with it? Another tear fell from her cheek and cut a cylindrical tunnel in the bubbles.

Then came David and his damned impulsive reaction to Ralph's infatuation. To the surprise of everyone but Maysun, Sana's blood weathered the pull of vampirism. She didn't know how she knew the young woman was impervious to the transformation. She just... knew.

As Maysun, the vampire, she'd heard about Jude's discovery of the peculiar girl who now lived in the States. The unusual, undetectable girl whom Jude had detected with the help of the Maleficence.

Maysun had confronted him about his fascination regarding Sana, who was then fourteen. Jude's only response was that he had her in mind for a future bride.

"She's a child," Maysun had argued.

"She's lovely," Jude said. "And she'll get older."

An uncommon, fleeting moment of concern came over her, but the memory remained elusive. Maysun followed Sana's story from afar as Jude had, waiting for twenty years. Jude's halfhearted interest in a future bride became an intriguing quest of discovery—how had this beguiling young woman resisted? How long would she hold out? Despite his claim, Jude never took her for his bride. Instead, she was a study, and David, her fieldworker, offered Jude weekly, then monthly reports on any changes. In the end, they barely remained in touch; the statements were brief and infrequent, as there were no changes to report. Sana grew no less stable, no more physically powerful. Only more beautiful.

Still, Jude waited. After twenty years, Sana showed no new strength, only resistance to the vampire strain. And then Jude had died.

Charles knows about Sana. Of course he did. Charles knew everything Jude had—or close to it. Charles didn't care about beauty or brides. He'd never loved, never hungered for physical pleasure, save the Death Rush. Sana held no use for him if she remained powerless.

But she wasn't powerless. Another memory dropped into place—that of a conversation she'd overheard between Charles and Jude.

"The girl has more value than that of a bride, Joseph. She may be the cure to vampirism itself. Think of the power we'd hold if we could threaten our opponents with humanity!"

She rubbed her face harshly and splashed it with water, wishing the memory was chalk, her hands and the water an eraser to wipe it clean. Charles had seen Sana as a potential lab rat to be studied and dissected. How long would he wait before gathering her up and sticking her into a cage in a Tribe laboratory?

She'd had a daughter. She'd abandoned her. That was easy enough to understand, if only with the detached logic used within the Balance. The universe had a plan for her offspring. Maysun had been the Balance for two thousand years. In that time, she'd played the part of a lover, a confidant, many times. Yet, despite her many sexual encounters, she'd never conceived before the widespread use of contraception.

Eoghan had held a pivotal role in the cosmic forces. The father of the Balance's child. Surely, she'd had other sexual encounters that year. Why Eoghan? Was his part merely due to timing?

No time for that now. You need to find your daughter and see if she's still alive, see if she'll let you back into her life.

She stood, prepared to hose off the bubbles with the showerhead and charge through her home, prepared to do whatever battle necessary to find her child.

But how to find her? She'd been meticulous about covering her tracks as the Balance, never leaving a trail linking her to Sana. She'd never kept a record of Sana's address, had never visited her daughter's home, and she didn't have a working phone number. Although Maysun had operational knowledge of the internet, information on Sana was inexorably linked to the Tribe and would make Charles' inevitable search for her simpler. Jude's tentacles undoubtedly reached into every part of her daughter's life—her associations, her friendships, right down to her credit cards. Hiring a private detective was pointless for the same reasons.

Using her connections within the *Shévet ha Dam* was out. With as little as a phone call, they'd sense her lack of bloodlust and loss of power. What explanation could she offer for that? *Sorry guys, but I'm not a vampire anymore. I could still use your help, though.* No. Not possible.

South Carolina. That was all she'd learned during her time in the Tribe. Her daughter lived within thousands of square miles of possibilities too time-consuming to contemplate.

An agony she'd never known clenched her heart, and she eased back down into the water, her legs weak with sorrow. This was worse than losing Eoghan. She was guilty of personal treason—the desertion of her own child. She buried her face in her hands and sobbed like a child.

How could I do that? How could I walk away from my baby?

She longed to have her power back, if only for a moment. Finding her daughter with the Balance was as easy as wanting the answer to a question; going to her side was as simple as a wish. She had limited resources, waking hours, and knowledge as a human. Limited brainpower. Limited strength.

Why didn't I record this information before giving my power to Eoghan? The answer was obvious: she wasn't supposed to. *Damn the Balance to hell and back. Damn it all!*

She sighed and eyed the razor on the side of the tub. Her gaze flickered to her wrist, the warm bathwater.

I could find Sana if I go to the highest Source, she thought. *All the knowledge I need is there.*

Like an angelic voice on her shoulder, her conscience stood up, indignant. *Traitor! That's cheating. It's wrong!*

Would the Universe allow her to return to her body or earth to save her daughter if she died? Could she stand it if she had to watch her daughter's life play out as a helpless spirit?

What's more helpless than being human? If I'm meant to be part of it, I will be a part of it, and the universe won't allow me to die. If I'm not meant to be... maybe I shouldn't be. Her chest grew tight, and she curled into a ball, her hands clasped to her chest.

Memories pummeled Maysun like stones. Giving birth alone in a forest glade in France. Taking the train ride with the tiny, wrinkled, red-faced child clutched in her arms. Handing newborn Sana, still wrinkled and pink, to an American couple living in Paris. The memory of that precious burden weighed on her as it could not then; the memory of the baby—her baby—in her arms.

A second voice on her opposite shoulder reminded her: *Death is not forever. If need be, there are ways to come back.*

With a shaking breath that stuttered around the tightness in her chest, Maysun lifted the razor and extracted the blade.

Chapter Twenty-three

Vivian leapt through the opening ahead of Crystal and Harmony, who held it open with matching grimaces of pain.. After the sisters eased through the narrow gap and released the edges, the tear in the fabric of space whooshed close, blowing Vivian's hair back from her forehead.

It wasn't until the fissure sealed that Vivian realized they'd entered a shopping mall. Right then, she stood in a utility corridor reeking of industrial soap that opened across from a Bath & Body Works and a clothing store—one of many that favored young, hip styles of urban youth. She didn't believe she'd seen this one before, though they all looked alike to her.

After dropping their bags—five small pieces of cheap black luggage that held everything of importance they owned—in a disused-looking closet, the new family gathered in the food court while Vivian tapped into the Source. The court was milling with shopping mall employees who worked at coffee machines, fryers, and electric countertop griddles. The smell made Michael's sensitive stomach churn.

Lukas paced in circles around their bags. "It's five forty-five," Lukas said with a glance at his watch. "Stores will still be open for another couple of hours, and the employees won't be leaving here for another half hour after that." He gave Crystal a weak smile. "Nice, public indoor place where the Tribe can't attack. Good thinking."

"I wasn't thinking at all," Crystal admitted ruefully. "This is Regency Square Mall. We come here whenever we drive to Richmond to visit my dad. He can be a prick. It's kind of an escape."

"Our safe place," Harmony said with an understanding nod.

"A car rental place would've been better," Megan said with a playful grin, "but this isn't bad."

"We can't rent a car," Michael said, his mouth tight with frustration. "We used the last of our liquid cash on Linda's funeral, and we don't dare use the charge cards or debit cards. If Charles is in Savannah, like Harmony said, he'll almost certainly find our ID machines, and then the Tribe'll—"

"Fuck!" Lukas barked, punching his thigh. "Those fucking machines are impossible to replace! Dammit, dammit, dammit!" He was so angry he hopped with each outburst until Megan laid a reassuring hand on his forearm. She murmured to him, her auburn head tipping back to peer into his much higher features, and Lukas received the words she uttered like a salve. In seconds, his grim expression appeared resigned.

"Cards don't matter anymore, anyway," Crystal observed. "If they find us, I can always cut a getaway hole."

"Huh," Michael muttered. "That's not a bad idea. If we spread out, the Tribe's search will be disconnected. They're looking for a group. Makes it harder for them to find a pattern. Good thinking."

With that in mind, Michael walked to a popular fast-food chain counter, ordered food for everyone, and paid for it with a credit card bearing one of his pseudonyms.

"Now *that's* an Irish-sounding name," said the cashier with a smile. Her curly red hair and bright green eyes stood out against her polyester uniform, and her smile was wide and straight. Michael grinned, careful not to show his fangs, as he read her name tag: Megan. "You must be Irish," Michael said with a chuckle. "I have a friend over there named Megan, too. Megan Jameson."

The young woman behind the counter laughed. "There must be a million of us."

"Probably more," Michael agreed, accepting the plastic tray of fragrant, greasy food she offered across the counter.

Lukas, who'd been standing at the exit looking into a sky sparsely dotted with light, crystalline clouds, hustled to his father's side. "Beautiful day," Lukas noted. "Are we close to D.C.?"

"Yeah, why?"

"Blu. He's got an apartment he sometimes uses when he stays with a guy named Byron or Bryan or…" Lukas rolled his eyes as he searched for the name. He snapped his fingers. "Brady! That's it."

"Talk about an Irish name," Michael laughed. Lukas looked confused, and Michael waved it off.

"We might be closer than we think if Vivian thinks it's best to find him. We wouldn't need to use Crystal. She's looking a little peaked."

"That would be good luck," Michael said. Neither of them mentioned what Michael was thinking—that luck hadn't often followed them as of late.

Michael set the tray on the table, and Harmony, Crystal, and DB dug in voraciously. Michael felt a pang of guilt for waiting so long to buy proper food. He'd forgotten how different it was, traveling with humans.

He'd held the role of the paternal figure for his small clan of vampires for so long. Now, Vivian sat at the head, and Gina was gone. With Cartaphilus so close in his chain, Lukas had power greater than Michael, and since Lukas had turned Megan, she, too, was stronger. Now, his troop extended to include Crystal, Harmony, and DB—an aerocleaver, a vessel of the Balance, and a young man with a mighty strange, fiery skill.

Life had turned on its heel since Vivian had entered their lives. Being allied with the Source's largest vessel had its drawbacks.

Charles lifted an empty fifth of whiskey and hurled it across the room. The thick glass bottle refused to cooperate with its destruction, bouncing off the parquet floor of Vivian's home with a dull, unsatisfying clunk.

The place was empty, but the evacuation had been fairly recent. The air was thick with the scent of human bodies. Telltale signs of a party lingered—the mislaid coat that was never retrieved, bottles of alcohol that hadn't found their way to the overflowing waste cans. A stack of folding chairs cluttered the rear garden, surrounded by crumpled napkins and crushed red plastic cups. A few mementos of a woman named Linda Goodson lay at the back of a living area.

A funeral, Charles noted with faint amusement. *They held it here. And they left only moments ago. Why didn't I hear anything? Where did my vampires go?*

Doyle puttered around nearby, held close by Charles' invisible leash. One glance at the photo told Charles that Doyle recognized the woman, but neither he nor Charles commented on it. Perhaps she was one of the many renegades who had asked for Doyle's help over the years.

Vivian had eluded him, but barely. The Blood Tribe had searched from alley to valley, but she and her family had vanished. He didn't know where she'd gone, or how. The Maleficence raged within him, a torrid fury that goaded him, threatened to envelop him.

He needed to kill something. Or someone.

"Mr. Dunning?" Doyle's voice was so pitiful and unctuous it barely penetrated his thoughts. Charles regarded Doyle, whose shaved head showed a hint of blond stubble and a light sunburn.

"What?" he snapped.

"Well, I just…" Doyle licked his lips. "Their clothes are still here. They aren't gone for long, I'd think."

"They *are* gone," Charles countered, "and I dare say they won't be back. They left their things here to fool us into thinking they planned to return." He scoffed. "As if that was enough to trick me." He lifted a cut crystal vase full of white roses and eyed the blooms angrily. "They're gone."

"But Mr. Dunning—"

Charles hurled the vase against the far brick wall. Unlike the bottle, the crystal exploded in a deafening, satisfying crash. Doyle scampered up the stairs using his arms to shield his head from the flying debris. Charles half expected him to fly, though shape-shifting was decades beyond a late bloomer like Doyle.

I can't home in on Jerusha. That blasted Source protects her. And Doyle's too stupid to make any good use of telepathy. She's probably shielded the whole damn group from me. Unless…

The slightest trace of a smile touched Charles' lips. It was a wild shot, but an outside possibility was better than no prospects at all.

Lukas, the son of Vivian's partner, doubtlessly traveled with them. She wouldn't let anything happen to Michael's son, and the safest place for Lukas to be was at her side. Lukas was only two generations removed from Jude Shepherd.

Two generations removed from Jude Shepherd, the previous host of the Maleficence. Hell, he might as well be my offspring, now that Jude is gone.

Surely all of that darkness hadn't escaped Lukas' immortal body. And if Charles understood young men the way he believed he did, Lukas had a weakness—a weakness for his blood spawn.

A plan was already taking shape in his mind. They may have escaped this time, but the victory would be his. Even with their best psychic walls in place, Lukas couldn't deny what he was: a child of darkness.

His cell phone rang. According to the screen, it was Susan Batista, one of his leading intelligence officers, who he'd sent to explore

Vivian's alternate Savannah home, a second-floor apartment on Waters Avenue.

He hit the speaker so Doyle could hear if he had half a mind to. No doubt the unfaithful bastard was counting the seconds until he could run to Michael and Vivian.

"Yes?"

"Sir, I've found some information you might find interesting," Susan said. Her nasally voice brought to mind her appearance: crisp, short, and businesslike.

"Well, that's good, because I've uncovered precisely zero."

"Sir, their identity card reproduction machines were downstairs at Waters Avenue. Computers, printers, lamination devices."

"That's good, Susan, but we already know they've created identification cards for the local vampires. What does it have to—"

"Sir, I have the names they're going by."

Charles couldn't believe his luck. Not one, but two ways to track them?

"You're sure?"

"Yessir. Vivian is posing as Melody Burgett. Two t's. Michael is uh… Dillon Moriarty. Lukas is Scott Moriarty. Supposedly, they're brothers. And there's another one, a Megan Jameson. She's traveling as… Ilsa Wolfe."

And now I have Lukas' offspring's name.

"Anything else?"

"We're doing a trace on the credit cards and identification now, sir," she replied. "So far no results."

"I'm going to do a trace of my own," Charles said, "but call me back with your results. It never hurts to have corroboration or, better yet, a pinpoint location."

"Yessir," Susan said, and hung up.

A smile touched Charles' mouth. "Doyle?"

"Yessir?"

The voice came from around the corner. As he'd suspected, Doyle had dashed out of view, but not out of earshot. "Doyle, are you ready to prove your loyalty to the *Shévet ha Dam…* or not?"

There was only the slightest of pauses before the reply.

"Yessir."

Chapter Twenty-four

Vivian paused, cocking her ear toward the furious whispers exchanged among the golden young man, Crystal, and Harmony. She had caught little of the content to that point, but she tuned in time to catch Harmony saying, "It wasn't my fault!"

"What?" Megan interjected, catching Harmony's hushed defense. "What wasn't your fault?"

"Tristan," Crystal sobbed, covering her face as tears overtook her—muffled quickly by DB's arms around her.

"What wasn't your fault?" Megan repeated, her chin jutting as she rose on her toes to loom over the smaller woman. Now it was Lukas' hand on her shoulder doing the calming.

Harmony sighed. "Tristan, our friend. We were there when…" her stoic guise crumbled slightly and then bounced back. "When he died."

"How?"

With Crystal's help, Harmony explained to them in more detail about the roundup of young vampires in Savannah, the short-lived battle, and Tristan's death. DB, who hadn't been present, listened as intently as the others.

"Crystal seems to believe that I may have gotten guidance earlier this morning that I withheld," Harmony said. Eyeing her sister levelly, she added, "But I didn't."

"The Blood Tribe rounded up our friends and killed them?" Megan said, appalled. "How did they not find us?"

"They weren't done," Vivian said. "That place you described sounds like a place near Broughton Street. They hadn't reached us yet. And Harmony, it *wasn't* your fault. Or yours, Crystal, for suggesting that you try to help. Forces greater than ourselves rule our lives when the impact is severe enough to tip the global scales."

"Like the Harmony," DB observed. He picked at a dracaena plant, plucking off one of the smaller leaves. With a practiced puff of air, he lit the tip with a tiny burst of flame and then shook it before it grew too dangerously. Michael grinned in surprise, and DB returned it with a flash of pride.

Charles had Krieg, his half-vampire, half-giant he used to transport vampires who couldn't fly. He evidently was aware of the existence of other beings besides vampires. *Why hadn't I looked for other kinds of beings before? Beings like DB and Tristan—what were they? More than human? Superhuman? Some hybrid?* She nearly laughed. *Does it matter, as long as they're on our side?*

No doubt Charles had spent the past few centuries devoted to studying anything with the potential to give him more power. In contrast, Vivian had spent them in servitude to Cartaphilus, often lying in her coffin for years, silent as death. When Joseph allowed her to wake up, it was in another life, with his instilled memories. She had only regained her memory of her life as "Jerusha," the second-oldest vampire, for less than a year, and had no reason to believe there were magical beings other than those she'd met—the vampires. She'd never thought to look or ask the Source about any different supernatural beings before.

She grinned. She knew now.

"A woman I used to call my mother was the Balance, too," Vivian explained to the newcomers. "It was one of a few roles she'd played. Joseph handed me to her, believing he was giving me to a widow who longed for a child and would do anything to keep me—even if it meant letting him control my life. She spent the next three years housing a being who could channel the Source—once I regained my memories."

"Our Mom, too," Crystal said.

"Your mother handled the Source?" asked Megan.

"No, the Balance," Harmony replied. "And she wasn't really our mother. She adopted Crystal and me when we were young. She said she sensed the power in us. Crystal—well, her difference is obvious. But mother—Laurel—she gave me my gift. The Harmony."

"Which guides you in everything," Vivian said. Harmony nodded, and Crystal's angry expression relaxed a bit.

The silence of the shopping mall was broken only by the occasional sound of mall walkers, background music, the occasional puff from DB as he toyed with the dracaena leaf.

"No car," Megan said, breaking the stillness, "and no money. Our friends are in danger or dead. What're we going to do first? Are we still going after Doyle?"

"What's wrong?" Michael asked, baffled by Vivian's expression.

Vivian tried to smile. "Nothing. Well, no, that's not true." She licked her lips, and her voice grew earnest. "I could go on ahead," she said, tapping the floor with her foot. "I use the Source, find Doyle, go on ahead and see—"

"No," Michael said. "You remember what happened last time you left me."

"A huge biker vamp kidnapped you and Blu and nearly killed you."

"Well, Krieg *was* a huge biker vamp," Michael admitted, "but he didn't exactly kidnap us. He told us he was a transporter, and he didn't say who he was transporting for. And he didn't nearly kill us—he was going to let Jude do that."

"Still," Vivian said, and stopped tapping.

"Still, not pleasant in anyone's book."

"But I could—"

"Please, don't go alone. Or, at least, not without me."

"No one needs to go anywhere alone," Crystal said. "I can take us anywhere, anytime. I don't need to see what a place looks like, either. But it helps."

"You'll wear yourself out," DB warned. "You know how you get when you cleave too often. And your hands are already burned really bad." He tried to take her hands in his, but Crystal withdrew and turned away from the group.

"It takes a lot to wipe me out," Crystal retorted. "I've never *not* been able to do it."

DB snorted. "No, but we've had to crawl through mighty tiny holes to get home."

Amused by the exchange, Vivian grinned, but her smile quickly faded.

Charles will launch an attack against us, against me, soon. He's already hunting down others.

"Vivian?" Michael asked, leaning forward to meet her grave gaze.

A quiet fell over the group again. Vivian took in person after incredible person in her group. Vampires. A fire-breather. Another Balance. An aerocleaver. There had to be a way to make it all work, but she didn't know how—and time was slipping away.

Chapter Twenty-five

Sana daubed a canvas bicep with diluted burnt umber and stepped back. The ambient light of the sun had softened under thick, blue-gray clouds, but the bright overhead lights still shone like a clear summer sky.

Too dark. The other men have darker complexions, but he's pale—much paler. And almost feminine.

She mixed raw sienna, yellow ochre, white, and a hint of blue until the color looked right. She brushed his oval face with gentle strokes, mixed a slightly darker hue, and added dimension and depth to the cheekbones, the temples, and the neck. When she stepped back to view her work from a distance, she was stunned to see what she hadn't registered as she'd hovered near her canvas, hypnotized by the pull of creation.

She'd painted her husband's killer.

Her breath shook and quickened. She leaned over the worktable, resting her head and arms on its surface, until the hyperventilation slowed. She waited for the voices to ridicule her, to say, of course she knew him. How else had Thom died? She must have hired him in an alternate state, while the Sana part of her was a suppressed persona. How much of a stretch was the idea of dual personality if she heard voices? But alas, for once, they were silent.

How pathetic am I? They aren't here, and I'm filling in their gaps, chastising myself and accusing myself of things I didn't do! Her eyes met the unmoving ones of the young man on the canvas.

Her lip curled up in horror at her behavior. How long until this constant barrage of accusations and inescapable taunting drove her to a padded cell? How long until her mind, made more fragile daily by the nonstop harping and repetitive mockery, snapped and drove her into the streets, babbling like a madwoman?

Some days it seemed her breaking point hovered only moments away. The closer that moment came, though, it seemed the resolution within her grew, drove it out, an exorcist banishing her madness like a demon. That strength was the reason she hadn't sought professional help. She prayed daily to gods she didn't believe in that her faith in her staying power was not unfounded.

Turning her attention back to her work, Sana scrutinized the faces. Three pairs of eyes, yet to be tinted, stared back. The painting—a thirty-six-inch square canvas—looked like the cover of a reverse harem novel. Still, once she envisaged a straight, black head of hair and robins-egg blue irises on the young man set farthest back in the group, the likeness was undeniable.

If he's Thom's killer, who are the other men?

She stepped away from the canvas. For once, she wished she didn't paint such lifelike images. The muscular men in her work looked ready to move and grow, to step from the taut canvas into her studio and cross the room, their arms outstretched as if to drag her into a passionate hell.

Stop!

Dropping her palette and brush onto the tarp, she raced to the sink on the far wall, yanked the knob, and splashed her face with icy cold water. The shock of the cold helped, but her heart galloped until she saw stars. She gripped the edge of the sink with white knuckles until it steadied.

A white towel lay on her work desk, and as she picked it up to dry her dripping face, she uncovered a pair of scissors, one she'd recently bought to cut away excess canvas from the frame. She dropped the towel on the floor absently and lifted the weighty scissors. She opened the blades and eyed the canvas. Hours of work stared back at her, and she fought the urge to tear the painting from its frame. With a sob, the sharp blades slipped out of her hand, slicing her left forearm as it fell. The cut burned like acid as it left a thin line of ruby liquid in its wake before clattering on the tile floor.

She lifted her head from the blood. Her eyes landed on the faces of the three men on the canvas. A cog in the wheel of her mind clicked, and her breath caught in her throat. For a fraction of a second, she was certain that was the answer. They were real, and they were somehow…

Somehow what? Invisible and able to get into my head? That makes no sense!

It didn't make sense, but it struck her as more accurate than any other notion she'd kicked around for the past twenty years. She didn't know who had killed Thom, but it wasn't her. Either there were invisible peo-ple—killers—prying into her head and planting thoughts, or she was dealing with a god-awful level of mental health problems and needed serious help. But which was it? Or if there was an option she hadn't considered?

She stood, grabbed the towel from where she'd carelessly dropped it on the floor, and wrapped her injury. Blood soaked through the fabric and tinged her fingers. She stood up, her back straight and resolute, and set off to find the first aid kit and Thom's book on self-hypnosis.

Maysun had killed during her time as the Balance, but she'd never lived through her victims' final moments after the glaze of death cov-ered their eyes. Throughout her time as the Balance, the aspects of cre-ation and death remained a mystery. Now and then she suspected she saw a divine revelation pass over her victim's faces as the final exhale passed their lips. Other times, death came quietly, like sleep.

It was almost with a sense of scientific discovery that Maysun expe-rienced her own death. Her body lay in the porcelain tub, peaceful and dreamlike, soaking in a cooling bath of crimson water. She saw without eyes, but not without sensation. It was almost the opposite of life as the Balance: peace and freedom enveloped her, and joy. The sense of being one with the earth and all the tenderness of its creators.

Creators?

Her point of view pivoted until she faced upward and traveled past her ceiling, her roof, and toward the sun. Her spirit quickened, soaring beyond the clouds, shuttling outside space and time and through a bril-liant tunnel.

In life, she'd believed she'd fly beyond the stars when her soul aban-doned her corpse, but in death, she torpedoed south and west, drawing close to the coast of the United States, then south, toward Puerto Rico. The blue-gray Atlantic hurtled past, white breakers churning on a foamy ocean. Thick cumulonimbus clouds hovered over her, gray billows gath-ering, preparing for a storm.

They were in the middle of nowhere, but Maysun saw where she was headed. The Bermuda Triangle.

A peculiar outcropping of land caught Maysun by surprise; a small tropical island with tall, green trees and lush foliage surrounded by a ring of white sand and covered by mist. Twin volcanic peaks rose above the hazy white film. A sense of serenity enveloped her as she floated toward the mountains and through the clouds. She sensed the moisture and warmth, but without a body, she discerned them without physical touch.

She traveled through the mists and onto the sandy beach, and then she discovered legs stretching below her as she gently touched ground on the powdery sand. Her body had been restored, by a mysterious power. The salty, lush air shone under the pleasantly hot, bright sun.

Thick foliage and palm trees in front of her, an infinite ocean behind, Maysun stood on the sunny beach, uncertain how to continue. *A sunny beach? What happened to the storm?* Was her eternity to be confined to a tropical island alone? The sound of crashing waves and a tropical breeze rustling the trees wouldn't be so bad, she supposed—if it meant Sana would be alright.

A childlike giggle emerged from behind the dense bush. Maysun's brow rose, and she swiveled her head in search of the source.

What was that?

The question was silly. She knew *what* it was, but not how it had gotten to this extraordinary place. Why would a child be hiding in the bushes on a desolate island with a dead woman on it?

She stepped forward and discovered her light, ethereal body—there, but not whole. As if it was waiting for a divine word before floating away into the atmosphere to eternal rest at one with the universe.

She neared the wall of flora where the sandy beach gave way to green. When she brushed the leaves aside, she was surprised to find the sharp-looking edges of the palm plants and tropical shrubs were softer than ordinary and moved under the slightest touch.

Instead of having to tackle her way through a deep jungle, after covering perhaps twenty feet of thick brush, Maysun found herself in a cleared space of grass with the sun beaming down. On either side of her, a level swath of grass cut a trail that curved along a towering, lush green wall encircling the island as far as her eye could see. Before her, a burning sword stood, its tip pointed upward. Though she stood several feet away, the sword's searing heat reached her. Flames crackled from pommel to point. The air was redolent with burning sulfur.

Another giggle erupted, this time from her right. She turned, and a small, chubby body emerged from behind a fat, green leaf. Tiny wings—surely incapable of flight—stemmed from its back. Rosy cheeks puffed on either side of its wide, childlike grin.

"This is what I'm supposed to look like, right?" it asked. It was an androgynous sound, like a six-year-old boy or girl, though the body appeared scarcely out of infancy. Maysun's mouth opened, but no words came out.

A cherub? They exist? She would have guessed the universe held no surprises after living for centuries as the Balance, but this was most unexpected.

"Or perhaps you'd prefer this?" The cherubic shape burst into flames that swelled to a height of around eight feet. A cloaked being—equally androgynous—emerged from the conflagration, clothed in a brilliant white robe. Wide, white, feathery wings spread from where the useless stumps had been. "This is how most folks nowadays think of me."

Words escaped her. None of this was as she'd planned when she'd taken her life. The mystery of death was more perplexing than she'd ever imagined. She said the only word that came to mind.

"…Hello."

The angel smiled, and the action seemed practiced. The facade of humanity on the serene face chilled her. This being had a depth of awareness that Maysun had never known, even as the Balance.

"Good morning, Maysun," it said. "We've been waiting for you." Learning that they expected her did not comfort her. If anything, it deepened her unease.

The angel swept its hand at the fiery sword as if unveiling a work of art behind a curtain. The enormous weapon moved at their command like a boulder rolling to the right with silent, laborious movement. Beyond where the hilt had been, an arbor of greenery in the towering wall arched over an entrance to the world beyond.

"Go ahead," it said. "This is what you came for, is it not?"

She willed her body forward. *Do it for your daughter. Do it for her!*

As she trod through the archway, she wondered if it was too late to pray.

⸻ ❧ ⸻

If there was one personal quality Sana prided herself on, it was her outstanding memory. It didn't matter if it was a phone number or the shade of green on a Douglas fir. Her memory held it as firmly as a photograph. Now, with the steps from Thom's book on self-hypnosis committed to memory, she set the book down on the oak coffee table. She relaxed onto the burgundy suede couch and stretched out, her head gently supported by a pillow. After taking a moment to test her position, she sat up, put a pillow behind her knees as well, and settled back down. Better.

She'd read that it could take weeks before self-hypnosis became easy, and she hoped it wasn't true in her case. Although the voices had been absent for hours, it was only a matter of time before they returned. They always came back. And once they did, she'd have a hard time finding a peaceful moment to try this.

Don't worry about that. Try it. What've you got to lose?

The answer, of course, was nothing. She'd already lost her mind.

She focused on her breathing, not forcing herself to relax, but allowing it to happen naturally. This step was relatively simple without the voices present to nag and berate her. A residual tension lingered, fear that they'd be back, but she pushed the fear to the back of her mind and told it to shut up.

Once relaxed, she began counting backward from 100, imagining herself sinking deeper into a tranquil state with each number. Thoughts tried to interrupt, but these were everyday thoughts, easy to ignore and bat away like butterflies, not invasive voices. She imagined her living room as the sea, her couch a soft raft drifting in lazy sun.

In minutes, she wasn't sure if she was hypnotized, but she felt more relaxed than she had in months—perhaps years.

Instead of probing the origin of the voices—an experience she suspected might be too traumatic for a first attempt—she'd decided she'd try to expose the basis for her painting. Were they classmates, movie stars, attractive men she'd seen in the grocery store? How had these faces eluded her typically flawless memory?

Faces reappeared in vibrant color, emotions blooming alongside them. She'd seen them all in the twilight before slumber, vivid shadows changing to corporeal forms emerging before she fell asleep and vanished before dawn.

Lean features, juniper green eyes, long, dark hair. A face that would look handsome, if not so filled with fury. *Angelo*.

Pale skin, black hair, wide turquoise eyes, thin lips. Prominent cheekbones that showed the adult the young man would soon become. *Perry*. His name was Perry.

And last, the foremost figure in her work. The one with the broadest shoulders, the tannest skin. Wavy, black hair, deep brown eyes.

"David."

Sana jerked upright, snapped from her trance by the thought—spoken aloud in a voice she knew too well, accent and all.

They were there. The men from her painting. The faces from her mind, plus one, a red-headed stranger she hadn't envisioned before. Why? Who was he? Why did the others feel so familiar when he was a stranger? Had she made a new one up by hypnotizing herself?

Her hypnotic state shattered as her heart galloped, but a nagging thought remained: was this another altered state conjured by a botched attempt to hypnotize her already fractured mind. The tremors which shook her body threatened to disable her. She curled into a ball like a pill bug, wedging herself into the corner of the couch as if she could disappear into a hollow behind the pillow.

I've done it. I've made them real. I can see those hallucinations! Oh, God, I should've left it well enough alone. Why'd I do this? What was I thinking?

"You're—you're not real."

David smiled, his teeth large and white, set in a mouth too perfect, too seductive. Romance novel cover quality handsome, exactly as she'd painted him. He sat at the edge of the wide oak coffee table before her, pried her arm from her chest with his firm hand, uncurled her fingers. With them, he stroked his face slowly, the stubble made her wince as if pricked by a cactus. She resisted the urge to scratch him to see how he responded.

"Do I feel real?" His voice was soft, but demanding. And god help her, sexy.

"You're not real," Sana murmured. Her wide eyes stared but refused to focus on what stood before her as she wished them gone, strove to see her world as it had been only seconds ago, before they entered it. God knew how. The front door was only feet away. Hadn't she locked it? Of course she had.

Her hands touched the rough texture of his chin, the softness of his lips, but she refused to acknowledge it. She tried to pull away, but David gripped her wrist and forced her hand to stay. "You're not real. You're not real. You're not real."

The one called Angelo cackled. "Cor, Davie. I think she's finally gone 'round the bend."

Chapter Twenty-six

One quick call with Batista, and Charles had more information on Vivian's whereabouts. A card embossed with "Dillon Moriarty" had been used to pay for purchases at a shopping mall in Richmond, Virginia, where they'd stopped at a fast-food restaurant. But stopped, how? How had they left the apartment only moments before and traveled nearly five hundred miles in time for breakfast? Was teleportation possible for vampires? Jerusha, perhaps, had that talent, though he'd never heard of her, or any other vampire, using any methods like it. The others were too young. Lukas, maybe? How long did it take for vampire blood to mutate, especially when confounded with both dark and light power?

Could the trail be a red herring? Very likely. They'd probably given the card to a friend to throw him off. Charles' intelligence had told him that their queer friend had a home near DC. It was more likely that another vampire unaligned with the *Shévet ha Dam*, Babu Ubora, known to them as Blu, had traveled out of his hometown with a duplicate charge card in Michael's alias to throw off the hunters.

He eased his body onto a step near the bottom of a maple wood staircase. Vivian's belongings surrounded him, her scent enveloped him, aroused, and provoked him. Might she be close? Might the search end tonight? *Vivian. Dead at last. Proof of my power ascertained in the eyes of the Shévet ha Dam.* The notion that her blood might be in his veins before the day's end excited him almost as much as the Death Rush.

Don't get too excited. They aren't fools. It'd be more likely they've used a false lead. But what if I'm wrong? Does Vivian have the power to travel long distances with her family instantly? Or is this a feint?

It didn't seem likely she had the power to teleport—which was why it was best not to eliminate the option. After the way she'd eliminated Jude, he knew never to underestimate her. He had no desire to share

Joseph's fate. Not that he risked dying the way Joseph had—allowing himself to love. Charles had more fortitude than Joseph, and no love for Vivian to manipulate.

Joseph's weakness hadn't surprised him, though. He didn't have the vision Charles did. Cartaphilus had always kept his vampires in the shadows, lurking on the outskirts, living in the dark. Charles planned to change that. Over the centuries, the *Shévet ha Dam* had accrued massive stores of money and strength, and with it, influence. Once he'd handled the situation with Jerusha, Charles would use both to bring his Tribe out of hiding and place them where they belonged—at the pinnacle of the evolutionary hierarchy.

He tilted back until his frame reclined on the stairs and then closed his eyes. Hard steps pressed uncomfortably into his shoulder blades and head, but he blocked out all thought, his mind receding to a place where his immortal soul became a mere amoeba in a sea of darkness. With all internal dialogue and sensation smothered, his thoughts quieted, Charles became one with the Maleficence.

Fire raged along his veins, and his body quaked with a hate-filled passion as the evil within him grew. Instinct consumed his body, his mind, his essence.

Lukas. The secret lay with Lukas.

Charles rode the current of the Maleficence, sensing the path followed by Joseph's descendant; his seed had not died with him. Lukas Graves harbored inner darkness, and the Maleficence traced this unrecognized hostility and rage.

It was a complicated trail to follow; the Source sheltered the family, so they were nearly impossible to locate, not to mention the strange leap in the boy's route from Savannah to Virginia.

Their new way to travel is worth investigating. Another time.

Batista's information had not let him down. Using Lukas' body as both a set of eyes and a homing device, Charles saw that Vivian in Virginia. He heard the words, though faint. She and Michael planned to meet with Blu and save their friends. The only question was which they did first.

Joy, or something like it, coursed through his body. The end to eight months of aggravation felt moments away. If they fled Virginia after speaking with Doyle, heading south to help their friends in Savannah, Lukas' proximity would enhance Charles' connection with the boy. Charles would have immediate insight into their actions and discern which roads they were likely to use.

Except that you have no clue how they moved from here to there so rapidly. Charles squelched the thought. He'd find out if he had to tear the family apart by their limbs to uncover their secret. It likely wouldn't come to that, though. Tapping into Lukas hadn't been difficult; it was only a matter of sticking with the boy often enough to learn what he knew. Once he learned the secret to Vivian's teleportation, he would either eliminate or duplicate it.

Vivian's family was on the run, uncertain, frightened, watchful… all those wonderful qualities that made the Maleficence so formidable and weakened the Source that fed Vivian. If they came back to Savannah soon, he'd be ready.

Perfect.

He begged the Maleficence to tell him how to imitate Vivian's jump from Savannah to Richmond, but the understanding eluded him. *What if the power isn't within her?* Charles pressed, scrabbled, implored, but he came no closer to finding out how she'd done it.

The fire in his veins surged until his body suffered like a burning corpse. Would she always escape him? Would Charles spend eternity hunting her, only to discover that she'd popped from one spot on the globe to another? Malice threatened to consume him like quicksand.

Enough! Stop!

The Maleficence receded with agonizing sluggishness. Once it released him, Charles' relief at being freed from its grip nearly matched his yearning to dive back in—drowning in the hate and evil that fueled him.

He jerked up with a start and pulled his phone from his pocket. The sensation of tiny flames lingered under his skin, matched only by the painfully exquisite silk blend of his slacks.

He pushed two buttons to reach Batista.

"Yes?"

"You were right. They're there."

Batista's silence struck him as resentful, her anger at his lack of faith in her job evident.

"Send in our air steward," he said. "But tell Krieg to use caution. We don't want to tip Jerusha off that we're there. If we can capture Lukas and Megan, do it. Not one or the other. If Lukas and Megan are isolated from the group, he will move in on them. They are direct descendants of Cartaphilus, and their power is beyond nearly every vampire of the

Tribe, so he should take great care. Do you follow?"

"Yes, sir."

"And Susan?"

"Yes, sir?"

"Make sure he doesn't get any idiotic ideas about taking Vivian out on his own. Jerusha is too much for any of our soldiers. She could easily take on a half-breed monster like him. She'd kill him and flee with her family before he so much as said her name."

"Yes, sir."

He ended the call and stood, pacing in his excitement. If Krieg captured Megan or Lukas alone, Charles had one hell of an advantage. Vivian would do anything to protect them—even if it meant her life. To use Michael as leverage would be better, but the odds of catching the inseparable couple apart were thin. Not to mention that stirring Vivian into desperation was a bad idea. Anger might be the food of the Maleficence, but Charles had no urge to face Jerusha's love-stoked righteous anger.

No, this plan was better. Faced with losing Megan and Lukas, possibly Blu as well, Vivian's grip on the Source might weaken enough that he stood a chance against her. He was not familiar with the depth of her power. Jude had never gone toe-to-toe with her, caving in to love like the weak being he was—but Charles trusted the Maleficence to guide him.

If he tore Michael from her side and threatened to take his life, he might persuade her to sacrifice herself. Not as satisfying, but an end to Vivian—any end—was better than knowing she lived and threatened him and his Tribe.

The Source would undoubtedly find another vessel, but so what? It'd be hard-pressed to find another rival to his power. And the body it used wouldn't be the body that had held Joseph Cartaphilus back from becoming the demon he might have been. Not the woman who had crippled the power of the Tribe and who had lived for two thousand years. By now, the vampire race should rule the Earth!

It wouldn't be Vivian. No, Vivian would be dead.

Savannah. Oh, how he wanted it to end in Savannah, bringing the story full circle where it should have ended eight months ago. He formulated and dismissed one plan after another. His Tribe had done well, imprisoning over a hundred young, unaffiliated vampires in Michael's hometown. She was bound to try to save them as well. It was unwise, though, to meet her there. The younger vampires, already braced for death, might rally to her aid to stop him from killing her. He likely couldn't stand a chance against such numbers. He'd have to choose another location once she'd made her play to save the young crowd.

Damn. So close! To know where she's going to be, and not to kill her! The pain of waiting was almost as powerful as foreplay. He simultaneously reveled and hated it.

They would come to save Doyle as well, no doubt. Perhaps it'd be wise to track the turncoat once he'd turned him loose and add him to a stockpile of imprisoned friends of hers. It'd been getting frustratingly challenging to follow the brat psychically. It was only a matter of days before Doyle realized his grip on the Maleficence was slipping. If he lost Doyle, it might be helpful to uncover where he'd been last.

"Doyle!"

"Yessir?" Doyle descended the staircase; the very sound rankled Charles' nerves. Did the boy never lift his feet?

"I'm hungry. First, we eat, and then you assume your new duties. Understand?"

The whites of Doyle's eyes appeared red, and the dread in his soul teased the Maleficence within Charles like an aphrodisiac. The boy would soon have a hand in the death of his friends, and he knew it.

Charles smiled.

Chapter Twenty-seven

"Her hands are turning purple," Perry noted, affecting the tone of an indifferent sod merely making an observation. His expression stayed placid as David turned from examining Angelo's knotwork to face him. Twenty years of hiding his moods had made Perry an expert at deception. That, and an ability to block David from reading his mind, had kept him alive for years.

David glowered, then glanced at Sana's hands, bound at the wrists with a pair of her pantyhose to the pipes that stretched between her bathroom floor and her sink. Angelo paused at his work, waiting to see what David decided.

"Loosen them," David said. "Not too much—don't do a bodge job. But don't cut off her circulation." He squatted to Sana's side and caressed the edge of her jaw, brushing aside hair stuck by wet tears to her face. "We don't want her getting away. She's more valuable than we thought."

Perry made a face, puffing out his cheeks before releasing the air in an exaggerated sigh. He wondered if his attempt at bravado worked against David as often as he hoped. Perry was used to wondering about a lot of things.

Like when it came time to bleed the girl. Every time it happened— her hunger, her need for sex, violence, and blood—David made sure he and his mates were there to quench it. More often than not, it was Perry he sent in to do the job. Why? Did David hope Perry might become as corrupted as he and Angelo by performing the act? Or—and this was what Perry feared most—was David afraid that she might turn after all this time and kill whomever she was drinking?

He cocked his head slightly as Angelo finished tying up their strange captive—the only victim who refused to transform, who seemed incapable of dying or going crazy, no matter what they did.

Her dark hair spilled across her face, gossamer strands like the finest silk. Her nutmeg skin was so unlike Perry's, dark and exotic. He'd always thought that her beauty was matchless, both physical and mental. It was why, when the time came for David to choose which one of them sated Sana, he never argued. He knew he'd be less beastly than the others.

Not that he hadn't taken her other times. *Don't pretend otherwise, Perry—you did the same as the other blokes.*

But he had to. It was that or death. He refused to give David a reason to kill him. Disgust at his behavior once again churned in his stomach like acid. He swallowed hard, almost choking on the block in his throat.

He should've chosen death. Only... if he had, he'd never be around to defend her. He'd suspected that a moment was coming—one where he'd play a critical role in her life.

He didn't yet know how important his role in her life might become. He had a suspicion this new red-haired friend of theirs was going to change things. He was mates with Charles Dunning, he'd met Jude Shepherd, and now...

"Perrywinkle?"

Perry looked up. He hadn't realized he'd been staring at Sana until David broke his concentration.

"Yeah, Dave?"

David's expression showed his humor at Perry's fascination. "No having at her whilst we're away, now," he said. "No fair not sharing."

Perry's stomach rolled again at the thought of forcing Sana to have sex. He'd never do that. When they did... what they did... it was her who was the aggressor, her bloodlust driving her into an alternate state.

"Wouldn't dream of it," Perry replied, forcing his voice into chipper tones. "Clear off then, you bums."

David smirked at Perry's cheekiness. "Alright then? You've got her until we get back?"

Perry nodded, his face carefully solemn. "I got it, Dave. I won't untie her, and I'll give her enough food to get her by. If she's got to pee, well, that's why she's in the bog to start with."

"You've got your phone?"

Perry lifted his cell phone from his pocket and jiggled it back and forth. "And it's on. The charger is in the bedroom. Dave, I'm set. Shove off."

David's grin showed his satisfaction with Perry's reply. "Alright.

We're off."

"Cheers, then."

As the crew turned, Eoghan gave Perry one last enduring stare. Perry refused to swallow the lump of fear in his throat until the newest vampire in their group turned to join David and Angelo.

Bloody hell. If I didn't know better, I'd think he realized what I was thinking!

David turned to Eoghan and gave the man a look he'd rarely given the others—one that bordered on respect. "So, how do we find Dunning?"

Eoghan didn't look at David, but his tone bothered Perry. It was as if he had no fear, no excitement. Deader than the undead had any right to be, like stone. All he said was, "He's closer than you think," but the words chilled Perry.

How much time do I have? Perry wondered.

Paradise was every bit as breathtaking as the greatest minds of humankind had ever imagined. Untouched by human landscaping, it sprawled with natural hills, cascading waterfalls, and lush, wind-stirred plains, and clouds topped blue and purple mountains in the distance. A curious mix of fauna grazed throughout the space. Maysun watched in awe as a black-and-white dog of indeterminate breed nipped playfully at a lion's heels, unafraid of reprisal. A peacock strutted at the edge of a creek next to a fox. A bongo pranced on the opposite bank. As she watched, a crocodile rose from the water and stretched out on the grass to sun itself, oblivious to the prey within its grasp.

The air carried a blend of Maysun's favorite scents—eucalyptus, ocean spray, and lavender. Each breath filled her with light. Her body sharpened with awareness, her spirit felt washed clean. With every inhale, she became purer. Lighter. More alive.

Near a moss-draped wall stood a man at an easel, painting the living panorama. His hair was white, his face gently lined with age. A brilliant blue bird perched beside him on an antique brass stand, its violet eyes reflecting an uncanny intelligence.

The white-haired man noted her presence, smiled and nodded, and then added another swipe of color to his work. The easel's back faced Maysun, and she wondered what style of artwork the universal creator found most interesting or challenging. Or, rather, one of the creators. She looked around, but the white-haired man was alone.

She approached God with caution, wondering why, to her, God appeared male.

She stood in silence as God continued his work. After a minute, he seemed content and stopped. In his hand, a fruit materialized, which he handed to the bird.

"Thank you for your patience, my Malham friend," he said.

To her surprise, the bird spoke. "Always a pleasure to watch you work."

God turned his attention to Maysun. "Not what you expected, is it?" he asked, indicating their surroundings with a wave. Maysun shook her head. God smiled, looked around, and the fauna vanished. Had it existed, or was the picture before her a heavenly hologram?

"I move the island around every so often," God continued. "Throws people off. It's interesting how humankind interprets what they don't understand. There are those who call this spot the Devil's Triangle. How's that for irony?" Maysun, unsure how to respond, remained mute, and God cocked his head in her direction. "Now, what do you wish to speak with me about?"

"Sir, it's my daughter. I don't know where she is—" The words tumbled out of her mouth like an opened floodgate.

God lifted a palm in her direction, and Maysun stopped. "That doesn't excuse your misuse of the knowledge between life and death to come here," God said calmly. "You should have prayed. That's what humans do, and you are a human now. I would hear you."

"That's like having a one-way phone call!" Maysun cried. "I know you hear me, but I can't listen to you! I need to locate my daughter. How can you expect me to find her without my power?

"You can't. Not as a human."

"But I'm here now. Talking to you. Can't you *do* something?" She shook her head at her verbal fumble. "That's stupid. Of course you can. *Will* you?"

"Maysun, that is not my way. You understand that better than anyone."

"Will you stop being so enigmatic for a second? I'm not a careless human throwing away her future over a single unrequited love. I spent over *fifteen hundred years* of my life in service to Earth and the balance of its forces. I devoted my *life* to it. You know as well as I do that humankind would not recognize the blessings given to them without Balance. Some would never pray at all with no need for Your help. Now I'm human, and I've come to you the only way I was sure would…. I'm begging for your help. Please, God. Help me find my daughter."

God's placid face might have angered her, but his eyes revealed a love she'd never known. A pure, unfathomable love that never died and never would.

"I'm sorry," she murmured, her eyes cast down to the impossibly green grass at her feet. "I took advantage of my knowledge to come to You personally. But—"

He tsked a few times and waved his hand. "You're here now. And yes, your daughter, Sana, is in trouble. Charles will soon discover who she is—or, rather, who her mother was. He'll want to find her. I suppose she needs a friend right now. Who better than her mother?"

A combination of dread and relief flooded Maysun, and her shoulders drooped. *Charles is going to find out that Sana is my daughter?* "Thank you."

God held up his hand once more, and Maysun stopped speaking.

"But you, of all people, recognize—no divine gift is ever free. This one must be paid for. It is the law of the universe. Sana holds a decisive role in the earth's balance, as you often suspected she might. Until you came to me, I intended to let her turn to the Maleficence. If she doesn't, to keep the globe in balance, I have to allow a measure of darkness to enter the world—dark by nature, if not in the heart. A body that wrestles with darkness at the core. This darkness would fall on you.

"Your role wouldn't have to be a sinful one—I can't decide the fate of your soul while you walk on Earth. Only you can do that."

"Anything," Maysun breathed. "Please let me keep my daughter away from Charles."

God's lips met in a firm line. His eyes, wise and caring, studied her, judging her conviction. Maysun's breath stopped as she waited for his verdict.

"Very well," he said. He held out his brush. Maysun stared at it blankly for a moment before extending her hand to accept it. As her hand brushed his, her body shot away from paradise, flying as if riding a lightning bolt.

In an instant, she slammed into existence—sprawled on tile, breath gone, mind reeling. The paintbrush still in her hand. The room was white: walls, ceilings, counters. Too clean. Too still. And at its heart, a canvas of three seductive men stared at her—eyes unfinished, but already unsettling.

With God's paintbrush still in her hand, she stumbled to her feet.

"Where am I?" she whispered. As her mouth formed the words, her lips brushed long canines protruding from her gums.

I'm a vampire! Oh, God, what have you done?

Chapter Twenty-eight

David and Angelo stood ready to take flight, but Eoghan held them back. A sudden, desperate need to separate from them slammed into him, his heart hammering like a panic attack was imminent.

Is this what emotion feels like, being the Balance? Urgency? That bone-deep pull, like my life depends on being somewhere—right now? It was possible. His life depended on the two vampires nearby never learning the truth about who he really was. He closed his eyes and let instinct take over, the Balance rushing through him.

Away. A phone. A conversation.

He became a marionette—strings tugged by an inside force.

"'Scuse me, lads," Eoghan said, already stepping away. "Need to make a quick call first."

David gave a curt nod. Angelo, as usual, brooded in stony silence. Eoghan stepped off the sidewalk a few paces and dug a phone from his rear pocket.

His carrier was European, but that was easy enough to fix. It wasn't his phone he needed, anyway. He held the phone flat in his palm and willed the Balance into its circuitry, weaving energy until it mimicked a similar device lost under a sofa in D.C. Soon, the icon showing the signal strength displayed all four bars.

If David believed his pre-call ritual was unusual, it didn't show. Eoghan didn't bother to acknowledge his peculiarity, but took several long steps away as he pretended to dial his phone. Meanwhile, the hand palming the phone was situated so his thumb adjusted the ringer from audible to silent, then to vibrate. The incoming call made his phone buzz within a heartbeat of silencing the phone, and he answered it.

"Hello?"

The voice was female and beautiful, and Eoghan took the call, careful to speak in tones imperceptible to vampire ears.

They lingered in the food court longer than anyone had patience for. After several minutes, Michael got the chirp on his phone giving them the word that it was time to meet with Vivian. She'd been hiding in a mall corridor as she contacted the Source.

"Any luck?" Crystal asked.

Vivian dropped her hands to her sides and shifted her weight on the bag. Michael fought the urge to pull her into his arms. The struggles they faced were wearing on her, and it'd hardly started. He didn't move, though. Her family stood in a semi-circle around her, waiting for an answer that he, too, was eager to hear.

Vivian waited to speak. The dreamy, yet resolute, expression reminded him of the last time she'd looked like this—right before the last war.

"No," Michael said. "I've already told you. You're not going alone." The words sounded more like a plea than an order.

"I'm not," she replied, her voice assuring him she meant it. "But we need to meet with Blu, reach out to Doyle, and try to save our friends— basically all at once. And we need to do it now."

"The ones in Savannah are OK?" Crystal breathed out, eyes welling with relieved tears. Harmony set a hand on her sister's arm. DB put an arm across each of their shoulders, and Crystal hugged them both.

Vivian rubbed her eyes as if waking up. "They're holed up in a warehouse and being tortured with sunlight. I guess Charles didn't give the order to kill them yet, so the Tribe is having fun with them while they wait."

No one spoke for a moment. Then Lukas said, "Damn."

Megan's hand met with Lukas', and their fingers twined.

Lukas opened the closet where their luggage was stored. He nudged a suitcase with the toe of his running shoe, absently spinning one of the wheels. "Shouldn't be hard to get to Blu. I was just telling Dad about a guy he's been shacking up with in DC. Why? What's up with Blu?"

"He's in the same trouble as our friends in Savannah. The Blood Tribe is on a witch-hunt, with the unaffiliated vampires as their goal. Blu—he's out there, but he's scared, paranoid. I reached him on his cell, and he wants us to meet him in DC at a pub called Brickskeller. He's on his way there now."

"I've heard of it," Michael said.

"You've heard of everything," Megan joked.

"But he's OK?" Michael asked.

"I think so," Vivian said. "We should go find out. He sounded weird. Maybe that's why I couldn't reach him telepathically. He's been injured."

"How?" Michael asked.

"The Tribe found his family," she said with a wince. "They shredded his wing pretty badly. He was lucky—Blu's the only one who made it out alive. He can't fly, and he said with his wing retracted, he's still got a hell of a backache. He's limited to vehicle travel for the next few hours."

"Or cleaving," Crystal said. "Which isn't a problem."

"Those hands are burned," DB murmured, gently turning her palms in his. "Lay off using them for a bit. Let us handle it. Please." Crystal nodded.

Michael asked, "It makes the most sense to head to Savannah first, yes?"

Harmony frowned. "What about the Dark I felt coming?"

Vivian let out a mirthless laugh. "He's there. Charles is there. But the Source is still pulling me back there."

"We could be headed to our deaths. We don't know what Charles has planned for us."

"It's possible," Vivian conceded.

"Tell me where we're going," Crystal offered, extending a finger in preparation.

"Next time," Vivian said, undistracted from her objective. "Right now, DB needs to head back to Savannah on a separate mission. We'll take him there, but then he's going to have to stay with—"

DB shook his head, clutched Crystal's hand, cautious of her burns, and winced in apology. "Leave y'all? But—"

"No," Vivian said, "No argument. Michael, give him Bully's business card."

"Bully?" Michael asked, confused.

"He's a genuine magician," Vivian said, "not a party performer. DB, you and he need to meet, to join forces." She shook her head as if shaking her thoughts together. "Along with any vampires that have escaped, and the others, the unusual ones."

"You mean freaks," Crystal said with a smile. "Like us."

"Superpowered ones like you, yes."

"Why?" DB asked. "I mean, I don't mean to question the Divine, but I'd like to know."

"We're about to be at war," Vivian said, "and Charles is doing his best to erase our army."

"Do you plan to recruit whoever you can? What if they're not undead?" Crystal said. "I mean, Charles isn't the nicest guy in the world, but that doesn't seem fair to the rest of us. Harmony, DB, and I volunteered, but why bring those who aren't involved into your battle? We're a lot more likely to die."

Vivian turned to Crystal, her face somber, more disturbing than Michael had ever seen. "Your blood's as tempting as anyone else's," Vivian said, her voice like steel. "Possibly more—because you've got superhuman talents. Don't for one second think you're not in as much danger as we are. After he wipes the earth clean of any vampire not willing to join the *Shévet ha Dam*, he'll come after you and your sister. Anyone with power he can use to his benefit. And like us, he'll give you a choice; use it for the Blood Tribe, or die."

Chapter Twenty-nine

After dispatching Doyle, Charles passed the time pacing outside St. John's Cathedral, waiting for his limo. A strange pickup location, but it was the first landmark that came to mind when he called for service. He'd need a method of transporting Michael's children once Krieg returned from his mission.

Something like Vivian's new way to travel would've been ideal—if anyone knew how the hell it worked. Charles grunted and kicked the nearest step. He hated himself for sulking like a child, but thinking about Vivian and her new ability made his blood boil.

He'd sent Doyle and four of the more loyal Tribe members to handle the detainees. With any luck, Doyle would find out where Vivian headed next, and report to him—and if he didn't say, Charles had the advantage of being able to pick Doyle's brain.

So far, luck was on his side; the Tribe was on track to corral wayward vampires. He'd learned about Vivian's new mode of travel (though not how it was accomplished), and Lukas was his unknowing tracking beacon. He was willing to risk that Doyle would refrain from turning to the Source before the day was out.

His strides slowed as his thoughts gained momentum. It was about time luck turned his way. Jude dead. Maysun was unaccounted for, likely dead as well. Half of the old Table was killed, replaced by new, untested members, and half of what remained of the Blood Tribe was uncertain who was in charge.

Vivian, you're a hell of a lot more trouble alive than you were half dead.

A gleaming white Lincoln limousine cruised into view, the late afternoon sun bright on its extended cab, as his cell phone jangled in his pocket. Charles lifted his hand to ensure the driver saw him and flipped his phone open as the car crept to a halt at the bottom of the steps.

The chauffeur rolled down his tinted window. His white suit matched the car—but not his ruddy complexion or dark mop of hair.

"Mr. Dunning?"

Charles nodded and motioned with an extended finger for him to wait. "Hello?"

"Mr. Dunning? It's Doyle."

As if his pleading voice wasn't enough of an introduction. "Doyle, why are you calling me? Wouldn't telepathy be easier?"

"With all due respect, Mr. Dunning, you know as well as I do that I don't do telepathy well."

Knowing how silence worried Doyle, Charles didn't respond.

Stuttering, Doyle continued. "Uh, Dominick, Brantley, and Bellina are here with me. Bellina said she's the head of the Southeastern region? We've gathered probably fifty or so in an abandoned place on Brough-ton Street. The other southeastern Tribe members have moved on and are corralling the ones they found toward Atlanta. We've got the local individuals rounded up. What do you want us to do with them?"

"What do you think? Do what I told you to do less than a damned hour ago. Kill them," Charles snapped. *As soon as they start dying, Vivian will show, and the sooner I get a lead on her.* This time, it was Doyle who reacted with silence. In his mind, he saw Doyle's mouth flapping. Why was he hesitating?

"But Mr. Dunning—Jerusha—"

"Is north of here. Trust me, if she or that stepson of hers was in your little group of prisoners, you and everyone who gathered that bunch wouldn't be alive to tell me."

Did Doyle suspect Charles believed Vivian would swoop in to their rescue? Doyle seemed to have trouble finding words, his unease about killing the younger vampires coming through the phone in waves. Charles reveled knowing that at least one of Doyle's friends was bound to be in the bunch. Probably several. He'd had connections in Savannah that had helped him more than once.

When Doyle finally spoke, his voice was tremulous. "Kill them *all*?"

"Are they willing to become part of the *Shévet ha Dam*?"

"A lot of 'em, sure. At least, that's what they said when Bellina and Brantley were at their necks. As far as the others—"

"The others can die."

A sniff came through the line. Was he trying not to cry? "Yes, sir," Doyle murmured.

"And then move west with the others. Don't waste my time with these petty calls until you've cleared out another city. Get with Batista, see what intelligence she's gathered, and move. I expect to have this country cleared of renegades within a week."

"Yessir."

"And Doyle?"

"Yes?"

"Stop feeling guilty about this." Charles snapped his phone shut.

The limousine driver stared through his windshield, pretending not to listen. Although Charles had used a company with connections to the *Shévet ha Dam*, he supposed it was rare that their human employees were privy to this sort of conversation.

Charles flashed the driver a smile that didn't reach his eyes. "You heard nothing," he said. The driver blinked as if dislodging an eyelash, then tilted his head.

"I'm sorry, sir," he said. "I drifted off, there. Are you Mr. Dunning?"

"I am," Charles said. The driver got out and opened the back door, allowing Charles to slide into the backseat and stretch out his legs. Charles allowed himself a relaxed breath and focused on releasing the tension from his shoulders. Once he had Lukas and Megan, Jerusha was only the fall of a domino away.

"Airport, please," he said.

Resentment coiled in his chest as the scenery crawled past the tinted glass. If he had the power that Vivian had, he'd use Lukas and be at her throat in an instant. Why hadn't the Maleficence allowed him the ability to travel the way Vivian had? Wasn't he the favored child, like Vivian was to the Source?

Charles checked his watch. His only comfort was that Krieg would arrive in Virginia at any moment.

Maysun scrambled to her feet and darted to a mirror above a narrow sink along the far wall. Gathering her courage, she pulled her lips back from her teeth and stared in disbelief. Staring back at her was the same image she'd grown used to during her darkest days with the *Shévet ha Dam*. Maysun Khatri—vampire.

God's words from the garden of Paradise echoed back: *I have to allow a measure of darkness to enter the world—dark by nature, if not in the heart.*

She wasn't playing the part of a vampire as the Balance anymore. She was a true descendant of Cartaphilus now, her blood the same as the man cursed by Christ.

Goddamn it.

She snorted at the accidental pun and stifled the urge to scream. Yes, she'd have to subsist on blood, but God had their reason. If it meant being a bloodsucker to find her daughter in order to shelter her from the Blood Tribe, she'd do it. At least God hadn't stuck her in a dying body again. It seemed she'd be forever in her mid-thirties. Or until she died for good.

She looked around the pristine studio. Was this Sana's? The white walls, the high ceilings—was she inside her daughter's home? For all she knew, Sana was in the next room. Her fingernails, longer now than she remembered, pushed forcefully against her palm.

Am I the same vampire I was before? Or did He make me a newborn all over again? Am I powerless, or am I as strong as the vampire I once was?

She eyed the sunlight streaming in through the window, noted how it hit her skin without incident. A small smile made its way to her lips.

Not a newborn, then.

She focused on the fountain of power that had imbued her with strength in her past and found that it repulsed her. An acid tang hit her tongue as her stomach clenched and her face twisted with disgust. The idea of tapping into that for strength—

No. Of course not. That's the Maleficence. The old Maysun used the Maleficence to fool Jude when she was a vampire. You're not that creature anymore. You don't have to pull from the same source now that Jude isn't watching.

She might be a dark creature who needed blood to survive, but at least God hadn't tethered her to the Maleficence. She was grateful, and she eased her shoulders and clenched jaw.

The Source was hers now, and it stirred emotions she hadn't experienced in ages, not since being locked in the emotionless grip of the Balance. Relief. Gratefulness. Excitement for life that she hadn't known was missing.

She closed her eyes and fell into the Source like it was a trusted companion, like she *was* every good thing in the universe—light, music, bliss. She had found her magnificent, joyous place in the Source.

A scuffing sound from behind her announced someone arriving to the room. If her senses were still human, she'd have missed the soft scrape of leather on tile. Instead, the sound set her nerves on edge. The hair on her neck bristled as her body braced for confrontation.

What's that?

Maysun reached into the Source of knowledge and confirmed what she had suspected—a vampire was in the house. The energy was black, but its intentions weren't clear—she received a notion of frantic, confused energy. A vampire she could probably handle, but there was something else.

What. In the hell. Is that?

Chapter Thirty

Crystal caught her breath as she crawled through the tear in space, joining the others on the other side. Her head spun, and she shook it to scatter the stars clouding her vision.

Crouching, she put her hands over her knees and took a few deep, shuddering breaths as she rose. She'd never used her power so frequently in such a short span. The strain was catching up to her. This last fissure had only reached scarcely over two feet tall, and the walls wavered, dangerously ready to collapse. Vivian, Michael, DB, and Harmony had been elected to hustle through—and her, of course, so the others had a way back to the mall, where Lukas and Megan waited. Lukas was too big to fit through the narrow opening, and Megan had chosen to stay with him until they returned.

Her sister laid a hand on her arm. "Are you alright?" she asked.

Crystal forced a smile and hoped it didn't look too fake. "I'll make it," she said.

She pushed off her knees and stood, taking in their surroundings. A small room, dark, cluttered, with a thin layer of dust. Velvet art on the wall, psychedelic shapes that made her unsteady eyes water—or maybe it was the thick aroma of incense. What was that fragrance? Patchouli? Sandalwood? She took a deep breath and let it out. Whatever it was, the odor was overwhelming. Nice, but overwhelming. Colorful blankets covered cushy seats. A bushy yellow plant stood in the corner, creating a massive bouffant atop a head carved into the stone vase. If she had to name the aesthetic, *African beatnik* seemed about right.

"Where are we?" DB asked, taking a cautious step forward. He stared at a golden clock under a jar that stood like a skyscraper among perhaps twenty small, hand-carved figures atop a chest of drawers. The clock gears spun in a hypnotic, liquid movement. He pointed at the glass, then quickly drew back, like touching it might set off the little army of wooden figurines.

"Right back where we started," Harmony said with a shudder, probably remembering the dark force that had driven them away only a couple of hours before.

Vivian nodded. "We can't stay long. Only long enough to find Bully and get him caught up—"

"Caught up on what, now?" a deep voice rumbled. "Or oughta I say *in* what?"

The sound of clattering beads drew Crystal's gaze to her left, where a massive dark-skinned man emerged as if through one of her holes in space. A colorful beaded curtain parted in his midst, and he strode to the chest of drawers before DB, checking to see if the contents had been disturbed. DB's eyes swelled at Bully's size, but Bully flashed the younger man a sly grin, and DB returned it.

"Now that was one hell of an entrance," Bully said, nodding at Crystal. "You got some serious talent."

"Bully, these are our friends Crystal and DB," Vivian said. "You've seen what she can do. He's—"

Bully lifted a hand, palm extended, toward Vivian. "Shh, hold on. Hold up. Lemme throw up a little extra protection before we get to talking." He withdrew a tall, black, tapered candle from the top drawer, rubbed it with an amber-colored oil, and set it inside a brass candleholder. Lifting a pack of matches from the dresser top, he discovered it empty and made a noise of frustration. Patting his pockets, he mumbled to himself.

Crystal watched, amused, as DB sent a pencil-thin flame from his lips to the wick, lighting it without melting more than a drop of wax. This time, it was Bully's eyes that grew.

"Bully," Vivian said again, "this is our friend Dorian Bradley. DB. He's—"

"A torch-tongue," Bully breathed, eyes wide. "You control the fire spirit. I heard stories about folks like you—but I never met one." His face lit up, his broad, straight smile impossibly large.

"He needs to stay with you for a while," Vivian said. "I don't have long to explain."

"Dark forces at work," Bully said with a solemn nod. "This whole town's crackling. I ain't slept right in days."

"I need to ask you a favor," Vivian said. "Can you do a spell that would help you find other unusual people? Others like DB and you and

Crystal? And can you try to gather as many as possible together?"

Bully grinned. "No problem. Yeah, I got something for that. Got a compass spell I trust. It'll do the trick."

Vivian gave a curt nod. "DB, can you inform Bully of our plans? I hate to drop that responsibility on you so fast, but we've got to go. There are vampires who need our help."

"Go on, now," Bully said, waving her off with hands the size of cast-iron skillets. "Go save the damn world. That's what y'all do."

"We should call them," Lukas said, pivoting on his heel for what had to be the thirtieth time in the last three minutes.

"Give them a minute, will you?" Megan said. "They should be back any second."

She was right. A drop-off was never as cut-and-dry as the expression sounded. There were curt explanations to add, hasty goodbyes to be said, and Lord knew what else. Lukas frowned.

Since Crystal had dropped the bomb about the vampires corralled back home, he'd longed to help his friends. Every passing minute felt like an invitation to their death. The Tribe members had their orders; surely, the vampires in Savannah hadn't long to live.

He wanted nothing more than to collapse into Megan's arms and perch on the luggage with her. They'd lay in their understanding silence, and she'd run her hands through his hair and stroke out the worries with that soothing way she had. Maybe he'd surprise her with a deep kiss, the kind she loved and responded to so well, and she'd wrap her legs around him, draw him close…

But as the mental movie played out, stirring him, he knew the timing was wrong. The tension of the day still clung to them, snuffing out their usual spark.

Why had the Source gotten so damn vague lately? It was fraying his last nerve. Their friends back home were being tortured, and he and Megan waited here. He was a direct descendant of Cartaphilus—his power should *mean* something. He wanted to act, move, and fight. Instead, he paced. Helpless. He hated having his future hinging on the whim of this force which, up to this point, hadn't done much but hand them vague clues and semi-coherent directions.

Megan reached for him and then dropped her hand, giving him a look that was an irritating combination of understanding and commiseration. He stifled the irritation; none of this was her fault. She was his strength, the only thing keeping him from ricocheting off the walls in frustration.

He glanced at the broad watch encircling his wrist and adjusted his butt on the tallest suitcase. His father, Vivian, and their new friends and only been gone for four minutes, but it seemed longer. How long until the sun reached the pinnacle?

A yawn reached his lips, and he gave in, stretching, a bear rising from hibernation. As he lengthened, Megan's blue-gold eyes shot a lusty look at his exposed abdomen. He grinned, unable to disguise his pleasure at her admiration.

"There's a vending machine around the corner," he said. "I could use a drink. Want one?"

Megan stood. "I'll come too." Not wanting to be apart. Understandable, given the situation. Truthfully, he was grateful for her company, even if the trip was only a few yards.

They crossed the corridor and turned right at the corner, passing an office with a glass door (Donald Strybecki, Mall Manager) and another unmarked room. The floors reeked of pine cleaner.

Lukas trailed Megan by about two steps as she sauntered to the machines at the end of the hall, gracing the beige cinderblock walls with an occasional tap.

"Stop that," she said.

"Stop what?"

"Starin' at my ass."

Lukas chuckled as she shoved open the door to the room that housed the vending machines and momentarily disappeared from view. "What are you, psychic? Or just vain?"

A muffled scream cut any further rejoinder. Lukas barely had time for the hairs on the back of his neck to stand up before he rushed into the room. A hulking mass of leather-clad vampire loomed, his head brushing the low ceiling. Under one arm, Megan wriggled like a cat on methamphetamines.

At six-foot-eleven, Lukas wasn't used to looking anyone in the eye— much less looking *up*. This man was the first to have that dubious privilege. A black handkerchief with skulls and crossbones covered most of his hair. The dun-colored sideburns that poked out from underneath reached the edge of his flushed jowls. Two narrow slits couldn't hide the brilliant green eyes within them. Despite their comparable height, the vampire who held Megan in his clutches had at least eighty pounds on Lukas, mostly muscle.

Lukas' experience in self-defense was limited to a single fight against Jude—a one-sided exercise in panic that would have failed, had not a miracle intervened, disabling his opponent. Now he froze, doubt and surprise rendering him immobile. Try as he might to think of a way to attack the man who'd seized his lover, his mind refused to cooperate.

The immense creature snatched Lukas up with ease with his free, baseball-mitt-sized hand.

Oh, God, I will die if anything happens to her! Lukas swung his hands and struck, but the unyielding monster holding him didn't flinch or blink. Lukas squirmed and fought, but the giant's grip only tightened, crushing Lukas to his side like a vise. His lungs, crushed and shallow, gulped at the air to no effect.

We're descended from Jude Shepherd, Lukas thought. *He shouldn't be a match for us. How can he do this?*

"Stop your bullshit, or I flatten the redhead like roadkill," the beast growled. Lukas went stiff as a mannequin, his eyes slitted with anger and his jaw clenched.

With one broad step, their captor cleared the distance to the door. He kicked the glass out rather than open it, balancing his hostages easily in a fierce hold as he removed a few tinkling pieces of glass with his boot. In two more steps, he cleared the threshold and dragged them down the hall, then turned the corner to the double doors at the end.

He kicked the door open, effectively disintegrating the deadbolt and bending the metal center beam. Then, pulling Lukas and Megan like large dolls, they were in the light.

Massive leathery, black wings unfurled from holes in a black vest designed to ease metamorphosis. Lukas tried to feign a startled jerk from the creature's grip, but it was as if iron bands encircled his arms and torso.

"I've been working out," his deep voice said. Lukas suspected he was telling the truth.

The enormous vampire made no running start, but lurched into the sky like a live bottle rocket.

Leather vest. Engineer boots. Massive vamp who carried those he kidnaps like carry-on luggage.

"Krieg," Lukas murmured. Lukas croaked, the name tangled in spit he couldn't swallow.

Krieg smiled, exposing his bright, white, elongated eyeteeth.
"Ah, you've heard of me."
Megan cut her struggle short once they'd taken flight,
"There's no such thing as giants," Megan said. "What *are* you?
Krieg smirked. "Don't be too sure, little one," he said. "You're about to learn there's more to this world than you dreamed. Of course, I don't suspect you'll live long enough to tell anyone."

Chapter Thirty-one

Doyle's phone hung limp at his side, Charles's voice gone, but the words still echoing in his skull.

The others can die.

Dominick, Brantley, and Bellina circled the edges of the young vampires like vultures. Every so often, Luzon—still marked with shiny pink burns—dragged one of the younglings into a narrow shaft of sunlight leaking through a crack in the boarded-up window. There, she forced their face or arm into the light, smothering screams with one thick hand. The others, paralyzed with fear, could only watch as the stench of searing flesh filled the room. The others, too frightened to move, watched in terror as the stench of cooking flesh permeated the room. Brantley laughed every time, the tight skin of his gaunt face making him look like a leathery mummy. The sight made Doyle as sick as the smell.

It would be nightfall soon. If he pretended he hadn't heard from Charles, he might buy the young ones a few more hours. But then what?

Kill the vampires. For what? Refusing to be like Charles? Like Bellina? For not butchering humans? The logic seemed twisted; join the *Shévet ha Dam* and kill, or die. But he had to admit, these younger vampires were brave. These young, untested ones were doing what he'd never had the guts to do—standing up for what they believed in. Most had chosen death over life in the *Shévet ha Dam*.

These vampires, most of whom had only heard of Vivian and Jude as folklore, who'd never known the joy of the Source or stood in the presence of one who had, still had more spine than he did. What was wrong with him? Had he become that detached? Or was he so scared of dying that he'd forgotten what it meant to be human?

Faced with their bravery, the standards he'd held sacred for decades shattered—and with them, his respect for Charles. Why was Charles killing these minor threats? Doyle's high opinion of himself—his belief in his cleverness, his ability to ride the fence between right and convenient—now struck him hollow and unearned. He'd lost his devotion to the Tribe in the fear reflected back at him from their innocent eyes.

He didn't want to kill them. He wanted to help them escape.

Doyle remembered the story of a strange spell Vivian once carried in a velvet bag. The spell released the Source in such quantities that it snuffed the life of anyone connected to the Maleficence within a hundred yards. Watching the three vampires circling… what was a group of vampires called? The only word that came to mind was clutch. *A clutch of vampires? What are we, chickens?* Didn't matter. No magic velvet bag, no Source. Just him and a bunch of renegades on their own.

How was he supposed to kill four vampires stronger than himself in a couple of seconds? He'd never killed anything that didn't pump warm blood through its veins, much less outlived him. Where did he begin?

Guard your thoughts, dummy. One of them might be telepathic.

He reduced his thoughts, as much as he could, into images. Ideas of death weren't new to vampires; blood and murder would be normal to this brood.

Doyle's bane was his bizarre weakness for his age. Did he even have years on them? Dominick—sure. Despite his youth, he was as strong as Doyle, possibly stronger, thanks to that pure-blood lineage. Dominick had the best. Dominick had maybe fifty undead years, tops, but the younger vampire still outclassed Doyle. Bellina? Probably five centuries older than both of them. Brantley was harder to peg. He might be ancient. He carried himself like an elder, but had the smug swagger of a newbie.

Well, then what? He wasn't that guy from Braveheart. Stirring the troops for battle in the face of death with a speech wasn't an option. He'd be dead before he managed a second sentence.

A trick? A trap? No. His telepathy sucked. Theirs was probably didn't. They'd be on to him in no time.

Now what?

He longed for Vivian's connection to the Source—something they couldn't…

…touch.

What was that?

But as soon as he wondered, he knew. The brown-haired girl in the peasant blouse, standing near the circle's edge, looked straight at him.

Her voice was weak, pleading, and pitiful, but it was there in his mind.

Help us.

Impossible. Nevertheless, he tried to send a thought back.

You're not Shévet ha Dam!

Neither are you. Her deep brown eyes met his across the room. Doyle's heart went strange and soft, a knot rising where his Adam's apple should be. Gooseflesh rose on his arms. He stretched out his hands, half expecting to find webbing—like this awakening had made him something new. No webbing joined his fingers, and no amount of breath made the strange pain in his chest subside.

Him? Not in the Blood Tribe?

Impulsively, he picked a member of the group—a short-haired young man still clad in the apron he must have worn to work—and used that part of his mind that always seemed a tad short-circuited. He imagined his brain as a shortwave radio, tuned to one specific frequency: scared, young vampires.

Can you hear me?

The young vampire met Doyle's eyes and nodded so slowly Doyle almost grew impatient and missed it.

They can hear me. They can—

His excitement faded. No Blood Tribe? No more Death Rush or sitting at Dunning's right hand. No more favors. No photoprotection. Life outside the Tribe meant he'd be constantly running and turning to folks of dubious loyalty who lived as he did—as he used to—to survive.

For the first time in his life, Doyle *felt heroic*. And it was magnificent.

Doyle focused on his telepathy and tried to crank up the volume. To his surprise, the power surged easily. Brantley glanced his way, as if sensing the Source flowing through him. Doyle smothered a grin. No way Brantley knew what was happening. The Source was as foreign to him as... well, Doyle had no idea what *was* foreign to Brantley. But regardless, he couldn't sense it.

The leathery-skinned vampire turned away, and Doyle focused on the group of captives.

Can everybody hear me? I think you can. Let me tell you about my idea.

Chapter Thirty-two

The newest hole—barely wide enough for Michael and DB to squeeze through—folded shut near where they'd left the suitcases. Vivian froze, her body rigid. Her nose caught something besides the scent of scorched clothing. DB hovered behind her, unusually still. His jaw worked in silence, as if tasting the tension in the air. Vivian's eyes panned from side to side searching for an unseen threat. Through a door leading to the mall corridor, Cary Grant had discovered an eye-popping spectacle in a window seat on a television screen. The appliance store had resorted to volume rather than color to draw customers.

"What is it?" Michael asked.

"Something's wrong," she murmured, rubbing her arms to fight her rising gooseflesh. "Don't you feel it?" Her ears twitched as if she expected to pick up an answer through echolocation. Michael held still beside her, half expecting her to hear what she sought in the quiet mall.

Crystal, whose hands rested heavily on her knees, looked up. "Are you talking to me?"

"No, but we should be," her sister said. "You okay? You look ready to collapse."

Crystal waved Harmony off. "I'll be fine. Vivian—what is it?"

DB appeared at her side before she could sway. "You're not fine," he said, offering a steadying hand. Crystal accepted his help reluctantly.

Vivian pointed to the exit, indicating the crumpled push bar between the double doors. In a surge of adrenaline, she bolted toward the door, barely registering the shattered glass lining the adjacent hall.

"Luke! Megan!" she screamed.

Michael unclipped his phone and punched buttons nearly as fast as his legs traversed the tile. Harmony and Crystal veered off down the glass-peppered hall.

Vivian crossed the threshold. Three large, green dumpsters Three green dumpsters, reeking of food court refuse, lined the building's side. Parked cars dotted the lot in the distance, and a couple of mall employees had stepped out for a cigarette. They regarded her with curiosity, but said nothing.

No sign of Lukas or Megan. A faint shimmer of heat rose from DB's lips—barely more than breath, but hot enough to warp the air.

Michael ended the call and slapped it back on his clip. "Lukas!" he bellowed, cupping his hands to amplify the sound. He and Vivian fell silent, as did a nearby bird. The hush that settled, although not complete, left the atmosphere heavy, eerie, like rain patter on the roof in the wake of a tornado. All she heard was traffic racing by on the nearby road. No footsteps. No voices. Only the white hiss of tires on concrete.

Harmony and Crystal met them outside. DB arrived beside them, watching the parking lot with fire lingering at the back of his throat, ready.

"Anything?" Michael asked.

Harmony shook her head. "The room with the soda machine—the door was blown out from the inside. Glass everywhere. No signs of struggle, though—I mean, other than the glass. It could've been a couple of juvenile delinquents, but I doubt it."

Vivian spotted a folded silver telephone on the ground a few paces away. She trotted over, picked it up, and brought it back. She flipped it open and powered it on. A chirpy tune welcomed them to the wireless provider, followed by a photo of Lukas grinning from the screen.

"Megan's phone," Michael breathed, taking it from Vivian's hand like a holy relic.

Vivian flipped open her phone and checked for messages. Nothing.

"They've found us," Vivian said. "We have to go."

"But Lukas—"

"He's gone, Michael," Vivian said. "He's gone, and if we're going to find him, we have to figure out how and where."

Michael smacked his forehead. "That damn credit card. We never should've left them behind. It brought the Tribe right to us. We knew it might, but damn, that was fast. Even for them."

Crystal breathed heavily and eyed the two employees grinding out their cigarettes under their heels. She flexed her fingers, gearing up for another tear.

"Where are we going?"

Vivian opened her mouth to admit she hadn't a clue—then it hit her like a fist to the back of the skull.

"Doyle!"

Michael's brows shot up in confusion. "Doyle? What about him? You think he knows where they are?"

Vivian wanted to sob, laugh, crumple up in despair, and dance all at once. Lukas and Megan were gone, but Doyle… Doyle was theirs.

"He's defected. I can sense him now! We still have time to save the vampires in Savannah but he needs our help."

"Damn it! We just left there!" Crystal snapped. Wagging her head, she puffed out her chest and pointed with a trembling finger. "Allow me."

Vivian held her hands out and placed them on Crystal's temples.

"First… allow me."

Krieg's grip was strong and painfully secure. Megan had no fear he'd drop her—not by accident, anyway. He hadn't followed them to Virginia for pleasure, and he wasn't about to lose his precious cargo. She feared she knew where they were headed. Krieg had been Jude's henchman recently; it stood to reason he was Charles' creature now.

Too frightened to fight, too angry to talk, and too far across Krieg's chest to meet Lukas' eyes, she focused on the scenery rushing beneath them—grateful she was hard to kill. Lots of woodlands, farms, ponds, and man-made lakes. Subdivisions. She suspected Krieg soared at the proper height to avoid detection by radar or human eye, and he often changed course to avoid flying directly over towns. Anyone with a decent telescope or binoculars would be in for a shock if they focused on the blurry speck rocketing past, but that chance grew smaller as night fell.

"Ever been shot at?" she asked.

"Only once," Krieg replied. "Some podunk farmer in Alabama mistook me for a duck."

She managed a half-laugh and wished she could go back and improve the poor sap's aim.

Within minutes, Krieg's grip made her ribs ache, and her arm throbbed. The scenery became blurry and repetitive and harder to make out in the dark. Soon her sides grew blissfully numb, and she almost felt ready to doze. The air at their elevation was chilly, and although she sensed the cold, her undead body didn't seem to mind.

Megan's ears began ringing. *I'm dead. I can't get tinnitus. What—?*

Then she knew. The last time she'd experienced this, Shepherd had sent a psychic All-Points Bulletin for Vivian. Every wicked vampire across the globe received it like a burst of telepathic radio. She and Lukas weren't evil, but their bloodline was close enough they'd felt it too. Could she pick up a mental conversation between Krieg and Charles Dunning?

Krieg adjusted course and began to descend. The landscape details grew clearer the closer they drew to the earth. Now she saw spots of the ground between the trees, the smallest limbs, and what looked like a gigantic bird's nest. Below, a two-lane highway cut through the forest, then emerged before a familiar bridge spanning a wide river. Megan stared in disbelief as the city of Savannah came into view.

What in the hell are we doing back here?

Krieg coasted until he hovered near the airport, and fear clenched her body like a vise. The last time she'd been here, she and Lukas had hidden safely inside while war waged in a nearby field until Gina had summoned Lukas away. She'd nearly lost her sire that night, the man whom she'd recently met, but intuitively trusted and cared for.

The lights from the dual runways came into clear view. Soon, Krieg aimed his feet at the tarmac. A white limousine idled beside a small plane. Megan already knew who rode in the rear of that machine, and crazily, she wished the door would never open.

Krieg alighted and air whooshed into Megan's lungs as he dropped her and Lukas on the broken concrete. She landed painfully on her feet, twisted her ankle, and broke her fall with her hands. Concrete and gravel scraped her palms raw. As the smell of her blood hit her nostrils, powerful emotions stirred in her: anger, hunger, fear.

Beside her, Lukas rose slowly. He, too, seemed to suffer the effects of the trip, which made her own pain feel less important. He gripped his side with a grimace, and she wondered if Krieg had cracked his ribs trying to hold her massive boyfriend in place. How long until he healed? A day? How long until his body recovered and he was ready to escape? She wouldn't leave without him. If it meant she died, she'd die, but she would never leave Lukas alone with Charles.

She tried to stand, but her ankle screamed. It might be broken—it'd take at least a day to heal—more if she didn't feed. Depression and helplessness sank into every pore. No doubt Charles' presence had a lot to do with that.

Her eyes met Lukas'. His held the same despair, the same fragile attempt at courage. Physically, he was stronger than she; emotionally, he was the more fragile one, and she wished she had the power to whisk them away.

If I ran, where would I go? Charles can find me if he wants to. I can't fly, and if I could, he's got Krieg!

She thought about the story Lukas shared about when he and Gina had dropped in on Jude. Gina told Lukas to think about anything but the facts Jude wanted to keep him out of their heads. Turned out, Jude hadn't needed any information—he'd invited them for a bit of sport. That night, Gina had her throat torn out and became Shepherd's slave. Lukas barely got out alive.

The limousine door opened. A leg extended: polished black shoes reflecting the overhead lights, tailored gray slacks with a sharp crease. A handsome middle-aged vampire unfolded from the car. Oval face, thick, arched eyebrows, and an unworried paternal expression.

The bastard looked as calm as Hannibal Lecter.

Every impulse screamed at her to flee, but if she did, Charles would kill her. She held no more value to him than a penny.

That can't be true. If it is, why bother kidnapping us?

Charles had a plan. He needed Megan and Lukas alive long enough to get what he really wanted—

Vivian.

The Source shielded her—he couldn't track her. But with hostages, she'd come. She'd always come to save her family. As long as they were alive, Vivian would come. And once she did, she and Lukas would become bait—ripe for cutting.

Or killing.

Oh, God. Not Lukas. Please, not Lukas!

Chapter Thirty-three

The moment Perry dreaded finally arrived as night fell and the room grew dusky. Sana stirred in her slumber, murmured a few incoherent words, and opened her eyes. She pushed herself up from the cool tile. The tile had left hash mark impressions on her cheeks that she caressed with her tapered fingers.

His breath caught in his throat. Although he'd prepared a dozen different conversation openers as he watched her sleep, the sight of her panicked, deep brown eyes obliterated every line. When her eyes focused on him across the narrow bath, she scuttled as far to the wall as possible and curled into a ball.

"Who—who are you?" she asked, her voice groggy with sleep. She ran a quick hand through her hair and checked for drool. Then her face grew more frightened as her index finger jabbed in his direction. "I know you! You killed Thom!"

Perry's hands opened into a pleading gesture, and he crawled toward her on his knees. "No! That wasn't me! That was—that was Angelo. And David. I just—I was the one who turned myself in, though." He let out the rest of the air in his lungs in a gush and added, "I took the blame. I couldn't let them…."

Sana's suspicious eyes weighed his comment. The worry lines in his forehead ran so deep he became conscious of the strain they caused. He raised a hand to touch the grooves, much as Sana had touched the tile marks on her face moments ago. He considered trying to smooth them out, and then decided not to, opting instead to shove his jittery hands in his pockets.

Seeming to take him at his word, she said, "The other ones killed Thom."

"Other ones. Yeah, they're bigger than me. And stronger. Older." He realized he was eyeing her toned arm appreciatively and stopped, berating himself for his insensitivity and moving his focus to the sink. "It was Angelo and David."

Her eyes narrowed, and Perry read the horrible memories lurking behind them. "But not all of it. You were there, too."

Shame flushed his cheeks, burning his eyes with a rush of heat and unshed tears. "David made me," he whimpered. "He'd have killed me if I hadn't. I'd—I'd…"

He slumped down along the opposite wall and took a seat on the floor. He didn't have the heart to look at her, to see the hate she sent to the only one of her captors present now that she was conscious—and bound. And now she saw and remembered who they were.

Why didn't I untie her? He was still following his sire's orders—even without David looming over him.

Frustrated, Perry kicked the tile wall and shoved the heel of his hand into his forehead. "Oh, you wouldn't understand."

To his surprise, her expression softened—not much, but it gave him hope.

"Try me," she whispered.

He did. Starting with the day Jude had found him in Hyde Park, Perry shared his tale of blood and brotherhood, of a curse that bound him to David through shared paternity to the father of vampires. As darkness fell, he told her of Ralph's involvement with David's clan and reminded her of details from the day they'd sought to sire her without success. When he wrapped up, Sana's lips were pursed, her gaze intent.

"We had nothing to go on but a half-baked description—a dark-skinned girl of about fourteen with an uncanny ability to draw people to her. I guess we thought we were looking for someone more… impressive." He gave a short laugh. "What does impressive look like? We had no clue. We found you by accident. Well, Ralph did."

"Did you ever leave?"

"Weren't there nights or weeks when you were certain you would be alright? When the voices in your head had gone on holiday, and you wondered why?" When Sana nodded, Perry did as well to help her draw the proper conclusion.

"But out of all the people in the world, why did Jude want to find me, the one person you can't turn?"

Crestfallen, Perry said, "I wish I knew."

"And once you couldn't sire me, why didn't you give up? Or hand me over to Jude?"

"He didn't expect us to," Perry said. "We were meant to watch for changes in you—but nothing ever happened. Jude planned to come and take you eventually, but I guess he lost interest when you never developed the thirst the way you were supposed to."

Sana considered this. "You said the three of you lived in London, right?" Sana asked. Perry nodded. "Well, with all of those thousands—or is it millions? —of people there to pick on, eat, whatever, what's kept you in boring Piper, South Carolina?"

Perry paused. He lived in Piper because Sana lived in Piper. But that wasn't what she meant. He frowned.

"You were our project," he said. "We're to observe you, and to tell the Tribe if you developed any special abilities other than being able to resist vampirism."

"You'd think you'd have gotten bored," Sana murmured. "Asked for another assignment. How boring is it to follow one woman around like that? To watch me work, cook, watch television, paint my nails…" She shrugged, uncomprehending.

"I think," Perry said, "That instead of making you addicted to us, it worked the other way around. We're addicted to you."

"Addicted to me?" Sana said weakly. Her expression revealed her thoughts: *My god. If that's true, I'll never be rid of them!*

Perry stood. "Time to go," he said, dexterously wrapping a cord around a mobile phone.

"Why?" Sana asked. "Why now? And where can we go?"

Perry paused. "Ever have the feeling that something bad—really bad—was going to happen?"

Sana lowered her chin and gave him a wise-ass half-glare.

"Oh," Perry said, momentarily stunned by his thoughtlessness. Embarrassed, he snatched a small bag a bit larger than a shaving kit, from its place on the bathroom floor. He shoved the mobile phone inside and grabbed her toothbrush and various toiletries as he spoke. "I had one of those. Only this time, it's worse. Worse than David in a bad mood."

Sana eyed her restraints, and Perry dropped to his knees and grappled with the hose. When their efforts only rewarded them with red welts on Sana's wrists, Perry snatched up a tiny pair of scissors Sana used to manicure her eyebrows.

"Those won't work," Sana said. "Get the big pair from the kitchen drawer."

That he didn't have to ask which drawer might have bothered her, but if his knowledge of her home perturbed her, it didn't show. His sense of haste seemed to have transferred to her; she was eager to get moving and showed no signs of trying to run from him. Hope soared in Perry's heart that she didn't appear to hold the same resentment for him as she did for David or Angelo. He didn't know what he'd done right, but she wasn't fighting, screaming, or glaring anymore.

He returned with the scissors and a grim expression, bent to his knees once more, and snipped the bonds. Sana rubbed her raw spots, but Perry snatched her hand and pulled her to her feet.

"No time to treat that now. I'm sorry—I'll get you what you need on the way. No time to pack."

"But what about—?"

"Go!" he exclaimed, veritably shoving her toward the front door as much as he urged her forward.

They left the house, shutting and locking the front door behind them. Sana followed Perry at a jog around the corner and got into the passenger's side of the Dodge he shared with Angelo and David. Perry scrambled for the seat adjuster. Seconds dragged as he fumbled, trying to remember where the switch was.

"You don't drive often?" Sana asked.

Perry shook his head. "Hardly ever." He found what he was looking for and let out an exasperated huff. After inching the seat forward, he plugged in the key and pulled out cautiously onto the dark street.

"You don't drive often."

"You Americans drive on the wrong bloody side of the road," Perry said. "It throws me right off."

"I thought you'd been Stateside for a while."

"Yeah. And you Yeah. And you Yanks still haven't figured it out." He pressed the gas a little harder.

Sana smiled. "Where are we headed?"

"Right now?" Perry said, crawling up to a stop sign. "Anywhere but here."

They'd only traveled another mile before she asked, "Why are you so nervous? We aren't where they left us. We're OK now, right?"

He shook his head, his face blank with fear. "No. We're not OK. That's what I'm afraid of."

"How far do we have to go before they can't find us?"

Perry glanced over long enough to say, "They'll always find us."

Chapter Thirty-four

"You didn't fly here?" Krieg said with a smile. He folded his leathery wings and retracted them as Charles offered a dismissive wave.

He folded his leathery wings and retracted them as Charles waved dismissively.

"Picked up a limo," Charles said. "Didn't want to ruin my suit. Had to get those two around anyway."

His voice was surprisingly friendly, and its sound caught Lukas off guard. Jude had sounded as evil as death on a good day: deep, alluring, but chilling. An old graveyard on Halloween. Charles sounded like he belonged on the nightly news—only friendlier, more sincere. It unsettled Lukas. Evil personified shouldn't sound like Dan Rather.

Charles moved away from the car and into the sunlight, toward him and Megan. Lukas' instinct goaded him to step between them, heedless of the danger. He recalled how Jude had used Gina to manipulate him only a few months before. Showing his love for Megan in front of Charles might be a bad idea. If Charles understood how deep his love for Megan ran, he might use it against him. Still, his drive to protect her outweighed anything else.

Charles closed the distance and positioned himself before Megan and Lukas. He tipped his head back and eyed Lukas' frame.

"My, you're a tall one," he said. Lukas declined to comment. Charles went on. "My Uncle Bran, he was a tall fellow, but he wouldn't hold a candle to you. How tall are you now? Six ten?"

"Six eleven," Lukas said. He wasn't sure if the words had popped out under Charles' subtle influence or if it was an impulse forcing him to behave as though he wasn't intimidated. The fact that he wasn't sure implied the latter.

"And fine-looking, too," Charles said, leaning to the side to weigh

Megan's response. Lukas and Megan both stood like paralyzed mutes. Megan glared, and the edge of Charles lip twisted up.

Charles shook his head. "Come, now," he said to Lukas. "The young lady has lost her phone, and yours is dead; you can't call for help. You're too inexperienced in using telepathy with much success, and you've both broken bones. They'll heal in a day or so, but meanwhile, you'd sit here in pain. And there's no telling when your folks are going to come—"

"They'll come," Lukas said from behind clenched teeth. How long had it taken Charles to assess their resources and physical conditions? One second? Two?

"They will," Charles agreed, "but we'll be gone by then. I won't meet Jerusha here. It must be under my terms."

"We won't go with you." Megan bit off each word.

Charles' expression grew cloudy. He held out one hand, palm up, fingers curved into a claw.

Agonizing pain, as if his head was surrounded with concrete, shot through Lukas' head, and he crumpled to the asphalt, his eyes shut reflexively. His body was being smothered from all sides by tremendous pressure that increased with every passing second. His arms, though untouched, hung pinned at his sides by an unseen force.

Megan cried out at his side. Whatever Charles was doing to him, she bore it, too. The knowledge made the torture worse.

The weight moved downward to include his neck, cutting off his windpipe and bearing down on his vocal cords. A choked sound came from his side—Megan gagging and coughing. His ears, eyes, and nose grew full of the hellish substance, too, suffocating, and the pressure, the horrible pressure…

Next will be our chests—what about our hearts? If this pressure's real, he might break another rib, or poke a hole in our hearts! It's not a stake, but we'd still die.

It had been several hours since he and Megan had eaten. Although fortified by Jude's blood at birth, their bodies were susceptible to death at the hands of a vampire empowered by the Maleficence. Lukas wasn't familiar with all the ways immortals could be killed, but he knew a vampire had it within his power to kill another vampire.

If they went with Charles, they might mislead him and save Vivian and his father. It was worth a shot.

Realizing Lukas was about to speak, Charles eased the crushing grip on his tongue. Catching a breath, Lukas croaked, "We'll go."

Instantly, the force surrounding him vanished. Beside him, Megan sobbed quietly as she collapsed. He staggered to her side and embraced her, stifling her sobs in his deep chest. "We'll go," he murmured.

Krieg peered at the cloudless sky. "Might want to hold off a second," he said. Charles turned his attention upward. Three dots, what looked like massive birds, gradually grew larger until their avian shapes turned more human. Lukas had the crazy notion that Icarus had come to life and spawned a sinister family.

Three vampires who appeared in their late twenties alighted beside Charles' limo. Their faces revealed little, but they emanated malice like steam. In a flash, their batlike wings disappeared. A tall, redheaded one stepped forward.

"Mr. Dunning," he said, his Scottish brogue worthy of addressing a dignitary, "I would like you to meet David Sheen and Angelo Vargas. You've heard of them through Jude, I'm sure. I think you'll find they're your new best mates."

A scowl crossed Charles' features, then vanished. He paused, his nostrils flaring. Like a predator discovering the scent of a meal on the wind, he grew alert.

"I smell Jude," he declared with a tone akin to respect, "On both of you. You aren't like his ordinary errand boys."

David smiled. "First in the bloodline," he said with pride. "I under-stand you know Kip—"

He turned to introduce his crewmember, but the red-headed one had vanished.

Chapter Thirty-five

Perry hustled, sensing an unknown vampire on the floor above him, but things weren't going according to plan. Without Eoghan's intervention, his carefully shaped outcomes would soon become a tangled web. If Eoghan didn't intervene, his controlled outcomes would quickly become a tangled web. His newest destination lay not far away, in South Carolina.

Within seconds, he found himself centered in a large white room. At a mirror on the far wall stood Maysun, her finger hooked under her upper lip as she studied her teeth. She released her lip as she turned away from the mirror and frowned.

Closing her eyes, she stood only feet from him. He considered speaking but sensed the inner exploration Maysun was engaged in mattered more.

Once again, disappointment covered her beautiful face, then her expression brightened. Without opening her eyes, she tilted backward at an alarming angle, then righted herself with ease. The Source swept through the room, bringing strength and joy to her. The entire white room glowed with a marvelous light. Even Eoghan felt its potency. As he watched his ex-lover enveloped in the divine energy, his heart lifted. Then, as the Source receded, so did the brief glimmer of emotion.

Maysun opened her eyes, unsettled. She pivoted, bracing herself for a dash across the room, saw him, and hesitated.

"Eoghan?" she breathed, as if she hadn't seen him in years instead of mere days.

"Yes?"

She took a half step forward, her eyes semi-squinted as she took in his form. "You look… so young," she said," she said.

He'd forgotten that he hadn't bothered to revert to his ageless body. "Would you rather I—?"

She shook her head and waved a hand. "No. No, it's fine. You—you don't have to…" The words died, and she dropped her head.

"What's wrong, May?" It was a dumb question, but he had to ask.

"Everything! Our daughter… I didn't know how to find her, so I killed myself. Brilliant solution, I know, but it was all I could come up with—I panicked. I spoke with God, one of them, and He said He'd help me find her, but at a price. He sent me back to Earth as a vampire. Now she's downstairs, but I can't approach her, because I'm a vampire, and a group of vampires tried to drive her out of her mind, tried to sire her, but failed. She's got to be terrified of vampires, and—" She stopped herself. "I'm babbling, aren't I? And all this is pointless because you knew it all to begin with."

He held out his arms, but she shook her head.

"It wouldn't be the same. You wouldn't mean it."

He tried to look consoling. "But you would."

She fled to his arms, burying her head into his chest, and breathed him in. The familiar scent of him was like a balm to her frazzled spirits. He wrapped his long arms around her, dug his hands into her hair the way he always did. Maysun clung forcefully, sobbed twice, then pulled in a long, shaking breath, preparing to speak.

"You feel… different," she said, easing her grip. "You're not you anymore."

"Neither are you."

She pulled away, still sobbing in shaky gulps, but more composed. She brushed unshed tears from the corners of her eyes and then put her hands on her hips.

"Why are you here? I'm guessing you're going to intervene in my life. Are you going to stop me from talking to Sana? Because let me tell you, it's going to be—"

"I'm here to help you."

Her arms fell to her sides as her tough posture dropped. "You are?"

Eoghan nodded. "She's left the house and locked you inside."

"I can open doors, Eoghan. I don't need a key. I'm the equivalent of a sixteen-hundred-year-old vampire. More or less."

"Yes. But can you find her?"

"What do you mean?"

"Try to find her."

Closing her eyes, Eoghan sensed her tapping into the Source, reaching outward for Sana, then the vampire with her. She frowned. Her brow creased. Her mouth pursed slightly as she tried harder to find them, but her search ended with a frustrated shake of her head.

"I can't do it. How is she able to block me?"

"She's not a vampire, for one. She's a new sort of creature, one the world's never seen. And Perry, despite his good intentions, has his roots in the Maleficence, which you've discovered you can't use anymore."

"She's with a member of the *Shévet ha Dam*?"

"Perry is a soul verging on becoming one of the good guys. He wants to do what's right, but he fears death too much to commit."

"Sana isn't in danger?"

"Not immediately, no. But Charles will be after her. He'll believe she can help him uncover the secret to vampirism and may also help him to tip the world to the Maleficence."

"Do you think it'll work?"

Her question surprised him. "No, I don't."

Maysun looked down, her eyes darting back and forth as she thought.

"You're not alone."

"What?"

"I said, you're not alone."" She eyed the door, clearly ached to dash through it, and then faced him once more. "There are several of you— those who control the Balance, and there are several souls like Charles and Vivian, affecting the balance of right and wrong. Charles might sway one of the others. He might be right."

Eoghan's mind reeled. Other Balances? He hadn't sensed them. Why hadn't he sensed them?

"I'd like to go now," Maysun said. Eoghan blinked.

"Yes, of course." He extended his hand. She accepted it, and before vanishing, he placed her in a moment where she couldn't go unnoticed—standing in the street of a suburban neighborhood, caught in the headlights of an approaching blue SUV.

Chapter Thirty-six

Crystal's return to Savannah was less graceful than she'd hoped. Her foot caught the edge of her portal, and she tumbled out like the worn-out woman she was. It didn't matter. No one's focus was on her. She stood to the side to let Vivian do what they'd come there for.

Her frowning sister joined her, pulling her from the dusty floor. Harmony then lay her hand on Crystal's triceps, discerning, the way she often did, what Crystal needed. The Harmony that motivated her had not asked her to intervene in this battle. Crystal didn't pressure her to change her mind; having her sister by her side eased her terror.

Vivian didn't need help. As she swooped through the hole in space, the four vampires who hovered around the circle of detainees turned toward the sound and motion. One—bald, average height and sinewy as a cheetah—grinned. The others, in whom Crystal sensed the Darkness, seemed to stare at their headstones.

"Jerusha!" the female one hissed. Crystal took in the presence of the vampire who'd killed her friend. The flames Tristan had engulfed her with had left a mark—her shiny pink face and charred clothing bore witness to Tristan's magical fire. She was an old one, but Vivian was older.

Young vampires in the circle bore torture marks, deep blackened gashes, as if held before a welder's torch. A shin-deep pile of ashes was all that remained of those who'd already died. Crystal's stomach twisted. This was her fault. She'd pressured Tristan and Harmony to join her half-assed attempt at a cavalry, and they'd pissed off the Tribe. Now Tristan was dead, and who knew how many others?

"Vivian!" the bald one cried, his mouth wide with a friendly smile. "Man, I was hoping you were coming."

Vivian smiled and tipped her head in greeting.

"Doyle," she said. "For once, it's a pleasure."

Chagrined, Doyle's smile turned down at the corners, but his obvious joy did not abate.

Vivian marched toward the vampires enclosed before her and raised her hands. To Crystal, it was as if the sun had cleared the building. Unlike the warm beams of the sun, these rays of light and bliss expanded until her heart filled with love to bursting. She felt weightless as air, luminous, free of the grief that had clenched her heart seconds ago.

"Wow," Harmony breathed, clearly impressed. The first time she and Crystal had seen Vivian tap into the Source back on Jones Street in Savannah paled in comparison.

"For real," Crystal agreed.

The linen-clad member of the Tribe snarled and leaped at Vivian, who blocked him with an effortless palm to his face. Elongated teeth snapped at her hand but couldn't find purchase. Instead, Vivian surrounded his skull with an extended hand and gripped it until his eyes bulged and he whimpered pathetically.

The second male jumped to his rescue. Vivian turned her attention from the man in her grasp to the new threat.

"Stop," she said. The word was so soft Crystal barely heard it, but the young vampire froze as if trapped in ice. "Down." He sat, clearly fighting Vivian physically, but incapable of breaking unseen bonds that held him tight.

Her charred dress billowing behind her, the female of the group charged at Vivian. Vivian hefted the trapped vampire by the head with both hands and swung him like a bat, slamming the charging woman into the far wall. The attacker slid down the exposed bricks to the ground.

"Damn," Crystal said. Harmony bobbed her head in agreement, her eyebrows arched.

Vivian handed the vampire in her hands to the seated Tribe member and turned her attention to the slumped woman lying in the dust a few yards away. The younger vampire dug his fangs into the neck in his lap.

Doyle and Michael, meanwhile, were using the distraction to cautiously herd the vampires out the door to the nearby Marshall House Hotel. Crystal tried to find the energy to help, but tearing her latest portal had worn her out.

"Peace," Harmony said, reading her mind as she often did. "They're doing fine without you."

As Vivian strode to the slumped woman's side, Crystal said in a voice choked with grief, "I hope she kills that wench slowly for what she did to us. To Tristan."

Head down, face covered by dark hair that hung in lank strings around her face, the large woman appeared knocked out. She wasn't. When Vivian reached an arm's length away, the body sprang to life—but Vivian was prepared. Gripping her by her dress front, Vivian lifted her feet off the ground and brought her nose to nose. The evil one's toes kicked inches from the ground and fought to throw Vivian off balance. Her fight was futile, and she stopped writhing.

"Don't kill me," she begged. "Don't drink my blood."

Vivian scoffed. "As if I'd enjoy that death-tainted swill," she said scornfully. "Don't flatter yourself. Not all of us live to kill."

"You'll let me go?" the female said, her face daring to brighten a little.

Vivian bit her lip, her eyeteeth showing for the first time Crystal could remember. Her face remained imperturbable.

"Not a chance," Vivian said. "I can see it in your eyes; if I set you down, you'd only kill again."

Drawing her left hand back, Vivian thrust her fist through her opponent's ribcage and withdrew a heart dark red with stolen blood. The sinister life within the vampire's eyes flickered and died, and Vivian threw her body to the floor. The charred dress and body ignited, this time never to regenerate.

Disgust contorted Vivian's features as she tossed the heart atop the pile of ash. Crystal wondered if the disgust was from the vampire she'd killed or at the act of killing itself.

Vivian dropped the burning heart at her feet, brushed her hands off on her jeans, and turned her attention to the young vampire who had drained his companion. The death of the undead didn't energize the way killing a human did, but it surprised Crystal that Vivian had allowed him to imbibe before taking him on.

The younger one stood over the body of his fellow Tribe member. "Brantley," he breathed. "Why did I...?"

"Because you wanted to," Vivian said flatly. She scooped Brantley from the alley floor and tossed his body atop the female's embers. His emptied body gradually caught fire as well, and the added smoke wafted toward Crystal, who gagged on the stench.

"No," the young one said.

"Yes," Vivian said.

"But he was a brother."

"And you wanted him dead, didn't you? Wanted his power?"

It seemed the man was incapable of lying when looking into Vivian's eyes. His expression softened, and he nodded.

"He's gone now," Vivian said. "How do you feel?"

"Scared," he admitted.

"Why?"

"Because you'll kill me?"

"Should I?"

He stumbled over a few garbled words but only managed a nod and a shrug.

"You might have the strength that Brantley's blood gave you, but compared to the centuries of power I have, you may as well be human." The words might have been bragging coming from anyone else; from Vivian, the words rang true.

"Will you fight me? Are you going to threaten my family?"

He shook his head hard, eyes wide, arms at his sides.

Vivian nodded. "I shouldn't let you live, and yet—" Her head tilted as if hearing words only audible to her. "Go."

He bolted, scrabbling to the door, his eyes wide in fear, his shirtfront painted in blood.

Chapter Thirty-seven

"Stop the car!" Sana cried, leaning over and cranking the wheel to the side to avoid the person in the road mere feet from the hood. *Where in the hell did he come from?*

Perry slammed on the brakes and wrestled with Sana for command of the Dodge until they halted with one wheel over the curb. Sana stopped, her body only inches from Perry, who still clung to the wheel. Though the near-miss lasted only seconds, both of them were breathless.

Wide blue eyes loomed before her. A beautiful face. A face she could—

She forced her mind to stop dwelling on the inappropriate thoughts, but it was difficult. *Don't be ridiculous! He's a vampire! He's done horrible things to you! Hell, you're out of your mind for trusting him.*

A picture flashed across her mental picture screen, and Sana fought the urge to cross the remaining inches and press her lips to his. She knew what they felt like. From the hidden trenches of her mind came the memory of his lips, thin but strong, on hers. Perry stared at her, either frightened, wishful, or both.

He'd been honest with her today. She didn't doubt that. But more than that, he sounded regretful. Painfully remorseful. And maybe a little like her—ready to break free of the shackles which had held her.

"We should probably go check on him," Sana said. Her body didn't move. With great effort, she eased back. The urge to kiss him subsided, but the longing lingered. She forced herself to find the door handle and leave the vehicle. She knew that her craving for the young man was ridiculous, but it was hard to fight against that uncanny instinct that came over her when she was near him.

Perry's eyebrows dropped, and he breathed out, leaning forward for the door pull. "Yeah," he said. "Be a good idea."

The person they'd nearly hit was a woman. An Indian woman,

judging by her complexion and the green silk kurta she wore. Long, wavy, black hair flowed to the center of her back. Her features were delicate, feminine, and not unlike Sana's own.

Sana had often wondered about her lineage. Her skin was too pale to be fully Indian, but she suspected some Indian ancestry. She'd always imagined that she'd had a dark father and pale mother. If she'd dreamed up a dark-skinned mother, this would have been what she'd hoped for.

"Ma'am?" Perry said, "Are you alright?" Though he sounded concerned, he kept his distance.

The woman hesitated. Her eyes, so black that it was impossible to tell where the pupil ended and the iris began, fixed on Sana, fascinated.

"I'm fine."

"It's—you weren't there a second ago. I swear. It looked like—"

"I appeared out of nowhere," the woman finished for him.

Perry surveyed the woman. Recognition set in, and he looked ready to bolt.

"Hey you're—"

"I'm fine," she insisted. Perry pulled back, and his wide eyes grew larger still as he measured the distance between the newcomer, Sana, and the SUV. Sana watched this exchange with trepidation.

Who is she? Why is Perry acting so funny? And why do they look like they're not saying something? She's not human. I'd bet on it. Is she part of David's group of thugs, or—?

"Sana?" the woman said.

Sana's heart leaped. *She knows who I am. She's here to kill me. She's the danger Perry sensed coming!* She backed a step toward the Dodge, wondering how fast the woman moved.

"Sana, I won't waste your time. I need to speak with you, and I hope you'll give me a chance. I'm your mother. My name is Maysun Khatri."

Sana's mouth formed "What?" and froze. Her foot stopped mid-step.

The woman continued, her tone pleading, her hands wringing in front of her. "I know what you're running from—which is more than you suspect—and I can help." She looked down and decided to change her words. "I have the power to keep them from seeing where you're going for a while. Divided three ways—to protect you, me, and your…" she balked at the word, "friend, here, my strength might last a day. Long enough to get a good head start and develop a course of action. What do you say?" As she finished her speech, she held her hands outward beseechingly.

Sana finished her half step back and considered her choices. Her life could absolutely get worse; it had turned on its end in the last thirty-six hours. First, they had killed Thom; then, for the first time in years, she knew she wasn't crazy, but only because she found out that vampires had been stalking her for years. Now, as she and Perry—the very man who'd confessed to killing her husband—fled the vampires who wanted to do God knew what to her, the mother she'd never met drops out of the sky.

If I wasn't crazy before, I will be before this is all over.

"I… I don't…"

"Sana, may I?" Perry asked.

She nodded. Maysun frowned.

This woman here says she's your mother. Right?" he said, motioning to Maysun. "I don't know if she's really your mother—but I can tell you she's a vampire."

"I knew there was something," Sana said.

Maysun glared at Perry, but he kept going. "She's a vampire, but she's not like me." He dropped his gaze, ashamed. "She's not *Shévet ha Dam*. She's honest. And good. I can tell. Because I'm not. More than that, she's old enough she could've given me a good fight and killed you if she wanted to, and she didn't. She's offering to help."

Maysun's gaze softened. Perry lifted his head to meet Sana's face.

"I don't know," Sana said. "So much has happened, and I'm so confused right now. First, you ask me to trust you, and now her. Trusting you was hard enough. Now she's asking me to trust her, too?"

As the words left her mouth, Sana knew they were moot. Despite their past, she had an ungrounded faith in Perry, and this newcomer, too. led against it, but her gut told her she wasn't wrong. Their goal was to protect her from David.

"Sana, think about it. If she isn't trying to help, why are we still alive? And you have to admit, the likeness is striking. If she can keep us safe from Dunning and David for a bit, that would be fantastic. If you aren't convinced in a few miles, we can always drop her off at the first petrol station and call her a cab. What do you say?"

The last sentence threw Sana off for a moment. Once she translated it to American English, she had to laugh. Hearing it, Maysun's expression relaxed as well.

"Alright," Sana said.

"Great. Let's get moving."

They climbed into the Durango. Maysun centered herself in the vehicle's backseat and belted herself in. Sana watched her close her eyes, place her hands into her lap, relaxing her body visibly. She exhaled slowly, which struck Sana as odd—did vampires breathe? She wasn't sure—but she recalled the instructions in Thom's self-hypnosis book about using the breath to visualize the removal of negative energy.

"I'm going to need silence for a moment," Maysun said, her eyes still closed.

"Is it OK if I drive, then?" Perry asked.

"Yes," she said, "that would be fine."

As Perry maneuvered off the curb and back onto the road, Sana watched the woman behind her, wondering if she sensed her stare. If she did, she gave no sign. She looked as calm as a sage.

A wave of cold washed over her, and her skin broke out in gooseflesh. Her ears rang as if a wet finger ran around the rim of a crystal glass. Sana's spirit lightened with a joy that had no place during such a stressful time. Was this the power Maysun wielded? Was this woman's presence going to keep them safe from Perry's sire?

Maybe there's hope for us after all.

Chapter Thirty-eight

Lukas consoled Megan as he looked at her ankle. Charles took pleasure in knowing that while Megan was grounded and immobile, Lukas would remain at her side. Lukas' wounds were more severe, but he had Jude's blood; he'd heal in no time. Megan had Lukas' blood in her, and they were bound by it—and, more powerfully, by love. Though they tried to mask it, Charles could see their bond ran far deeper than sire and progeny.

Charles stood with one hand on his chin, the other tucked beneath his opposite arm as he assessed David's strange account of meeting the vampire who'd disappeared, Kip MacConin.

"And he said he knew me," Charles repeated.

David's steady stare told Charles he had no intention of retracting a word. But it explained little, the least of which how this Kip MacConin had known where to find him. Strange.

"David," Charles said, dropping his arms, "what makes you think I give a dead rat's shriveled balls about anything you've got to say? Apart from your lineage."

"MacConin told us something," David said.

"And what makes you think it's true?"

David's nostrils flared, but he kept his voice level. "Because it explains why my mates and I haven't been able to turn this woman into a vampire for over five years. Not completely."

"You mean the little babysitting job Jude gave you?" Charles said. "Let me guess: suddenly this woman has developed a new talent. What—she added a page to the Kama Sutra while high on vampire blood?"

"Mr. Dunning, I wouldn't waste your time if I didn't think it was worth it. If you recall our relationship with Jude at all, you remember that we rarely bothered him in person. He came to us. And in the time you've been the one holding the Maleficence, have I tracked you down? Harassed you, pestered you?"

Charles considered David's claim and nodded. "Go on."

David, satisfied, shared what he'd learned from the mysterious Mac-Conin.

Charles listened intently. He covered his mouth with his hand to save it from fidgeting as he reflected.

When David finished, Charles spoke. "He said she's the daughter of the Balance? Maysun, who used to be part of the Tribe? Are you saying the Balance infiltrated the Tribe?"

"Yes."

"And you say you've never seen this MacConin chap before today?"

"Never."

Charles snapped his finger. "Maysun was the Balance, and that's why I can't find her, can't see her. And I'd wager that she's off the job. This new guy—this MacConin—he's the new Balance."

"You sure it's not Maysun in fancy dress?" David asked.

"No, no," Charles said, his head swimming now. Where was all this coming from? His surroundings took on a strange gray, like dusk triggered by gods dimming a switch at midday. "That Kip chap had a distinct energy to him."

He stopped when he realized that everyone around him was staring at him with expressions ranging from reluctant curiosity to terror.

"Cartaphilus was studying Sana," Charles said. "He suspected she might harbor a power he could use, but he'd given up on that long ago…" He stopped, not wanting to share more. "Do you know where she is now? The daughter of the Balance?"

David snorted. "Sana? Sure. She's tied up in a loo a few hundred miles north of here."

How much power did Sana have? Was it growing stronger now that Maysun was no longer the Balance? Or weaker? Had an occurrence in her life triggered abilities she hadn't shown before? Had the Maleficence caused outcomes that offered Sana to him so easily?

It's almost too easy. He thought of Vivian's jump from Savannah to Virginia. Maybe the Maleficence was compensating for his inability to travel like Vivian—offering him the same power by a different path. Who knew what Sana was the key to?

Vivian will head to Blu's home; she'll be there in only moments at the rate she travels now. Perhaps with Suna's power added to mine, I, too, can travel the world in a moment.

"Krieg, you're free to go," Charles said. "The rest us will be taking the plane."

Dawn would be coming too soon for some; the best Vivian could do to protect the vampires she'd saved was to rent rooms for all of them until nightfall made it safe for them to venture home. Michael, who already blamed himself for Lukas and Megan's capture, argued against using his charge card again. To Vivian's surprise, Doyle had the best solution. Whipping out a thick wallet, he pulled a wad of hundred-dollar bills from within. Vivian refrained from asking what he was doing carrying such an enormous stash of money in his pocket.

"Clean, easy, and untraceable," Doyle said with a twinkle and a sly eyebrow wiggle.

Fifteen rooms, and several thousand dollars later, they'd settled the grateful vampires who'd been rounded up from nearby towns with no easy way to get home soon. An exhausted Michael, Vivian, and crew took seats in rolled-arm sofas in the plush ivory lobby.

Michael slouched low in his seat, eyes closed against the chandelier light—but the steady undulation of his aura told Vivian he was awake, and his bearing was too full of tension for him to be dozing. Besides, Michael was too much like her. There was no way he'd slumber with his son trapped by the *Shévet ha Dam.*

He'd always looked so handsome when he slept. The way he'd poised himself now, head tilted to the side, his eyes closed and immobile, she could almost believe he'd taken a nap. The stress lines at the corners of his mouth and eyes gave him away, though. She longed to remove his tension.

"Michael?"

His eyes stayed closed, but his eyebrows raised. "Hmm?" His lids lifted, and he started to put his feet on the white coffee table, noted the clerk at the check-in counter observing them, and decided against it. He pushed his hair from his forehead and it stood up in messy, dark spikes. "Lukas–"

"Is strong," Vivian cut in. "And he has Jude's blood. If we knew where he was right now, Crystal is half-dead from all the work she's done. I could give her another jolt, but it's not a good idea to do that again so soon. We have to wait."

Michael frowned so hard every wrinkle in his face came to the fore.

"It's going to be alright," she put a hand on his. "You get that, right?"

His eyes, more bloodshot than any vampire's should be, opened. "How can you be so sure?"

Vivian shook her head. "I can't say. It's a crap shoot, this power of mine. It didn't save Lukas and Megan from being kidnapped, but it's telling me to go north, find Blu, and take all of you with me. That we're on the right track. This is all part of a plan."

Michael shook his head. "It's not that I don't trust the force behind your power. But Vivian, I thought I'd lost him once before. Now, it's happening again. All because—"

"All because you met me," Vivian finished, her mouth tensed at the corners.

"No!" Michael said, the sincerity in his voice deepening the timbre. "No, not because I met you. Because of the Maleficence. Vivian, this was a battle that was centuries overdue. Because of you, the vampire world lost its first—and most powerful—leader. You are one of the most influential beings on earth, and because of you, I have a new purpose in life. I'm part of that battle, the war against the Maleficence." He sat up and wound his fingers through hers. His fingers were only slightly longer, but much more masculine.

Vivian smiled a meager smile. "Charles is worse than Jude was," she said.

Michael's hand tightened on hers, and she saw the tension in his eyes grow, although he tried to hide it. "How can you be sure?"

She hated telling him, but she needed him to grasp what Lukas and Megan were up against. "His soul is far more evil, and his reason for hating still exists."

When Michael didn't convey a grasp of what she was trying to get across, Vivian continued. "Joseph—Jude—his hatred wasn't of me. He wasn't what did the hating at all. It was the power that motivated him, the Maleficence. That was what Yeshua cursed, not Cartaphilus, the man. Joseph wasn't an evil man until the Maleficence supplanted his personality. The Maleficence found a person who had terrible potential and climbed aboard, using Jude like a person riding a horse. Charles, unlike Jude, was born evil. The Maleficence is probably having a hey-day with him."

"I've never asked you—who is Charles, anyway? What was he

before Cartaphilus got a hold of him?"

"Oisian Drummann," Vivian answered. "Originally from Scotland. Joseph found him around the year 1066."

"Why does that year ring a bell?" Michael asked.

"Battle of Hastings?" Vivian ventured.

"Ah," Michael said. "Was he there?"

Vivian shook her head. "No. He was a feudal nobleman and what we now call a serial killer."

"What?"

"I knew him in the area as the 'Unlucky Nobleman.' Guests who visited his land were often reported missing or lost. Why do you think Joseph singled him out as a good right-hand man? He had a way with people—often rich people or other noblemen. He had a talent for leadership—he ruled his lands effectively, even as his guests vanished. Joseph offered Oisian riches and all the blood he wanted. In exchange, Oisian created the Table, the first formal law-making body of the growing *Shévet ha Dam*, and he supplied them with many of their laws. Jude was a figurehead. Oisian couldn't beat him in strength, and he didn't have the Maleficence behind him, but he had a deeper motivation: a pure hatred of humanity."

A stunned look painted Michael's face. "So, we're dealing with a creature that hated people even before he was turned."

Vivian disagreed. "Charles has been many things, but not one of them was human."

"And he has Lukas," Michael breathed, seeming to force the words out. "And Megan. And killing him might bring on Armageddon. What the hell are we doing? Can we even stop him?"

Vivian pressed her lips together. "I have to trust the Source, Michael. I won't say it's never let me down, but it's right. In the end, it's always right, in the greatest sense of the word."

Michael tried to hide his skepticism, but his pained look and too-quick smile that didn't reach his eyes gave him away.

"I suppose triggering Armageddon would be better than living under the rule of anyone powered by the Maleficence," he conceded.

Doyle strolled back into the lobby, a glass of something that looked like an old-fashioned in hand. Vivian peered at him curiously.

"Bit early for a cocktail, isn't it?" she joked. "Is the bar even open?"

Doyle chuckled. "It is for me. I met the hotel manager when we both lived in California a few decades ago."

"Vampire?" Michael ventured.

"Yep," Doyle said. "Nice gal named… Darcy, I think is what she's using now. She keeps a stash of blood to add to her personal drinks and the drinks of a chosen few."

Vivian's thoughtful frown evolved into an inquiring gaze. "Doyle, you're pretty resourceful. Would you be willing to help us?"

Doyle shrugged. "Yeahyeahyeah. What'd you have in mind?"

"I doubt it'll shock you that Charles is up to something," Vivian said, leaning forward.

"Nope," Doyle said. "He appointed me head of the U.S. division of the Tribe—mostly because he could manipulate me better that way."

"Damn," Michael said. "That didn't last long."

Scoffing, Doyle took a sip from his glass. "No, sure didn't."

Vivian leaned forward until she sat on the edge of her seat. "Can you tap your network—vampires, werewolves, anyone strong enough— who'd be willing to help us take down Charles?"

Doyle nodded and crossed one arm around his chest. He seemed to grow smaller for a moment as fear tightened the planes of his chiseled face. He sucked in a deep breath and pulled himself up.

"Sure. What did you have in mind?"

Chapter Thirty-nine

One moment there was a shuffle among the crowd, and then Eoghan appeared in the spot least likely to cause a stir. He reached the Theodore Roosevelt Island pedestrian bridge, slowed to a leisurely pace, and took in the view of the Potomac River. DC commuters and tourists buzzed past on bikes or jogged by, chasing work, home, or the next landmark—but he didn't mind their frantic pace. Instead, he leaned on the wide, white rail and sighed.

Maysun was safe with Sana and Perry. David had surely told Charles everything by now. Eoghan's plan was unfolding as designed—though he still lacked confidence in his ability to measure emotion, especially the inhuman kind. Was the plan foolproof?

Charles' strategy to take out any vampire unaffiliated with the *Shévet ha Dam* was working better than he'd bothered to find out. If Charles took a moment to see how his scheme was going in North America, he'd revel in the depths of his power, the breadth of his reach, and his strength would grow. Instead, being the animal he was, his concern was concentrated on developing more power and eliminating the only being likely to kill him. Jerusha.

Charles was tipping the scales heavily—more than he realized. But Eoghan knew, and had done what he must to level them. It made little sense, sending Charles after Sana—unless the plan worked. A plan that relied on a heartless, unpredictable madman. So much hung in the balance. Billions of lives, thousands of undead.

The battle he faced was coming to a head. He took a slow breath and leaned against the rail, letting tension slide from his shoulders. Charles was… oh, Charles was close to unraveling all of his hard work. Very close. Vivian… it would take time for Vivian to reach Sana. He had to move, and fast.

With one last glance at the pieces in play, Eoghan made himself the pawn, and vanished.

They had to rest. There was no way they could continue at the pace they'd been going for the past two days. After risking a few short hours of fitful rest at rooms in the Marshall House, Vivian and Crystal introduced Doyle to Bully and DB. They made quick introductions, and Vivian's heart swelled with hope when she saw the group of fighters that Bully had amassed so far. After a quick briefing, Crystal cut another portal for the next leg of their journey, and Vivian and Crystal ducked back through the hole to Savannah.

They emerged in an alley in DC, and Vivian allowed Michael to navigate them through the city until they saw a wide, burgundy awning that read "Dining House & Down-Home Saloon." Below that was "Brickskeller" the name of the bar Blu had mentioned on the phone. Black iron rails flanked stairs the same color as the awning.

"We made it," Crystal puffed.

"Oh, sorry," Vivian said. "Too fast?" Crystal waved her off, but Vivian noticed how the morning sun highlighted the heavy circles under her eyes.

They passed beyond a heavy wooden door and down a narrow staircase. Antique brick and stone walls set up the framework. Worn hardwood tables and chairs accented by red and white checkered tablecloths covered the dining areas, which smelled of a tasty standard pub menu—burgers, pizzas, and breaded chicken in various dishes. Mirrored pub signs, countless shelves lined with beer bottles, neon lights, and beer-related embellishments that ranged from tasteful to tacky, filled the space.

At the edge of the early lunchtime rush sat Blu, a man whose every detail looked as if it were drawn in black ink. A dark complexion with lids lowered around beautiful, wide, black eyes. Thick legs clad in black leather stretched under his table and ended with large black boots. A black shirt with a wide V-neck exposed his broad chest. Blue-black dreadlocks tipped with sapphire dye hung behind his chair back. In one hand, he held a bottle of Dragon Stout beer. In the other, he cradled a pen with which he unremittingly assaulted a napkin.

Everyone took seats at the sides of the table. After brief introductions, Blu looked up, his expression grim. "It's getting worse, isn't it?"

he said. "The war's over, Jude's dead, and the world's still spiraling." There was no trace of doubt in the question. "They killed my family. Nearly got me, too. Found us on our way home as we walked through the park."

"They've taken Lukas and Megan," Michael replied in a similar grim tone.

Blu's troubled eyes dropped back to the napkin. "Shit," he hissed.

On the worn napkin, scenes from the Blood War played out in graphic black-and-white detail: severed limbs and wings were strewn at the edge of the paper, fangs tore at lunging necks, claws ripped at the flying bodies. This was not the same carefree man Vivian had met a year ago. Then, Blu had embodied joy—both in the old sense of "gay" and the modern one. Now, he was war-torn, tired. Almost defeated.

Blu tore himself from his rendering and drew his attention back across the table to his friends. "What's the plan?"

Vivian pushed back her heavy chair and extended her legs. "I was hoping you might have an idea."

Blu's incredulous scoff bordered on a laugh. "Me? What makes you think I got answers?"

Vivian shrugged. "I couldn't say, Blu. The Source guided me to come to you. To talk to you."

"Me?" Blu repeated as the implication sank in. His eyes darted behind him to the nearest occupied table. He set down his pen and studied his work as if a spirit hand had illustrated it. "The Source sent you to me?" He sat up, consternation evident in his jerky movements and uncharacteristically awkward posture. "That doesn't make a damn bit of sense."

Vivian took in his haunted expression. "Maybe it wants you to come with us," she suggested.

Blu shrugged. "Maybe it does. I don't have a family to keep me here anymore."

"Do you want to join us?" Michael countered.

Blu's frown flattened into a frustrated line as his brow lost its worry lines. Regret pained his handsome face. "Sorry, Michael," he said. "I wanna say yes. I do. But shit's been tense here since the war. After that ambush last night…"

"We're your family, too, B," Michael reminded him. "And we need you now more than ever. First, we lost Gina. Now Lukas and Megan are in Dunning's hands…" His voice choked, and he could not continue.

Blu's head dropped to near shoulder level, then rose again. "Let me tell you what I've heard. Can't name names, but they're solid."

"Go ahead," Vivian said.

"Maysun isn't the Balance anymore," Blu said. "I figure you already knew that. But what you probably don't know? She passed it to her man—Eoghan. They had a kid. Her name's Sana."

"The Balance can procreate?" Vivian said. "I thought they were like us."

Blu's palms turned skyward. "Guess not. Turns out they can," he said. "Anyway… Sana's about to be the center of some heavy shit. Some vamps tried to turn her. Couldn't do it. Not all the way. She resisted it. She's got some of the perks—speed, strength, allure—but almost no thirst."

"Man, she lucked out," Michael said.

"Yeah," Blu agreed, his voice almost envious, "Except those same vamps stuck around for years. Jude told 'em to. They didn't know why, just knew she mattered. And now? They've met Charles Dunning—"

"Charles?"

Blu's dumbfounded face said volumes. "I think he's planning on studying her. Pick her apart, see how she works. She's lived like a regular human, feeding only a few times a year. No breakdowns, no wild binges. Even with her sires poking around her head. They stalk her. She thinks she's got some kinda mental illness—but she's holding it together. Barely. Charles wants to understand why she's a freakin' anomaly. And you better believe he wants to crack her open."

Michael's jaw dropped. Vivian turned her attention to him.

"What?"

Michael sat up in his chair. "That's bad. Think about it. If Charles, through Sana, learns how the Balance works, what does he have? He's got a handle on how two-thirds of the universal power works. Or he might learn enough to keep the world tipping his way—keep the world darker." Michael slapped the back of one hand on his palm. "If Sana is a key to the Balance or holds the secret to what makes a person into a vampire, he adds major weight to his side of the Good versus Evil scale."

"You think he can manipulate the Balance?" Harmony said, incredulous.

Michael exhaled sharply. "Think about it. Charles won't care what the odds are of success. If he has the slightest chance of getting a tiny toehold in this war, he's going to take it. If there's a shot that he can learn how to influence the Balance, even a little, he's going to try it. Anything to help the world swing according to his plan."

Vivian's brow furrowed. "Do you think Charles might kidnap Sana the way he did Lukas and Megan? To use her as a pawn to draw Eoghan?"

Blu shook his head. "Nah. Eoghan ain't wired like that. Can't feel emotion—it's part of the whole Balance gig." Harmony nodded her concurrence.

"Incapable," Vivian said, her head slowly wagging back and forth as her eyes met Harmony's flat ones. "That must be awful." Vivian straightened in her chair. "So, there's a young woman whose life is in danger, and we may be the only people wearing the white hats who know she's in trouble. What about Maysun?"

Crystal's voice broke in. "What about this vampire round-up he's doing? That will affect the Harmony—Balance—whatever that way too, right? Knocking off good guys has got to be swinging the Balance his way. If he gets a hold of Sana, and she helps him learn how the Balance can be affected or toyed with…"

The discussion lulled, leaving them with only the sound of tinkling bottles and glasses and the jovial conversation of those nearest them. The chuckles and laughter contrasted starkly with the gloom that had settled over the group.

"So," Michael said, staring pointedly at Blu, "are you coming?"

Blu exhaled and hesitated, then grabbed another napkin from the next table. He jotted down an address and phone number and slid it across the table to Michael. "Gimme an hour."

Michael and Vivian stood. "Good to have you back, man," Michael said, taking Blu's hand in an elaborate handshake.

"Good to be back," Blu said.

Chapter Forty

He watched the group retrace the steps they'd taken upon entering, his eyes locked on the one with the light brown hair. Vivian radiated the Source so powerfully it hurt, and Michael and Crystal were easy enough, but the other one…

In the fraction of a second that every eye in the pub looked away, the body at the table in the heart of the pub changed to a photographic negative of its previous occupant. Stout limbs grew lean and lengthened, deep brown eyes shifted to crystalline blue. Ebony skin grew pale, and long black hair became short and red.

The server entered his corner of the bar and stopped in her trek as if pushed by an unseen hand. She motioned to his table with an inquiring wave.

"The—the man who—"

"I've got it, lass," Eoghan replied. He put the empty bottle of Dragon Stout on her tray. "Can I get a Harp's, please?" He pulled a slim wallet from his back pocket, handed her enough to cover both his former tab and this one.

"Right away," she said in a puzzled daze. She made a note on her pad as she followed Eoghan's eyes toward the door shutting behind Michael and Vivian.

He'd had contact with three major players in the war between the honorable and the corrupt in less than a day: Maysun Khatri, Charles Dunning, and Vivian Black. With one look at each, he'd read their minds and souls, knew their fondest wishes and most heart-wrenching fears. He grasped—to some small degree—the method of each competitor for the earth's power, and their limits. Maysun's, of course, was much smaller now that she'd surrendered her power to him. Smaller, but still significant.

Harmony. A snippet of conversation came back to him. Crystal had called the Balance the Harmony—the same name as her sister. Maysun had mentioned another Balance. Could it be…?

Another Balance on the same task as he? How influential was this battle going to be?

A frustrating delay at the airport had left Charles sitting on the tarmac far too long. Fortunately, the plush interior of Charles' chartered Falcon 900 jet was made waiting tolerable, if a bit smaller than he'd prefer. The colors were largely a relaxing beige, the seats leather, the miniature table a shiny brown wood. Charles and David waited for Angelo to shuffle Lukas and Megan to the rear of the cabin before taking seats on opposite sides of the table.

"So," Charles asked as everyone settled, either comfortably or begrudgingly, into their places, "Tell me more about Sana, David."

David accepted the bubbling glass of champagne from the attendant in a sharp navy-blue suit before turning his attention to Charles.

"Jude said there was some bird in Piper he wanted us to keep tabs on. Reckoned she might turn into something proper dangerous later on."

Angelo's mouth opened, then closed without saying anything. Charles noted Angelo's hesitation and remembered how he'd held his own tongue as Jude's second-in-command. Charles knew the game well. He'd played it for centuries and hated every moment. However, the less one spoke, the more one learned.

Charles scrutinized Lukas and Megan at the stern of the plane. The flight attendant spoke to them ardently, shaking her head. Her navy uniform stretched pleasingly across her narrow hips as she leaned forward. Charles almost hated to interrupt her.

"Miss?" he said, digging into his jacket. The attendant righted herself, torn between her current conversation and the one offered by the man who'd chartered the flight. Charles produced a thin black wallet from his pocket as she strode to his side. A gold tag pinned above her right breast read, "Henny Carter."

He pulled five one-hundred-dollar bills from his billfold and handed them to her. Her blue eyes widened.

"Thank you, Henny. That will be all. My companions and I will be happy to attend to our own needs. It is a short flight."

"But, sir—" her eyes shot to the rear of the plane where Lukas and

Megan huddled together like frightened children.

He thrust the bills at her. "Please. I insist."

Henny eyed the bills with her bottom lip clenched under a row of straight teeth. Charles dug back into his wallet and produced a second set of bills to match the first. The temptation was too much. She took them and swiftly exited the plane, as if afraid he'd change his mind.

"Aren't you afraid she'll tell someone?" Angelo asked.

"Tell them what? That we had passengers on board who were asking about how to exit in the event of an emergency landing? No. She might have her suspicions, but Lukas was a good boy. Just asking questions because his girlfriend is terrified of flying. Weren't you, son?" Charles directed the last words toward the rear of the plane, where Lukas cradled Megan's head in his arms.

"Tie them up," Charles said to Angelo. "There's bound to be rope, or the like, tucked away in one of these compartments that will do fine. Bind them good and tight. They're only second and third generation from your sire. The ropes won't hold them long if they decide to struggle."

Disbelief of Charles' words showed on Angelo's arched eyebrows, half-hidden under his shaggy forelock but he was too eager to do the job to mull over the paternity of their captives. He headed off in search of rope.

Charles resumed his seat, facing aft, and leaned toward David.

"You hadn't recognized Sana as the one you'd been looking for?"

"There was no way to tell," David said; his belief was indisputable. "She looked like any other pretty young woman I'd seen, and it wasn't as if I tried to psych her. Why bother? Sana looked almost twenty, and we were told the girl we were looking for was fourteen."

"What happened when you took her? Was it just you?"

David's steady gaze wavered. "We all went in, but she didn't show any spark at first. I was brassed off at Ralph for wasting my time and Jude's. I was also more than a little afraid that Jude would be angry with me for taking so long on what should have been a quick mission. So, we dog-piled her."

"She didn't fight back?"

"I put her under. That one's one of my stronger tricks. Felt odd, though. Like trying to hold on to smoke. Still worked."

"Weird how?"

David thought for a moment. "Cold. Almost absent. As if her mind was there, but ghostly. Not as concrete as a regular mind, not as easy to sink my hooks in. I should've known then, I guess. That was Jude's big clue; she'd likely be a hard person to read."

Charles sipped his champagne. "In all this time, she hasn't shown extrasensory perception… no superhuman power at all."

"She doesn't age," David said. He set his flute on the table and wiped his hands on his jeans nervously. "Well, not as fast as a human. And there's the fact that she hasn't turned." He was equivocating.

"Mm," Charles said, his lips a straight line. "But no clairvoyance, no hypnosis—"

"She can hear us in her head, but she's not taken to the leash since the shift. Hypnosis is a bust. And she's a proper siren, too," David said with a shrug. "I mean it. Watching her work, it's something else. No human pulls that off. Not like her. Especially before she got herself hitched."

"Really?" Charles said, his face brightening.

"Yeah. Before she met Thomas, she was a bit of a goer."

Charles chuckled, then grew somber. "But she hasn't turned."

"Not really, no."

"What do you mean, 'Not really?'"

"Well, there's this… thing. Now and then, she goes a bit mad. Fangs come out, but she doesn't touch humans. It's our blood she's after."

"Not human?" Charles' voice was skeptical.

"No. That's what's odd. It's like she senses us more than usual. She keeps glancing our way, even though she can't see a thing. And she gets… properly randy. But she never remembers a bloody thing after. It's insulting, if you ask me."

"She didn't escape all of her vampire heritage." Charles said, leaning back in his chair. "Do you think—"

"We, erm… we fulfilled that need a couple of days ago."

Ah yes. They did, and I felt it. Discouraged, Charles asked, "How long until she craves it again? Another year? Another month?"

"It depends on how much blood Perry gave her. He says she didn't feed much this last time. If she barely touched him, she could have a craving tomorrow. Tonight, maybe."

Charles looked out the window as the jet taxied down the runway. *I can use her to my benefit. What if Sana holds the cure to vampirism? Vivian would be effortless to kill as a human.*

"This is good. This is very good."

Chapter Forty-one

If someone had told me two weeks ago that I'd be helping in a revolt against the Blood Tribe, I would've said they were out of their goddamn minds.

But he *was* helping, and damned if it wasn't going better than it had a right to. Doyle had spent decades using cloak-and-dagger strategies to balance the needs of both the Tribe and a handful of rebel factions, and now those strategies might keep him alive. For a few more days, anyway. Once the Big Brawl happened, either the world would fall apart under Charles's thumb, or... whatever Armageddon was. He didn't know for sure, but it didn't sound good.

Burner phones. Clandestine websites. Meetings with people using names that were clearly aliases. Doyle would locate them, Bully would pop them to their new location, and DB would use his persuasion skills—and sometimes a little pyrotechnics—to convince people that this battle was one they didn't dare spend on the sidelines. By combining Doyle's covert skills for pinpointing rare and hidden people with Bully's magical relocation talents and the silver-tongued fire-breather's gift for persuasion, they were gaining momentum fast. In very little time, they'd already recruited nearly twenty fighters to their cause, and they'd only begun.

"What do you say? Are you in? We could really use your skills." DB held a ball of fire on his fingertips while the group of... well, Doyle wasn't sure what they were. Demons, maybe. Or ghouls. One of his old friends had once called them jinn, whatever the hell that meant. Maybe they were right. The humanoid creatures' reddish skin, sharp features, and black irises had always unnerved him, but they'd always been unsettlingly proficient at locating illegal items he needed to procure over the years—especially drugs.

The unusual beings exchanged a silent conversation with furtive glances, their brows furrowed, their dark eyes squinted in scrutiny.

"We'll come," the stoutest of them said. Stout for these beings only made him about as wide around as a water pitcher, but for all of their slenderness, they were surprisingly wiry and strong. Their build and fluid, confident movements sometimes reminded Doyle of Bruce Lee.

"Excellent," DB said with a smile. "How soon can you be ready?"

"Now," the stout one said with a carefree cock of his head. "We can acquire whatever we might need when we get there."

I'll bet you can, Doyle thought.

As they approached the concrete staircase attached to the three-story red brick townhouse, Vivian checked the address on the napkin in her hand. A somber expression crossed her face. The conversation she'd had with Harmony as they strolled the D.C. streets had changed her demeanor from hope to that of uncertainty.

"This is it," she said. "This is the address. If he was right, this is Blu's boyfriend's place."

Harmony's face was stolid. "You sound surprised."

"I am," she said. "Knowing him, I expected something more…"

"Flamboyant?" Michael ventured. Vivian managed a giggle, and a smile crossed his face. Vivian was not one to giggle often, and the sound was the first sign that perhaps she was hopeful, which brought to mind why she'd been despondent. His smile faded.

"Man, this is weird," he said. "How can you be sure it wasn't Blu?"

"He felt absent," Harmony said. "If he was Blu, I'd have sensed it. Vampires have an aura—an undead one, sort of grayish where humans tend to have colors that glow, but an aura, nonetheless. He was blank."

Michael turned to Vivian.

"What?" she said. "I didn't feel him out. It was Blu, for Pete's sake. At least I thought—"

He held up his hand, pressed the doorbell, and his smile reappeared as the chimes sang out the melody to the first lines of a Gloria Gaynor tune.

"That's a good sign," Vivian said with another giggle. She tried and failed to suppress her smile as Blu opened the wide wooden door to the townhouse. His eyes searched for the source of her mirth, then realized what must have caused it. He chuckled as he shambled onto the steps to take her in a hug. Gone was the black leather from before; his muscular, barrel frame was housed in a teal t-shirt and baggy jeans.

"Michael! Vivian! Lord, y'all don't know how good it is to see familiar faces," he said.

Michael took in Blu's wardrobe, the interior of his home, his arms embracing Vivian as if he hadn't seen her for weeks. Harmony had been right. "Good to see you," he said.

"I haven't seen my phone since the Tribe rolled up on us last night at our other house," Blu said, rubbing the back of his neck. "Between the fight and the mess after… I think it's gone. I'm gonna have to get another one. That pisses me off. Y'all are lucky you caught me. I only stopped by to grab my stuff and bounce. Sorry I look a hot mess—if I'd known you were coming, I might've thrown on some real clothes…" he let the sentence trail off, unfinished. He caught the knowing looks shared back and forth. "What's going on?" he asked, the words rushing out in a single breathless sentence.

Vivian turned to Michael. "Eoghan."

"What the fuck is an Eoghan?" Blu asked.

"The new Balance," Michael replied.

"Wait—there's a *new* Balance?" Blu said, blinking. "Okay, who told y'all that?"

"You did. At Brickskeller, an hour ago. Vivian called your phone, and you told us to meet you there. Only we know now that it wasn't you."

"You're telling me the Balance got my phone?"

Vivian burst into laughter.

"What's so funny?" Blu queried.

"The way you look at life," Vivian said. "I love it. One of the leading forces in the universe impersonates you, and you're worried about them stealing your cell phone."

After shooting a glance up and down the street, Blu smirked, let out a quick snort of laughter, and waved them inside his spacious apartment. With a sense of odd déjà vu, Michael introduced Crystal and Harmony as they stepped inside.

Blu shut the door and led them under a winding iron staircase into a comfortable living room with wood floors so shiny they nearly reflected. Vintage movie posters flanked a wide fireplace on an exposed brick wall. Overstuffed seating was arranged around a large entertainment center with a plasma television. A first-aid kit lay open on the coffee table, and Vivian noted a lump protruding near his shoulder blades that she suspected Blu had bandaged under his shirt.

After moving a blue chenille blanket out of the way so his guests could sit, Blu flopped onto the armchair, elbows on his knees. The others took seats around the coffee table.

"Tell me what's going on." Blu's large, brown eyes reflected such sensitivity, Vivian wondered how she'd ever mistaken the Balance for this deep-feeling vampire.

"First," Michael said, "I want to make sure all of our facts are straight. Is it true the Tribe killed your entire family but you?"

Blu nodded somberly. "All the vampires, and a few of our human friends, too. Everyone there last night. Brady—he got away. He wasn't here when it happened."

Michael then divulged their tale, starting from when they left Savannah and concluding at their exit from Brickskeller. Blu took it all in without interrupting.

"Do you think you need me?" he asked when Michael finished.

"I don't think it's a coincidence the Balance impersonated you and gave us your address," Vivian said.

"Yes, but…" he dropped his head a moment as he rested his hands on his thighs. "Whose side do you think the Balance is trying to favor by suggesting that I come with? I'm injured. I'll heal quick enough, but do you think you'd be better off without me?"

"No," Michael said. "Look at it this way: Charles is heading to South Carolina to get Sana to improve his chances at affecting the balance of good and evil in favor of evil. He's killed off hundreds, maybe thousands, of vampires who've refused to join the Tribe. If the Balance sent us to you, it's likely to improve the odds for good."

"I hope you're right," Blu said. "I hope y'all are right," Blu said quietly. "I don't know what help I'm gonna be, but if the Balance said I'm part of this, then I'm in."

He looked at his house as if surveying it for the last time. "We made it through the last war, alright. And while this one doesn't seem to be going in my favor, at least I'm still alive. I hope my luck holds out." He rose. "Let me get my bag and turn stuff off, OK? Brady left town yesterday morning and…" his eyes looked down as he recalled the last night's unpleasantness. "Well, he hates it when I waste electricity. At least he made it out alive. I'll be right back."

Michael and Vivian nodded, and Blu headed upstairs.

Michael asked, "What's wrong?"

"He knows something, Michael," she said. "Maybe he can't touch the Source the way I can, but he knows something bad might be about to happen to him, or someone close to us."

"Are you sure?"

"I don't feel it. He's the one who senses it, and I sense it through him."

"Harmony?" Michael asked.

Crystal interrupted, her mouth a flat line. "Don't bother. She won't say, even if she knows."

"I can at least say that I don't know this time," Harmony said. "But I'm also not free to speculate."

Michael's mouth turned down at the corners. He leaned forward and put his elbows on his knees. Turning to Vivian, he said, "Do you think he's—"

"Lightning fast and every bit as brilliant," Blu said, appearing at the landing with an olive-green overnight bag slung over one shoulder. He'd thrown on a black cap stitched with interlocked, rainbow-colored rings. "To be fair, I was mostly packed already. Let's roll."

He paused near the door, taking one last look around. "This place was ours, you know? Me and Brady. Doesn't feel like home anymore."

Vivian waited to see if Michael would finish his sentence. He didn't. He rose and then offered his hand to Vivian to help her stand. As she reached her full height, Vivian wavered on her feet, and she gripped Michael's hand tightly. Harmony and Crystal rose as well.

"Are you alright?" he asked.

Her free hand left her temple and motioned for quiet. Crystal and Harmony exchanged a fleeting, confused look. Vivian winced, and Michael cringed as her hand—centuries stronger than his—crushed his fingers. He swallowed a yelp.

Vivian swallowed. Her lips tight, she managed the word, "Lukas."

Michael forgot the pain in his hand. "Lukas? What about him?"

Vivian's eyes opened. Noting the contorted shape she'd forced his hand into, she loosened her grip. "I don't know. I think—I think he tried to reach me? It didn't come through well."

"What did you get?" Harmony asked. "Any impressions?"

Vivian shook her head, frustrated. "A plane. Megan. Fear. Pain. He's—he's hurting."

"We knew most of that," Crystal said. "It's why I can't cleave us to him—you said he's on the move."

Saddened, Vivian put her head in her hands. "I'm sorry, Michael. I wish there was more. It's gone."

He wished that, too, but knew it wasn't the time to say it. He rubbed the back of her neck and drew her close, not sure who needed more consoling. "It's alright," he said. "It's going to be alright."

Chapter Forty-two

Charles and David descended the short staircase of the Learjet into the humid South Carolina air. Lukas and Megan followed, their legs for the moment untied, trailed by an attentive Angelo. The receiving airport had spared no expense: Charles and his crew stepped onto a crimson carpet. A limousine had approached as they touched ground, and now the driver all but leaped from the driver's seat to reach their side.

"Good evening, Mr. Dunning," the eager attendant said. "Welcome to Columbia." He ran a hand through close-cropped brown hair fixed in place with too much gel. "Your limousine is right this way."

"Give us a moment, please, if you will," Charles said. The young man bobbed his head and hastened back to his automobile, where he waited by the rear passenger-side door.

Charles turned to David. "Do you think you and your boy can manage carrying our captives in flight?"

"What if they fight?"

"They'll be too afraid of falling to try."

"You mean they can't—?"

"They haven't tried, and I don't expect they will once we're airborne. An aerial escape is too risky. On the ground, however, they might get scrappy if given a chance, and I'd hate for you to lose your… mate. It's better to carry them right now, for speed. Can he do it?"

David eyed Angelo, vigilantly guarding Lukas and Megan from a few steps away. "He can do it," he said. "I'll give him the girl."

"Very good."

"What about the limo driver?" David asked.

Charles shrugged. "Are you hungry?"

"Starved," David said with a laugh.

"Problem solved," Charles said with a snap of his fingers. He paused, his senses attuning to his dark intuition. Although his plans were going well so far, something was amiss. The Maleficence requested his undivided attention. It had knowledge to share immediately.

"Excuse me, David," Charles said. "I need a moment."

"Mind if I make a phone call?"

"As you wish. But watch them."

Charles turned his back on his protégé and paused. Clearing his mind of any distracting thoughts, sounds, or visual input, he focused on the virulence that steered his heart. Cautious, unwilling to surrender his body, he opened his mind to the Maleficence.

As the dark power surged in him, an acrimonious smile touched his lips. When he learned what the Maleficence intended to share, the smile flickered, then faded.

Lukas. Lukas is... contacting Vivian! He strained to hear the context of the conversation, if only Lukas' portion, without success. The Source protected him through Vivian. Still, it didn't take a great leap of logic to guess.

Charles severed the link to his dark power and pivoted on his heel.

"Mr. Graves!" he barked. Lukas jumped as if goosed, his eyes wide in alarm. "Care to share your thoughts with the rest of us?"

Terror crossed Lukas' face. His eyes bugged as his body instinctively inched toward Megan's.

"Lukas," Charles crooned with a single arched brow, "you've been speaking to Vivian, haven't you?" He pressed his fingers together, a spider-like motion he'd picked up from Jude over the centuries.

Lukas kept a poker face as he watched the way Charles pressed his fingertips together, and his Adam's apple bobbed in his throat, but he didn't speak in his defense. Charles had caught him off guard.

He's frightened. Good, Charles thought. *But I can't kill Lukas. He's my greatest bargaining chip, and the one most closely linked to Cartaphilus. Still, it wouldn't hurt to carry one less prisoner.*

A smug grin turned up the corner of Angelo's lips as he followed Charles' eyes like a wolf awaiting a signal from the pack leader to take out the weakest deer in a herd. Lukas edged closer to Megan, who cowered behind him, fear radiating from her in waves. She crawled backward, stumbled on her wounded ankle, and grabbed Lukas' arm for support. Her fear pheromones carried in the sultry air, tickling the Maleficence in Charles like an aphrodisiac. She'd scraped herself in her fall, and the scent of blood triggered his hunger.

"Kill her," Charles snapped.

"No!" Lukas cried. He spun around and scooped Megan in his arms as enormous, sleek brown wings burst through his t-shirt. Although his face revealed his surprise, his body reacted as if he'd done it a thousand times. He crouched for take-off as David and Angelo reached him. Each leapt on a wing and kept him earthbound.

With his hatchet men gripping Lukas' wings, Charles wrenched Megan from Lukas' grip with a yank to her arm that issued a *pop* from her shoulder socket. Megan screamed in agony.

Lukas cried out, yanked and pulled frantically for release, and gasped in horror as Charles lunged for Megan's throat before she had a moment to fight back. His wings retracted without warning, leaving David and Angelo grasping at air as Lukas lunged at Charles, arms outstretched for battle.

Charles foresaw Lukas' plan. He dropped Megan's lifeless body and slugged him full in the face. As Lukas stumbled backward toward David's cronies, Megan's mouth worked, releasing wet gasps and the heaving sounds of desperation.

Angelo and David each gripped an arm, trapping Lukas again as Charles heaved a foot at Megan with the intensity of an NFL kicker. She let out a forceful huff of breath and dropped to the tarmac with a weak groan, her strength gone.

Angelo turned to Charles, eyeing Lukas with hope and hunger.

"Not him," Charles said. Angelo complied, but it didn't stop him from taking a swing at Lukas' face with his free hand. The blow hit Lukas on the cheekbone, the heavy ring on Angelo's finger drawing blood from Lukas' cheekbone. David added a sharp blow to Lukas' groin, sending him crumpling to the carpet, arms wrapped tight around his ribs. The blood from his cheek flowed and blended with the crimson fibers, and he reached for Megan as he crept in her direction, desperate to help her. David and Angelo gave each other a wolfish grin over Lukas' prone body before pummeling him with blows to his stomach, kidney, and head, determined to immobilize him. He was a vampire. He wouldn't die. But he could suffer immensely.

Charles leaned down and gripped Megan by the hair. She screamed as he yanked her to her feet.

"Please," she whispered with tears in her eyes. Her arms flailed weakly in front of her, seeking a body part to beat. Charles easily held her at a distance. Blood streamed from the gaping wound on her neck.

"Please don't. Please don't."

Lukas struggled for her, crawled in her direction with his broken body, agony shooting through every joint and muscle. She was twenty feet away. He'd never reach her in time.

"Megan!"

Charles yanked her toward him and tore out what remained of her throat. The light faded from her eyes as David and Angelo joined Charles in a feast of Megan's blood.

Chapter Forty-three

Perry believed Mexico was their best bet, and Maysun pushed for Canada. Sana was ambivalent about their destination. Every strategy tossed around only seemed as if it postponed her unavoidable capture by Charles Dunning, she said. Perry continued on Highway 20 west without a destination to head for, hoping they'd reach a resolution soon. In the meantime, they kept moving.

A silence descended over the Dodge until they crossed the South Carolina border into Georgia. Nobody seemed to want to be the first to chat. Conversation came in fits and stops, always nonconfrontational and simple. After they'd passed through Augusta, Perry, unable to stand the quiet any longer, broke the stillness.

"So, Maysun, tell us where you've been, and what brought you into Sana's life now."

"You mean now that the world's going straight to hell?"

Perry met Maysun's gaze in the rearview. Her expression revealed little. "Yeah, that."

Over the next three hours, Sana and Maysun spoke more frankly to one another than Perry suspected they had to anyone. Maysun explained her work as the Balance, about Joseph Cartaphilus, the *Shévet ha Dam*, and Sana's father, Eoghan. She described how Charles probably now knew about Sana, and how, thanks to David, he learned about where she was. She ended her story with her suspicion that Charles would want to find out how she might be turned into a weapon to turn the world in his favor.

"That's ridiculous," Sana said. "I'm nobody."

"That's not true," Maysun said.

"Not true at all," Perry murmured. Sana didn't show any sign she'd heard him.

Sana told Maysun about the voices she'd heard for so long, her nightmares, Thom's death, and how she'd learned that what she'd thought was schizophrenia was much worse. She ended with the story of how Perry had helped her break free.

The talk grew easy as the women discovered how similar they were. Perry wondered if they noticed how their mannerisms echoed one another, the way they each pushed their hair back behind their neck with the same smooth motion, or that their eyes averted contact as they recalled the sadder memories. Even their laughs matched—a womanly sound, pleasant, not quite a chuckle.

Their conversation continued with hardly a break until mid-afternoon. Only the pit stop Sana demanded because she needed a bathroom gave them a moment's rest from their flight westward. When they neared Birmingham, Sana asked if they could pause for a moment and eat.

"Although I guess you two don't need to," she laughed.

"Food is good," Perry said. "And no, it might not be the same, but it's still a good idea. We wouldn't want Maysun to lose her strength."

They walked together to the truck stop, and Maysun laid a hand on Perry's arm.

"Sana, why don't you go ahead while we…?" Maysun nodded toward a place where a trucker slept upright in his rig. Perry saw him so clearly, he could read the Peterbilt logo on his hat, saw his arms crossed on his ample stomach, the red and white pattern of his flannel shirt.

"But why?" Sana said.

Or was that wishful thinking—that she didn't want to be away from him, even for a moment? He wanted to tell Maysun he'd be OK with no sustenance, go ahead, I'll join you next time, but his strength was waning, and today was not a day to be caught with old blood in his veins. How long before he risked a burn, or worse? The sunlight on his skin felt hot as they stood outside the door and waited.

"Maysun's right," he said. "Oh, and don't use your debit card. Here…" He took out his wallet and handed Sana money. "We'll be in shortly."

He knew she wanted to argue. A word or two formed at her mouth. She took a breath to utter them, but didn't.

"You have to eat too, huh?" she asked, noting people wending their way through the door behind her.

"We'll be careful. I promise," Perry said, adding an emphasis to the final syllables he hoped she recognized. With her eyes, she measured the distance from where they stood to the truck and back before heading inside.

He and Maysun stepped away from the doorway. "You see him?" Maysun asked.

"I see him."

"What are your gifts?"

The question caught him off guard. "Oh, uh… telepathy. Flight. Uh…"

"Mist?"

"Come again?"

"Mist," she said. "Can you evaporate? Become one?"

"Uh… no. I mean, I've never tried."

"It'll look less suspicious if you're walking alone. I'll meet you there." And she was gone.

Impressive. He wondered if he had that talent. Maysun might be older than he, but he had Jude's blood in his veins. He considered trying it.

A carload of vacationers, judging from the suitcases strapped to the roof of their car, pulled in a few yards away.

Maybe later. He noted Maysun at the semi where she had pulled open the passenger's side door. The driver didn't stir. He picked up his gait, eager to feed.

Maysun had already sunk her teeth into the vulnerable skin at the man's neck as Perry eased the door nearest their victim open. The heady smell of blood filled the cabin, and Perry closed his eyes, savoring it.

Maysun detached herself.

"Be careful," she warned him. "Don't take too much."

That's right, I don't have to kill him! His delight at denying himself the Death Rush, what had become such a central part of his life, surprised him. This one would live. He didn't have to worry about what David and Angelo thought anymore.

"No problem." He leaned in.

Moments later, after lying the man down for the rest of his nap, they walked together to the restaurant where Sana waited. The few sips of stolen blood left Perry barely revived, but it was a gratifying sort of deprivation. The man lived.

The noises of the hash-slinging joint resonated in Perry's refueled system. The fluorescent lights made him wince, and the smells, although appetizing, made him feel as if he'd thrown dessert and drinks on top of a meal. He spotted Sana at a red vinyl booth near the kitchen and felt like dancing all the way to her.

Maysun slid in next to her daughter, leaving Perry on the opposite side of the booth.

Sana had ordered an enormous plate of smothered hash browns and sausage with a side of toast and orange juice and a cup of coffee. "I'm so hungry, and I couldn't decide," she gushed.

"That's alright," Perry said. "Eat all you want. That's why we're here. If you don't finish, we can take the rest to go."

Sana looked up and smiled. She leaned in and gently wiped a drop of blood from Perry's lip. "Missed some," she said. Her cheeks were bright, and Perry smelled the blood in them.

Chapter Forty-four

Consciousness came slowly, like surfacing from a chloroform stupor. As Lukas stirred, his limb and head pain returned with a throbbing, mind-splitting fury. The physical suffering was bearable. The agony that rendered him lifeless came from the way his mind replayed the light going out of Megan's eyes as he laid there, physically incapable of saving her. How the gaping crimson wound under Charles' mouth poured.

It might not be over. She's a vampire. She can regenerate. Jude brought Gina back after tearing her throat out and nearly killing her. Megan is their way of keeping me prisoner, isn't it? So they can use her against me? They can't kill her yet.

A spark of hope flickered, and he lifted his head from the hard, red carpet, still damp with blood. Before him, Charles hoisted the limp body of the limousine driver into the front seat of his car. He removed a plastic-wrapped hanger from the back with a new black suit draped on it. After locking the vehicle, he circled toward the jet with a severe expression on his horribly handsome face.

Lukas turned over slowly, wincing in pain with every movement, and craned his head in the other direction. Megan's empty eyes stared skyward. Angelo's back was to him as he drank from Megan's left jugular. David—

Lukas felt like he'd fallen into a cavern he might never crawl out of. David held her heart in his hands. Angelo coughed as Megan's body devolved from an undead shade of human pink to gray and turned to ash in his mouth.

"No! No, no, no…" Lukas crawled a step and collapsed as unbearable pain shot through him from groin to sternum. Bile seared his throat as his stomach struggled to vomit. With nothing to regurgitate, the result was a trail of pink spittle and burning stomach acid that dripped from his mouth.

She's ash. Ash! There's no bringing her back now. No bringing her back!

Misery racked his mind and body, and he curled into a ball and sobbed in agony. Megan was gone. His girlfriend, his progeny, his everything, turned to ash like so much firewood. There was no hope he'd ever see her face laughing again, ever hear her sweet voice, or see her look at him with desire. He'd never hold her again, never kiss her. Never.

Damn them! Damn Charles! Damn the Shévet ha Dam and every vampire in the fucking thing. I hate them! I wish they were dead, every one of them! I'd tear every one of them apart with my hands if I could. I'd kill them!

His lungs heaved with deep, burning breaths that twinged the sharp pains in his ribs as he ground his teeth in anger. He longed to be anywhere other than where he was, any place that might take him away from Charles and his horrible underlings that prevented him from saving her and who'd feasted on her body. He longed for death that, for all he knew, was years—centuries—an eternity away. Centuries he'd spend without Megan. Second generation from Jude Shepherd that he was, he stood a chance to live an eternity away from the person who had made death most bearable.

His vision blurred behind a pink-tinged veil of bloody tears. *I can't do this. I can't... God, please, get me away from them. Please. I beg you.*

A peculiar tingling sensation came over his body, his nerves shot through with white energy, his mind went blank, and then he was gone.

David lifted his gaze from the heart in his hand, now a misshapen oval of ash. Lukas had vanished.

He blinked, dropped the gray flakes, and rubbed his palm on his Levi's. He leaned to the side to view the carpet from a different angle— a ridiculous notion, considering the chap he sought had to be over six and a half feet tall. There was no way hiding behind Angelo was an option. As he suspected, there was no one there.

Charles reemerged from the jet dressed in a clean suit. He stopped at the top of the stairs, noted their captive's absence, and hustled to the place where Lukas had lain as if expecting to find a trail of footprints leading to Lukas' position. Charles rushing anywhere would've been amusing under any other circumstances, the man was a study in poise. As it stood, David froze in fear.

He's going to blame me. He'll think it's my fault.

Charles stared at the empty spot, incredulous.

"What happened?" Charles barked. Angelo stopped coughing long enough to turn to David, then Charles. He saw Lukas had vanished and came to a standstill.

"I— sir, I haven't the faintest," David stuttered, his hands gesturing wildly. "He can't have gone far. We worked him over good and proper—you saw the state he was in."

Charles took this in. True, Lukas had appeared almost dead when they walked away from his bleeding body. So how had he disappeared?

"He's inherited Joseph's ability to evaporate," Charles said.

"He can do that?" David said. *How can he do that? None of us can bloody do that!*

Charles motioned to the vacant carpet where Lukas had lain. "Obviously, he can. Unless you can come up with a better explanation."

David had to admit, no, he couldn't. "So what's the next move, then?"

"He won't reappear and fight—he's too much of a coward. We'll go to Sana's apartment and remove her before Vivian and Michael arrive."

David flinched. This was going to be painful. "Right. Small wrinkle, sir."

Charles glared.

"I rang him while you were handling things—before all this," he gestured vaguely at Angelo, the limo, and Megan. "He said he was fine, but it didn't sound right."

"Why is that?"

David hesitated. "Sounded like he was in a car."

Charles closed his eyes and clenched his jaw. He rubbed at his forehead with his fingers, massaging the worried lines. David sensed Dunning's tension. It not only stiffened his body, it surrounded him like a live shadow ready to attack. David braced himself—for what, he wasn't sure.

Charles let out a slow breath. "Can you find him with telepathy?"

David swallowed. "It's possible. I sired him." He didn't want to tell Charles about his trouble sorting through Perry's mind of late. The boy, though his child, had been impervious as soon as David's blood was diluted with new.

"Find him." Charles stalked off to his jet, leaving David shaking on the tarmac.

Chapter Forty-five

"Try Megan," Blu said gently.

Vivian nodded. Her pretty features scrunched in frustration. After a second, she huffed and banged her fist on her crossed legs. "Nothing. Nothing—it's like—"

"We lost them?" Michael asked. His heart twisted in a crippling vise at the thought of his son dead, but Vivian shook her head and the vice loosened.

"They're not gone, exactly, but… they're unreachable. Like can't even touch them."

No one but Vivian sat; they all paced Blu's living area. Every so often, the sound of a loud pedestrian or startling noise caught someone's attention, and wide eyes shot to the corners of the flat. That the *Shévet ha Dam* had tracked down Blu's D.C. family and had killed nearly everyone in it left them jumpy and paranoid. Michael knew everyone longed to leave, but until Vivian or Harmony had a fix on a location, travel was moot. There was no point in hurrying off for the sake of travel. Poor Crystal, brave as she tried to act, was wearing out with every trek.

"Want me to give it a try?" Blu said. "Maybe he's shut you out on purpose. Trying to protect you."

"Please," Vivian said. "You may be right. There's a chance he's putting up a wall to protect us. He doesn't know we're with you. It's worth a shot."

"Take a break," Blu said, tapping her on the knee and sitting next to her place on the couch. "There are drinks in the fridge. Grab a cool one and try to relax."

Vivian nodded and headed to the kitchen with weary steps. Michael followed while Crystal and Harmony continued pacing next to the coffee table as quietly as possible so as not to disturb Blu.

In Blu's kitchen, Vivian helped herself to a can of soda and pressed it to her wrists, her forehead. She leaned against the sunny yellow countertop heavily.

Michael leaned against the opposite counter, crossed his legs at the ankles, and said, "I have no clue why you accommodate me the way you do."

Vivian blinked and snapped back to the present as she tore her eyes from the spot on the wall where she'd been staring. The framed print of an artistically rendered, icy pitcher of lemonade had not been what she was paying attention to.

"What in God's green earth do you mean?"

"I mean, out of all of us—me, you, Lukas, Harmony, Crystal, Megan, Blu—I'm the one with the least to offer. Luke and Megan came straight from Cartaphilus through Gina. There's no telling what all they'll be able to do once they put their minds to it. Crystal's been damn useful from the second we met her. Harmony told us about the 'other' Blu, and hell, she's like having another powerhouse traveling with us. Blu is over five hundred years old. He can fly. He can withstand the sun way better than I can. I'm barely twenty undead years and generations removed from anyone remotely useful."

"Most of our family hasn't had much reason to use their supernatural power."

"Until now." The thought that Lukas harbored potential power that neared that of Charles Dunning—before his possession of the Maleficence—had been what kept Michael hopeful that his son had a chance at surviving. As the hours ticked by without a word, his optimism dwindled. "You and Blu, Crystal and Harmony, you're useful in this fight. You have gifts. You're like a superwoman, Vivian, and you have an enormous strength of spirit because you can tap into the Source. I'm— I'm pretty much useless."

Vivian chewed her lip thoughtfully. "I'm not sure how to tell you this, Michael—"

"Then *say* it."

"Let me start by saying that I'm not trying to change the subject or take away from what you've said. We can get back to that. But I'm afraid there's another reason I'm having trouble reaching Lukas. He didn't have what I had when he inherited Joseph's blood. The Source didn't protect him. Gina, either, and that's why Jude could corrupt her. Lukas wasn't an immediate heir, and that he didn't die when exposed to the Source is a good sign, but I think he may have inherited a touch of the Maleficence as well."

The words hit him like an arrow in the chest taking his breath away. "No! No way."

"Michael, it's true. Listen to me. There's a part of him I can't touch. When I contact you or Blu or Megan, it was like putting my hand in a stream; I could flow through you. Lukas has a spot, a small spot, that's like a rock. I can't penetrate it. I doubt he's aware of it, but it worries me."

"Why didn't you tell me this before?"

"Because I don't know for sure what it is!"

"And the Source can't break through?"

Vivian shook her head. "I've worked with him on it a couple of times. Nothing deep. I asked him if I could heal any lasting psychological damage from his experience with Jude. Being Lukas, he laughed and said sure. After the second time, though, I couldn't come up with another excuse to try. He's over the incident as much as anyone can be and still be somewhat healthy. I didn't want to worry him, and I didn't see any reason for me to worry or make him second-guess himself. He's never displayed outward signs of any evil. He's still Lukas. Have you noticed anything different about him?"

Michael had to admit he didn't.

"Still," Crystal said, emerging from the living room, "if the Source can't reach it—can't get through—then it's gotta be the Male-Mali-- whatever. The Darkness, right?"

Michael put his hand to his face. *What might be too hard for the Source to break through? A memory, maybe? The memory of his mother's death? He was only two.*

Vivian slammed a palm onto the counter as her face lit up with an expression of eureka. Her ears perked up as if listening, her eyes seeing beyond Blu's kitchen, her face happier than he'd seen it since saving the lives of those in Savannah.

"What the—?" Crystal exclaimed, and then cut herself short as if afraid to interrupt whatever epiphany Vivian was experiencing. The woman practically glowed with relief.

"Sorry," Vivian said to Crystal. She flew past her and Michael and burst into the living room. Crystal and Michael followed, eager to hear what Vivian had grasped.

"Blu, you can stop now."

"Thank the goddess," Blu sighed, letting his weight fall back into the couch. He caught sight of Vivian's beaming face and gave a wry smile. "Girl, if you weren't you, I'd tell you you look clean outta your mind."

"If I weren't me, you'd still be struggling."

"Mm-hmm." He grinned. "What'd you see, hon?"

Instead of answering, Vivian marched to Crystal and set her hands on top of the smaller girl's head. The energy level in the room peaked in less than a heartbeat, and everyone broke out in gooseflesh. The air sparkled with universal intensity, sending tiny particles of what appeared to be ball lightning floating like fairy lights on a slow summer breeze.

Crystal gasped, puffed herself up as if bracing for a race, and drew a powerful, shimmering line. Vivian widened it, allowing autumn air full of traffic sounds into Blu's home.

"He's here!" Vivian exclaimed. "I found Lukas!"

Hurriedly, they all stepped through. They emerged at the side of a freeway in a triangle of highway ramps and the highway itself.

"Look around!" Vivian shouted over the rush of traffic. "Lukas is nearby!"

After long moments of looking and several passes up and down the ramp, a patch of what might have been blond hair caught Michael's eye. "What's that?" he asked, pointing.

The group waded through thigh-high weeds to a spot in the center. Amid the wildflowers sat Lukas, hunched and weeping. Elbows on his thick knees, hair tousled, his eyes swollen and red, head bowed, he epitomized anguish. The back of his shirt was torn from shoulder blade to hem, the tears placed as if two wings had sprouted from his back. *Why not? If he has grown wings, should that surprise me?*

"Lukas?" Michael murmured.

His son looked up. Bloodshot blue eyes in a face reduced to childlike helplessness pleaded with his father to make the wrong right again. Michael's heart broke. With Lukas' adulthood, his ability to ease pain with a simple kiss or kind word had vanished.

Blu's said, "Where's Meg—?"

Out of the corner of his eye, Michael saw Vivian minutely shaking her head. Gone was the joy she'd exhibited when she'd pinpointed Lukas; tears now shone in her eyes as well. Blu gasped as Michael understood what had caused his son so much suffering.

Megan too? When will this stop? Must I lose everyone I love?

Now crying as well, Michael leaned down and put his arm under Lukas' and strained to lift him. Blu dropped to the opposite side and lifted as well. Together, they carried Michael's son to the wide berth at the edge of the road where they'd emerged into this world of Lukas' pain.

Lukas never stopped sobbing.

Chapter Forty-six

David swore. Not even with both of his feet on the foyer tile, surrounded by the walls of Sana's home, could he pick a bead up on Perry's trail. Not that he was surprised. He'd never had much reason to read Perry's mind; the boy followed orders verbatim and showed no sign of holding secrets close to his chest.

"Still no luck?" Charles asked, his face barely masking his irritation. David shook his head.

"I want to say he's close but…" David said, throwing his hands up. "I've no idea how—or why—he's scarpered. It's not like him to defy orders. Perry's never had the backbone to pull a stunt like this, let alone the power to hide from me."

"The Balance must have interfered," Charles said.

"I don't get it. That Kip bloke led us straight to you."

Charles contemplated Lukas' sudden disappearance, and now this unfortunate twist in his plans. "I can't assume what that Kip character had in mind. You say he knew me, but I don't recall ever meeting the man." David's chiseled expression dropped at Charles' words.

Charles frowned. What was MacConin playing at by setting him after Sana? If he'd found her, would she help the Maleficence—or put the world in Balance? Perhaps tilting against him entirely?

"It's probably a trap," he said. "The Balance must have a strategy in mind. My Tribe must have killed hundreds of those penny-ante blood suckers by now, so the Balance is planning to level the odds."

David didn't have a solution. He put his hands in the pocket of his jeans and began pacing, the soft soles of his sneakers soundless in the tile foyer.

Charles cursed under his breath. *I kill off hundreds of vampires, and now, the Balance wants to kill me, or take away the advantage I'd gain with Sana. I must be more cautious. If I run into this too hastily, it might cost me my life*. He stopped before the window in the entryway and stared out over the manicured lawn to the street beyond.

"Mr. Dunning," Angelo said, "What do we do next?"

Charles felt his glare chilling Angelo, and the small satisfaction turned his mouth up into a smile. "We meet a few of my associates at my nearby cabin and see if they can't help. I've sent out my dogs to challenge those who don't want to join the Tribe. Let's see which ones come."

Lukas sat next to Michael by the side of the road, his body hunched over and motionless, his eyes still. Vivian's heart ached for him. Lukas and Megan had held a love that went oceans deeper than that which typically linked sire and progeny. *If it doesn't match what I feel for Michael, it has to be close.*

Harmony and Crystal stood by, neither of them sure where to look, but both trying to respect Lukas' grief. Crystal's hands crossed over her chest as sympathetic tears glistened in her eyes. Harmony placed a hand on her sister's shoulder, and Crystal wrapped her hands around Harmony's waist before resting her head on her shoulder. Vivian wondered about the emotion in that embrace. What was it like to hold a person whose display of sentiment was more out of habit than genuine emotion?

Michael rested a hand on his son's shoulder that went unacknowledged. For a moment, Vivian wondered what life without Michael might be like. The idea made her feel the way Lukas looked.

She stretched a hand toward Lukas. "I can try to heal—"

"No!" Lukas snapped, his voice choking on the word as he knocked her hand away. "I deserve this. It was because I tried to contact you that Charles made his move. This is my fault. I didn't do enough—didn't fight like... like... I should've tried harder! It's my—"

"If you say 'fault' again, Lukas, I swear I'm going to knock you out. I don't care how old, how big, or whose descendant you are," Michael snapped. Lukas raised his head, startled, as his father continued. "I have not one doubt, not one iota of reservation, not one scrap of uncertainty, that you did everything in your power to save her."

"More than I thought I could," Lukas admitted after a beat. His eyes turned back down, and he finally blinked.

"What do you mean?"

"I can fly," Lukas admitted, sounding ashamed. "At least, I sprouted wings. I never made it off the ground."

Wonder covered Michael's face. *And why not?* Vivian thought. *This man is used to leading and teaching his family. He was the strong one. Now, the few members of that family still alive overmatch him.*

The awkwardness vanished the moment Blu spoke. "Not to rush anyone, but aren't we in a hurry?"

Lukas shook his head. "Last I knew, Charles was headed to Piper, South Carolina." A scoff escaped. "But I don't think that turned out."

"Are you sure?" Blu asked.

Lukas looked away. "Pretty sure. It's weird, but since…" his mouth flapped a moment, "since they took Megan, it's like… like I have an idea…" His voice trailed off, and his eyes fell to the long grass at his feet. "Probably nothing."

"'Probably nothing,' huh?" Crystal said, arms crossed. "Yeah, that sounds totally normal. So what now"

"Yeah, why don't we ask the Source," Lukas muttered, bitterness sharpening his voice.

Vivian understood why he sounded so resentful. It had to be difficult to believe the power that guided their lives had directed him and Megan into Charles' hands.

"Lukas?" Vivian said.

Lukas looked up, eyes blazing, his set features holding back a torrent of anger and frustration.

"We're likely about to be in another war," she said, keeping her voice calm. "That means there will be battles. Sometimes we win, but we will lose battles as well. Today, we lost a horrible one."

"She wasn't supposed to die!"

"Lukas, Megan was a tough woman who would have laid her life down to save you or any of the rest of us without hesitation. And maybe that's what she did. Maybe she died because the Universe needs you to live."

"That doesn't fucking help!"

"It's the truth. We've seen more than any human out there how the world works. Charles won't be happy until he's overridden it with evil. We need to stop him, to end the *Shévet ha Dam*, if it's in our power. It's up to us."

Lukas looked away, his jaw jutting out and clenched. Vivian wished she had more insightful conversation, but she'd reached the end of her consoling platitudes.

"So what's the move?" Blu asked. "We heading back to Savannah to find Bully, or going after Sana?"

"Unless Harmony has gotten guidance, I'll look into the Source," Vivian said, "but not here. The energy isn't conducive, and there's too much of a chance we'll be spotted by a good Samaritan who'll stop to see if we need help."

"Oh sure, tons of good Samaritans out here these days," Lukas said, voice hostile.

"Harmony?"

She shook her head. "No guidance yet. Sorry."

"Where to?" Crystal asked, stretching a finger.

Vivian shook her head. "There's a state park near here," she said. "Let's go there. Save your energy."

Everyone nodded, but Lukas refused to meet her eye.

Chapter Forty-seven

Around Eoghan, the sounds of Ritchie Valens, Elvis, and Chubby Checker permeated the greasy air of the chrome-and-checkerboard diner. Before him sat a half-eaten plate full of hash browns covered in whatever the kitchen offered—a craving he'd developed as he mentally tracked his daughter on her journey.

Most recently, he'd eavesdropped on Charles Dunning's plan through the mind of Angelo Vargas—easy enough to do. The younger vampire was eager, open, and nearly soulless. Sana had gotten away, but now Charles suspected she was a trap laid for him by the Balance. Charles' shift in thinking wasn't what Eoghan had expected.

He'd been helpless to intervene in the sweeping number of vampire deaths in the eastern part of the country. To do so would have drawn Charles' attention from Sana. Now, Charles had an alternative plan to capture her, which did not involve himself so intimately. He still hadn't called off the Tribe; the number of vampires resisting the Maleficence was diminishing swiftly.

Eoghan reclined as much as the booth allowed and frowned. As with all probabilities, he'd contrived a contingency plan. Several, in fact. A minimum of two scenarios for each player; one, for if events went as he steered them, at least one other to compensate if they diverted from the original plan. Other contingencies had blueprints buried deep in his mental archive of tactics. His head swam with prospects, and other complications and deviations grew with each new possibility. Charles knew Kip MacConin wasn't who he'd said he was. Changing his appearance… yes, he could do that. But the problem was that it would take at least two dozen unfamiliar faces to make the tables turn, all within the space of the next twelve hours.

He thought of the young woman who'd traveled with Vivian and Michael to D.C. Her empty expression had stuck with him all afternoon, mostly because it mirrored the hollowness he carried inside.

"You alright, hon?"

Eoghan opened his eyes as a server in a rumpled uniform strolled to his table. Her hips were pointy, her neck long and thin, but she wore what meat she had on her bones well and topped it off with a light daubing of make-up that barely escaped looking overdone. She put her pad in the pocket of her apron and leaned in. The name tag inches from his face read *Lily Belle*. "You want some water or sweet tea, sugar? You look a touch parched."

Eoghan declined.

"You need anything, just let me know," she said with a wrinkle of her nose, her voice earnest and friendly. She beamed at him. "You know, I love listening to you Irish people talk."

"Thank you," he said, not bothering to correct her, "I will."

No one had said that simplicity was part of his job description. Maysun may not have told him every nuance of the work, but she knew he'd learn quickly. Understanding came with the power he'd accepted, along with a blankness where his heart used to be.

Foreseeing what lay ahead, he was grateful for that inability to feel. It made it simpler to focus on his job than on the effects it'd have on those he'd lived alongside what seemed like a lifetime ago.

He would need privacy if he was going to do what the Universe called of him next. Privacy and proximity. He dug into his wallet, paid the server with a generous tip, and headed out of the diner.

He focused. A Native American name. A copse of oak trees.

He blinked, and a forest painted by in autumn colors at dusk surrounded him.

A primitive log and white-on-brown painted sign welcomed them to Pocahontas State Park. Michael paid the requisite entrance fees, tossing in a tube of sunblock while he was at it. Vivian noted the reddish tint to his skin; he was acquiring a sunburn. As the weakest one of their group, he needed to feed more often. It'd been too long. Why hadn't he spoken sooner?

They bought an armful of firewood from a seller at a picnic table near the gate and hiked a while down the road with their arms full of firewood. As they marched, Harmony and Crystal munched fast food burgers and fries out of a paper sack. Vivian let her heart guide them, and they found a path.

"Anybody up for a walk into the woods?" Michael asked, breaking the sunblock out and slathering it onto any exposed areas.

Blu looked at his clothes—which looked as if they hadn't seen a drop of sweat before today—and arched his eyebrows. "I'll go," Blu drawled. "But if one mosquito so much as looks at me funny, I'm breaking into a cabin with air-conditioning and satin sheets."

"I doubt we'll need that long," Vivian assured him.

They trekked only far enough to find an isolated campsite. Michael set to work on striking a fire in the steel fire ring provided by the campground, lighting a cigarette for himself while he was at it—a sure sign of his stress, as he had no physical addiction. Harmony and Crystal shared a log bench upwind from Michael's smoke and huddled together. Michael and Blu occupied the other nearby seat. Lukas had all but turned from the group, his depression a stifling, physical presence muzzling conversation.

"Blu, would you call Doyle, please?" Vivian asked. "I'd like to find out what he's up to."

Blu nodded, and Vivian rattled off the number. As he dialed, Vivian excused herself from the group and walked through a wooded area ankle-deep in piles of crunchy orange leaves, until she found a small clearing a few yards away. Sitting cross-legged on a patch of dry foliage, she tilted her head back and willed her body to embrace a fuller portion of the Source. It came. Her body prickled with energy. Her breath came quicker, now emitting from her lungs in puffs of warmed air. She felt alive. Human, but better, stronger, eternal.

Good. Now let's see what Sana is up to.

She found her face pointed in a direction, one she sensed led to Sana, but how far did they have to go? She strained to see a face, hear a voice, sense a distance, or gather thoughts. Pictures and impressions swam before her eyes, but the images blurred. It was not enough.

Reluctantly, she let go of the Source and joined her family at the campsite, where Michael was still trying to get his pyramid of wood to ignite.

"It's time we feed," she said. "I'm only getting a few blurred pictures of faces and an inside of a Dodge SUV. They're running, but I can't say where. Who else is hungry?"

"Not me," Blu said. "I fed last night. I'll be good for a couple more days. Doyle's good, by the way. He, Bully, and DB? It sounded like DB. They're moving now that the sun is low. Bully's got some crazy means of getting them from place to place without leaving a trail. The crowd they've gathered is so big now it's getting hard to hide, Doyle said."

"Good," Vivian said. "The more they can keep from the Blood Tribe, the better. Lukas? Hungry?"

Lukas shook his head, his pursed lips unwilling to form words.

Michael touched his cigarette to a stack of leaves and pine needles and grunted in frustration as they flickered and died, clearly for the umpteenth time. "Where's DB when I need him?" he said with a comic glower.

"May I?" Vivian asked.

Michael offered his butt. "Go ahead."

Vivian grinned, crouched, and extended her flat hand until it was inches from the wood. For a moment, nothing happened. Then a small glow emerged from the center. The fire crackled, then grew. In seconds, the flame was large enough to sustain itself.

"Girl, you are downright magical," Blu said with a wink. "I'm keeping you around."

"Come on, Michael," she said. "Time to introduce, identify, impress, ignite, and imbibe."

Michael chuckled at Vivian's mention of his first lesson to her in hunting. They bid the others a brief farewell and set out in search of warm blood.

The air grew colder as the sun descended behind the trees, setting long, red-gold shadows across the path. Vivian knew that Michael, as she did, grew aware of the drop in temperature without enduring the discomfort that humans did. Poor Crystal and Harmony were undoubtedly chilly back at the campsite without a jacket. Vivian was glad they had a fire to help and resolved to hurry.

The sound of voices grew nearby, that of a couple on the verge of arguing. From the sound of it, there were people behind the bend of saplings at the edge of the wood.

"Gimme the lighter," one of them, a female, said.

"Jacqueline, I'm telling you, this is how I learned to do it in Boy Scouts. Now gimme a second."

"Kyle, you've been trying for five minutes now without giving me one damn chance. Now give me the effing lighter!"

A sound of male frustration erupted as Vivian and Michael rounded the corner. Jacqueline was bent over a small pile of wood stacked haphazardly in a metal ring. She lit the flame, and a small gust of wind blew it out. She growled in aggravation.

Vivian eyed Michael, and he smirked.

"Excuse me?" she said. Two heads popped up, suddenly aware of the others' presence. "I know I'm a complete stranger, and I'm sorry for butting in and all, but I have a method of lighting fires that never fails, if you could use a hand."

"She does," Michael said with a hint of sheepishness as he took a step off the path, careful not to infringe on anyone's space. "It's amazing. Puts me to shame every time."

Jacqueline and Kyle, despite their disagreement, shared a reserved look that said they weren't the type to make friends readily. Kyle's eyes danced from Jacqueline's face to the cooler, where Vivian guessed their dinner sat on ice in anticipation of a campfire.

Please let this work. Michael's hungry.

Vivian hesitated, unwilling to join Michael in that step toward them yet. She inhaled deeply but subtly, willing the Source to give them a gentle push. "I promise. One try, and if it doesn't work, I'm out of your way."

The promise of a time constraint seemed to warm Jacqueline enough to extend the orange lighter toward Vivian.

Thank you, thank you.

Vivian approached the woman with almost the same respect as a shy dog, taking the lighter with a modest smile. She knelt over the stack of logs and did the licked-finger-exposed-to-the-wind trick.

"Yeah, I told him it's awful windy," Jacqueline said cattily, then stopped.

Vivian's eyes met hers across the steel ring in a show of female solidarity. "Yes, it is."

She rolled her thumb across the ignition wheel of the lighter and extended her hands toward the wood, her second hand moving under the pretense of sheltering her flame, but in actuality, generating the energy she needed.

She held her hand there until she dared to extend the heat in her fingertips into the stack. A small blaze emerged.

Come on, come on. The heat in her hands grew intense as she fought to contain it. The lighter went out, but she didn't take her finger off the pedal, focused on sending the heat to the center of the wood.

Whoosh!

Vivian dropped the lighter, her hands suddenly awash in flame. She patted them on her slacks until the fire subsided.

"Oops," she said. "I guess I owe you a lighter."

"My God!" Jacqueline said, rushing to her side. "Are you alright?"

"I'm fine, I'm fine," she said, but Kyle was in the cooler, grabbing ice cubes and dashing to her side. He offered them to her, and she accepted them, holding them in her palms as if nursing wounds. The three of them stood side by side, eyeing the campfire, now crackling heartily.

Silence. Kyle shrugged and grinned. "Well, the fire's lit," he said.

Everyone chuckled, and Vivian dropped the ice to the ground. With a smile, she waited to see if the fire had caught well. The quiet lasted long enough for Vivian to grow ill at ease. As they prepared to excuse themselves in search of other, more social prey, Kyle spoke.

"Y'all want a beer or something?"

Chapter Forty-eight

Harmony knew her sister had troubles on her mind, but she didn't press. So much had happened in the past few days—Tristan's death, fleeing their home, volunteering to help Vivian and Michael, meeting Megan only to hear of her death hours later. It was a lot, even for a person familiar with the bizarre.

Watching Crystal hunch over the campfire, her empty gaze fixed on the flames, Harmony was tempted to start a conversation, but Crystal was not the type to respond well to pushing. Though outspoken in many ways, she wasn't one to divulge her anxieties. It was as if she believed that by giving voice to her fears, she risked speaking them into being. Like a true Cancer, Crystal wore a tough outer shell that hid a deeply sensitive core.

"What?" Crystal snapped, breaking her stare-down with the fire. As if on cue, the fire popped as a log rolled down, scattering embers into the sky as a tendril of smoke curled in their direction, making Crystal jump.

"I'm sorry?" Harmony said.

"You sighed. You never sigh. What's wrong?"

Though Harmony attempted to smother it, a derisive snort escaped. "I might ask you the same."

Crystal returned her attention to the fire. Her fingers twiddled in her lap. "What's wrong? Oh, every-freaking-thing."

"You're tired," Harmony said.

Dark ringlets shook back and forth. "Not like I was. I mean, I'm mentally exhausted, sure, and that doesn't help. But that jolt Vivian gave me back at Blu's…" she let out a curt laugh. "Man, that was like getting my batteries recharged. She's amazing." Crystal held out her healed palms as proof.

Harmony hated to add to Crystal's list of problems, but putting it off any longer was foolhardy. "Crys, I have to go."

Seeing her sister's heartbroken face made Harmony oddly grateful for her own emotional armor.

"No!"

"I have to. There's no other way."

Crystal scoffed. "You're not leaving us to work for… them, are you?"

"I can't say yet," Harmony said. "If I have to, I will, but like we've been saying, it doesn't seem likely that I will. I'll be back as soon as I can."

Crystal closed her eyes. The campfire let out another loud pop, but neither of them paid it any mind. "Go, then."

Harmony squeezed her sister's hands, then hugged her, and Crystal returned it almost as dispassionately as Harmony felt. As she turned to walk away, Crystal spoke.

"What, no vanishing act this time?"

Harmony pointed. "He's right over there."

Crystal knew better than to ask.

He was good-looking. That, Harmony hadn't foreseen. When she'd first met him as Blu, the friend of Michael, he'd been extremely attractive, but this was a different sort of beautiful. Tall, red hair, sky-blue eyes, lean, he was the kind of man who would have turned her head had she not inherited the Harmony. He stood in the clearing's twilight, the dim moonlight seeming to glow on his fair skin.

Her approach hadn't caught him unaware—but why would it? She'd known he was there, as well.

His eyes met hers, and her heart stopped. In that instant, it was as if she were almost human. The wall of impassiveness cracked and fell, shattering into splinters and flying in the wind. Emotions she'd been without overwhelmed her—almost a decade of stoicism broken in a glance.

What the hell…?

Fighting to keep her expression blank—it seemed unprofessional not to—she continued her approach.

"Why are you here?" she asked, stepping into the clearing where he stood. He faced her full-on, and her heart stirred. She was startlingly aware of his good looks. What was he doing, and how was he doing it?

"I'm Eoghan O'Rourke," he said, not extending a hand or presenting any sign of friendship. His brogue carried an appealing timbre.

"Harmony Novak," she replied, resisting the peculiar urge to cross her hands in front of her self-consciously. "And I know what you are. Why are you here?"

Eoghan kicked at a stump restlessly. She'd never met another Harmony before; it was odd watching him with emotions. Or was he not weakened by her presence as well?

Harmony's brows knit together. "If we're going to have a lengthy conversation—"

"It's done," he replied. "Nobody's getting anywhere."

She almost hated to admit it. "There's still work we need to do—"

He held out his hand, and she knew from his reluctance that even if he wasn't as drawn to her as she was to him, his emotions had returned as well.

He let out a resigned sigh. "Let's get to it."

Chapter Forty-nine

Vivian and Michael hiked back to the campsite after they'd fed and laid their prey next to one another, encircled by a halo of aluminum beer cans. Surrounded by the vivid autumn leaves and brisk air, Michael realized how much he enjoyed this time of year in northern climates. His senses, primed with fresh blood, now picked up the clarity of the night sky, the crispness of the air, the smell of the vegetation that had fallen and lay, crunchy and fragrant, under their feet. The sound of each bird, insect, and animal roaming the surrounding forest seemed to present itself to his ears alone.

They rejoined their friends around the campfire. Michael scanned the circle. Something was off. "Where's Harmony?"

Crystal sniffed and wiped her nose with a crumpled tissue pulled from a denim pocket.

"She was called?" he ventured.

Crystal responded with a slight nod.

Michael was clueless how to react, so he said the first words that came to mind. "I'm sorry."

Crystal's grateful, glassy eyes told him that his instinct had been a good one.

Vivian excused herself, mumbling hasty words about going back to the solitude of a small clearing in the woods. Michael agreed. He took a seat on a flattened stump in silence alongside Crystal, Blu, and Lukas. They stared at the campfire, each lost in their own thoughts, their faces blank with fatigue.

An hour of arduous waiting passed with no word from Vivian, only the sounds of the woods at night and the crackle of the fire to break the stillness. Unable to stand it any longer, Michael sought her out and found her slumped in a circle of moonlight.

He crouched beside her, but she didn't move. "I can't do it, Michael," she sobbed. "I don't understand. The Source—it's like it has cut me off!"

Vivian, the most remarkable being he knew, had lost her ability to touch the Source. The sound of her anguished voice tore at him like claw hooks, striking him dumb. What could he, a member of the undead for a mere twenty years, do to help?

What if this severance was more than temporary? How much of a chance did Lukas—did any of them stand against Charles without Vivian's most significant asset?

He patted her hand, an action that struck him as trite as he did it. He stood. "Be right back. I'm going to check on the others. Keep trying."

Feeling like a useless putz, he headed back to the campground, where their fire lay dying. Blu, Lukas, and Crystal stared at the fading embers as if enraptured.

Michael froze. *Where's Harmony?* He closed his eyes as the reason for Vivian's barrier clicked into place—Harmony was the one keeping her away. *How on earth did she have the power to do that?* But why, if Charles was so far ahead of them? None of this made any sense. Charles had hurt Lukas, possibly beyond healing, and had killed hundreds— maybe thousands—of vampires who resisted him. What did the Balance hope to accomplish by cutting Vivian off? Why had it led them to Blu, allowed Megan to die?

No sense dwelling. Noting the drop in temperature and how Crystal had wrapped herself into a ball to conserve body heat, Michael gathered a few pieces of wood from the forest's edge and placed them on the embers. He grabbed a seat on the log next to his son and turned his way, but remained quiet, respecting Lukas' grief. Finally, Michael's steady gaze stirred Lukas from his false slumber.

"What?" Lukas barked.

"It's me," Michael said, keeping his voice from sounding confrontational. "We've always been able to talk before. Why can't you talk to me now?"

"What would I talk about?" Lukas said.

"About what happened? What's been on your mind? The skirmishes in the Middle East? The World Cup? The skyrocketing cost of American education? Hell, I don't care. Say *something*."

"Like how the Source is as useless as… as…" Lukas waved his hands as if swatting insects as he spoke. "Oh, hell. You know what I mean. What's the fucking Source done since we've left Savannah? Led us on a wild goose chase? Gave you vague directions to D.C. where Charles had Megan and me kidnapped instead of leading you to where you might help? Hell, it took the Balance—one of 'em—to step in to tell you to get him," he waved at Blu. "And for what? So we could have another stop-over in Virginia while the Source gets its shit in one bag?"

Michael searched for the right words to say. Platitudes were useless. Telling Lukas that things happened because they were meant to hardly sounded reassuring, regardless of how true it was, and telling him he'd get over it in time was worse. Time was all they had right then.

You've got every right to be angry," he said.

"Damn right I do," Lukas muttered, aiming his words at a tree to the left

"I'm angry, too. Lukas. We all loved Megan. You're not alone in your grief."

Lukas stuck his jaw out. Although he remained quiet, Michael knew he listened, waiting for the philosophical answers his father was so well-known for. Unfortunately, this time, he had nothing to offer. "Lukas, I can't say why it happened. It seems as pointless to me as it does to you, believe it or not. And I'm confused, too."

"I just—I—" Lukas stammered as tears ran down his face. "Do you understand what it's like to have someone you love die in front of you while you sit there, helpless?"

The tears Michael had held back until that moment broke. "Yes," he said, "I do."

Lukas turned away from the darkness as understanding set in. "Mom," he said, his face draining of color. "Oh, Jesus Christ, Dad, I'm sorry. I wasn't thinking. That was really shitty of me."

Michael nodded. "I had to lie there on the ground, drained of blood and dying, while they killed your mother." He sniffed, looked unsuccessfully for his handkerchief, and finally wiped his nose with the back of his sleeve. "All the while, you're sitting there with this unsuspecting look on your two-year-old face. Like it was a game, and you were ready to play." The tears burned, and his son was lost in a fuzzy sea of saltwater. "You said, 'Wake up, Mommy...'" he choked, then stopped. Lukas leaned in, his blue eyes huge and shedding tears.

"They nearly took you, too, only they were too gorged to bother. One looked at the other, saw that I was still alive, and asked his friend what to do with me. That was when they turned me. They turned me so that I'd—" he swallowed hard.

Lukas recalled the hunger that had overwhelmed him after waking the first time as a vampire. "They thought you'd kill me. That you'd become one of them."

"They thought I'd kill you," Michael agreed.

"My god," Lukas whispered. "But you didn't. How did you manage?"

"I'd die before I hurt you."

Lukas' mouth turned down as he thought about his father's story. "I'm sorry. I'm so sorry," he said, scooting as close to Michael as he could without falling off his log.

"And I'm sorry you had to go through what you did today," Michael said. "But I made it, and you will too."

A moment of awkwardness arose; an adult son encompassed in grief, a father still grieving but trying to help, both wanting to comfort one another. Lukas leaned forward and embraced his father with arms so powerful they forced the air from Michael's lungs. Michael returned the hug.

"Thanks, Dad," Lukas said. "For everything."

It took a cosmic wave of power to leave Vivian without as much as a finger on the pulse of the Source. At the height of Vivian's effort, Eoghan sprawled on the forest floor, praying she hadn't heard him collapse in her zeal to touch the power she so deeply relied on. Harmony kneeled beside him, took one hand, then the other, and together strength flowed between them that dwarfed even Vivian's. Their combined efforts built a wall around her that encapsulated her power.

Breathless and weakened, Eoghan rose again with Harmony's help. His eyes met her green ones, and to his astonishment, he noticed her tanned skin, her oval face, her cheekbones. The way her tawny brown hair fell smooth down her back. She was pretty, and he knew it. He would've thought himself too callous to notice beauty.

Emotions. From another Balance. That was new. The entire job was new, and every hour seemed to hold a new lesson in how to handle the change.

He brushed the leaves from his denim slacks. "Well, they're talking. Michael's cooking up a brilliant idea while Vivian's distracted. I hope that's what you had in mind. I hope that's what you had in mind. Are we in this together, or—?"

"That depends," Harmony said, her voice professional. "What are your plans? From here?"

"Plans?" Eoghan repeated, flustered. "I've just been following the flow."

"Me, too. But it's come to my attention, and yours, I guess, that the Darkness is gaining ground way too fast."

Though he hadn't heard it called the Darkness before, Eoghan understood. "Are you thinking we should work together?"

"It felt pretty good." She flushed; the color in her cheeks visible even in the twilight. "Strong, I mean. When we worked together."

He hesitated. Why was he waiting?

"About these emotions," Harmony said. She crossed her arms, seemed to recognize her posture was unfriendly, and untangled her arms. "I have a theory."

"I'd be glad to hear it."

She gave him a wan smile, and his heart galloped.

"I've only been doing this for five or six years, but I've never come across another one of us. I've had to intervene for the Source with one or two like Vivian—what I call 'fountains,' and I've had to deal with other hosts of the Maleficence, but I've never seen another Harmony— a Balance."

"Aye, go on."

"It makes sense to me that the Universe bringing us together is significant."

Eoghan frowned as he tried to make the leap of logic she had. What had their meeting to do with emotion?

"Maybe," she said, "the universe has a default for us. Like, if we meet, it's a bad sign for the world. What if it's about to end, or get heavily out of whack?"

"That's bad, where do emotions come into it?"

"Maybe, when a Harmony meets another, the Universe is allowing us to feel in order to drive home the urgency of our jobs."

There was a certain logic to her argument, but he hoped she wasn't right.

It was unsettling—not getting a bead on her thoughts like he could with everyone else he'd encountered, but she must have the same vacant spot on her mental radar with him.

Did she have hidden motives? Not if she handles her portion of the

Balance the way you do.

He took a moment to reach into her sister's mind and flipped through the memories where Harmony dwelled. Love. Trust. Faith. No suspicion or deceit.

Eoghan nodded and offered his hand, this time in partnership. Harmony swallowed. Was that reluctance he saw on her face? If it was, she hid it well.

Eoghan put his mind in the place where the Balance lay as their hands touched, and lightning struck. Eoghan vanished into himself and rode the current of the Balance with Harmony, together as spirit-bound Gemini twins riding a roller coaster down a track careening down a sharp spiral. He'd thought the information he'd held before was vast; this was as if God had handed him the keys to the universe.

Michael. He's the weakest member. Leafing through the infinite files, they found what he believed was the right path to the desired end.

Will Michael go along if it means discovering his worst fears about his child?

Eoghan and Harmony scanned together. Michael, though not powerful in the conventional sense, was a formidable being. Maybe there was their answer.

Chapter Fifty

Dusk had settled over Atlanta like a swarm of locusts coaxed down by a cloudy Georgia sky. The sunset had been magnificent, Charles observed, a good omen. Brilliant gold, orange, fuchsia, and purple extended to indigo, where the sun's descent met the city's night sky.

Inside, over thirty members of the *Shévet ha Dam* congregated in the Table's former meeting place, the vast basement of a Gothic-style home in Atlanta. Renfields had removed the books, which were now housed in Charles' library. The polished mahogany table itself was conspicuously absent. Only the crystal chandelier above and the parquet floor beneath them remained.

The younger vampires, Charles noted, harbored a few new battle scars. Cheng had lost the top of an ear, but it was already growing back without a hint of scarring. The elder members, though exhausted, appeared unhurt.

Charles waited while his Renfields scurried about, offering cold cocktails and warmed blood. He paced at the fringe of the circle with his tumbler of Dalmore until the beverage service was complete, then stepped soundlessly to the center of the group. He took each step in a calculated fashion before turning to note faces, postures, thoughts. What he gathered was a room full of legions who'd grown exhausted from fulfilling his directive and a few who wondered what had happened to the ones who hadn't made it.

Obedience. Good. Perfect.

Hatshepsut Keket rested her dusty feet on an ottoman, one of the few remaining pieces of furniture, her long black braids trailing to her triceps. The absence of Domevlo Ghedi by her side was a blatant gap in their usual number. An untouched snifter rested in her palm. "Charles," she said, her voice scarcely a whisper, "we are here again after so much progress. Why?"

"How much progress, would you say?" Charles asked.

"How much?" Errando asked, fidgeting with the sleeves of his jacket. "Well, I'd say we've eliminated over one hundred groups."

"Closer to two," Wynda said with a stubborn tilt of her chin.

"*Si, si*," Errando said, his head bobbing, "The reports aren't fully in, but there have been several hundred killed."

Charles smiled at the news. "Good."

"Where's Doyle?" Cheng asked, more to Errando than Charles, avoiding his superior's gaze. His brazen posture was gone as he sat near the feet of Lan Chiu, but his voice revealed his bitterness at the presence of another young vampire holding a close bond with the vessel of the Maleficence.

"Doyle," Charles said, lifting his glass of scotch, "will not be joining us." His tone was asperous, and he took a sip and dared Cheng with a fiery glare to ask why. Cheng slouched but didn't interrupt.

Doyle's absence was regrettable, but not unforeseen. Charles had hoped to prolong Mr. Christy's cooperation long enough for him to help with Vivian's capture. The young one's anguish had been delectable, but now the traitorous youth was another casualty of the Source. Disloyal Doyle had chosen a side and was now useless.

Charles paused to see if anyone else had something to add. No one did. Good. He needed more time to decide who would fill the seats at his Table—this was not the time for rash decisions.

"For the next few hours, we'll take a more leisurely pace," he said. "What I need now is information. For you to set your legions in search of a woman."

Wynda's eyes closed, and her head dropped to her chest, her thoughts broadcast into Charles' mind almost as if she'd meant them to reach him. Not another search for a woman. Jude had asked the same when Jerusha escaped days before he died.

He held a hand up. "Relax. This isn't Armageddon waiting to unleash the way it was with Jude when he lost control of Jerusha. This is strictly a favor," he said, turning to Cheng. "A big one. And the woman isn't a vampire—though I suspect she's more than human."

Cheng straightened, his face sharpening with focus. He winced and pressed a hand to his ear, as though a spike of pain from the regeneration had struck. Charles waited until he had the group's full consideration before speaking.

"Allow me to tell you about Sana."

Michael reentered the clearing where he'd left Vivian, only to find the circle of trees silent and empty. The moonlight, which had shone so brightly here before, now cast silvery shadows on the leaves and the trees. But there was no Vivian.

"Vivian!" he cried. Then he spotted her lying on the ground in the dark, legs crossed, eyes closed, focused.

"I'm here, Michael," she said, her voice eerily calm and exhausted.

"What's wrong? What's—"

"Shh," she said. "I need a moment, please."

Michael froze in a gauzy mix of moonlight and shadow. Vivian hovered inches above the leaves, motionless, her back stiff and perfectly straight. Bit by bit, she descended until she'd shaken the trance. She stretched her arms over her head and sat upright.

"The Source?" Michael asked, "Did you contact it? Did it say anything?"

"Yes, and yes," Vivian replied.

"But the light," he said, "you didn't—you usually produce light. Or the Source does."

"Not this time," Vivian said. "What it had to convey was brief, not to mention a little vague. The connection was weak." She shook her head. "I'm afraid it's not good."

"What's not? Tell me what's going on."

"Maysun has found Sana, but she's formed a psychic barrier around them that makes it impossible for Charles to see them."

"What's not good about that?" Michael sat on the clump of leaves nearest Vivian.

"It's made it hard for me to pinpoint her, too. All I can say is that they are south and west of us."

"It's a start," Michael observed.

"Yes, they won't stay in one place. They're running, and we're running after them. Same as Charles. We might benefit from Crystal's ability to put us on her doorstep, but she has to stop for us to get to her. And it won't do us a bit of good if the Tribe has made it so that they're driving straight into Charles' arms."

Michael put a hand to his chin and rested his elbow on his knee. He rubbed his brow with his other hand, smoothing out the thoughtful creases that had formed there. Vivian said she suspected Lukas had a connection with the Maleficence, a suspicion he hated to give credence. But if it helped, it was an idea worth exploring.

"What if we didn't need to find Sana?"

Vivian straightened her legs. "You mean we find Charles, see what he's planning? I can't do that. With Jude's blood out of my system, I have no connection to him."

Michael rose and smoothed his jeans down with his palms. "Wait here," he said. Vivian agreed, and though her expression begged for more information, she knew the answers were forthcoming.

He crossed the stretch of woods to where his son sat by the fire, his stomach already twisting with the thought of lying to Lukas. He trampled through the underbrush, and Lukas turned at the sound of his approach.. This time he wasn't as sullen, but his slouched body and tightly curled hands showed Michael that his son was still far from happy.

"I need your help," Michael said. "We do. Vivian and I. You too, Blu," he said almost as an afterthought.

"What about me?" Crystal said.

Michael nodded. "You can touch the Source. It's worth a try."

Lukas motioned his father to the seat beside him. "What can I do?"

Michael braced himself. He'd never believed he was a good liar—clever, maybe, but not good. He'd prepared his phrasing during the walk to Lukas' side and forced himself to use it before his courage wore off and the story sounded too phony.

"We think we might have a way to locate Charles. If we get to him before he finds Sana, this whole debacle might be over—at least for now."

Blu and Crystal were following, but Lukas frowned. "I don't get it," he said, crossing his long legs. "Where do I fit in?"

The first part was simple; this was where the Big Story came in. Michael stirred up his courage and spoke. Never had he told his son such a bald-faced lie.

"Vivian thinks that if we all focus on Charles at once that it might concentrate the Source powerfully enough that she can overcome the Maleficence and pinpoint his location. Especially if he's not actively blocking her."

Lukas looked skeptical. "Sounds pretty iffy."

"It's a theory," Michael admitted, "but if it works, we're one step ahead of him. We've never tried anything like this with Crystal helping us. Blu—you're pretty old, so you can offer a few centuries of power.

And you—" Michael cut off his sentence, not wanting to remind Lukas of the short branch of the vampire family tree that led him straight to Cartaphilus.

Lukas hunched over and put his elbows on his knees. "What the hell? I'm game."

"Good," Michael said. "Blu?"

Blu looked puzzled, his tight lips and narrowed eyes telling Michael that he knew his friend was hiding his true motivations but agreed to cooperate.

"Crystal?"

She shrugged. "I'm game."

"Good," he said. "Vivian's already doing her part. Are you ready?"

"Go ahead," Blu said.

"Sure," Lukas said. "What am I doing?"

Michael, who'd only heard secondhand what it was like to use telepathy, tried to recall what Vivian had told him. "Okay, try to relax. Let your mind go wherever it's inclined to. Breathe deep. Focus on what you remember about Charles. What he looks like, sounds like, every detail. If you need to close your eyes to focus better, then do that. Block as many external stimuli out as you can, but don't stress if you can't."

Lukas closed his eyes. His face grew somber, then angry. His hands clenched. He looked ready to kill.

"Relax as much as you can, Lukas," Michael encouraged, not liking the expressions he saw crossing his son's face. Lukas loosened his fists, but his jaw remained tight.

"Can you see him?"

"Mm-hmm," Lukas said from behind tight lips, his anger so forceful it was palpable.

"Do you know where he is?"

Lukas cracked in eye and regarded his father dubiously. "Aren't you going to do this, too?"

"Yeah, yeah. I'll be quiet and focus. Tell me if you get a hit, though, okay? Any detail that might help."

Michael settled in and behaved as though he was taking part in the exercise. Crystal and Blu sat, faces impassive, as they cooperated, but it was Lukas that Michael observed. Seconds ticked by. Michael alternated between closing his eyes and watching his son's shifting expressions as he attempted to pinpoint Charles.

"He's in Atlanta," Lukas said flatly, his eyes fluttering open.

Michael sat up, his esophagus burning as his stomach roiled. He made his voice steady. "You're sure."

A single massive shoulder rose and fell. "Yeah. There's a place inside the city. Used to be used by Jude. The place is filled with Tribe members right now."

Such detail! Michael almost winced, but fought to maintain his poker face. "Any chance you've got an address?" he asked, forcing a chuckle.

"No, but I'd bet I can get us almost to his door once we're nearer."

Michael stood. "Good, good. Blu, you get anything?"

Blu shook his head. His eyes had grown wide, but he prudently was not voicing his reservations. "Nothing new," Blu said flatly.

"Crystal?" She shook her head, her eyes wide and her lips pressed together and biting back questions. Michael knew Crystal understood more than she said, but silently thanked her for not voicing her concerns.

"I'll go tell Vivian."

"I think… I think he's telling them about Sana. The Table. He wants their help in capturing her because he thinks she's a key to him tilting the Balance."

Michael's brows arched, the air in his lungs froze. He gave himself a second to compose before responding. "Well, let's get ready to go, then. I'll get Vivian." He'd walked several steps before adding, "Good job, son."

"Did you get anything, Dad?"

Michael licked his lips and said, "No, but I'm not as strong as you." Lukas nodded and started gathering his few possessions.

Michael made the trip to Vivian's side on shaky legs and joined her in the clearing. Once there, he slumped onto the ground, fighting the urge to put his head in her lap and cry. His hands balled into fists in the leafy ground, crumpling up dried oak and maple leaves and ravaging them in his palms.

"What's wrong?" Vivian asked, drawing close and placing a wary hand at his temple.

"Lukas. He found Charles in Atlanta."

Vivian withdrew her hand and put it on her mouth with an arched brow. "You taught him to use telepathy?"

Michael's eyes burned, and he brushed at them with the back of his forearm. "I tricked him. Vivian, you should've seen the look on his face. He was livid. There was no way he used the Source. And not only did he find Charles, but he also knows what he's thinking."

Vivian stood and rubbed the dirt from her palms onto her shirt, then began swatting the leaves from her clothes. "Well, that's a–"

"Vivian, he used the Maleficence!" The words tore from a throat raw and burning with emotion.

Vivian stopped brushing and lifted her head. Empathy radiated from her eyes, and he noticed a glassiness there, too. "Michael, we need to save Sana before Charles gets a hold of her. Maybe he's wrong, and she's useless to him. Or he's right, and Eoghan led Charles to her for a reason. But if Sana will give him an undue burden on the Balance, there's more than your son at stake. After this is over, we'll make sure Lukas is alright. For now, his ability to point us to Charles is helpful, and it gives us an advantage. I hate it, too, but Lukas is dealing with a lot."

Michael clenched his jaw. She was right. *But why does all this seem to involve Lukas? First, Cartaphilus had Gina turn him into a vampire. Then Jude toyed with him, killed Gina in front of him. Now, Charles has had him kidnapped. He killed Megan while Lukas watched. Why my son? Why is he going through all this hell? What does the Source want with him?*

"So, we go to Atlanta?" Michael asked.

Vivian shook her head. "Charles is in Atlanta. According to Lukas, he's using the Blood Tribe to track down Sana, right? Which means he has no more clue where she is than we do."

"But if we stick close to Charles—"

"We risk Charles sensing Lukas."

Michael found himself without words. He plopped down on the ground as the gravity of Vivian's words became real. His son had a grain of evil in him, and they didn't dare bring him near Charles. Vivian said, "If Charles senses us nearby—"

Michael interrupted. ""He'll fight us. He'll try to kill you," Michael cut in. "Same reason he took Lukas before." He tongued the points of his eyeteeth. "You don't think he can use his telepathy to find Lukas now?"

Vivian joined him on the forest floor. "Possibly." He gave her his sternest look. Her hands went up in protest. "Probably. He probably can. How else did Krieg find him before? We suspected the credit cards, but that mall was a big place—he had to have more guidance. If we get within twenty miles of Charles, we might as well hire a brass band and buy huge beacon lights and blinking signs that point right to us."

Michael understood. "We're still stuck."

"Until we find out where Sana is, yeah."

"So much for my brilliant plan."

"Not nothing," Vivian said with a sigh. "We learned we have to be concerned more about Lukas."

"Do you think we'll lose him?"

Her eyes clouded. "I think we already have."

Chapter Fifty-one

Every few hours, Perry, Sana, and Maysun switched seats, so they each had time to rest in the back seat alone. The highway carried them through one bland southern town with a strange American name after another. The only constant was the choice of direction—always west. It was all they'd agreed on so far. As long as they headed west, they had a direction, if not a destination. I-20 turned into 78, became 40, then 30. The numbers weren't important, only the continuous motion.

Other than the rare break for crowded, anxious city traffic—Augusta, Atlanta, Birmingham, Memphis—roads were surrounded by forests, shrubs, and kudzu and interspersed with towns, harvested fields, and the occasional abandoned car. Peaceful, silent, and boring. Billboards advertised locations from churches to strip clubs and anything in-between. Rolling hills flattened out into farms, level woods and trees, so many trees, Perry never wanted to see another forest in his life.

They crossed the broad Mississippi River into Arkansas, and as they traveled down the neglected roads, they gradually found themselves back in hilly countryside again.

After nearly ten hours of steady driving, truck stops, and gas station restrooms, seventy miles an hour felt like a crawl to Perry. He pushed the speed limit more and more, and forced himself to slow down every time. A speeding ticket was exactly the kind of thing the *Shévet ha Dam* could use to pinpoint their location, regardless of the psychic protection Maysun gave them.

Stopping for any reason was nerve-racking, so they kept their pauses to a minimum. Though Perry and Maysun both knew the Tribe had rules against attacking humans—or any enemy—in public, there remained the chance that a Tribe member might spot them and report their location. Worse, in towns as undersized as these countryside pit stops, they risked there not being any witnesses. No witnesses meant no rules.

They paused in a town called Forrest City so Sana could use the facilities and grab a snack while Perry filled the tank. After they'd satisfied their reasons for stopping, even running the risk they took lingering at the side of the truck, no one seemed eager to get back in.

Conversation lagged as they stood around the side of the vehicle under the guise of stretching their legs. As much as he hated the lengthy pause, Perry dreaded the thought of getting back behind the wheel. The setting sun had tormented him as he pushed westward, his head throbbing from the glare off the shimmering pavement. Hours after dark, his skull still pounded with the lingering effects of the sunlight on his retinas.

Maysun broke the silence. "At our next stop, I think it's best if we check into a room for a while. We all need to rest."

"You mean in an actual bed?" Sana asked hopefully, massaging her sore shoulders.

"Is that wise?" Perry asked.

Maysun nodded. "I'm nearly out of juice, for lack of a better term, so my ability to block the *Shévet ha Dam* is weakening. Blood has helped, but it isn't enough. I need to recharge for a couple of hours to continue to block Charles' and David's searches."

"Will you still be protecting us while you do that?" Sana asked.

"Not as well, no."

"How long will your guard be down?" Perry said.

"Not completely down. Just weaker."

Perry rocked on his toes, misgiving etched across his face. His restless hands swung from front to back, springing off one another as if in perpetual motion. "I don't think that's a good idea," he said. "All they need is a general idea of where we are, and the whole *Shévet ha Dam* will find us."

"It'll be alright, Perry."

Perry's hands stopped, but his fingers still danced in agitation. He turned from Sana to Maysun, then back again.

"Fine then," he said. He didn't believe it was fine at all.

Sana drove for another two hours, still due west, until around one in the morning when they reached a small town past the city of Little Rock, Arkansas. They rented two motel rooms for two nights under false names, using the last of the cash Perry kept in his wallet.

The doughy man behind the counter handed over two keys and watched with keen interest to see who took them. Perry took one, Maysun, another. Sana wondered which of them they expected her to follow. Judging by the nosy look on the fat man's face, so did he.

They exited the lobby into the silent, gorgeous, starlit night and walked single-file along the sidewalk to their rooms. Sana's stomach started twitching with nerves.

Who am I staying with? Is it understood that I'm going to stay in my mother's room because— She cut the thought short, ashamed of where her mind had gone. Stay with the boy? Was she crazy?

Sana was so nervous her teeth rattled. She nearly ran into Maysun before she saw that they'd stopped outside their rooms. Maysun held her key in one hand, Perry his key in another. They looked at her in anticipation. Sana's head swiveled, uncomprehending.

"Would you rather stay in your mum's room?" Perry asked, his voice uncertain for the first time since they'd talked in her bathroom. Had that been only half a day ago?

Sana blinked. They were looking to her to tell them! She wanted to back up and ask for a third room. They should have asked for another room. She longed for the slick tongue of a motivational speaker—or poor, dead Thom, self-proclaimed King of Sales. Instead, she stood mute, her tongue unmoving.

"Oh, uh…" Sana felt sheepish—a grown woman acting like an awkward teenager. She eyed Perry, who *looked* like a young twenty-something, though his body had stopped aging when he was seventeen. How old was he, though? He'd been seventeen when they'd tried to turn her. She was sixteen then. Despite his youthful appearance, Perry was, in fact, older than her by a year.

"I think I'd better stay with Perry. I wouldn't want to distract you from your—uh—shielding."

Oh God, did I just say that? That sounds ridiculous!

"I understand," Maysun said, opening her door and stepping across the threshold in a manner that said she'd known all along she'd be alone.

I'm glad somebody does.

She trailed Perry into the hotel room. There was only one bed, she noted. A queen-size bed, and a single chair, but still.

Perry double-checked the lock and made sure the thick curtains blocked out the bit of remaining daylight. Sana's heart pounded, and every nerve in her body seemed aware they were alone. Her nipples tightened against her bra and blouse, and she folded her arms across her chest. She wanted to move across the room and shut herself into the bathroom until she'd regained her self-control.

"Perry, I—"

He turned, grabbed her by the waist, and pulled her against him, kissing her hard. Her arms fell to her sides, then to his hip bones.

Any self-restraint she'd clung to vanished the moment their lips met. She clapped her hands on his head and pulled him closer.

"Amazing what a little push will do."

Eoghan, seated on a fallen stump beside Harmony in the midnight woods, nodded. Her hand in his felt natural now, like vines twined together. "They make a strange couple," he added.

"But they fit," Harmony said. Eoghan could not disagree. "And it would have happened in time. We couldn't wait for them to get their courage up."

"That would have taken years."

"Years too long."

Overhead, the thrushes and warblers sounded unnaturally loud. Times like now, when so much hung in the balance, the weight of his new role crushing, the life force in him felt almost too powerful. When combined with Harmony's extra force, he thought he might lose himself under the weight of its potency. Together, they could twist the earth on its axis until they stood at their chosen pole.

Eoghan traced the lines of undead power back as far as they ran, but the roots of the family trees were often severed or shortened. Most of the eldest vampires who'd fought the *Shévet ha Dam* were dead. The ones left were too young, too green, or had scurried back to the Blood Tribe for safety.

This battle would need more than a handful of bloodsuckers less than two centuries old if it was going to thwart Charles from tipping the scales. And Eoghan knew a battle was brewing; it was only a question of where and how. Where, it appeared, was in a tiny town in Arkansas, and soon. He had to move fast.

"We'll need more than vampires. More life forms than last time," she said. "I think your friend was the only Balance in that fight. She was enough. The fact that I'm here now means this one will be far worse."

Life forms. The word, a few days ago, might have sounded odd. Now, Eoghan had to agree. He hadn't been the one to hold the Balance then, but the knowledge that flowed through him coincided with Harmony's viewpoint. Vampires had held the Balance last time. Now, the price of peace rested in more than immortal hands They would need anyone with superpowers that they could find. Shifters. Magicians. Psychokinetics. Anyone with speed, strength, or gifts that defied the human norm.

"All of them," he said. "As many that will come as we can."

"It's the only way to restore the Balance. Anyone who can play a role or who can make it to this battle has to be there. Tell as many vampires as we can, but add more. Vivian has already started it—we need to help her."

"Not humans," Eoghan muttered.

"Superhumans," Harmony corrected. "Like my sister. Most of them would agree that this is crucial."

Who are my power players? Vivian, of course, is on her way. Blu. Lukas is strong, but his resentment is spiraling so quickly he might only feed Charles more hatred—he can't be relied on to help the Source. Crystal Novak. Bully Bosworth—he's already gathering an army. It was as if Vivian had sensed what was coming, sending DB and Bully as ambassadors to rally those threatened by the Blood Tribe. Perhaps she had.

As much as he hated it, it was time for them to cross the lines. Each species would need its own reason to fight—otherwise, this war could spiral beyond his control. Beyond either of theirs.

Eoghan drew a long breath of autumn air and summoned the names of those closest to the front of this conflict. Harmony leaned in, gripping his hand, and the stomach-clenching descent into the Balance began again.

Chapter Fifty-two

Maysun tossed her keys onto the long table inside the motel room door, where they nearly slid under a television bolted to the fake wooden surface. Before her, in the tall, age-spotted mirror, stood a vampire whose exhaustion had aged her two decades in the last two days. *I suppose dying does that to a person*, she thought, settling onto the edge of the bed.

She needed to rest before they set out again. The Source might be a limitless store of power and energy, but she was not.

The canary-yellow cinderblock wall between her room and Sana's had been freshly painted, and the smell of fresh paint still hung in the otherwise stale motel air. She supposed the intent was to lend the space a cheerful atmosphere despite its shabby interior. Instead, the bright hue only emphasized the contrast between what was new, and what was not.

The thought of her daughter next door with Perry raised conflicting emotions. On the one hand, she knew Sana was physically and emotionally stunted, a woman frozen in time—or, at least, as close to it as one can get. From what the Source had shown her, Sana's mind had matured around one year for every five since David and his gang tried to take her. That would make her…

Eighteen. A perfect age for Perry, if he wasn't maturing, either. Which he wasn't, physically. He looked perhaps twenty, but he was closer to thirty-seven, and who knew how old emotionally? Sana looked like a woman but felt like she'd scarcely reached womanhood. Perry looked young for her, but he was closer to her "age" than any man she'd been with in adulthood.

On the other hand, Perry had a history of hurting Sana—badly. He'd run with David, took part in the day Sana was nearly turned, and never left David's side. Why hadn't he turned his back on his sire? Or stood up to him and said he wouldn't share in Sana's torment anymore? Why had he never defended her, if he cared about her at all?

Maysun shed her clothes and laid down. *I'm not here to psychoana-lyze my daughter's life. I'm here to protect her. I got her into this by choosing to give her life without knowing how my power might affect her. It did, and now it's up to me to keep her safe.*

It took several minutes before her turbulent thoughts subsided. Failing to clear her mind might be deadly to them all. She forced her mental debate out of mind.

The five steps to the bed were too far to walk. Perry turned and backed Sana to the table along the motel wall. Without taking her lips from his, she sat down and wrapped her legs around his hips, pressing his body to hers.

They scrambled out of their clothes, barely paying attention to how they disrobed, so intent were they that something—anything—was touching one another; her hands on his lips, his cheek on her stomach, her mouth on his chest. Sana thought about birth control for a fleeting moment, then realized he was a vampire—she'd be willing to bet he was incapable of fathering a child. Not to mention his body would have healed itself of any STDs.

What am I worried about? We've done this before, right? He'd said they had, but she didn't recall it. It felt like the first time to her, and from his zeal, it felt that way for him, too.

It thrilled her to discover that he was as faultless without clothing as he was with: muscular chest, narrow waist, perfect limbs, and gentle hands. His pale skin was an exciting contrast to hers.

Once divested of clothes, they discovered the table wasn't conducive to their plans. Perry hoisted her easily from the tabletop and carried her to the bed.

Sana's heart hammered in her chest. Perry's body was cool to the touch, a testament to his lack of life, and yet he felt so vital! Everywhere his cool hands touched her brought fire to her skin, and when he caressed her most intimate parts, she cried out with pleasure she'd never experienced with another lover. Within minutes, using his hands and mouth, he'd sated her urgent needs, and she set about satisfying him.

She directed him to put his back against the headboard, swung a leg around his body, and mounted him. Once he'd penetrated her, her body shuddered, and she knew another orgasm was imminent. She resisted the urge to ride him at a frantic pace and bring the climax on quickly, but her willpower only lasted so long. Once Perry put a breast to his mouth, then the other, the impulse to finish again won over.

Sensing her building climax, Perry gripped her hips and met her rhythm. Sana felt wild, primitive, mad with need as a strange stretching sensation emerged above her eyeteeth. As the wave of pleasure crested, Sana found a new longing joining that of her orgasm. Although she didn't understand what she did, even as she did it, Sana lunged forward, her lips clamping on Perry's neck as her teeth broke his skin. Blood trickled into her mouth and down her throat, and it was the most delicious thing on earth.

As one, she and Perry reached an earth-moving finish.

David had never seen Jude's home, so crossing into the Table's cavernous old meeting place scratched an old itch in his life, filled in a mental picture that had been blank for years. This was where his sire had met with his immediate subordinates. The infamous Table. No doubt it looked different then. Milling vampires waiting for direction spoke in small clusters around the room, but there was no furniture, save a handful of barstools, no art on the walls, no sense that the room was used anymore.

When they'd arrived in Atlanta, a handful of remaining Renfields provided Angelo and him with every necessity—a place to clean up, a telephone charger, fresh blood from their veins. Still, David knew he was being used, despite what appeared to be favored status. The only reason Charles kept him close was his bond with Perry, and Perry's proximity to Sana.

Back in Sedona and around the world, the *Shévet ha Dam* worked, using cell phones, telepathy, fax machines, and the internet, all hard at work locating Sana. Anything resembling a sighting was given periodically by cell phone. Meanwhile, Charles and David stood at the bar while Angelo poured drinks. David saw no need to top fresh blood with tasteless cocktails, but didn't want to seem ungrateful or interrupt Charles. Besides, most of the alcohol was gone, too.

David resisted the urge to eavesdrop as Charles walked past on the phone. Whatever he'd been told, the news wasn't what he'd hoped for.

"Try again," Charles barked and hung up the phone with an angry stab at the End button.

David fought back an exasperated sound, or any sign that he believed the search was pointless. He accepted the glass from Angelo, but set it down without taking a drink.

"Do you mind if I head outside?" he asked. "I think better outside."

"Think wherever you like," Charles said, "but I'm coming along."

Does he think I'll try to leave? I'm not stupid.

David pursed his lips, rose up from a barstool, and took the two flights of stairs to the porch. Charles followed, his steps disturbingly silent in David's wake.

David opened the doors and stepped out under a sky bejeweled with stars. He enjoyed a mild breeze caressing his bronze skin before he tipped his head back and sought his spawn.

No compass directed him, no spirit left his body. Only his mind traveled, searching the skies for a hint, a scent, any small clue. He discerned a vague direction in the miles that separated them, then the trail went cold. West. Perry was west. He fought back a laugh. He'd found him.

Narrow it down, try to get a more direct answer.

David pictured Perry in his mind, every detail he recalled, but all he got was a strange sense of arousal.

Rage surged through David. *Oh, no. That little bugger better not be doing what I think he's doing!*

"David?"

David concentrated, but it was futile. He felt as if he was banging his head on it until he retracted his focus and returned to his body.

"Well?"

David pointed a finger westward. "He's that way."

"You're sure?"

"Positive."

"Any more details? A town? An address?"

"No. No more. He's almost straight west, though."

Charles headed back inside. This time, David trailed, shutting the door behind them.

"Well," Charles mused, already heading to the lower level, "it's a start. And once we get closer, your sense of direction will undoubtedly prove more fruitful."

David hoped Charles didn't pick up on his lack of confidence. Perry's reluctance and taciturnity were growing into outright stealth and evasiveness. It wasn't a secret that the only thing keeping Perry in his group was his fear of death. His caring for Sana must have grown to the point they now pushed him past giving a shit if he lived or died.

They reached the basement room, and David hitched a finger toward Angelo, who hopped over the bar, leaving two half-filled crystalline scotch glasses on the countertop. David waited to see if Charles had more to ask him, but the man was gathering the Tribe and directing them to the surface.

Together, David and Angelo joined vampires already filing back up the flight of curving stairs and out the front door. The crowd of Blood Tribe members billowed in their wake as the word spread that they had a target. David felt the announcement ringing in his mind as Charles used telepathy to contact his Tribe, and other beings tied to the Maleficence, directing them to follow his lead.

David resented knowing he was only Charles' bloodhound. Still, living at Charles' side as a working bloodhound was preferable to being killed for losing track of Sana.

One by one, the *Shévet ha Dam* rose into the starlit night. Without a word, they waited for David to take the lead, a cloud of predators on the trail of wounded prey.

⁓❦⁓

Move! Move!

They raced—hastening, flying, loping, marching, or driving—against a timeline they felt in their bones from Atlanta, Memphis, Shreveport, Dallas, and all points around. Creatures of all variations, vampires, werecreatures, spellcasters, beings that existed without human labels, all pulled by an inner force the Balance didn't permit them to ignore.

Time was short. Their instincts drove them to spend whatever power they had left, no matter the cost. They knew that their lives, the lives of their friends, the right to live free of tyranny, all of it hung on this strange pilgrimage.

Some traveled alone, believing themselves the last of their kind, not sure what force it was that inspired them to make a pilgrimage, but voyaging by a course provided in their wary hearts. Others traveled in packs, the journey of families which had moved by instinct like gypsies for generations to survive. Some came in clans or similar units, bonded

*by blood or likenesses and motivated by dreams, ideas, visions, signs.
They shared one imperative etched into the core of their being.*
   Move.

Chapter Fifty-three

For the first time since Linda's wake, Bully laughed.

DB stirred, his golden eyes adjusting to the light of hundreds—maybe thousands—of flickering Technicolor sparks dancing above Bully's palm. It was like waking to a forest full of fairy lights, and although he was tired, stressed, and full of bodily aches from his neck to his ankles, he smiled.

The odor of hundreds of sleeping bodies and musty canvas tenting, which had served as bedding, hung in the air of the abandoned airplane hangar. DB had no clue where they were—Bully had a trick similar to Crystal's that helped them move from place to place, miles from one another. It was handy but confusing, and DB gave up trying to keep track of how many people they'd gathered after the fifth or sixth city.

Thankfully, they'd saved a few groups of vampires before the Tribe found them. So far, they'd found shapeshifters, spellcasters, and countless others with talents that ranged from mind-blowingly useful to questionable at best. Freaks always knew where to find more freaks. Like the strange, paunchy middle-aged man with the two-tone hair who had the power to influence animals. ("Gives new meaning to 'animal control!'" he'd cracked.) Sure, it'd help if the war took place in the wild, but DB doubted there'd be too many critters sticking around once the Blood Tribe descended. Animals knew predators when they smelled them. Still, they brought him along. One never knew.

A young man—a thickset ranger from Hunter Army Airfield named Brooks—had joined their numbers during the night, and he'd told them of an abandoned hangar that would hide them as they rested.

Only one of their new charges had refused to go to sleep, a wiry man with puffy, prematurely white hair who introduced himself as Lightning and who reminded DB of a walking white pipe cleaner. When asked why he didn't want to rest, Lightning merely said, in a voice that sounded charged with an entire pot of coffee, "I-I-I d-don't s-sleep." He didn't shake hands, crossing them against his chest protectively, but he offered to stay up with Bully and pull guard. He didn't strike DB as untrustworthy, just… jittery.

DB ran a hand through his tousled golden curls.

"Whassat?" he asked Bully, pointing to the fairy lights and keeping his voice down so as not to disturb the hundreds of bodies sleeping around them. The whisper woke Doyle, who pulled himself up to a seated position as he squinted at the shifting, glowing pinpoints.

"That," Bully murmured, "is the cavalry." He studied the dots for a moment, nodded, closed his hand, and the darkness in the hangar swallowed them.

When DB expressed puzzlement, Bully said, "You don't feel that?"

DB shook his head. "Feel what?"

"Yeahyeahyeah," Doyle said with a nod. "How far away are they?"

Bully scoffed and waved his hand. "Don't matter. I can get us to Arkansas like I did California."

"California? Is that where we are?" DB asked, but Doyle was already on his feet, rousing the rest of their charges. DB rolled onto his Vans and helped.

Michael lit a cigarette, his nerves driving him to old, if no longer deadly, habits. The three crumpled butts in his shirt pocket were stale, but the motion of lighting it, flicking the ash, inhaling, all kept his hands occupied. Sleep was out of the question; his nerves were a tangle of live wires.

Blu leaned forward and motioned that he'd like to bum a butt off his friend. Michael offered the pack, eyeing where Crystal and Vivian huddled nearby, slumbering the best they could in the cool night air. Lukas reclined against a stump bench with his back to the fire, half-asleep.

Poor Crystal's gotta be freezing, Michael thought. Sure enough, he saw the slight movement of her jaw as her teeth chattered. Their lack of life protected the rest of them from the cold.

"Atlanta, huh?" Blu asked, flicking his ashes toward the fire. "How do we find him once we get there?"

Michael gave a halfhearted laugh and shot a nervous look from Blu to Lukas. If they were going to get a fixed position on Dunning, Lukas was their key. The problem was, he was completely unaware. He dreaded telling his son about his tie to the Maleficence, but they didn't dare wander about Atlanta and hope for the best, and so far, Vivian hadn't been able to get a fix on Sana. The woman must have never stopped moving.

Nearby, Lukas mumbled worriedly in his sleep, and Michael turned his attention to his son. From behind drooping eyelids, Lukas' eyes darted in REM sleep. He tensed, sucked in a quick breath, and moaned, rolling over but not waking. He spoke, but the words were garbled.

"What?" Michael asked, leaning in. Whatever Lukas was experiencing, Michael believed it was more than a typical dream.

"There," Lukas said, jabbing at the air with an extended finger and waggling it violently. "There! He's there!" Lukas jerked upright, jolted from the dream and disoriented to find himself in the woods. Vivian and Crystal, roused by Lukas' zealous cries, sat up.

"Oh, honey, please tell me that was what I think it was," Blu said.

"I don't know what it was," Lukas said.

"Sounds like you had a revelation," Michael said. "Was it a dream, or a premonition? A connection?"

Lukas scoffed. "How'm I supposed to know?"

"It's possible," Vivian said, her voice thick with slumber. "I used to get them all the time when Jude held me captive. Psychic dreams. Telepathic connections to other vampires."

"Me? Telepathic? Since when?"

"You found him last time," Michael said softly.

"With your help. All your help."

Blank faces met his statement, and reality dawned on him.

"You mean I—?"

"You did it on your own," Vivian confirmed.

"That means I've got… something you don't," he said, shoulders slumping as the truth hit him.

"I'm sorry, Lukas," Michael said. "I didn't want to mislead you, but I wasn't sure my theory would pan out. It did. It sounds like Charles is closing in, and we need you to lead us the rest of the way."

Maysun jerked awake, her rest interrupted once more by the certainty that she wasn't alone. Peering into the shadows was simpler this time.

Remarkable visual acuity came with vampirism, as did a heightened sense of smell. She probed the corners of her room with her eyes, scanning for a potential hiding place. The odors of old carpeting, fresh paint, and clean sheets didn't seem to mask any unfamiliar scents.

It's a hotel room the size of a playpen. They blocked the underside of the bed so people don't lose their things underneath it. Where in the hell is anyone going to hide?

The undisturbed lock on her door gave her no comfort. A flimsy motel room lock wouldn't deter vampires as deeply bound to Cartaphilus as Charles and David.

She focused on her shield. It was in place. Weaker than she'd have liked, but in place.

This has happened before. This feeling I'm not alone. Why would I— David! This is how Sana said she felt whenever David was nearby.

The dream she'd been having didn't help. In it, she'd been a transient vampire, a young one who'd lived by shunning daylight, who walked alongside a hairy man on their way to a huge fight. To a van, which would drive them to a battle. A green van, already full of friends of varying strengths and abilities.

It was no dream. They're coming. The ones who want to fight for the right to live a normal life, to fight for their undead friends to live free of the Blood Tribe. They're coming.

But how? How did they learn where to find them?

Eoghan.

Was it Eoghan leading them? If so, to whom? To Charles? To Sana? Did it matter? *Not if he's in your bathroom. It'd be the same now, wouldn't it?*

She swung her legs over the side of the bed and tiptoed to the bath, feeling stupid as she did so. If Charles and David had found her, she'd be dead. Playing hide-and-seek in the lavatory was beneath them. The idea was asinine. Still, she wouldn't rest until she looked.

She'd reached the door to the bath and decided it unwise to enter the small room alone. It was a ridiculous overuse of power, but she'd use the Source to detect any hidden evil beings.

She pulled in a slow, full breath, clearing her mind of external distractions. Her vision blurred as she focused inwardly on the power that surrounded and now flowed through her.

Her body, which had only had perhaps two hours of sleep, rode the waves of power like a cork in rough waters. The Source had given her plenty of strength and protection in the past day, but now it wasn't enough. Though she was sure that she'd be able to focus well after resting, her connection with the Source had diminished.

She learned two things before she let her tie to the Source fade. She was alone in her motel room, and her psychic force field had dwindled worse than she'd thought. If David's power was as strong as she feared, it wouldn't be hard for him to get a general fix on Perry.

They had to move, and fast.

Perry slept, stretched out nude underneath the comforter of the multicolor bedspread, his lips parted, and his hair askew. He was as breathtaking sleeping as he was awake. More, if that was possible. Sana loved the sight of him.

She sat up on the edge of the bed and turned on the light above the table. Checking to see if the glare bothered her lover, she smiled as his thick eyebrows raised a touch before falling back into place. Other than that, there was no movement. He slept on.

Beyond the sex—which had been kinkier, and far stranger, than anything she'd experienced before, a new fullness had swelled within her during her intercourse with Perry. As if her body had become chock-full of kinetic energy, making her incapable of sitting still or sleeping.

And the sensations that surrounded her! Lights seemed brighter. Perry's masculine scent near her drove her wild. The purr of every engine on the nearby highway sounded like the roar of a monster truck. But it was so much more than that. Electricity crackled beneath her skin, like it could light the whole room if she willed it. Her fingers held lightning bolts under the tips. Although she'd often fantasized about flying, tonight she believed she could soar with one look into the infinite sky.

The desktop at the edge of the bed held a sparse amount of the typical supplies. Despite being a budget motel, the management had tried to provide at least the bare necessities: two pads of paper—one large, one small—a pen, a pencil, and two paper clips near a laminated list of nearby restaurants and their phone numbers.

Sana held her hand flat above the writing supplies and, on a whim, willed a connection between the two. She lifted her palm, and, as if suspended on invisible marionette strings, the pen, pencil, and clips rose. Her jaw dropped with delight and spread into a grin. She wiggled her fingers, and they bobbed in tandem. She stilled her fingers and focused intently on her floating toys. The smile that crossed her face was so wide it hurt. Envisioning them spiraling in her control, she sent them into a miniature orbit.

Perry stirred beside her and rose onto one elbow, watching silently as she spun her newfound playthings.

"My God," he whispered, "what are you?"

"I don't know," Sana said, grinning. "But whatever I am, I just got a whole lot better at it."

Chapter Fifty-four

He'd seen Bully tap into the Source only a couple of hours before, but it brought Doyle to tears this time, too. To think he'd shunned this for the Death Rush, and his was only a second-hand experience! The Source was so much more; deeper, yet lighter, a freedom born from knowing his role in the grand play of life, a love, an awareness of the force that bound the universe moving through him, using him.

Bully's voice broke through the fog of excitement and happiness. "Ready?"

"Oh, yeah," Doyle said.

Beside him, DB waited, his foot tapping a rapid cadence. He nodded, too hyped on adrenaline to voice his readiness. Brooks, the soldier who'd told them about the hangar, waggled his head so vehemently that his entire upper body shook along. Around them, a sea of faces watched, waiting for Bully to work his magic.

Bully chuckled and extended his hands. Ten beams of light shot out, found purchase in the air, circled until they met one another like laser beams tearing a ring into the atmosphere. In front of the hangar door, a circle of a motel parking lot appeared. Brooks, the ranger, leaped forward and tugged at the hole, stretching it to allow more people through. No one wanted to go first.

"Go," Bully breathed. "I can't hold it forever."

"You heard him!" Doyle yelled, "Go! Go!"

A hive of beings of all shapes, colors, and types poured through the rip in space.

"Hot, huh?" DB asked the ranger, knowing full well it was. He was just killing time waiting for others to jump through.

Brooks grunted and twisted his face in a sweaty grimace. "Pain is weakness leaving the body."

Bully advanced with the crowd to the hole he created. "Lord," Bully muttered, "don't make me any stronger than I already am."

"How do we do this?" Lukas said. "Crystal needs to know where we're going, and I only have a mental picture of supremely evil anger and a general direction."

"Touch me," Crystal said.

"Squeeze me?" Lukas asked, more reflexively sarcastic than genuinely teasing.

"Touch me," Crystal said. "Show me where you were. Use your telepathy."

"Does that work? I mean, you're not a vampire. Can I—"

Crystal shrugged. "Worth a try."

Lukas laughed in disbelief and covered his mouth with a long-fingered hand. "You're kidding. This is so jacked up." Still, he stopped and set his hand on Crystal's shoulder. The heat from her human body radiated from under her hoodie.

"Got it?" Crystal said.

Lukas pressed his lips together. He closed his eyes, pulling back the memory of flying through the night, an army of hellish beings behind him. It was impossible to conjure the memory of the impressions from that sinister dream while looking into Crystal's innocuous face.

His cheeks flushed as if he'd had a sip of fresh human blood. His neck grew warm, then his arm, as if life flowed through him from the mind, down his body, to his point of contact with Crystal. The mental picture streamed into him, along with the recollection of the evilness.

"Oh," Crystal said, her shoulder shuddering. "Oh, God."

The pressure under his palm vanished. Lukas opened his eyes to see Crystal retching, clutching at her stomach. Michael raced to her side and asked if she was alright.

"I'm fine, I'm fine," she said, her voice strained as she waved him off. "No time. They're there. We have to move."

Crystal, still heaving, covered her mouth with one diminutive hand and tore a hole into space with the other.

The woods were silent now, hushed as if in honor of the vast power between the two concordant beings. The quiet and darkness were so deep that as Eoghan stirred from his meditation, he needed a moment to recognize that he was in his body again.

He caught his breath, and life flowed through him as if a defibrillator jump-started his heart.

"Are you okay?" Harmony asked. Though the connection had ended, she hadn't released his hands. Small, soft, and feminine, they reminded Eoghan of Maysun.

"Fine," he replied, taking another deep breath. The woods stirred, blurred at the edges, and then came into focus.

Harmony paused and fidgeted. "We can't go to them now." It wasn't a question, but it sounded like one.

"No. They're on their own."

Harmony let out a laugh that might have been a whimper as she twisted in her seat on the ground. How long had they sat there? Minutes? Hours? She'd lost track of time.

"On their own," she echoed. "Sometimes… not often, but sometimes… it's hard."

"Hard?" It was his turn to echo.

"It's my sister. She's one of them." Harmony's fingers twitched, but she made no move to let him go, reluctant to part with the strength he lent her. Eoghan was aware of every finger, every ounce of pressure from those tiny hands. How was it that a being that had left him with no impression only hours before now stirred emotions in him?

Harmony went on. "She's had to deal with me going on these undertakings before, but I've never had to see her involved in one."

"Mm. And my daughter, as well. And my lover."

Harmony's blank face said so much through her downcast eyes. She gently peeled her hands from his. "Why? Why are so many people we love caught in this fight?"

"Because we're not normal," Eoghan said quietly. "Not even close."

They sat in silence. Harmony leaned over and looked Eoghan full in the face. "There's no stopping what's going to happen now. The most important parts, at least."

"We'll have to wait until the end and see if we've finished."

She slumped back against the log. "I don't like it," she said, biting off every syllable. "I *know* we had to do this—but why are my emotions betraying me *now*, when it matters most? It may have to be that way, but I don't have to like it."

Vivian reached for the Source in case the battle on the other side of the tear had already heated up. Meanwhile, she pulled Michael and Lukas through the portal before Blu. After the others passed through, Crystal darted in behind them. The portal sealed with a sound like bellows—an exhale of wind that blew her hair into her face.

Vivian pushed her locks back from her eyes and studied the landscape. It was an odd one: hundreds of mismatched people standing in the parking lot of a motel, with more descending from the heavens and pulling into the lot by the second. Young and old, every race, background, and style of dress—all stood side by side in the same parking lot, silently awaiting her arrival.

Eoghan and Harmony had sounded the alarm then. Good.

From the way her stomach fluttered in fear, the *Shévet ha Dam* were seconds away. Blue-black clouds blanketed the sky. If the Tribe was up there—

But they were. Already Vivian detected deaths of uncorrupted ones, a silent loss of life in the skies as airborne assassins stalked inexperienced renegades that hadn't landed yet. How long did she have?

The air held an eerie silence like predawn in a small town, just before the sun breaks over the horizon. Everyone seemed unsure what to do. *This is my army? It'd take me hours to find out everyone's strengths and talents! How am I supposed to coordinate an offensive? The battle has already begun!*

Vivian did not want to fight Charles for Sana—especially not with an untrained army in an unfamiliar area. The conflict had escalated in mere hours, as the Maleficence had planned.

Where's Charles? Where's Sana? I've come to save her, and don't know where she is!

Which room to try? The parking lot was packed with members of their army who had driven to the fight.

The door to number 58 opened, and a dark, wide-eyed woman rushed through, so intent on reaching the neighboring unit, that she failed to notice the enormous crowd only a few meters away.

"Maysun?" Vivian called. "Oh, thank God."

At the sound of Vivian's voice, Maysun spun on her heel. She backed into the motel wall with a thud that made Blu wince. When Maysun saw Vivian among the crowd, her features no longer looked panicked, but she appeared more stressed than Vivian thought possible. Maysun had always struck her as quiescent, unflappable.

"Vivian," Maysun breathed. "Thank god. I thought you were *Shévet ha Dam*."

"They're here," Vivian said with a hasty glance at the skies. "They'll be landing any second. Are you alright?"

"No," Maysun said. "I let my guard down for too long. I'm sure we don't have too long before—"

"You have no time at all," a deep male voice interjected.

Maysun's eyes grew wider still as the familiar form of Charles Dunning emerged from the skies, trailed by a descending army of the Blood Tribe.

Chapter Fifty-five

Sana and Maysun were on her left, her family on her right, and her inexperienced army behind her. Who to protect first?

David and Angelo flanked Charles on either side, joined by the throng of Tribe members. His minions landed behind him: centuries old vampires, hulking beasts like Krieg, and towering vampire-giant hybrids. The clutches of many of the larger ones held other, flightless creatures about whose natures Vivian could only speculate. Although Vivian's group was larger, they appeared less threatening. Maybe it was because the crowd behind her seemed to be ready to bolt while the Blood Tribe looked prepared for a five-course gourmet meal.

Vivian willed them to have courage. She had no fear of death or pain for herself—she'd experienced both before—but a battle would raise anger, violence, aggression. Fuel for Charles and the beast that powered him and the *Shévet ha Dam.*

Send them a message. Let everyone behind you understand what they're battling while you stall Charles as long as possible.

It meant dividing her attention, but she trusted the Source. She had no time for history lessons; imagery would have to do. *Give them the basics, show them Charles' plan. They'll see what to do.*

Through her, the Source gently tapped the consciousness of her army, and through a series of rapid-fire images combined with corresponding emotions, helped them to understand what had drawn them to this spot. Anything not drawing their power from the same fount was a threat. Their life—all life—hinged on their ability to stop the fearsome beings who were there to harm Sana.

"Don't do this, Charles," Vivian said. "We outnumber you. It'd be nothing but pointless bloodshed."

"Outnumber?" Charles said. "Perhaps. But not by much. One plus three equals seven—strength enough in the one and the three," Charles said with a laugh," Dunning said with a laugh. "And mine have much stronger blood than yours. Your lover is a child by comparison. And he," Charles motioned to Bully, "is a parlor magician. Do you think that you could hope to defeat me by recruiting witches and werewolves? How many of your dog fighters are capable of a full change now the moon is waning?"

Bully's and Maysun's faces mirrored the strength and determination of David's gang.

Vivian perceived the Source's readiness to lend her more power than she had already wielded. It waited patiently for her. Charles didn't.

"David, go." Charles motioned to the motel door numbered fifty-six.

David went.

"David's here!" Perry cried, scrambling to find his clothes. "Oh, god. Oh god." He yanked his shirt over his head, skipped the boxers, and went straight for the pants. He didn't bother with socks, but slipped his shoes onto bare feet.

"What are you doing?" Sana asked.

Perry stopped. "Well, I—I—" Scanning the room, he saw what Sana saw. The room had only one door and one window, no vents, no alternative escape routes. He slumped back onto the bed.

"We have to face them, Perry," Sana said gently, brushing his cheek. "Or they'll keep hunting us forever. And I don't know about you, but I plan to live a long time."

Perry groaned, misery and uneasiness contorting his face into a frown. His hand joined hers, and the frown grew determined. To Sana's surprise, tears appeared in his eyes.

"You're right," he said. His turquoise eyes searched hers. "I'm scared, Sana. Are you?"

"Terrified," she admitted.

The door burst open with a thunderous boom, sending wood splinters across the room. David stood in the doorway, a smirk on his sinister face.

"Hello, Perrywinkle." His smirk widened like a blade being drawn.

Charles stared at Vivian, who found herself speechless. Not in Joseph's vilest moments had he reveled so much in the promise of death. The Maleficence had driven Cartaphilus to inflict pain; Dunning reveled in the malice behind it.

"I've so been looking forward to this," he said. Startled by the suddenness of his action, Vivian nearly forgot to react. He vanished and then materialized before Vivian, with her throat in his hand. His forcible grip cut off her windpipe; his claw-like nails dug into her throat, threatening to tear out her vocal cords and sever her jugular.

"No!" Michael screamed, lunging forward as Vivian vanished within Dunning's grip. So strong had Charles' grip been, her lack of presence emitted an audible clap of his fingers against his palm. His action set off the other players like the snap of a clapboard on a Hollywood set.

As Michael jumped to Vivian's defense, Krieg stepped in, covering the distance between him and Michael and pinning Michael's arms at his sides, lifting him off his feet. He swung him around with a cackle of glee as he dove for Michael's neck, but an enormous silver wolf knocked the giant off balance. Michael brushed his arms vigorously as if shaking off creeping bugs and slapped at his neck where Krieg—Vivian assumed—had sunk his teeth. Twin trails of blood oozed down his neck.

Around Vivian's ephemeral body, it appeared as if she'd stepped backstage at a combination Fourth of July and horror show. Lycanthropes dropped to their knees, hastily yanking off clothes and crying out in inhuman voices as their bodies transformed into giant wolves. It surprised her to see others changing into panthers or bears that dashed into the fray with claws bared.

As the Blood Tribe surged forward, blinding rays shot from the fingertips of a pale, towheaded man with a face intent on nailing his targets. Vivian saw the head of a dark, squat Tribe member fall to the ground, severed as if by a laser beam. Spellcasters brought out wands. Others, it appeared, needed only the wave of a hand as they sent various spells at their foes. One young man took out two others by simply laying his hands on them. The sickening smell of burning, bleeding flesh was rampant.

Charles must be in heaven.

One man with a wide middle-aged stomach and thick glasses gripped the sides of his temple and absorbed the gaze of one of the massive cats—this one, a leopard. Strangely, it stopped charging and dove back into the Tribe group, clawing and biting as if hypnotized to act against its will.

Angelo dropped into a fighting stance, faced Blu, Lukas, and Bully, and prepared to do battle with all of them. They scattered into the crowd of monsters, now rushing into the foray of supernatural beasts.

Vivian re-materialized atop the Durango above Krieg's head, which she jerked back with a sudden crack. He dropped to the ground as the damage to his spinal cord made it impossible to hold on. He'd recover if no one killed him sooner, but the giant was out of the battle.

Charles turned and found Vivian crouched on the SUV's roof behind him. "One down," she said, her voice colder than she knew it could be.

Bully ran forward with his arms posed to grip Angelo, but his opponent quickly responded. He twisted around like a dancer on speed and covered Bully's head with his jacket. Blinding Bully made it easy to grip him under the chin, cutting off his wind.

Lukas and Blu ran to either side of Angelo, who shook off Blu's first two blows. When Lukas pummeled him, his response was less blasé. His face contorted with deeper pain every time Lukas' enormous fists hit home. Blu yanked on Angelo's elbow. His grip on Bully's windpipe loosened, but didn't quit. The sound of a chant came from under the jacket.

Charles sprang atop the Durango with grace and faced Vivian.

"Why do this, Charles?" she asked. "You lost so much in the last war, now this?"

Charles, who looked down in time to see Angelo fumbling with an empty spot where his prey had been, frowned. Lukas and Blu took Angelo by the arms and pinned him. Angelo let out a frustrated grunt and glared at the vampire who'd led him to his defeat.

A small smile covered Charles' face, his eyes flickering to the open door to Sana's room.

"So nice to see you again," David said with jovial sarcasm.

Perry rose. "You can't have her, Dave."

Ignoring Perry's insistent voice, David said, "Just tell me one thing. Just one fucking thing before I rip your ungrateful head off for being a traitor to your sire and your bloody tribe." He took two more steps forward, knocking a lamp from a table as he closed the distance between him and Perry. "Why?"

"All my life, I've wanted nothing more than to get shot of you!"

"Was life with me that bad?" David asked, pointing at Perry like a parent reprimanding a child, then directing his finger at Sana. "After all, you got to spend it around her."

"You can't have her!" Perry circled, inserting himself between Sana and his sire. "Not anymore."

Sana shot a venomous glare at David as she climbed onto the bed behind her.

"Ah," said David, directing his attention to her for the first time. "Climbing onto the bed won't work. You see, there's a wall behind you."

With David's attention diverted, Perry dove, plunging his shoulder into his midriff and driving them to the floor. Perry got in two solid blows to David's chin before David bucked him off, rolled on top of Perry, raised his elbow back to hit him, and then his arm broke.

He cried out like an animal and turned to see the creature that had done it. On the bed stood Sana, one arm extended. But she hadn't touched him. Not physically.

"Back up," she said. "Get off him."

"Or what?"

Her answer came in the form of a fierce blow to his head. When he recovered, with his left hand clutching his now bleeding temple, his eyes searched for what had struck him, but the space was empty.

"Back. Up," Sana repeated. He did.

From the splintered doorway came the sounds of a ferocious fight. Perry turned for a moment before returning his attention to the battle before him.

David scrambled to his feet and then reeled as another blow from an invisible foot struck his chest. Perry had seen her move, but her foot was at least a yard from David's body.

"You fucking bitch!" David cried, and dove for the bed. Perry again made a lunge for David, bringing them to the ground inches from the bed. The two battered each other for a minute until David gained the topmost position, at which point Sana lunged and yanked David back by the hair, dragging him off Perry with a primal scream borne from years of torment and fear.

Perry thrust his hand at David's chest, only to have David's hand seize him as his fingertips brushed the fabric of David's shirt. Perry brought his knee up and delivered a blow to David's groin that brought them both to their knees, as David refused to relinquish hold of Perry's wrist.

Sana watched them struggle once more. As soon as David gained the top position, she stepped forward and yanked him off, dashing him to the floor.

"Where in the hell did you get that str—?"

David tried to rise, but Sana kicked him back down, this time by the chin. David's head lolled to the floor, his eyes vacant and unconscious.

He didn't have to shake Vivian, only put her off long enough for David to drag Sana out of her room.

Charles sprang into the air, leaving his opponent below. Above, two of his Tribe tore apart a weaker vampire, the air thick with blood and shrieks. Charles swooped down, bathing in the blood that showered to earth, reveling in the coppery smell. He laughed at the surrounding casualties. Hatred, resentment, fear, agony, and death everywhere. He'd never been stronger.

"We should go," Perry said.

"It's not over," Sana said. "It won't be over until he and the rest are dead." She turned to Perry. "How many ways to kill him? All of them? Vampires?"

Perry's expression looked both relieved and disturbed at the thought of taking David's life. His mouth flapped a few times before he found his voice. "Decapitation," he murmured, "removal of his heart. Uh, fire."

"Fire," Sana echoed with a grim nod. "Help me wrap him."

Together, they removed the comforter from the bed and hastily wrapped David's body from foot to forelock. Twice he stirred, and both times, they rendered him unconscious with another heavy blow to his head. Sana pushed Perry toward the door once they'd encased him in his cloth cocoon. "Stand back," she said. "I've never tried this."

She took a few steps and paused. All those voices she'd heard for years, self-doubt, and nightmares were tied up in the helpless being before her.

Strangely, she hesitated. With Thom dead and the voices silenced, she would be alone—truly alone—for the first time. The idea frightened her a little.

She reached out until it was only a few feet from David's form. The tips of her fingers trembled. His fate was hers to decide. It was more difficult, since he wasn't actively attacking her. Still, she knew what had to be done. He would not give up, though she could defend herself now. What was it that Perry said about their addiction to her?

The sight of David's helpless form triggered a long-buried memory of a night when four vampires, led by the one prostrate before her, had decided her fate. Though she no longer cursed him for what they'd done to her, she'd never forgive him for not allowing her to decide for herself what her future would bring.

"May the gods grant you mercy. Because I can't."

Fire shot from her fingers and ignited David's clothing and hair in five tennis-ball-sized circles. It wasn't enough. She hated him, but was a better person than one that'd let him suffer. He let out a horrific cry that raised gooseflesh on her skin. She winced and imagined David's body consumed in an inferno. Without warning, the comforter blazed as if doused in kerosene.

"Thought that might happen," she said.

Perry's eye rounded with fright as he watched his sire and former friend—if he ever considered David a proper friend—burn.

He shook his head, as if dislodging his gaping eyes. "What are you?" he repeated.

"I think I get it now," she said. "I have this power because I've touched all three—evil, good, and Balance."

Chapter Fifty-six

Smoke billowed from Sana's room as she and another vampire stepped into the parking lot.

From above, Charles dropped from the sky with a predator's pounce and a malicious grin. With a flick of his hand, he sent the dark-haired vampire flying, his body skidding down the sidewalk several car lengths away.

Though he made no move to restrain her, Sana didn't run. She didn't fight, didn't scream. Despite the chaos erupting around them, she showed no fear. He put his hand under her chin and rotated her face toward his, but her placid expression remained. The streetlamp light flickered in her dark eyes, but still—no fear.

Her calm ignited his fury. He struck her. Maysun cried out—but Sana didn't fall. The carnage didn't distract her. Her focus lingered on Charles as much as his on her.

Michael moved to intervene, but Vivian threw out a hand to stop him.

"She's still mortal," she warned. "And she's in his grasp. If we rush him, he might kill her just to keep from losing."

"You're even prettier than I imagined," Charles said, his voice almost wistful. "Either I'll be a lucky man… or deeply disappointed when I have to kill you."

A door crashed as a Blood Tribe member burst into one of the motel rooms. Vivian heard a human voice rise in panic—an instant before a silver-gray wolf launched itself onto the vampire's back.

"I'm not going with you," Sana stated.

"Then you'll die," Charles replied flatly.

Behind them, a heavy *thwump* echoed as Angelo unfurled his leathery wings, knocking Blu and Lukas aside with a single sweep before launching into the air. Lukas and Blu exchanged a quick, wordless agreement and bound into the air after him, Blu with a cry of pain from the use of his wounded wing.

"Lukas!" Michael yelled and pressed forward to the spot where his son had once stood. The air near him rippled like a broken water surface as a spell passed, and he ducked to avoid getting hit.

Vivian clenched her fists. She'd never felt this level of frustration. Dunning was dragging it out—reveling in their helplessness, soaking in every drop of despair. Meanwhile, beings were dying, wounded, miserable. It was a Maleficence banquet, and everyone was on the plate.

Several of their fighters on the ground stood ready, waiting for the right moment to act. Vivian considered using her power of disappearing and reappearing, but that had substantial risks. Charles was no minor soldier of the *Shévet ha Dam*, and his ability frightened her. If she materialized behind him, there was a chance he'd snuff Sana's life with a swipe of his hand to her throat. Unlikely, but not implausible. He'd prefer her dead to her turning to life in the Source.

To Vivian's surprise, Sana spoke.

"You didn't turn me," she said. "You didn't order the experiments. You didn't stalk me like I was a lab rat. So I don't need to hurt you. Yet. I've made my peace with most of the vampires who abused me." Tears glistened in her eyes. "Back down now, and I'll spare you."

Charles guffawed, an amused twinkle in his brown eyes. "Listen to her! So sure of herself. Yes, I can tell by the smell that you've burned my boy, David." He gripped Sana by the wrist. "I will be much more difficult."

With that, he leapt into the air, yanking Sana skyward. The movement was so sudden, so violent, Vivian was sure he had dislocated Sana's shoulder.

Vivian, Maysun, and Michael all dove for Sana's feet as Charles moved up, nearly colliding in their zeal to bring her down.

It all happened in a blink, yet to Vivian it unfolded in slow motion.

"Don't be so sure," Sana said—Then Charles screamed. A scream of pure agony.

Fire erupted across his body.

With no wings to support her, Sana fell after him. She looked like a child miraculously chasing after a falling star.

Vivian rocketed into the sky after Sana, lifted by the Source and nothing more. She swerved midair, dodging Lukas and Angelo locked in a brutal brawl ten stories above the ground.

Where's Blu? The thought hit hard, dredging up her premonition. Was he hurt—or worse? Her senses stretched outward, scanning frantically for any trace of him.

Then she saw him on the ground below.

One blue-feathered wing lay detached, like a broken angel's. If not for that, she wouldn't have recognized the ruin of his face and body.

God, no—Blu!

Angelo let out a cry like a wildcat and clenched Lukas' wing. Vivian heard an audible crack, and Lukas screamed in agony, instinctively retracting his wings to avert further damage and losing his grip on Angelo. He dropped like a falling angel.

Vivian whipped into a dive. Sana forgotten, her only thought was saving Lukas, the boy who'd become her son in every way that mattered. As her fingertips brushed his pants leg, a set of firm hands clenched her ankles, adding drag to offset her thrust.

Angelo.

She kicked, but Angelo had the flexibility of a child of Cartaphilus. Lukas' pants slipped through her grip.

Vivian's tormented cry split the midnight air, an uncanny, almost divine sound of righteous anger. Angelo's grip faltered. She didn't wait for him to let go. She folded herself midair, twisted hard, grabbed Angelo's wrists, and wrenched them from her body, her only concern freeing herself before Lukas hit the ground.

Angelo pulled his hands to his body with a woeful sound and dove to the ground after easier prey.

Vivian surged ahead and caught Lukas under the arms, yanking upward as his toes brushed the ground.

Hovering, not wanting to wait any longer than she had to, she asked if he was alright.

"Fine," he said. "Go. I'll check on Blu. You've got Sana—"

She was already gone.

Vivian locked down every stray thought to keep her flow to the Source steady, and shot after Charles like a missile.

He was easy enough to spot. Even if he hadn't been carrying the Maleficence, the trail of fire that clung to him blazed like a comet against the night. He descended fast, reached the ground, and dropped, rolling in the dirt to douse his body.

Vivian wrestled with her instincts. She loathed the idea of battling Charles or gaining a sense of satisfaction from his death. It went against everything the Source stood for. Still, allowing him to escape only meant this battle was the first of many.

She thought of Blu, his body bloodied, perhaps dead, Michael nearly dying at Krieg's hands, Megan's death, Maysun now a vampire, and Sana…

Sana, who'd arrived already, seemed to be doing just fine.

Charles struggled to his feet, looking like a scarecrow dragged from a harvest bonfire. His blackened body was already recovering from the fire; charred bits of flesh dropped like ashes to the ground as Sana squared off before him, her jaw set.

"I need to know," she said. "What did you think I'd be to you? Some secret weapon? Do you know more about me than I do?"

Charles didn't speak, his recuperating body either incapable of replying or unable to come up with an answer.

"You don't, do you?" she said, bitter laughter escaping her lips. "You don't know a damn thing. You want to own me. Use me. Like David did. Like Thom. Like my father."

His jaw, no longer blackened, now flexed as if each millimeter of motion was painful. "You are a beautiful—"

"Shut up," Sana said. "Just… don't. It's pathetic." Her dark eye narrowed as she watched him in horrific fascination as the flesh inched from black to red. "The sad part is that if you'd shown up sooner, I probably would've fallen for it. I might have even fallen for you. You were handsome enough. Smooth, in that slick way. I was naïve."

With every sentence, Charles grew vaguely more human-looking. Vivian suspected that his strength drained with the effort to repair his corpse, but did he still have the muscle to overpower Sana? Vivian wanted to intervene, but not with Sana's cathartic dialog. She held off, looming in the distance and staying downwind, hoping the dark hid her from them.

"All you want is to make me afraid, so you can use me. Well, guess what?"

He didn't answer. Did Sana hear his thoughts?

"I'm not scared of you. Not anymore."

Sana dashed forward. Her foot snapped up in a clean, brutal roundhouse that exploded Charles' chest in a spray of ash, blood, and bone.

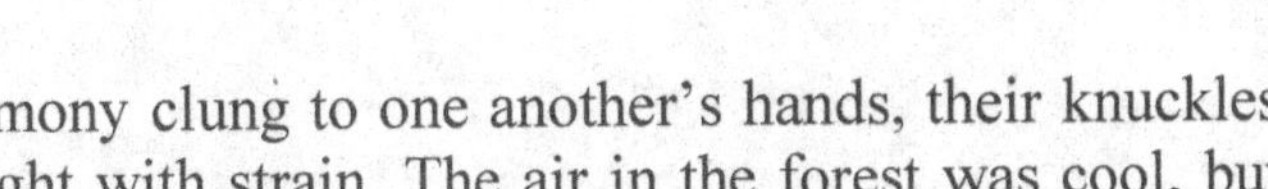

Eoghan and Harmony clung to one another's hands, their knuckles white, their faces tight with strain. The air in the forest was cool, but their faces were lined with streaks of sweat, tears of exertion, and dust from the blowing fall air.

The Maleficence, now free from its bodily form, spread its shadowy tentacles wide in search of a dark host. Invisible to the eyes of mortals, or semi-immortals, it flitted from soul to soul, but every form it touched was engaged in a perilous battle, its lifespan uncertain.

Frantic for survival, the dark energy flitted from body to body like a minnow through murky water, but found no host. frantic to root itself in something—anything. But unknown to it, two forces worked in concert, warding off the union of darkness and flesh, pushing back the endgame of good versus evil.

"How much longer, do you think?" Eoghan choked out, teeth clenched, a tear cutting through the grime on his cheek.

A wave of effort poured over them like molten lead and they gripped tighter, falling to their knees but not letting go, their hands cutting off circulation but not noticing it over the agony of the fire that consumed them.

"H-host," she said, her teeth gritted as well. "You know who. Just hold on. Hold on. It's coming. It's coming."

It *had* to be.

Chapter Fifty-seven

arnage lay everywhere. Bodies and blood-covered detritus were strewn on the asphalt parking lot and in the nearby grass for yards around. The doors to every motel room had been knocked, ruined, from the frames. Vivian had no doubt that anyone who'd spent the night in those rooms was either dead or newly undead. A gunmetal-gray police cruiser sat half in a ditch, its lights still flashing. The responding officer hung halfway out the window, throat slashed grotesquely, arms spread wide like Saint Peter's cross.

As she approached the battle with Sana at her side, Vivian heard a female of the Tribe roar. "Jerusha," she cried, her voice panicked. "She has the target."

Vivian thought of Sana's courageous stand against Charles. *No, I don't.*

In seconds, the skies were spotted with the shadows of fleeing vampires, some holding the flightless bodies of evil compatriots. With the host of the Maleficence dead and Sana by her side, the tide was turning for the renegades. The Tribe had no leader and the Maleficence no vessel; their drive to live outweighed their urge to satisfy their now-dead leader. Vivian dispatched Michael to check on Blu and Lukas as the remaining Tribe vampires chose flight over a losing fight. Immortality had its limits.

The vampires who were ashed didn't pose a problem, but this war differed from the last. Now there were new beings with semi-human bodies that lingered after death. Corpses lolled, naked, in uncomfortable positions—shape-shifters, she supposed, who'd shed clothes and sprung a pelt, but reverted to their human forms after death. More human bodies were missing limbs, hearts, or heads. The wounded were too many to count.

How many had once been Tribe? Sana's dark-haired friend and

another man she didn't recognize—probably a soldier, she guessed, based on the haircut, musculature, and bearing—were dragging out blankets and sheets to cover the corpses.

What are we going to do with them?

Vivian climbed atop the Dodge and scanned the crowd, mentally counting friends and family. Sana was fine, of course. Michael was off to see to Blu and Lukas, and Maysun still stood as well. Bully was okay. DB sat up bleeding and clenching his arm, but he was alive. Doyle would make it, though he walked with a limp, and it appeared several fingers were missing from his right hand. Blu might be gone; she'd know soon. Her head dropped. She was so tired.

"Is he dead?" Perry asked, his eyes moving to where they'd all last seen Charles, arching through the sky. Sana nodded, not sure how she felt about it. Was it murder or self-defense? Charles didn't stand a chance of beating her in his condition, but once he had…

"And he's—" Perry motioned to Angelo, splayed on the asphalt, too wounded to crawl away. The war had done a number on Jude's child—several creatures must have taken him on at once to inflict damage this extensive. Rib bones protruded from his t-shirt, and she wondered if she might be able to use one to stake his heart.

"Going to heal, sooner or later," Vivian said, "unless something happens tonight to stop it."

Sana looked up in surprise. "You won't kill him?"

"Not now. He's helpless at the moment. It wouldn't be right."

"What're we going to do with him?" Sana's eyes narrowed. She didn't share Vivian's sympathy.

As if she knew which way Sana was leaning, Vivian asked, "What do you think we should do?"

Sana regarded Angelo, whose face, for once, expressed panic.

"He's fixed in evil," she concluded. "He won't change… he's entrenched in it, enjoys it. How many people will he kill if we let him live?"

Vivian's appearance grew glum, as if the idea of an irredeemable soul hurt her personally.

The sound of footsteps drew their eyes to two men shuffling heavily through the long grass near the hotel. Vivian's face lit up as her friends, one tall with a bear-like build, the other closer to an average frame and very striking, staggered under a burly black vampire who had one blue wing extended; the other wing was gone, save a skeletal stump.

"What's the score?" the injured one groaned. He tried to grin, but the result was a macabre farce, a slit of white in a pool of red and dark skin.

"Christians two, Lions nothing," Perry joked glumly. Nobody laughed.

"Lost the same fucking wing," the injured one said. "This shit's getting old."

Sana stepped toward Angelo. "If he's going to die, who'll kill him?"

"I can't kill him," Vivian said. "He'd have to fight me first."

"Which wouldn't be a problem if he was in top form," the tall one said, rubbing his shoulder while his eyes strayed to the stub of his friend's wing.

"Still," Vivian said, "It's not my place. It'd be like taking a pot shot. Do you understand?"

Sana advanced toward Angelo. Perry rushed to her side.

"I'll do it," he offered. Angelo's eyes flew open. "Let me. That way, you'll see how much I hated what they made me do."

Sana took his hand and considered Perry's offer. Would watching Perry kill Angelo prove his caring for her? Or would it only bring images of him killing every time he drew her near?

"No," she murmured. "I have to do it. If I don't, I'll wish for the rest of my life that I had. These things tortured me, Perry–"

"I know. I was right beside them."

Silence. In the distant trees, an owl hooted.

Sana covered Perry's hand with both of hers. "Remember how I told you I thought I got my new abilities from touching all three of the world's major influences?"

"Yeah, so?"

"My birth… that gave me the Balance part of me. When David tried to turn me, that was the Maleficence. Last night…" Perry turned a brilliant shade of scarlet and turned away from the crowd of listeners, "that was the Source. You helped me realize the full potential of the good part of me. That's how I can tell you're telling the truth when you say you weren't one of them."

"You mean—"

"You're not part of the *Shévet ha Dam* anymore, Perry. Don't go back to prove yourself to me."

Perry nodded and stepped aside.

Decapitation. Removal of the heart. Fire.

The last one—removing his heart—felt right. But the idea of touching his cold, broken body made her stomach churn.

Did embracing the new person she'd become have to mean death to those who'd tortured her? Was this really the start of her new life—proving she could be as ruthless as the ones who'd tortured her? Or was she more than that?

"Sana?"

Sana turned and faced Vivian's dark-haired friend. "Yes?" She hated the frail sound of her voice.

"There is another way. Vampires can drain other vampires to death. Removal of his blood would make the sunlight enough to kill him."

Sana swallowed and nodded, stepping back from Angelo's body. All the vampires present—nearly everyone—stepped forward to relieve Angelo of his blood. All of them except Perry, who stood by her side, gripping her hand.

The cooperation made quick work of their last enemy. Once done, Vivian's handsome friend cleared his throat. "Does anyone have any suggestions for the corpses?" He looked at the crowd for input.

A petite, dark-haired woman stepped forward and swallowed hard. "We have to move them from here before we decide. We're about a mile outside a town, and morning can't be far off. This time of year, there's a million harvested fields; I can get us to one if you want to burn the bodies."

"There's a quarry nearby, too," another one said. "We drove by it on the way out here. It'd be a good place to stick a few."

"I'll cut another hole," a burly man in a bright red athletic suit said. "We'll get them out of here, at least."

"I can set them on fire," a slim, golden boy said.

"Me, too," said another, much paler man. "Well, they'll cook, at any rate, and they'll burn up if I touch them long enough."

"We can start a team collecting identification," Michael said with a bob of his head. "Check for wallets, that sort of thing so families can be notified. Write it down. There should be paper in the lobby—check the desks or an office printer. Plus, someone will have to go to a drugstore or a Walmart for first aid stuff."

"I'll go," a lean, bald-faced man, said. "I've got money."

They set to work as if they'd done it a hundred times—dragging bodies, covering the fallen, tending wounds, salvaging what was left of the night. No one asked for orders. No one needed to. Vivian watched them move and nodded, a quiet swell of pride in her eyes. Sana saw it too. These people—some friends, some strangers—were scarred, bleeding, exhausted, but not broken. They were survivors. Fighters. Chosen family, bound not by blood, but by battle. And as she stood there among them, hands stained and heart hammering, she realized: this was what a real Tribe looked like.

EPILOGUE

Disposing of the dead went faster than it had any right to. The vermilion dawn sky encroached upon the hills as the last of the bodies were ignited in a nearby field that must have recently hosted a bonfire. The pile rose taller than Lukas's head, easily twenty feet across, and the stench drove everyone back through the hole Crystal had made. DB and Lightning had stayed behind with Bully to ensure none of the bodies remained.

Lukas and his family showered in the broken motel rooms and changed into clothing they rinsed free of blood in the sink. They patched Blu's back with a first-aid kit found under the check-in counter—all the supplies Doyle had bought were already gone through. No one knew whether he'd have use of his wing again. None of their friends had suffered an injury that grave and lived.

Once most of the vehicles had cleared out, Michael discovered a key in a wallet of one of the deceased that matched a Chevy Tahoe in the parking lot. Crystal would not have to cleave for a while, at least.

When DB and Lightning returned from the field, they torched the hotel. No trace of blood or battle could remain.

At last, they were ready to go. Lukas had never felt so done in.

"Now that Charles and Jude are dead," Michael said, handing the keys of their newly gained SUV to Vivian, "are we relatively safe? Where do we go?"

Vivian didn't answer. Her eyes, glazed with exhaustion, stared dazedly at the blaze of the motel room before them. Beside them, Perry and Sana prepared to leave with Maysun. DB shot a ray of fire from his mouth to one end of the motel as Lightning laid his hands on the opposite side. A bolt shot out and ignited the siding as the scent of smoke filled the air.

I never want to smell that, or anything like it, ever again, Lukas thought.

"I don't think so," she said. "The Maleficence didn't die with them. And as long as I'm a walking carrier of the Source on earth, it will try to kill me."

"We'll fight them," Blu assured her. "To the death if we have to."

"Damn straight," Michael said, taking her hand. "I might not have the power you do, but you've got me, for what it's worth."

Vivian smiled, weary and grateful. "It's worth the world to me. The love we all have for each other? That's what fuels the power I have, and those like me."

"They say 'God is love,'" Michael observed. "And I am nothing without it. Nothing special. Just another undead soul walking the planet."

Lukas' lip curled up at Vivian's serene face. *Dad, you need to lose her. I can't believe what you're saying. You think you're nothing special because you can't tap into the Source? That's bullshit!*

"How long until it finds you again?" Blu asked.

Vivian shrugged. "I can't say. It depends on who the Maleficence uses and whether it labels me as a priority this time. Maybe the person it inhabits next will have a different Source host to pursue."

"Maybe we'll get lucky," Blu said, his voice daring to reflect his hope.

Michael pointed to the ignition switch. "If you don't start the truck soon, I'm going to think you're waiting for it to find us," he said. Blu and Vivian laughed.

From his place in the backseat, an icy wave washed over Lukas. Suppressing a shudder, he rose slightly in his seat, fighting the impression that his body was encased in a vise. The sense of desperation poured over him, as if part of his soul was desperately looking for a home. But not his soul. *What is this?*

Must merge. Must be hidden. The Source is too close.

His thoughts weren't his own. A crazed animal had sunk into his mind and was searching for shelter, its claws scratching at his consciousness. He wanted to gasp, scream, and warn the others. He'd lived through the worst battle of his life, and now, safe in their escape vehicle, he knew he might die, his mind exploding with this intense change.

It passed. As quickly as it had swept over him, it vanished, leaving him covered in gooseflesh as the sweat evaporated from his skin.

Lukas' breath caught in his throat. What had happened? *God, I feel sick. Whatever that was, it can't be good. I should say something, tell them.*

His eyes caught Vivian's large brown ones in the rearview mirror, and as they did, a surge of sheer hatred coursed through him. He wanted to lunge forward, rip out her throat, make her undergo the humiliation his father felt as being lowest on the pole, to make her feel the pain of every loss he had ever known. To see her weep and scream and beg for mercy—and then die.

Not yet, something dark inside him whispered. *Not this time. This time I wait… until I have them all.*

Lukas vanished.

HERE IS A LOOK INTO THE FINAL BOOK OF

IRIS KAIN'S BLOOD TRIBE TRILOGY – BLOOD TREASON

Melissa Vartalidis woke to the sensation of sand weighing down her every part, from her heels to the thick, long hair now heavy with earth. She extended a slender arm and pushed upward, stretching her slim fingers until they broke the surface, then followed that arm with the other, swimming upward through a sea of dirt, a grave of her own making.

Crawling, she made her way into the air and emerged from her sandy burial place. Stars in a black sky free of the jealous moon shone pale light on the skin that nearly matched their ethereal hue. Melissa extended her muscles, atrophied with sleep, and gathered her thoughts.

Sending out psychic feelers, she checked the status of the latest war and Charles. The power of the Maleficence had shifted once more. The war was over, and Charles, the leader of the Maleficence, had been killed. Her shoulders slumped. She'd been so confident of Charles' victory that she'd dug her grave outside of his home, following him like a paparazzi stalker.

Charles is dead. I should have fought. I should have helped. Who cares what the Shévet ha Dam *thinks of me or might have said? Now I have to hunt down the head all over again.*

It seemed like such a waste. Charles had been a brutal serial killer in Scotland when he was alive over a thousand years ago, propelled into vampire ferocity and bloodlust after death, and held the Maleficence for less than a year. The being who had possessed it previously—Joseph Cartaphilus, the father of the vampires—had held it for over a millennium.

Fucking Cartaphilus. At least with Charles, I'd have had a chance to come back to the fold. Maybe. If I'd tried.

She studied the massive French chateau-style home before her, Charles' home, a colossal edifice wholly out of place among the typical adobe styles typically found outside Sedona. He'd chosen his home for its exclusive location and elaborate privacy measures, but his security hadn't considered someone willing to dig under the fence to be close to the dark power of the Maleficence. Melissa had tracked him down a month before and studied the head vampire, learned more about him, and waited until the right time to come forward and win her place back in the Tribe.

Charles was gone. Who held it now? How long would it take her to track down the next leader and win their favor?

She might have been depressed if not for the foolish urge that overcame her. Brushing and shaking the dirt from her limbs, hair, and clothes as she approached, Melissa changed her walk from the stagger of a woman who had recently evacuated a grave to the sure saunter of a queen. She set her shoulders back, elongated her neck, and added a switch to her stride. She could do little about her protruding eyeteeth, but the servile Renfields who scuttled about Charles' home cared nothing about the trivialities of appearance. She held the royal blood—the blood of the vampire—and that was what they obeyed. It was what they craved.

Never mind that she no longer held the strength she used to wield. No doubt Charles harbored an adequate amount of Renfields within his walls to overpower her, should they wish. If they thought about it, one or two might recognize how far down the family tree Melissa was. How far removed from Cartaphilus. How weak.

The trick was never to let them think.

Melissa reached the side entrance and paused. The smell of the *Shévet ha Dam* was strong here. Only hours before, members of its Table had launched themselves from Charles' stoop in preparation for last night's battle as she watched, hidden in the yard below. A war which, judging from the Charles' absence in the flow of the Maleficence, had gone poorly. Had many vampires had they lost? How many members of the Blood Tribe were gone?

None of them had any reason to return to Charles' home. Would they? Surely, they had fortresses to return to, Renfields to tend to them.

Melissa's hand started for the knob. *No. The front entrance. Give them no reason to doubt.*

Melissa veritably skipped to the side of the home which faced the road—a road nearly out of sight down a lengthy drive. Composing herself, she approached two massive, carved wooden doors with old-fashioned iron hinges. They quickly came unlocked under the influence of her hand.

Some power she had retained.

Strolling into Charles' former home, she cocked her head assuredly and did her best to look even taller than her five foot eight inches. She threw her shoulders back and placed a stiff smile on her face. She caught herself stepping on tiptoe, and brought her bare feet flat to the floor. No need to go overboard.

Charles had fantastic taste. Before her sprawled a home seemingly drawn from the earth itself; earthen tile, natural paint and wallpaper tones, plenty of wood and leather. Huge rooms, all of them open, flowed from one setting to the next. Boxy seating had been painstakingly arranged around heavy wooden tables. Thick, masculine window treatments no doubt blocked out any trace of daytime sun. Tasteful wall décor in medieval themes had been hung as if by a decorator—and probably had been. Not a speck of dust or fingerprint to be seen. The place just screamed money, and all of it, every inch, was faultless.

However, having enough servants desperate for a swallow of vampire blood would do that.

A tiny female Renfield caught her eye from the opposite side of the living area and skittered down the hall. Melissa smiled, wary of broadening it too far and exposing her youthful trait, and rolled forward.

After she'd wandered the floors for less than a minute, one of the larger, male Renfields stepped forward. No doubt chosen for his size to intimidate any human intruders. Tall, robust, he'd probably been a handsome man before he'd been roped into his blood fixation. Now deep blue circles ringed his eyes, and his skin was drawn and pale. His hands twitched and jittered at his sides, and his eyes had trouble focusing on her. Could he smell her last meal dried on her dress?

"Madam?"

It'd been a while since she'd been addressed so, and she felt a small measure of pride. These lot had no idea who she was, only that she had the blood they craved. A half-smile curled at the corner of her mouth.

She peered down her nose at him, a challenging feat, since he was the taller between them. "Yes?"

He swallowed. He had at least four inches and fifty pounds of ropey muscle on her, but she had the power, and he knew it.

"Would madam know if Master Charles will be home this evening?" Hands twitching, jittering, restless, danced from his side to his chest and back. He scratched his forearm unselfconsciously. His eyes shot from corner to corner as if afraid to meet hers. When he did, he looked away, too fearful to hold her gaze for long.

Does he care for Charles, or is he in need of a fix? Melissa wondered. How to tell them Charles was gone? Did they earnestly want to know, or would any pretext she offered suffice? Her servants had harbored no loyalty toward her. Did the leader of the *Shévet ha Dam* treat his help better than she had? *Might as well be honest. He'll find out in time. If he*

"Master Charles is gone," she said, "and will not be coming back."

"Dead?" he ventured, his voice turning up in the short syllable. Jerky speech. Yes, this one was withdrawing badly.

"Dead," she confirmed.

He let out a frustrated breath followed by an anguished groan and then sucked in another at his display of insubordination.

"Sorry," he said, his voice pleading. Melissa wasn't fooled. He longed for her to take his blood in exchange for hers, to shed his dependency on vampires, and finally become one of the *Shévet ha Dam*.

There were two types of Renfields: takers of vampire blood and those who had their blood taken by the undead. Neither was completely made, but hovered on the verge of death in the life of a Renfield. The takers of vampire blood were mere addicts, junkies whose dependency on their sire was nothing more than a devotion to a drug. Any vampire would do—and often did, if they needed a servant of their own. Those who were drained were fiercely loyal and dependable once they revived from their anemia—not the jittery mess she saw. He was a taker.

"Hungry?" she asked, offering an arm.

The man's eyes glowed in disbelief at his luck as he studied the veins under her pale skin, tracing them with rough fingers. What was his position here? Caretaker and handyman, perhaps? Chosen for his size because of his brute power to be useful for lifting and intimidation?

Melissa withdrew her arm and, careful to keep her face impassive, she cut a shallow trench in her forearm with her fangs. A trickle of blood flowed, then a small stream. She proffered her arm once more.

The young Renfield didn't hesitate. Snatching her arm into his calloused hands, he held the ruby flow to his lips and drank deeply. Melissa closed her eyes at the sensual feel of his lips brushing against her flesh. The sexual feel of his tongue as he drank gave her a pleasant tingle down her back that ended in her feminine parts.

Her head tilted back, she opened her eyes a crack and saw the longing faces of others who peered from the hallway behind walls and countertops and furniture, clearly drawn by the smell of the promise of vampiric blood. Pale faces. Curious, dependent beings in need of a new leader. In a humongous, paid-for house with no one to head it.

Melissa had shown herself willing to satisfy their cravings. She was more than welcome.

She was the queen of the castle.

"Well, he's got it," Harmony Novak said. She ran a hand through her hair and flopped down on the edge of a bed in the studio apartment she and Eoghan O'Rourke had entered illegally blocks from where the battle had occurred. It wasn't the best place to hole up in, but it would do while they watched the teams choose their next steps. Thankfully, the April weather was mild, and they could open the windows, letting the stale air out of the disused home and letting in the mild Arkansas spring air.

Honey-colored strands escaped her finger comb and tickled her nose; she brushed them away and turned to Eoghan.

Tall, Scottish, with bright red hair and eyes as blue and intense as a butane flame, he was a more beautiful man than a handsome one. His pale skin contrasted deeply with the dark tones of the imitation Reschi painting behind him. Ageless, as she was, they both embodied the Balance—what she had been raised to call the Harmony—the force that fought to keep the earth in spiritual check.

"Aye, but who'd have thought we'd have to send it to Lukas?" Eoghan said with a grimace. The corners of his eyes wrinkled as he frowned with displeasure. He took a seat across from her in a beige leather armchair that almost, but not quite, clashed with the yellow rose-striped wallpaper. The apartment they'd borrowed was a strange collaboration of masculine versus feminine; the home was either owned by a couple vying for decorative control or a gender-confused individual.

"Anyone should have seen it," Harmony said in a huff. "Us. We saw it coming. I did. Didn't you?"

Eoghan let out a huff as well and copied Harmony's absent hair-tousling gesture. "Aye, I had it sussed. The way Megan had died in front of him must have been a big push. He loved her deeply." His eyes met hers, locked for just a moment, and then jerked away. "Any road, we've done the right thing. Lukas was a good chap, and the Balance was going far too long in favor of the Maleficence. Now the Source has a chance to catch up."

"It might be at the cost of Lukas' soul," Harmony observed.

Eoghan wet his lips and refused to meet her gaze. He set a capable pair of freckled hands on his knees that bobbed up and down. He whispered, "We've got to get away from each other when he finally spoke."

"What?" Harmony said, taken aback, her head shaking softly.

"You. Me. Apart." He stopped bouncing and met her eyes. "Look, it's nobody's secret that I thought you were the bee's knees when you made me feel emotions. I'd only been away from them a day—minus the part where I was a vampire—and I missed them. I can't imagine what it's been like for you. How long had you had to survive without feelings?"

"Two years," Harmony said.

"Two years, right," Eoghan said. "So, you had to be missing them, too, right? I mean, as much as you could, being a Balance."

Harmony didn't know how to tell him the hole where her emotions had laid had been vacant for so long, she'd forgotten it was there.

"We ran into each other there in the woods, and *bam*," he hit a forceful fist against a palm. "It feels like we're human all over again, emotions and all. Only we're super-powered."

"Power we strengthened by combining them," she pointed out.

"Right," Eoghan said. "So now we're like ten Balances for the cost of one, which is fantastic, since Charles has been acting beastly and had been multitasking rather effectively, sending his mates to kill off vampires who won't join the Tribe while he hunts down Karin—"

"Is there a point to this?"

Eoghan paused. "I think that… Well, it's been a great ride, love, but… we can't do our jobs properly around each other, can we? You make me feel human again, and I can see I do the same for you. If we're acting like we're human instead of balancing the world, it's going to be impossible for us to do the job we need to do. Our position allows a certain amount of evil to run amok. That's hard to do when you know how it will hurt some people."

"You're saying I don't have a spine," Harmony said. "That I can't do what's right if my 'emotions' get in the way."

"I'm saying you're a kind woman with a good heart," Eoghan said. "And I don't mean that as a gender thing—don't take it like some sexist nonsense. But who could blame you for not wanting to hurt people, even if it's for the good of the planet?"

Harmony had no answer to that. Eoghan was right. She'd allowed her emotions to let her feel guilty for guiding the Maleficence into Lukas even if she knew it was the correct thing to do. Not the "right" thing. The correct thing. She'd been the Harmony long enough to know the distinction.

That handsome face. Those perfect features. Yes, there was no doubting that Eoghan made her feel. Now it was her turn to have a hard time making eye contact. She stared at the thin, mustard-yellow carpet below her Keds and willed her mind to focus, but couldn't.

"Maybe I should go back to my family."

He scoffed and picked at a thin scratch in the leather sofa. "With Lukas at the helm, it'll take the Tribe years to get straight. I imagine that will give the Source enough time to gain some more momentum. At any rate, I can't be fagged to deal with any more of this horse crap today."

Harmony giggled with tears in her eyes. *As if Lukas and his family are the only ones that might need us. Eoghan, you still have a lot to learn about what it's like to be the Harmony.*

"I need a kip," Eoghan said, nodding toward the bed. "You?"

"I'm bushed," she admitted.

"Well, let's kick off our shoes and get some sleep. We can worry about parting company another time."

Harmony stood and pulled back the cheap brown comforter. Eoghan joined her on the other side of the bed. They met in the center, wrapping their arms around each other, Harmony's head on his chest.

"Why don't we wait it out together?" she asked, "See where the Harmony leads us?"

Eoghan traced gentle circles on her scalp with his fingers. "Shh," he said. "I imagine we'll know soon enough."

About the author: Over the years, Iris Kain has called Michigan, Arizona, South Carolina, Georgia, and Germany home. She is a fan of horror movies and hard rock, and enjoys playing the piano (albeit poorly). She currently resides in Alabama with her husband, son, cats, and two adorable Swedish Vallhund dogs.

Follow Iris Kain on:

Instagram / Facebook / Threads / TikTok @ authoririskain

Goodreads: @goodreads.com/author/show/20996798.Iris_Kain

Support
Indie
Authors

BUY

READ

REVIEW